ABC

Julia Bell lives in ... \
Cruel Suspicion is h ... s \
have included work ... ĭ \
at St James's Hospital in Leeds and also Darlington Memorial Hospital and she has also worked as a civil servant in the Prison Service. She has two children and five grandchildren and when her children were young, she successfully completed an Open University B.A. degree studying psychology and sociology. She is a proud member of Promoting Yorkshire Authors and has also signed-up for the Ethical Authors' Code.

As well as writing, she loves country walks and travelling abroad (she adores airports, ferry terminals, railway and bus stations – any place where people are on the move).

Contact the author on her website on
http://www.JuliaBellRomanticFiction.co.uk

1

ACKNOWLEDGEMENTS

I would like to thank:

Anna Faversham for her excellent proof reading along with some very sensible advice.

Also Mae at Cover Fresh Designs for a beautiful front cover.

A CRUEL SUSPICION

by

Julia Bell

*To Slennis
Best wishes
Julia Bell
2/12/2023*

For my grandson, James
Kick boxing champ, video game YouTuber
and aspiring musician

"You're only seventeen, my dear and as such you must live with your next of kin."

Mr Dodwell's soulful expression told her everything she needed to know and his words confirmed it.

"I didn't know I had an uncle. My mother never mentioned her family."

The solicitor studied the young girl sitting across from his huge and rather busy desk almost obscuring her. She was growing into a beautiful young woman, with auburn hair and the widest blue-green eyes he had ever seen.

"Your mother had... difficulties with her family. She was estranged from them for many years. But yes, she had an older brother."

"And now I'm expected to go and live with this uncle and his family? A family I've no knowledge of!"

He glanced down at the letter. "Your uncle says he's happy to provide for you until you decide to marry." Seeing her disdainful expression, he added, "Although you must admit your father gave you an excellent education. You know Latin and Greek and you could very well teach." He coughed slightly. "It would be up to you, of course."

"But this uncle lives in Lancashire you say. Isn't that in the north of England?"

He nodded. "The north west to be precise. It's a beautiful part of England I'm led to believe. Not far from Morecambe Bay. A wonderful habitat for butterflies and birds because of the coastal salt marshes and..."

Antheia stopped listening, her mind in turmoil. Did she have to leave Herefordshire and the village in which she had been born and raised? How could she bear to leave Bromyard with its medieval half-timbered houses, market square but most of all, how could she leave her friends and those she had known her entire life? And to live in a place where there were 'coastal salty marshes' whatever they were. It sounded bleak and cold and worst of all, quite dangerous. She blinked hard and tried to concentrate on what the solicitor was saying about her uncle showing such kindness to send the funds, so she may buy her train ticket for the journey to the north of England.

She couldn't hide from the fact she must leave the vicarage. The new vicar of St Peter's and his wife had been kind to let her stay with them since they had no family of their own. However, to discover her father had stated in his will she must go to her maternal uncle had come as a shock. But the biggest shock was losing her mother and father in only ten days. The cholera outbreak in Leominster had swept into Bromyard and it didn't seem possible such a terrible illness could strike a pretty village in the valley of the River Frome where farmers grew their hops. Tainted water had tainted her life and she sighed, knowing she had to accept it.

The Reverend Brown and his wife were more upset than Antheia as they waited outside The Falcon Hotel for the stagecoach bound for Leominster. The day before, the young girl had said farewell to friends and neighbours and their touching parting gifts were to be packed up and sent on the next mail train.

"Have you got everything? Did you pick up the clean handkerchief I left out for you?" Mrs Brown wiped her eyes with her own lace handkerchief. "Such a long way for a slip of girl to travel."

The Reverend Brown agreed. "Why didn't your uncle come down for you? He shouldn't have left you to travel on your own. If I'd had the time, I would have accompanied you myself. And what about your solicitor! Surely Mr Dodwell could have…"

The Browns had been a delightful couple to live with these last six weeks, but she didn't want them to fuss. "I'm old enough to make the journey on my own. And I'll write as soon as I arrive at my new home."

The Reverend nodded. "Yes, you must. I've made a note of the trains you must catch. Do you have it?" Antheia patted the carpetbag. "Good! Good! Now you refer to that itinerary often then you won't go astray."

"And I've packed you sandwiches and a flask of orange juice. You must purchase something to eat at the stations. But please don't miss your train when you do." The concern on the face of Mrs Brown was painful to see.

Antheia kissed her cheek. "Please don't worry, I'll simply catch the next one. I will be all right."

The stagecoach came round the corner; the four horses ready for a drink as they pulled up outside the hotel. A few young men seemed to have the same idea as they dropped to the ground from the cheaper seats on the roof, bound for a quick ale in the hotel before continuing their journey.

"At least your luggage has gone before you. It'll be there ready for you when you arrive, my dear," said the Reverend, peeping inside the coach. "Two seats available. Come on, let me help you inside."

Antheia was glad when the horses were watered and the young men returned to take their seats. Pulling away from the front of the hotel, she waved until the stagecoach swayed and lurched its way round the corner and out of the village. Suddenly she felt afraid. She had visited the market town of Leominster many times in her seventeen years, but had never travelled further than that. She looked out of the window and decided to enjoy the beautiful August weather. The sky was a brilliant blue and as they rumbled along the country lanes, she knew the twelve miles to Leominster would take about ninety minutes. But she had caught the coach at six-thirty and she delighted in the early morning freshness. Asking the two couples who were travelling with her if she may, she pulled down the window sash to allow fresh air to circulate the carriage. The scent of the hedgerows drifted into the interior along with the birdsong.

Precisely at eight o'clock, the coach pulled up outside the small railway station and Antheia climbed down clutching her carpetbag to her with one hand and holding up her skirt with the other. How glad she was she had chosen to wear a modest crinoline cage since she couldn't contemplate travelling with wide encompassing skirts. Even so, she had worn her best white blouse and black skirt with a short jacket that didn't quite reach her waist. Her straw bonnet was simple in design and tied with a black ribbon. But in her luggage, sent ahead of her, she had placed her favourite Sunday hat; with a small crown and narrow brim and decorated with ostrich plumes and a long veil tied round the brim that hung down the back. This was her best hat and she was determined to look smart when attending church with her new family.

She passed the time waiting for the train in a tearoom with a cup of tea and a currant bun contemplating the large piece of paper on which was written the Reverend Brown's itinerary. It was impressive and detailed. Smiling at the fact he had not only written down the stations, times and platforms, but also the railway companies that would take her north, she wouldn't have been surprised if he had listed the number on the locomotives. Kissing the paper in memory of the life she had left behind, she tucked it back in her carpetbag.

The next part of her journey was quite pleasant as she kept her eyes on the scenery outside of the window, munching the sandwiches Mrs Brown had packed for her. One hundred and twenty-three miles to Manchester Piccadilly Station. It seemed an unbelievable distance; almost like travelling to a foreign country.

She climbed down from the train to use the facilities and stretch her legs at Shrewsbury and Crewe, but it was after Crewe the landscape deteriorated into factories and mills, belching smoke. The 'engine house' of the country Reverend Brown had called it. But Antheia knew the war in America had almost destroyed the cotton industry, to the detriment of the workers' livelihoods. Although she couldn't believe how people tolerated the working conditions in these huge buildings and lived in a place where the sun disappeared in a haze of grime, the accounts in the newspapers of starving people, tugged at her heartstrings.

How relieved she was to arrive at Manchester Piccadilly and board the next train that would take her to Lancaster, passing through countryside more pleasing with undulating hills and vast fields where sheep grazed. And then she was embarking on the last part; Lancaster to the small station of Carnforth and further into the wilds of North West Lancashire. When she stepped down from the carriage at four o'clock that afternoon she felt as though every muscle in her body had been pummelled. She stretched on the platform, raising herself up on her toes to ease the ache in her legs and then made her way out of the station. The sharp tang of salt air made her breathe deeply. Thankfully, the good weather had stayed with her all through her journey, but how glad she was it was done with. Outside she searched for the transport her uncle was supposed to have sent for her.

At first her eyes swept over the sumptuous landau waiting at the roadside, pulled by two black horses. As well as the driver and a liveried footman standing by the door, a woman of ample proportions was sitting in one of the red plush seats. Antheia looked about for a waggon or dogcart. Her mother had been forty-five when she had died so Antheia expected her uncle to be a few years older. A farmer perhaps, or a blacksmith. A man of the cloth would be wonderful. If she were to live in a vicarage she would feel very much at home. She should have questioned Mr Dodwell more thoroughly.

The woman in the landau waved to her. "Miss Vale? It that you? Come over here, my dear." Clutching her carpetbag, Antheia walked across to the waiting carriage. "Ah, you look so like your mother, you must be she."

Was this the wife of her uncle? She looked the right age, perhaps in her forties or fifties. Antheia smiled up at her. "Have you come to meet me?"

The woman nodded and a pleasant smile filled her face. "Indeed I have. Jump up here and we'll be on our way. It's only four miles to Brawton and we'll have a little chat while we travel along."

Antheia climbed in helped by the footman who then took his place at the rear on the footboard. She settled comfortably on the seat across from the woman, her back to the driver and studied her companion dressed in a plum coloured coat and elaborately decorated black bonnet. She had an authority about her, plainly shown when she called out a command to the driver to 'get us home and quick about it'.

It was Antheia who started the conversation. "Are you my aunt?"

The woman threw back her head and chuckled. "Goodness no. I'm Mrs Hadwin, the housekeeper."

The housekeeper? So, her uncle had a housekeeper, which meant he might not be married. She felt pleased hearing such news and realised she could be some help to an unmarried uncle. Perhaps she could help with his accounts and paperwork? She had helped her father in the same capacity and prided herself on her skill and efficiency.

She glanced at the footman, feeling confused. "Mr Dodwell, the solicitor said I was to live with my uncle, but I didn't ask for any details I'm afraid."

"I'm not surprised after losing your parents within a few weeks. How you were able to breathe, I have no idea. It must have been a terrible shock."

Antheia noticed the smell of the sea was getting stronger. "I was devastated and there seemed such a lot to do. Thank goodness for the Reverend Brown and his wife. They were wonderful helping me through it."

The housekeeper leaned forward and patted her knee. "You'll be happy at Sedgwick Abbey. After all, it was where your mother was born and raised."

Sedgwick Abbey? She was to live in an abbey? That was impossible. She must mean her mother was born and raised on the estate of the Abbey. Perhaps her uncle worked on a farm or was a stable hand. Although he could be the butler.

She swallowed hard and decided to ask about her new home later. "You remember my mother?"

"I do indeed. I was heartbroken when she left, especially when we heard nothing from her for the next twenty-five years. In fact, not until she died and Mr Dodwell wrote to your uncle."

"Goodness, you've been a housekeeper a long time."

"Thirty years at the Abbey, my dear. Started as a kitchen maid, then housemaid and then parlour maid and finally housekeeper."

"So, you work alongside my uncle?"

The housekeeper chuckled with delight. "I do try, but he can be a contrary individual and often won't take advice. But he is the master."

Antheia licked dry lips. "My uncle is the master?"

Mrs Hadwin stared at her. "Mr Dodwell did tell you your family connections?"

She shook her head. "No nothing. And I failed to ask him."

One of the wheels hit a large stone and the carriage lurched slightly to one side.

"Mind how you're driving, Wilson," the housekeeper called, straightening her bonnet. Wilson turned his head and muttered something inaudible over his shoulder. Mrs Hadwin shook her head in exasperation and her blue-grey eyes sparkled. "He does it on purpose, you know. Now, where was I? Oh, yes, your uncle is the Earl of Sedgwick and Sedgwick Abbey is your family seat. Before her marriage your mother was Lady Anne, the only daughter of the late earl."

CHAPTER TWO

The housekeeper had told her it was four miles from the railway station to the village of Brawton and for the rest of the journey, Antheia felt she couldn't speak. Her mother was Lady Anne and daughter of the late earl. And the late earl would be her grandfather! This was a revelation she hadn't expected. She could have accepted living in a small cottage belonging to a tradesman. But to live in the ancestral home of an earl? Suddenly she felt inadequate and unequal to the position. Did she have a title? She decided she didn't since her mother had married a humble clergyman.

As the carriage rumbled through the pretty village of Brawton with its cottages, shops and church, she wondered if the Abbey was within walking distance. She would like to visit the village since it did remind her of Bromyard. But they continued on down the lane and yet more lanes until they turned in at elaborate wrought iron gates decorated with swirls of metalwork in the shape of leaves and flowers. Passing woodland and lawns, the Abbey came into sight and Antheia felt shock sweep through her. It was huge and ugly. It seemed to have at least two three-storey wings adjacent to the main part of the building, jutting out like wayward limbs that seemed out of place. To one side was a tower and at the other the windows of a conservatory. A portico sheltered the main door and Antheia couldn't take her eyes from it. It was a monstrosity.

"Over four hundred years old," said the housekeeper, nodding in the direction of the building. "It has a great deal of history. In the fifteenth century the earl fought for the Plantagenets during the Wars of the Roses and as we know, the Lancastrian side won. The family then went on to support Henry Tudor at the Battle of Bosworth."

"An enterprising family! Has the building any hidden nooks and crannies?"

Mrs Hadwin stared at her in amazement. "How strange you should say that, my dear. During the time of Elizabeth the family were of the catholic faith and hid their priests away in priest holes."

Antheia smiled. Perhaps it would be exciting living here? It would take her days to explore the whole building and the grounds. She could still taste salt on her lips and decided she must find the sea. She had never seen the sea and suddenly happiness filled her. The earl was her uncle and the only family she had left. For that she had to be grateful.

Why was it called the Blue Room when the décor was cream and chocolate? The cream wallpaper was printed with vertical bands of small blue and pink flowers, but as far as she could see the room was mostly painted cream with brown trim. There was no fire in the grate and a large vase of chrysanthemums filled the space. At the side of the room, next to the armoire were the two trunks that had arrived before her. The room was comfortable with a large window overlooking the front of the house. The land seemed fairly flat and she hoped the sea was out there waiting for her to explore.

She untied her bonnet, shrugged off her jacket and placed them on the chaise longue, before stepping across to the trunks. "I'd better unpack."

The housekeeper looked about the room and pulled the bedspread straight. "Already done, my dear. You'll find everything in the armoire and chest of drawers. I'll get one of the footmen to take the trunks to the storeroom. However," her face flushed with embarrassment, "as we were unpacking your clothes, I noticed your skirts and gowns are…simple and plain." She coughed and pulled a handkerchief from her pocket and wiped her lips. "I think we should get the seamstress to make you a full wardrobe of clothes. You'll need evening gowns and warmer clothes for when the colder weather arrives. The winters up here can be quite harsh."

"My mother taught me to sew and we made our own clothes," said Antheia. Her cheeks became hot with humiliation that the housekeeper had gone through her clothes and passed judgement on them. "I'm sorry you don't feel they're quite up to scratch for such a prestigious family home as Sedgwick Abbey!"

To her surprise the housekeeper chuckled. "My, you have your mother's temper." A frown crossed her face. "Yes, I remember. Your mother was quite adept with the needle."

Antheia nodded. "Yes and she made all my clothes when I was a child and then we made our clothes together." She bit her lip. "We couldn't afford a seamstress and unfortunately, I could afford the cloth for only a few mourning clothes. Crape is so expensive." She turned her attention back to their former topic. "So, you think I need more fashionable clothes?"

Mrs Hadwin gave a bright smile and pointed at the skirt and blouse the young girl was wearing. "I can see you're fashionable already, although I can never understand the attraction of a crinoline. They take up far too much room. But I saw no evening attire in your luggage and you'll need some gowns when you take dinner with the family and while she's at it why not let the seamstress make you some day dresses too? All within the parameters of your mourning."

It made sense and Antheia nodded in agreement. "What time does my uncle dine?"

"Ah, not this evening, Miss Antheia. It's been decided you'll have a tray in your room since you've had such a long day of travelling. Now, I'll get one of the maids to bring hot water so you may freshen up and also a cup of tea and sandwich to keep you going till dinner."

"Would it be all right if I explored the building?"

"Of course, but this is a big house so try not to get lost. This floor is the bedrooms and upstairs is the servants' quarters. The ground floor houses all the main rooms." She turned on her heel to leave the room, but stopped in her tracks. "Oh, I nearly forgot. His lordship wants to see you at five-thirty in his study. That's the room by the main door." She looked at the fob watch pinned to her black dress. "You have forty minutes. Don't be late, his lordship doesn't care for tardiness."

After she had left, Antheia went to the window and looked out. The sweeping lawns and winding drive gave her the view of where they had arrived and looking up at the sky she calculated her room must be facing east, therefore should get the morning sun. She shivered. It was getting chilly and she could have done with the fire lit. She stepped across to the fireplace and removed the chrysanthemums, discovering they were made of silk. The grate had been swept clean and there wasn't a scuttle nearby filled with coal. A knock on the door made her start and she went to open it. Outside stood a young girl in apron and frilly cap, strands of red hair springing out of its lace confines; her cheeks and nose peppered with faint freckles. She carried a large pitcher from which steam arose, making her cheeks shiny with the moisture.

"Good afternoon, miss. I've brought you hot water so you may freshen up." Antheia smiled and opened the door for her, watching her walk towards the oak washstand by the window where she placed the pitcher by the large ceramic bowl. The young girl turned to her. "You have soap and there's a towel ready for you on the rail. Just pull the bell by your bed if you need anything else."

Antheia stepped forward her hand outstretched. "My name is Antheia Vale. I'm so pleased to meet you. What's your name?"

The young girl stared at her hand as if it were a snake and bobbed a curtsey, grinning. "My name is Mathilda, miss. But I get called Matty. Mrs Hadwin said I'm to be your personal maid and help you dress for dinner and deal with your needs."

This was an eye opener for Antheia who dropped her hand quickly. "I won't be any bother I promise," she said hurriedly.

Matty gave a giggle. "It's no bother, Miss Antheia. It's my job. I'll just bring in your tea."

"Thank you, you're very kind."

Matty gave her a quizzical look, before bringing in a tray containing a plate of sandwiches and a pot of tea.

Antheia waited until she could hear the rustle of the maid's skirts moving down the corridor before crossing the floor to the washstand and pouring water into the bowl. As she washed her face she peeped behind the ornate Japanese screen and smiled at the large hip-bath surrounded by towels and bottles of bath salts and oils. She devoured the sandwiches and tea in five minutes, so hungry was she.

Glancing in the mirror, she sighed at the untidy strands of hair falling from the pins and searched through her vanity case for the gold-coloured silk hairnet and tucked her hair inside so it looked tidy and out of the way. It was time for her interview with his lordship.

She descended the wide curved staircase slowly, her hand slipping along the highly polished banister until she reached the newel post at the bottom. The hallway was huge with quite a few doors leading off plus passageways to other parts of the house. Antheia waited for a moment to get her bearings. Flowers adorned the vases standing on the three occasional tables round the room and on the walls were many portraits Antheia supposed must be her ancestors. She would study them later.

The minute hand on the tall grandfather clock was approaching the half-hour and she looked at the doors either side of the main entrance. Remembering she had seen huge bay windows at the left-hand side, she decided that door must lead to her uncle's study. She stepped across to it and knocked, as the clock struck half-past. There was a sharp call of 'enter' from within and she turned the handle and stepped into an extensive room filled with light from the bay window. This room also faced east and she wondered if the morning sun warmed the room since there was no fire lit and the chill made her shiver.

The man sitting behind the desk was slender in build and clean-shaven on his top lip but sported a beard. In many ways he reminded her of the drawings she had seen of the American president, Abraham Lincoln. His clothes were neat and tidy with dark blue trousers and frock coat, a black silk waistcoat, pale blue cravat and white linen shirt. She was surprised to see he wore a black armband on his left arm and felt touched that he should show such respect for a woman he hadn't seen for a quarter of a century.

He stood as she entered the room and she could feel his grey eyes appraising her. "So, you are Antheia, my niece? Daughter of my late sister, Anne?" Was he unsure? She decided his question was rhetorical and nodded. "I would ask you to take a seat, but I'm rather busy at the moment. I'll have to find time to get to know you better. You must be tired after your long journey so I've told Mrs Hadwin to arrange a tray in your room tonight."

"Yes, I know. And I'm happy with that."

"Good! You may join us for luncheon tomorrow. Is your room comfortable?"

She wondered if she should tell him her room was a bit on the cold side, but decided against it. "It's a lovely room. Thank you."

He grunted and stroked his beard, his gaze flicking over her clothes. "I've informed Mrs Hadwin to commission new clothes for you. I expect evening attire at dinner and I also expect good timekeeping. None of this ladies' prerogative of being fashionably late." She didn't know how to reply and stayed silent. "So, we'll talk more tomorrow." She felt as though a disgruntled headmaster had dismissed her when she had done nothing wrong.

But she needed to ask him one thing. "How must I address you?" He looked puzzled and she explained. "Should I call you my lord?"

For the first time he broke into a smile and his severe expression disappeared. It was as though the sun had come out. "Certainly not! You're my niece and therefore you may call me Uncle. If needs must, Uncle Henry."

Uncle Henry! It sounded wonderful and made her feel more like a member of the family instead of part of the staff. Dipping a quick curtsey she left the study and fled into the hallway, closing the door behind her. Standing with her hand on her hip, she tried to catch her breath not realising she had been breathing shallow all through the interview, so scared had she been.

The doors round the vast hallway intrigued her and crossing the floor she decided to try the one on the far side of the main entrance. Opening the door, she peeped round and found herself in the library where three long windows cast shadows on the walls of shelving filled with books of all shapes and sizes. She gasped and stepped inside, gazing at the shelves that dominated three walls from floor to ceiling. There were comfortable armchairs and sofas round the room and a large table in the middle scattered with volumes.

And then she saw him. Lounging in a leather chair was a young man, one leg flung over the arm of his chair in a casual manner. He had a book on his knee and seemed to be reading it by skimming through the pages. He was dressed almost identically as her uncle except his fair hair was too long and the fringe kept falling over his forehead, which he would flick back occasionally.

He lifted his head and blue eyes stared at her until he remembered his manners and hauled himself to his feet, placing the book on the table.

"Ah, the country cousin I assume. Ariadne?" He was tall and slender and moved awkwardly as though he couldn't work out what to do with his arms and legs.

Antheia bristled at his impertinence and rudeness. "The name is Antheia and I don't see you living in a bustling city so what kind of cousin does that make you!"

He lifted his chin. "I'm Felix and I take your point."

If it was an apology it was given grudgingly, but she decided to accept it. "How do you do, Felix. I'm pleased to meet you, Cousin."

He stepped towards her and gave a sharp bow. "So, you've come to live in this monstrous pile. I pity you. I'm going up to Cambridge in October and I've never been so relieved in my life."

She looked round the room, breathing in the musty smell of books. "It's not a very attractive building but I'm sure it has its advantages."

"I fail to see any."

She decided to change the subject. "So, you're eighteen? And the…heir?"

His reply came in a snort of derision. "Yes, I'm eighteen and no, I'm the spare."

"You are Lord…Felix?"

"My goodness, I go back to my earlier observation. You really are the country cousin."

Antheia sighed. "Then why don't you enlighten me."

"I'm nothing more than The Honourable Felix Martindale."

"Not Sedgwick?"

"Sedgwick is the title, Martindale is the family name." His eyes swept over her clothes, one corner of his mouth lifting slightly. "My elder brother is the heir. Viscount Keasden. You may call him Lord Keasden if you wish, but I'd stick to calling him Will as we all do."

"And where is Will may I ask?"

"In foreign parts."

A thought flashed through her mind. "Ah, yes. It's called the Grand Tour, isn't it? Young men go abroad to see the world." She frowned. "I didn't think they did that any more."

"My dear brother isn't on a Grand Tour as such. He's gone to dig up dead bodies."

"Oh, what's he going to do with them? Sew them together like Doctor Frankenstein?"

"Ah, the country cousin knows Mary Shelley's work."

She pulled a face at him. How she wished he wouldn't keep referring to her humble but happy life in a Herefordshire vicarage. "Yes, I do. So, why has he gone to dig up dead bodies."

"I exaggerate," he smirked. "Actually he's studying archaeology and he's on the dig at Pompeii. You'll have not heard of Pompeii I take it?"

Blinking rapidly, her words came at him like bullets from a rifle. "Pompeii. An Italian City where Vesuvius erupted in 79AD burying the inhabitants under volcanic ash and debris."

"Well done. I'd ask your opinion on the war in America, but I'm sure…"

She raised her eyebrows at him. "You mean the one that started at Fort Sumter in Charleston Bay in April 1861? The Confederate army opened fire on the fort claiming it as their own…"

Felix made a quick bow. "I must take my leave, dear cousin. I need to get ready for dinner." It seemed he wanted the last word. "You do know your mother married your father out of spite? She hated the late earl. Little wonder since he murdered his wife, our grandmother."

And then he was gone leaving Antheia with a sour taste in her mouth. How disappointed she was with herself, since her reaction to her cousin had surprised her. It seemed as though he brought out the worst in her and she didn't relish the feeling. They had had a battle of one-upmanship and she had never encountered that in her life. But it was obvious he felt superior. He thought her an ignorant country girl with little education, in her plain clothes and her hair tucked inside a hairnet.

But the one thing she was sure of was her mother certainly didn't marry her father out of spite. They loved each other and besides, her mother had been employed as a governess in Leominster for two years before meeting and marrying her father.

She left the library and immediately met Matty. Her bright smile cheered Antheia and she could have kissed her for lifting her spirits.

"Oh, there you are, Miss Antheia. I'll be bringing your dinner to your room in ten minutes and then I thought you might like to bathe after such a long journey. It'll help you sleep."

Antheia nodded in agreement and made her way up to her room. To her surprise the fire had been lit and she warmed her hands over the welcoming flames. Matty brought in her dinner tray and placed her meal on the occasional table already set with a white tablecloth, cutlery, napkin and a crystal wineglass. A small vase containing a bunch of deep pink peonies sat in the middle of the table. The maid pulled up a chair so she could be comfortable and Antheia noticed everything on the table was beautiful. She might not be dining with the family that evening, but she was certainly receiving first class service and as she tucked into her meal she realised the 'family' comprised only her uncle and cousin. Perhaps she was better off dining alone in her room. When the maid returned forty minutes later, Antheia had enjoyed a bowl of chicken soup with a bread roll, salmon salad and was finishing off a slice of chocolate cake. And all washed down with a glass of white wine.

She smiled as the maid knocked and entered the room. "You lit the fire, Matty. I'm grateful for that."

Matty tilted her head and thought about it before replying, "I put it to Mrs Hadwin this room hasn't been used for years and being on the east side of the house does get a little chilly in the afternoon. Sometimes a fire is needed in these old rooms even though it's August."

"I can imagine." She took the last mouthful of chocolate cake, licked the spoon and noticed the maid turning her head away as if to hide a smile. Perhaps licking the spoon was not polite and she must remember not to do it in future. She placed the spoon on her plate and wiped the corner of her mouth on the napkin. "Please tell the cook the meal was delicious. My uncle is very lucky to have such excellent staff. Are there many of you?"

The maid grinned and began to count up on her fingers. "There's the housekeeper, Mrs Hadwin and the butler, Mr Winder. There's about twenty indoor servants. Maids for house and parlour and those for kitchen and scullery. There's five footmen. And then the men in the stable and the grounds."

"I've met...Wilson," smiled Antheia. "And one of the footmen."

Matty nodded. "Wilson is the driver and it'll have been Charlie what accompanied Mrs Hadwin when she met you from the station. He's the tallest footman I've ever seen and usually takes the footboard. And then there's his lordship's valet and her ladyship's maid."

Antheia stared at her. "Her...ladyship?"

The maid's expression became pained. "Oh yes, I forgot. Her ladyship wishes to see you in her parlour tomorrow at ten o'clock." Seeing her stunned expression she explained, "The Countess of Sedgwick, your uncle's wife?"

"I assumed my uncle was unmarried. I have an aunt too?"

Matty thought about this before saying, "I suppose she's more your step-aunt. The second wife of his lordship since the first countess died shortly after Master Felix's birth and when Lord Keasden was only a nipper. That was before I came to the Abbey, of course. I've been here only three years." She peeped behind the screen. "Now I'll take your tray away and prepare your bath."

It felt lovely to be pampered and spoiled and she allowed Matty to do her work, filling the bath with at least two full buckets of hot water brought up from the kitchen and sprinkling jasmine oil in the water. Antheia lowered herself into the scented balm and relaxed, enjoying the feel on her skin as she washed away her cares. It had been an eventful day, starting at five o'clock that morning and although it was only eight-thirty now, she decided to get straight into bed after her bath.

As she snuggled under the covers she thought about her interview with Lady Sedgwick the following morning. How would that turn out? Would they like each other and become close? Or would she be like Felix? But perhaps she was being silly worrying so. No doubt her ladyship would be a lovely, sweet lady who would welcome her into her new home with a gracious smile and a cup of tea. Felix was a different matter. To say such things about her parents was unforgivable.

Antheia thought back to the many morning services she had attended and how when they arrived home for lunch, she and her parents would debate her father's sermon. The fact they challenged him didn't upset him at all and he enjoyed the heated discussions they had and the exchange of ideas. Her father's eyes would gleam with delight as he proposed counter arguments. It was round the table as they ate their meal that Antheia thought her mother the happiest and her opinions were as much respected as her daughter's.

Was her life at Sedgwick Abbey so confined and stultifying she had to escape to Herefordshire when only twenty years old? Felix's declaration her grandfather murdered their grandmother was poppycock. He might be a year older than her, but he was years younger in maturity. She would ignore him until he went to Cambridge. Only two months and she wouldn't have to suffer him any longer.

Antheia shivered and lifted her head from the pillow. The fire was dying and there was no coal to build it up. Jumping out of bed she fetched her coat and black cape, spread them across the bedcovers and clambered back under. Reaching out she turned down the oil lamp beside her bed, smiling at its beautiful glass fluted shade and ceramic base depicting a pastoral scene. She would become warm soon but at least she now knew why it was called the Blue Room and it had nothing to do with the décor.

CHAPTER THREE

Antheia stood in front of the Countess of Sedgwick suffering her scrutiny as she viewed her through a lorgnette hung round her neck on a silk ribbon. She was getting used to censure although she was becoming heartily sick of it and she hadn't failed to hear Lady Sedgwick's gasp as she walked into her private sitting room. Dipping a curtsey, she surveyed the green and yellow room with chintz curtains and soft furnishings, before turning to study the stern middle-aged woman sitting straight backed on the sofa, dressed elaborately in a purple silk gown with silver buttons down the bodice and lace adorning the cuffs and neckline.

She was about to say 'Good morning, Aunt,' when the countess held up her hand to stop her speaking. And so she stood there, wondering if she should have dressed in her best gown instead of a plain blue dress, again with her hair tucked inside the gold-coloured hairnet. But she wanted to save her best until dinner that evening. She was to join the family for luncheon and it would be the first time she would sit down with them. Since Matty had brought breakfast to her room, she had toyed with the idea of requesting all her meals in her room. The idea of meals with the family didn't appeal to her one bit.

"Your uncle tells me you're to reside with us."

Was it a question? Antheia decided it was. "Yes…Aunt. If it pleases you."

"I have little say in it. But you're only seventeen and have no trade at your fingertips to keep you in Herefordshire."

She sounded disappointed and the young girl knew she would be living under sufferance at the Abbey, especially where the countess was concerned. Antheia prayed she wouldn't mention her clothes.

"I'll learn a trade, Aunt. Perhaps I could teach. I can read Greek and Latin and…"

"Yes, I'm sure Greek and Latin will come in handy at the poor schools in this area," she drawled in amusement.

"Then I can teach the poor children to read and write and also enough mathematics to get them by."

"Education is wasted on the poor. They'll only get above themselves." Antheia stayed silent; there wasn't anything she could possibly say to this woman. "You're dismissed. Don't trouble his lordship with petty matters and keep out of the way of the servants."

Antheia dipped a curtsey again and hurried out of the room almost colliding with a middle-aged woman with salt and pepper hair, who seemed startled. Antheia got the impression she had been listening at the keyhole. But when the woman saw the young girl, her face broke into a bright smile.

"My name's Patience, miss, lady's maid to the countess. And patience is something I need in spades. Don't you mind her ladyship. Her family ain't aristocracy and she thought all her birthdays had come at once when she bagged the earl. There's a lot here who remember your ma, the cook and butler amongst them."

"Do you remember my mother?"

"Ah, no. I've been here fifteen years so I don't. But she was the daughter of an earl and you're the niece and granddaughter of an earl. Aristocracy is in your blood. Her in there only married into it." Her ladyship was heard calling for her maid and Patience grimaced. "Better go and see what the old trout wants."

Antheia stood outside the sitting room for a few minutes more. How was it the family treated her so horribly; indifference from her uncle, contempt from her cousin and disdain from her aunt and yet the servants were more friendly and welcoming. Perhaps they saw her as an innocent outsider. A lamb thrown to the lions, as it were.

In her room she collected her black cape and decided to find the sea since she had no stomach to explore the house as she had planned. Making her way to the main door she pulled it open and stepped out into a glorious day, lifting her face to the warmth of the morning sun. She had been right and her room had warmed as the sun rose, but she knew as it passed across the sky it would be plunged into a deep chill by the afternoon.

In front of her were the wide drive, a good stretch of lawn and the trees beyond. If she followed the driveway she would reach the gate and by following the lanes she would eventually arrive at the village of Brawton. But it was the sea she wanted to visit and that must be in the opposite direction on the far side of the house. No doubt there were many exits in this huge building but she had chosen the main door simply because she was familiar with it. Now she realised she must go round the house to the west side. No matter it would allow her to examine the architecture.

Following the path she passed the library windows and then those to the main rooms, before coming across a pleasing conservatory. Shielding her eyes, she peered through the glass and saw a profusion of potted ferns and aspidistra as well as an assortment of comfortable chairs and sofas.

Finally, she rounded the corner to the rear of the house, still in shade, but would be glorious when the afternoon sun reached it. She gasped at the wonder spread out before her and blinked rapidly as her senses tried to take in all she saw. There was a terrace in front of wide French windows filled with flowerpots brimming with blossom. A few steps took her down to the paths leading her through red, pink and white roses trailing over wooden trellis. Beyond were herbaceous borders of irises, delphiniums, lilies and hollyhocks. She followed the garden paths stopping to smell the various blooms until she turned a corner and stopped.

He was an older man wearing brown fustian trousers and a checked shirt, the sleeves rolled to his elbows. A flat cap sat on grey hair and as he dug a patch of soil he would stop now and again to lift his cap and wipe his brow with a handkerchief he stuffed in his trouser pocket. Next to him was a wheelbarrow full of tools and next to the wheelbarrow, lying patiently on the path was an Irish Setter which rose to its feet as she approached.

"That looks like hard work, but the garden is beautiful," she approached him with a gentle smile. The other servants she had met had been friendly, but she felt wary. She stroked the dog's head and he licked her hand.

"Thank you, miss. We do our best to make it pleasing."

"I'm Antheia Vale, Lord Sedgwick's niece."

He gave a smile showing missing teeth. "Aye I know, miss. The news got round."

"And you are?"

"I'm George Dent, the head gardener." The dog whined. "That there is Fred. He's getting on a bit now and is allowed to potter where he wishes. He wanders about the house and grounds at will, but you'll find him mostly with his lordship. It was he who found Fred half-starved on Warton Sands many years ago and brought him home to live here."

It seemed her uncle had a soft spot towards animals at least. As she stroked the dog's head, she nodded across the garden. "I thought I'd try and find the sea."

He lifted his cap and scratched his head. "Not so much the sea as an estuary for the Lune, Wyre and Ribble rivers all flowing into the Irish Sea."

"I'd still like to find it."

He pursed his lips before saying, "It's an interesting walk, but the estuary is tidal so don't go far if you wish to walk on the sandbanks."

"Coastal salt marshes?" she nodded, remembering what Mr Dodwell had told her.

"Aye, and quicksand. But good for spotting the wildlife. Many marshland birds like bitterns and bearded tits. And butterflies of course."

"Sounds lovely."

He smiled and plucked a few pink roses from the trellis and taking some twine, cut a strip with his knife and wrapped the twine round the stems.

"Flowers for a flower," he said placing them in her hands. He pointed to the far side of the garden towards woodland. "Follow the path through the woods, but keep to the path for now, I think."

She thanked him and wondered if she could kiss his cheek. Deciding against it, she put the roses to her nose and inhaled the scent before meandering through the rest of the garden passing a stunning stone fountain showing Puck filling the cup of Oberon, the king of all the fairies, lounging on a bed of moss and leaves. Antheia smiled. *A Midsummer Night's Dream* was her favourite play by Shakespeare.

Eventually, she reached the woodland and stared up at what she supposed were conifers, horse chestnut and cherry birch. Hadn't the Reverend Brown mentioned those when researching the area? Something about them being hardy and able to survive the salty conditions? She was surprised she remembered.

She found the path leading to an open field without any difficulty and crossing the field she noticed the hardy plants with thick stems and small leaves. Yes, cordgrass she recalled with delight, perhaps she had absorbed more information from the Reverend than she had realised.

It took her a full ten minutes to cross the field but there was a well-used track she could follow. She realised the field was inclined and when she reached the edge she gasped at the sight spread out before her.

The breath she inhaled was deep and long as she surveyed the vast expanse. The tide was out and the sandbank stretched for miles; the sharp tang of salt and wet sand assailing her nostrils. She could taste it on her tongue and she licked her lips. The sun came out and every rockpool glistened and attracted the many birds that wheeled above the magnificence of the estuary. This was nature in the raw and she knew it was uncompromising in its danger, giving and taking life as it wished.

She raised herself up and flung out her arms as if to welcome this astonishing sight into her life. The breeze fanned her face and a memory stirred. When she was a little girl she had asked her father why she had been called Antheia in the hope it was a family name. Being devoid of all family except her parents, she yearned to know about her grandparents and any uncles and aunts. Her mother was unhelpful, but her father more forthcoming.

While he had been waiting for her arrival into the world, he had occupied himself with a book from his library. Being a clergyman he was well versed in Latin and Greek and he was especially enthralled with the Greek gods and goddesses.

He was deep into the chapters concerning Greek mythology and especially the goddesses, when the midwife called him in to meet his new daughter. His mind still in ancient Greece, he pondered on the name of Antheia, goddess of flowers, blossoms, vegetation, swamps, marshes and most importantly human love; a goddess of humility, gentleness and kindness. When he suggested the name to his tired and dishevelled wife, she nodded and smiled down at the small human being with tufts of auburn hair, sleeping peacefully in her arms.

Antheia didn't mind being named for flowers and blossoms and as for human love? As she had grown she had seen her father spread a great deal of human love when she occasionally accompanied him on his visits, her heart swelling with pride at how he comforted and supported his parishioners in their times of trouble and grief. But Antheia was troubled by the swamps and marshes part of her goddess name. It made her think of slimy, crawly creatures. In fact, she had wondered if her new home would be surrounded by swamps and marshes. But now seeing this awesome wildness she knew how wrong she had been.

Her mind returned to her encounter with Felix and she grimaced. So much for being named after the goddess described as humble, with tender ways and setting a good example of gentleness and kindness. She certainly wasn't living up to her name. Perhaps being the goddess of marshes and swamps was more suited to her nature? She had certainly been pulled

35

down into the swamp of pride and arrogance. She sighed and resolved to show her cousin more tolerance and understanding when their paths crossed again.

She decided to find a way down to the sandbanks and continue her exploring. There was a path leading to the shingle and she followed it carefully, mindful not to slip. Once on the sandbanks she stared around her feeling so small against such enormity of space. She approached a rockpool and peered in, but couldn't see anything of interest except small shellfish. Continuing for half a mile, she followed the shingle until she saw another path leading to the top of the limestone cliff and glancing out to the estuary once more decided to take it. It was probably better to be away from the water's edge and she was curious what was up there. She was disappointed there was yet another field, but in the distance was a structure and she went to investigate. It turned out to be a small chapel, unused as the windows were broken and the roof had fallen in allowing the birds to nest inside. A small cemetery surrounded the chapel and Antheia could see the graves were old, some of the stones leaning over. Towering over the gravestones was a large sarcophagus, the inscription almost erased by the wind and salty rain coming up the estuary.

Suddenly the sun disappeared behind a cloud plunging everything into a profound gloom. Along with this a slight breeze stirred and Antheia felt a despair that made her gasp. Sadness swept over her as she glanced around the old burial ground and she couldn't help lowering herself to the plinth surrounding the bottom of the sarcophagus, her legs suddenly having no strength to take her weight. Her head in her hands, she couldn't stop tears trickling down her cheeks. What was the matter with her? She was happy on her walk. She stared at the bunch of roses George had given her. Had the last twenty-four hours taken its toll on her? She felt unbelievably sad and so very weary she could hardly hold up her head.

The sun came out once more and she turned her face to its warming rays. She must lie down and an idea came to her, so bizarre it was ludicrous. Lifting herself up onto the marble sarcophagus, she stretched herself out and closed her eyes, listening to the sound of the crows in the old church and feeling the gentle breeze on her face.

She was almost drifting off to sleep when footsteps crunching on the gravel made her freeze with fright. There was someone there and her heart pounding she lay quietly hoping she wouldn't be noticed and they would pass her by.

The footsteps came to a halt and a male voice echoed across to her.

"Well, I'll be damned! You really should have a word with the gravedigger, Will. He's obviously not aware he should bury bodies below ground not above." There came a pause before he added, "But the flowers are a nice touch."

CHAPTER FOUR

Antheia had to admit it was a pleasant voice with an accent that seemed to drawl in a slow and easy way.

Another voice answered in cultured English and with a chuckle. "Perhaps she's just asleep and needs a kiss to awaken her?"

This was too much for Antheia who gave a yelp, pulled herself upright and swung her legs over the side of the sarcophagus. "Don't you dare!" She held out the roses as if they would protect her.

Standing in front of her were two young men, one much taller than the other. The taller one had brown hair peeping from under his hat, his laughing blue eyes gazing at her appreciatively. The smaller man had black hair and the steel grey eyes of his father. Antheia knew she was looking at her elder cousin.

He smiled. "We should introduce ourselves. This is my good friend Joel Newton and I am William Martindale." He gave a bow. "And we are at your service."

She held out her hand. "Miss Antheia Vale."

He took her hand, surprise spreading across his features. "Wait a minute! Aren't you the…"

She smacked his hand playfully and tried not to chuckle when he pulled back, his mouth turned down in a boyish sulk. "If you say the country cousin then I'll hit you with these roses. I've had enough from Felix!"

"I was going to say the delightful cousin from Herefordshire we've been expecting."

"Well saved, my friend," murmured Joel Newton.

William gave him an annoying glance and took her hand once more. "Let me help you down." He eased her to the ground.

"So, you are Viscount Keasden?"

"Will, please. We are family."

She smiled at the two handsome men who seemed to tower over her. "I think it's getting near luncheon. We'd better be on our way. I know my uncle wouldn't want us to be late."

"Perish the thought," said Will, feigning horror. "Take my arm, dear cousin." He tucked her hand into the crook of his arm.

"And you may take my arm too, ma'am, then you'll be sure not to trip." Joel Newton took her other hand and did the same, narrowing his eyes at his friend.

She decided not to ague and held onto them both. They were dressed smartly; carrying their jackets over their arms and wearing cream linen shirts with turned down collars, their black ties in a bow and pale coloured waistcoats. The only difference was their headgear. Whereas her cousin wore a Bowler, Joel Newton wore a black felt hat with a wide brim, one edge secured to the side of the crown by a metallic eagle.

"So, my brother has been making a nuisance of himself?" asked Will with a grimace.

Antheia nodded. "Put it this way, I'll be glad when he leaves for university."

"Yes, he'll be ready for Cambridge."

"But is Cambridge ready for him!" The two young men burst into laughter and Antheia glanced at Joel's hat. "Your hat is unique. I've seen photographs of Union officers wearing them."

Joel's expression hardened. "It was my pa's. He fell at Williamsburg in '62 and my ma sent it to me in his memory."

Tears sprung to her eyes. "Oh, I'm so sorry. It was a dreadful battle, as they've all been. Before I left Herefordshire I read about Gettysburg and the terrible losses there."

"He was a colonel in the 7th Maine Infantry Regiment."

"You come from Maine?"

Joel lowered his head. "Yes, ma'am. Cape Elizabeth. Born and bred."

Will had remained quiet as they traversed the field and made their way across to the wood of horse chestnut and cherry birch.

His voice when he spoke had tension in it as well as anger. "Perhaps a sensible girl like you can talk him out of returning to join the war. It's crass stupidity, but he won't listen!"

Antheia turned to study the man who held her arm firmly. "You want to enlist?"

"I've been offered the rank of captain in my father's regiment."

"But you're not a soldier," said Antheia thoughtfully.

"No, he's bl...certainly not! He came to Britain when he was only seventeen to study at Cambridge and only returned to visit his mother," snapped Will. "And he stayed to become a Doctor of Archaeology. Ten years in England and now he wants to return to America to fight in a damned war!"

"It's my country and the bugle calls me home," said Joel softly. "I feel I must do my part and support the Union."

Antheia caught the glance between them and realised this was an old argument. "When must you go?"

Joel smiled. "They've given me a few months to decide, but I must be gone by October. We've just come back from Italy so I need time to make up my mind."

The three stayed silent for a few minutes until Antheia spoke. "How was it in Italy?"

Will cheered up immediately. "Splendid, but hard work in all that heat and one reason why we left the dig now. Couldn't suffer the burning sun. But Pompeii was unbelievable. Lots still to do, of course. It was a substantial town and absolutely fascinating."

"Felix said you were digging up dead bodies."

"Only if we came across them. Mostly amphitheatres and houses and street upon street of small shops." His eyes took on a faraway look. "You could almost imagine how they lived…and died unfortunately."

They were through the woodland and back in the beautiful garden, approaching the house. Fred bounded towards them and allowed the three young people to make a fuss of him. Antheia could see her uncle and younger cousin talking together on the terrace and they hurried to join them.

The earl held out his hand. "Will! You're home at last. And Joel too. That's wonderful."

The warmth between the earl and his elder son was palpable. "We sailed from Naples, sir, and docked in Southampton yesterday morning, but decided to travel up country and divert to Morecambe for an overnight stay. We walked along the coast this morning."

"Ten miles! You should have sent a telegram and I would have had the carriage sent to meet your train."

Lord Sedgwick clapped his son on the back. "No point in wearing out good boot leather when we have carriages aplenty."

"Joel and I enjoyed it. After Italy Lancashire seems like a breath of fresh air, literally." He fluffed his brother's hair and was rebuffed, but ignored it. "And how's my little brother?"

Felix shook his head and gave his brother a disgruntled look. "Glad you're home, I suppose. I need help with my Latin, so you can tutor me while you're here."

Antheia had remained silent throughout the greeting, but now spoke up. "I could help you with that. I'd be happy to." The men stared at her as she explained, "My father taught me Latin and Greek."

Joel looked impressed, but it was Will who said, "Of course, your father..." he stopped for a moment, thinking, "who I suppose was our uncle by marriage since your mother was the younger sister of Father." He was speaking more to himself and shook himself as though he suddenly realised he was in company. He smiled brightly. "Yes, your father was a man of the cloth and would be versed in Latin and Greek. But how wonderful he should pass his knowledge on to his daughter."

Felix wasn't of the same mind. "I don't think Antheia can help me with my studies."

"Don't show such ill manners!" said the earl, gesturing towards his niece. "I know many women who are versed in Latin, although not so much in Greek. And my mother was one of them."

Felix muttered a begrudging apology and Will took Antheia's hand and kissed her fingers. "I've known our cousin for barely one hour and it's plain to see she's a cut above the rest of all the young women I know."

Antheia bowed her head in thanks and heard Joel say, "Here! Here."

Lord Sedgwick pulled out his watch from his waistcoat pocket. "Luncheon will be served in thirty minutes, so come along everyone. Freshen up and get yourselves to the dining room."

"Will Stepmother be joining us?" asked Will and Antheia detected tension in his voice.

The earl shook his head. "No, she's requested to eat in her room, but she'll be joining us this evening for dinner."

Antheia pulled off her dress and removed her hairnet. Washing her hands and face she sprinted over to the armoire and pulled out a grey and purple check gingham dress and placed it on the bed. She rushed back to the huge piece of furniture by the wall and slid her hands through the pile of fabric in the drawer, groaning with despair.

A sharp knock on the door was followed by Matty appearing. "I've come to help, miss."

Antheia gave out a wail. "Oh, Matty, what am I to do? I have this for luncheon, but what shall I wear for dinner? I've nothing suitable and I need to look acceptable this evening."

The maid tried to hide her grin. "Yes, I heard Lord Keasden and his American friend were back."

Antheia spun on her heel. "It has nothing to do with that!"

"No, miss, if you say so. But please sit at the dressing table and let me do your hair. Yes, the gingham will do well for luncheon."

Antheia sat on the stool and faced the mirror as the maid undid the pins and allowed the auburn tresses to tumble over her shoulders, before brushing it firmly and coiling it at the back of her head in a neat style.

"That looks lovely, Matty. Usually I wear it in a bun."

"I've noticed. But I thought this way would set off your eyes, especially if you wear this too." She dipped into her apron pocket and pulled out a comb, decorated with purple silk flowers.

Antheia studied herself in the looking glass and realised she had never thought much of her eyes. Yes, they were blue-green, but nothing remarkable. "It's so pretty. Where did you find it."

The maid tapped her nose. "Ask no questions, tell no lies, miss."

Antheia went back to her former problem. "Oh, but what shall I do about this evening?"

"You could wear the muslin."

She shook her head. "It's so plain and dreary."

Matty helped her into her dress and did up the buttons. "There, miss, as pretty as a picture if I say so myself." She thought for a moment. "I'll have a word with Mrs Hadwin. She might have an idea."

Leaving it in the maid's hands, Antheia made her way down the stairs and found her way to the dining room; an easy task as the door had been left ajar and she could hear the murmur of male voices from within.

It was at lunch she met the butler, Winder, a rather small and austere middle-aged man who knew his importance in the household of the Earl of Sedgwick and his family. He showed her to her seat at the large table as the other men rose to their feet to greet her.

She was more than pleased she was placed next to Will and also relieved her step-aunt was absent. After her interview, she felt anxious at being in her ladyship's presence, although she knew it would be inevitable at dinner. But what delighted her the most was the conversation round the table. She dreaded the fact they might have to eat in complete silence, but as it was it was lively, her uncle more than happy to engender a heated discussion.

They were enjoying the final course of cheese and biscuits when Will turned to his cousin. "Is your room comfortable?"

Antheia felt she could be honest with him and whispered, "Actually, it's a bit chilly."

He frowned. "Which one did they give you?"

"The Blue Room."

He looked aghast and raised his voice slightly to attract his father's attention. "Father, Antheia has been put in the Blue Room. Did you know that?"

The earl shrugged. "I leave those kinds of arrangements to your stepmother and Mrs Hadwin."

"But the Blue Room, Father! Antheia must be moved at once. Why, it's east facing and gets very little sun."

"Where do you suggest, dear boy?"

It was plain to see his elder son and heir was the apple of his eye and the earl's manner changed remarkably when he was in his presence. Antheia wondered if that rankled with Felix. Suddenly she felt sorry for him. Perhaps she would be kinder and more sympathetic towards him in the future.

"The Pink Room. It would suit Antheia down to the ground and it's south-west facing."

Lord Sedgwick beckoned to the butler who scurried across to attend his master. "Inform Mrs Hadwin my niece's possessions must be moved to the Pink Room immediately."

"Thank you," whispered Antheia, her heart lifting to the ceiling.

"Oh, Matty, it's perfect." She danced about the room full of sunshine from the two huge windows. The room was decorated with silk wallpaper printed with pink orchids and cyclamens. Everything seemed to glow in an ethereal light and the dusky pink curtains added warmth to the room. "All I need is a gown for this evening and I really will feel like a princess."

"Mrs Hadwin and Patience are working on that as I speak, miss. And if I may, I'd like to join them."

Puzzled, Antheia allowed her to leave while enjoying her beautiful new room. A knock on the door shook her back to reality and she called for them to come in.

"It's me, Antheia. Will." She grinned knowing a gentleman must never enter the room of an unmarried young woman and she went to open the door. "Joel and I were wondering if you'd like to go out riding with us."

"I'm sorry I don't ride. But I'm an excellent driver. A dogcart or waggon poses no problem for me," she said, her chin held high.

"What about a phaeton?" he grinned.

"I think I can manage that."

"A four-seater, so Joel and Felix may come with us?"

She nodded. "Yes, I can handle one of those too. But where to?"

"Brawton. We'll meet you outside."

As he left she decided she would keep on her checked gingham dress and probably take her black cape with her in case the weather turned chilly. Snatching her bonnet from the dressing table she made her way down the staircase, nodding to the butler.

"Thank you, Mr Winder," she said, as he opened the door for her.

"Winder suffices, miss," he informed her sternly.

She smiled and continued outside where a phaeton pulled by two horses waited at the front of the house. She noticed her uncle standing at the bay window, watching. It seemed she was to have an audience. The three young men stood near the vehicle and Will took her hand and helped her up into the driver's seat before jumping into the seat next to her. Joel and Felix hauled themselves into the back seat. She took the reins and entwined them through her fingers and glanced at Will. He was leaning back, his elbow resting on the backrest, his expression one of complete confidence in her. She looked over her shoulder and saw Joel grinning in reassurance. Felix's expression was of annoyance and she wondered if he had argued with his brother about allowing a woman to drive.

Calling a command to the horses and snapping the reins, she manoeuvred the vehicle away from the front of the house and at a walking pace, the horses made their way along the drive, finally trotting and then cantering towards the gates and onward to the village of Brawton.

CHAPTER FIVE

They had wandered round the small shops and Antheia decided to buy a box of treats from the confectioners. She thought the box pretty; the painting on the lid depicting a young woman from the Regency period surrounded by flowers and enjoying a garden swing. The box was decorated with a satin ribbon and inside was an assortment of peppermint drops, butterscotch and marzipan hearts. She decided she would give it to Matty as a thank you for all her help.

"So, what about a drink at the Red Lion?" suggested Will.

The other two agreed, but Antheia was horrified. "I can't go to a public house! My reputation would be sullied."

"Isn't being out with three young men without a chaperone just as bad?" said Felix.

His brother shook his head in exasperation. "Our cousin is in the company of family, you idiot! We're chaperoning her."

Joel grinned. "Yes, you're saving her reputation from me."

Antheia smiled at him and then became serious. "Even so, I mustn't go to a public house."

Will tucked his hand under her elbow. "Leave it to me, Cousin dear."

They arrived outside the stone-clad public house with its swinging sign and while three of them waited, Will ran inside and was gone a few minutes. When he came out he was smiling broadly and ushered them round the building to the rear where there was a tall wooden gate. The landlady was waiting for them and welcomed them into her small but beautiful garden making them sit on the ornate metal chairs round a matching table by a gazebo. They ordered three tankards of ale and one glass of ginger beer for Antheia. As they waited for the landlady to fetch their order, they enjoyed the wonderful sight of lobelia and busy lizzies in the pots and hanging baskets.

"This is an inspired idea," nodded Antheia, looking about her as the landlady bustled out of the rear of the public house and placed their drinks in front of them. "I can enjoy all the public house has to offer whilst not being associated with it. But what my father would have said, I can't imagine."

This statement made Will thoughtful. "It would have been nice to meet my aunt and uncle."

"You knew nothing about my mother?" She felt she needed to ask.

Will shook his head. "No, nothing. Our father never mentioned her. We thought he was an only child."

"So, what did you think when you discovered I was to live at the Abbey?"

"I received a letter from Father whilst in Italy and I was stunned. But happy too."

Joel raised his tankard and took a sip of his ale. "Actually, he was overjoyed. It was all he could talk about for two days."

Antheia squeezed her cousin's hand. "I was dubious I must admit and rather cross. I didn't want to leave my home."

"Are you pleased now," asked Will, smiling.

"I think I'll be happy, although if Felix is going up to Cambridge and Joel back to America, the Abbey is going to seem empty."

"I was thinking of returning to Italy and rejoining the dig." Will studied the contents of his tankard.

Antheia felt dismay. "Then I will be on my own. I must find something worthwhile to do to fill my time."

Will gestured towards his friend. "I'll go only if Joel decides to accept his commission."

"If Cambridge doesn't suit I believe I'd like to serve my country," piped up Felix and three pairs of eyes turned to him. "The Navy I think would suit me."

"You became sick in a rowing boat when we visited Morecambe as boys," pointed out his brother with a smirk. "Perhaps studying law at Cambridge will be enough for you."

"You want to become a lawyer?" repeated Antheia impressed. Somehow the law suited her younger cousin. "You will need good Latin for that."

Felix blew out a breath and a snide look crossed his face. "Perhaps. But there again, I could join the Constabulary and as a policeman, discover the whereabouts of our grandmother's body. Our grandfather must have stashed her somewhere after he'd finished her off."

A shock went round the table and Antheia glanced at Will. His expression was thunderous. "How dare you say such a thing in front of our cousin and my friend!"

Felix was unabashed. "It's true and you know it. Our grandmother disappeared and she was never seen again. I believe…"

Will jumped to his feet, picked up his tankard and threw the contents in his brother's face. "Don't repeat servants' gossip and not in front of me."

Antheia felt a chill despite the beautiful weather and amazing garden surrounding her. Her grandmother had disappeared? Felix believed their grandfather had murdered their grandmother, but if she had disappeared, then where had she gone? Was all this true or just servants' tittle-tattle? She remembered the proverb; there's no smoke without fire. The rumours must have a foundation somewhere. She glanced at Joel.

"Terrible waste of good ale," he said, smiling and draining his tankard.

There was no doubt their idyllic afternoon was spoiled and the conversation was subdued while they drove back to the Abbey. But the atmosphere warmed once they were in the drawing room enjoying afternoon tea and later she decided to find a place to write a letter to the Reverend and Mrs Brown. She hadn't yet told them she had arrived safely and knew the reason; she had been too taken up with her cousins and Joel Newton. The butler directed her to the morning room and the writing desk by the window.

However, Antheia felt anxious when she went to her room to get changed for dinner. What would she wear? She nearly skidded to a halt when she saw what was lying across her bed.

It was the most beautiful dress she had ever seen. In white satin that shimmered in the sunlight, it had a wide skirt to fit over a crinoline cage and lace entwined with lavender-coloured thread decorated the low neckline and short sleeves.

She picked up the gown in awe. "Matty! This is unbelievable. Where did you get it?"

The maid walked across to her, grinning from ear to ear. "Well, Mrs Hadwin remembered the trunks in the attic full to the brim with gowns her ladyship had finished with. She likes to renew her wardrobe every year and that dress is about two years old."

Antheia turned to her in horror. "But she'll recognise it."

Matty shook her head. "No, she won't, miss. Besides, Mrs Hadwin, Patience and me have been working on it all afternoon. We shortened the skirt since you're so much smaller than her ladyship and we took in the waist. We also snipped off the decoration and added the lace round the sleeves and neckline. She'll not notice, believe you me."

"It's…I have no words except thank you." She pointed to the dressing table where she had left the gift she had bought in Brawton. "Please take the box of sweets with you and share them with Mrs Hadwin and Patience and tell them I couldn't be more delighted with my new gown."

"Hardly new, miss."

"New to me and that's what matters." She thought for a moment. "Is white acceptable for mourning?"

Matty's eyes lit up with delight. "It was Mrs Hadwin who said so. She looked it up in one of her books. White can be worn as well as black when the situation dictates."

Antheia felt she couldn't doubt the housekeeper's wisdom and the next hour was spent with bathing and getting her hair done, before she stepped into the white gown and Matty fastened her up. They had also found matching shoes, evening gloves and a fan in the trunk and looking in the chevel mirror, Antheia couldn't believe her eyes. No longer did she seem a clergyman's daughter.

"You're the granddaughter and niece of an earl, miss and now you look quite the part." She grinned. "I think the American gentleman will be delighted."

She didn't feel quite the part as she made her way down the stairs and towards the drawing room where they were meeting before dinner. The countess would be present tonight and would she be under her scrutiny? Perhaps, but it was a certain young gentleman from America she wanted to impress. A man who would probably leave and go off to war. She couldn't bear the thought of it, even though she had met him only that morning. That morning? Yes, in the old graveyard when she had felt so melancholy almost to tears. Why that had happened she couldn't imagine since she had never felt such desperation before. She walked steadily across to the door of the drawing room and when Winder saw her he opened the door wider to allow her to enter.

As she stepped into the room all conversation ceased and eyes turned in her direction. She tried to smile, but suddenly wondered if she had got a bit above herself. Matty had entwined a spray of silk daisies amongst her auburn locks, telling her an unmarried young woman must look fresh and innocent as a daisy. Antheia felt she could only comply. After all, the maid seemed to know better.

It was her uncle who came forward, a smile filling his face. "There you are, my dear. And how enchanting you look. Now, I'm sure a small sherry wouldn't hurt you." He called for Winder to bring her a glass as he guided her to the centre of the room.

The men were dressed in evening attire, in black trousers and tailcoats, their shirts white and ties black. The only colour in the room besides her own gown was the countess who was sitting on the sofa in regal splendour. Her gown was purple and elaborately decorated, the many jewels she wore on her person and in her hair made her look like a Christmas tree Antheia had seen in a shop in Leominster. But how thin she appeared. Antheia had only briefly noticed it at their first interview. But now in her off-the-shoulder gown and short sleeves, her shoulders seemed angular and pointed, her arms emaciated.

"You do realise she shouldn't be in evening company since she's in mourning for her parents." The countess didn't mince her words and Antheia felt shocked.

Lord Sedgwick tried to pacify his wife. "My love, we're enjoying a private family dinner not a soirée in London."

Taking the sherry the butler offered her from a silver tray; she felt she needed to clarify the situation. "Is it so against protocol for me to be here?"

He squeezed her hand and whispered. "This is Lancashire and we have our own customs in the Abbey. Anyway, I think I would have a rebellion if I disallowed it."

In moments Will and Joel were at her side, complimenting her and suddenly she did feel like a princess. Even Felix crossed the floor to kiss her hand.

The meal was delicious and the company delightful, except for the countess who would stare at her occasionally making her feel uncomfortable, her pale blue eyes always scrutinising her. Antheia tried to ignore her and made conversation with all. But sitting at the long oblong table with the earl at one end and the countess at the other, she was happy to be placed at the earl's left hand. Will was opposite on his right hand side with Joel and Felix adjacent to the countess. How pleased she was Joel was seated next to her and was constantly attentive to her needs.

The earl had imbibed a few glasses of wine when he turned to her. "I have deep regrets I never wrote to your mother. Whatever the circumstances between my sister and our father didn't mean I should have behaved so. It was unfeeling of me."

Antheia felt she must speak the truth. "She never mentioned her family. I had no idea you and my cousins existed."

Lord Sedgwick studied the pale liquid in his glass, swirling it around as if looking for inspiration. There was a hush round the table and Antheia glanced at Winder and the two footmen serving them. Should the earl speak like this in front of the staff? She wasn't sure, although they seemed to be keeping their eyes forward and standing almost to attention. Surely they must hear what was said round the table?

The earl nodded. "Twenty-five years is a long time to be estranged. My dear, was your mother happy?"

"I believe so. She loved my father and he loved her. I'm sure about that."

"She left when only twenty years old. She saw me married to Frances, the boys' mother, but declined to attend…" He glanced down the table at his wife and then coughed. "I knew she lived in Herefordshire as the solicitor, Mr Dodwell, had been instructed by your father to inform me of your birth. He thought it only right."

"Father got in touch with you?"

He sighed. "Not personally. Our communications were through the solicitor only. Your mother must have told your father about her family and he wanted you to have a guardian should you need one until your twenty-first birthday. I agreed you'd become my ward. Of course, I thought the situation would never come about. It was more a formality."

"That was kind of you."

Will broke into the conversation. "But you never told Felix and me about our cousin?"

"Thought it better, my boy. It would have provoked awkward questions."

"But I could have visited Antheia in Herefordshire when I was at Cambridge!" He turned to Antheia. "You said you lived near Leominster?" When she nodded, he added, "Indeed, the train would have got me there in under three hours."

"I didn't want your aunt to spurn you and hurt your feelings," said his father firmly.

Antheia thought for a moment. "I don't think Mother would have spurned him. In fact, she might have been delighted to meet her nephew."

Her uncle sighed. "How bitter is the harvest sown in youth and reaped in maturity. How we regret the decisions made in springtime when autumn comes." He pursed his lips. "If Will had turned up on the doorstep your mother would have had some explaining to do."

Antheia took a sip of her wine. The footmen were serving them dessert, but her stomach was churning. How delightful it would have been if Will had turned up at the vicarage door. She would have thought herself blessed. But how would her mother have explained a viscount for a nephew? What an interesting conversation that would have been.

She cast her uncle a bright smile. "True. But I would have been delighted to discover I had more family. My mother and father were married six years before I was born." She looked round the table and saw everyone watching her intently. "You see, I would have had an older brother and sister if…"

She couldn't finish and stared down at the tablecloth. Her uncle squeezed her hand and nodded sadly.

How grateful she was the evening passed pleasantly in the gold and red drawing room. Her step-aunt played Chopin on the piano, before Felix sang *Cherry*

Ripe and *Heart of Oak*. To Antheia's surprise, he had a good voice and she clapped enthusiastically. Afterwards they played cards until it was time to retire.

As she snuggled under the bedcovers in her new room, she felt happier. And yet mystery seemed to pervade the very stones of Sedgwick Abbey. Why had her mother left at the age of twenty? Certainly not to marry her father. So, what was the reason behind the rift between her mother and grandfather? Antheia yawned and turned over in bed. It was a long time ago and yet she had a feeling whatever it was still rankled with the family. Especially with Felix who believed their grandmother's disappearance had something to do with the late earl. Was that why her mother had left? She believed it too? Servant's gossip Will had said. But servants watched and listened.

Her eyes closed and drifting into sleep, she decided she would try and glean some information from Mrs Hadwin the following day.

CHAPTER SIX

"It's an exciting day, Miss Antheia, the seamstress is arriving after breakfast and she said she'll bring some readymade gowns with her as well as samples and designs for further dresses."

It was an exciting day and the thought of having an entirely new wardrobe thrilled Antheia. The only person who had measured her for new clothes was her mother. And the cloth they had bought was mostly cotton, muslin and wool.

In the breakfast room, next to the library, she helped herself to the tureens laid out on a long table against the wall. This was a lovely room, facing east and decorated in eggshell blue. The table was set with places, but the residents of the Abbey could sit anywhere they wished. Winder fussed over the residents, sending the maids scurrying to serve coffee or tea in stunning silverware.

Only Joel was sitting at the table, perusing the morning paper he placed to one side as Antheia entered the room.

"Good morning. Did you sleep well?" He stood briefly until she gestured for him to remain seated.

"I did," she said, helping herself to a plate of eggs, bacon and mushrooms. She took her place next to him and Winder beckoned the maid with the teapot. Antheia shook out the napkin and placed it across her knee. She smiled a thank you and turned to Joel. "I'm to be fitted for new clothes this morning."

"Why, what's wrong with your old ones?"

"It seems my old ones are not suitable for the niece of an earl." She grimaced.

He blew out a breath "Well, as far as I'm concerned, you always look wonderful. And yesterday evening, I thought a princess had walked into the room."

"Thank you," she smiled. She looked down at the gown she was wearing. A simple grey with long sleeves and a velvet collar. "The gown I wore for dinner is a secret."

"Is it indeed, ma'am. Perhaps one day you'll tell me its secret?"

She grinned and became thoughtful. In a whisper she said, "I think there's a secret in this house. What did you make of the conversation at dinner? About my mother leaving and never seeing her family again?"

"That was...interesting. But sad."

She bent her head towards him. "My mother seems to have left after a disagreement with my grandfather. I know it was a long time ago, but everyone still seems to be living with the consequences."

He grinned. "And you would like to discover more of the family secret?"

"Well...yes. I would. You heard Felix yesterday. He's convinced our grandfather murdered our grandmother."

"I wouldn't hold much store with what Felix says. He's always been an...interesting boy."

"Even so, I think I'll have a word with Mrs Hadwin. She's worked here for thirty years and she knew my mother when she was fifteen or sixteen by my calculations. She must know something."

"If you want any help with your investigations then do ask."

"Are you offering?" she grinned.

He inclined his head. "Yes, ma'am, I am."

"In that case, I gladly accept." She paused, thinking. "Have you decided yet about crossing the Atlantic to follow the drum?"

"I'll be writing my letter in the next week."

"You're going?" Her heart sank into her shoes.

"I am and I only ask one thing." He took her hand and kissed her fingers. "Will you write? I would so enjoy receiving your letters."

"Where would I send them? Armies move about."

"I'll give you my ma's address in Maine. She'll be happy to send them on to me."

Antheia didn't know how to answer, but her feelings were torn. She didn't want him to go and yet how could she feel so when she had only just met him? He was a stranger. But she couldn't forget the descriptions of the battles and number of casualties reported in the newspapers. The thought of Joel lying amongst the dead and dying young men on a battlefield made her hair stand on end.

"What's Maine like?"

He thought for a moment before saying, "It's a big state, over thirty thousand square miles in area so about half the size of Scotland."

"Is it a lovely place to live?"

"I think so, but of course I reckon I'm biased. But, yes, wide-open spaces and woodland and of course it's a coastal state."

"You said you were born and raised in Cape Elizabeth. That's obviously on the coast."

He smiled. "It is and a very rugged coast, dangerous to shipping. We've had a lighthouse since the 1820's, but Cape Elizabeth is a quiet town. The native Indians lived there first and then us white folk in the early seventeenth century. My ma likes to attend Spurwink Meeting House, although I find it rather a plain church compared with the churches and cathedrals in England. It's made of white clapboard with a tower and I feel it might blow away in a strong wind."

She chuckled. "Well, it's lasted so far."

Winder appeared at her elbow. "The seamstress has arrived, miss."

Antheia rose to her feet. "I'd better go. No please don't stand." She stared down at Joel, who resumed his seat, with a smile, his blue eyes sparkling. It was on the tip of her tongue to ask him to reconsider a military life, when she realised it wasn't any of her business. Besides, if his good friend Will couldn't persuade him otherwise, then how could she?

Joel watched her as she left the room. For all he loved England and had some wonderful friends, he felt he must go back and help the Union. It was his duty. But meeting Miss Antheia Vale was making him waiver. The thought of leaving her broke his heart. Damn the war, he thought, flicking open the newspaper to the report that Grant had captured Vicksburg in July. Perhaps the war was nearly over? But why hadn't he travelled straight to America from Italy?

Miss Liza Sill was a tall, slender woman and greeted Antheia with a smile. The seamstress had arrived minutes before, the footmen helping her carry all her wares up the stairs to Antheia's room. But she had already arranged three or four gowns on the chaise longue and samples of material were lying on the bedspread.

Matty was examining the gowns and commenting on the style and colours as Antheia walked into the room.

"Oh, miss, aren't they lovely!" She held up one. "This olive green is beautiful and just look at the silk buttons down the front."

Antheia agreed and felt overwhelmed. "These are all for me?"

Liza Sill nodded. "These are the readymade day gowns, miss, and should fit although I can make alterations in no time. I hoped they would suffice, since I chose the colours that would suit your year of mourning."

"That's wonderful. Thank you."

Matty giggled. "Miss Vale isn't like her ladyship, is she!"

Miss Sill knew better than to comment on a client and simply smiled and got down to the job in hand. In minutes she had measured Antheia and written the figures down in her notebook. Showing her the material samples followed this and although Antheia did her best to choose those she liked, she felt spoiled for choice. Everything she saw delighted her.

Within two hours Miss Sill had left, informing her new client she would bring the garments to the Abbey for a fitting as soon as possible.

Antheia looked at her fob watch. It was nearly eleven o'clock and she would like to see the housekeeper and ask her the all-important questions about her mother.

"Where would Mrs Hadwin be now?"

Matty stopped her work of placing the new gowns in the armoire and thought for a moment.

"She might be in her parlour, miss."

"I need to speak with her."

"I could fetch her if you like."

"Oh, no. Please don't disturb her. Our paths are sure to cross sometime today."

She descended the staircase knowing most of the household would have had their breakfast by now and her uncle would be busy in his study. Wondering where the others were she was alerted by laughter from the library. Her cousins and Joel must be looking at the literature available or perhaps Will was helping his brother with his Latin. She was about to cross the floor to join them when she faltered. She might not be welcomed and turned on her heel, glancing about at the portraits and landscapes on the wall. The main rooms were on the south side of the Abbey and she decided to explore more of the house that was now her home.

Walking along the corridor and past the dining room and drawing room, she knew she was now in an area she had never been before. She turned the corner and found herself in a small but impressive hallway. The plastered ceiling was sculptured into panels with an elaborate leaf and flower motif in the middle. Along the walls were half a dozen occasional tables on top of which were vases of flowers and exquisite Chinese figurines. The walls displayed another seven or eight portraits depicting men and women in different period clothing and a plush carpet softened her footfalls.

Antheia went across to one of the windows and looked out. To her amazement, she found herself staring at an inner courtyard and she let out a gasp of pleasure. It was like the drawings she had seen of an Italian courtyard and although surrounded by the main part of the building it looked like a place to find peace and solitude.

She pressed her forehead against the glass and tried to absorb as much a possible. There was a tiled path of blue and white and Mediterranean-style terracotta pots planted with what looked like rosemary and lavender and the borders were filled with citrus and olive trees. She spotted a bed of aromatic herbs and at the far end were palms near a small limestone pergola adorned with engravings of grapes on the four supportive columns. The wrought iron cupola was almost covered with climbing tamarisk and campsis; plants she recognised from her endless reading of her father's books on foreign gardens. But what delighted her most was the marble fountain in the middle of the courtyard. It was smaller than the one in the garden, but it still seemed to have the Shakespearean theme. The entwined figures portrayed a young girl and boy as if dancing; their right arms raised above their heads and their fingers barely touching. They stood on a plinth in an overflowing basin of water; the water cascading into a larger bowl which never seemed to fill.

"I wonder if that's Romeo and Juliet," said Antheia, sighing.

"Yes, it is and you can go out there to sit if you wish."

She hadn't realised she had spoken aloud and her cheeks flushed as she saw the housekeeper, skirts swishing, walking towards her.

"It's lovely...I didn't realise it was there."

Mrs Hadwin nodded. "Well, this is only your third day, my dear. And it takes a while to explore the entire house." She joined her at the window and smiled as she studied the wonder beyond the glass. "I'll show you the door to the courtyard later, however, Matty tells me you wish to speak with me."

Antheia turned to her. "I wanted to ask you...about my mother and why she left her home and family and never saw them again."

The housekeeper sucked in a deep breath. "Are you sure you want to know?"

"I know they say it's better to let sleeping dogs lie, but where's the harm in knowing? My mother and grandfather are gone, so why shouldn't I know. I'm part of this family now and I want my mind to be at peace."

Mrs Hadwin tilted her head and her lace cap slipped slightly. She adjusted it and said thoughtfully, "Come into the ballroom and I'll tell you what I know, although I'd appreciate it if you didn't mention this conversation to the family."

"Of course. This is between you and me."

The housekeeper turned and stepped across to the huge double doors on the far side of the hallway and Antheia followed her into a room that delighted her. From the large French windows on the far wall and the terrace beyond, she knew she had stood outside these windows when she had first found the garden and talked to George. In the distance she could see the trellis that held the beautiful red, white and pink roses.

She looked about her at the wonderful parquet flooring and at the end of the room to the enormous fireplace she could have stood up in. The walls were of walnut and from the ceiling three crystal chandeliers hung, glittering in the light from the windows, their sconces devoid of candles. Any furniture was covered with white dustsheets.

"What a beautiful room!"

"Not used much now," sighed the housekeeper. "But there used to be balls and parties in here nearly every week when your mother and uncle were young. Now your uncle prefers a quiet life and his sons seem destined to live away from Sedgwick Abbey."

Moments of silence passed until Antheia said, "I think now is the right time to tell me what I need to know."

CHAPTER SEVEN

The housekeeper walked to the centre of the room, her expression of someone who was now remembering a lost, forgotten time.

"Your mother loved this room and in those days…she was just a girl when I came to the Abbey. In fact I wasn't much older. I would come in here to dust and polish and find her dancing round and round, her skirts spinning about her, her hair down her back and swaying about her shoulders with the music in her head."

Antheia followed her not wanting to break into her memories.

"She would call to me in that singsong voice of hers, 'What do you think, Edwina? William or Victoria? Victoria or William?'"

"William or Victoria?" queried Antheia.

Mrs Hadwin turned to her, grinning. "At the time old King William was on the throne and her father had said she could be presented at court when she was seventeen. We all wondered if the king would last and a young queen would take the throne. That's what she meant. Would she be presented to William or Victoria."

"If she became a débutante at seventeen," Antheia quickly calculated, "that would have made it 1835. The queen didn't take the throne for another two years."

The housekeeper nodded. "Indeed. So, your grandparents accompanied her down to London for the Season and your grandmother sponsored your mother since she too had been a débutante and Lady

Anne was presented to a doddery old king who was bored out of his mind."

Antheia tried not to smile and then realised she too could have met the queen, being the granddaughter of an earl and her mother a former débutante. She forced the idea away; she had been happy as a clergyman's daughter.

"I'm sorry, what does this have to do with the rift between my mother and grandfather?"

The joy left her face. "Oh, yes, of course. Forgive me, my dear, I was lost in reminiscence."

Antheia stepped closer and linked her arm through the housekeeper's. "I understand. Memories are so precious."

Tears came to her eyes. "It was what happened the year after." She shook her head. "Your grandmother disappeared never to be seen again."

"What do you mean disappeared?"

"Exactly that. She left with no warning. Just gone."

"She didn't leave a letter explaining her actions?"

Mrs Hadwin blinked rapidly and tears dripped onto her cheeks. "Nothing at all." Fear welled up inside Antheia and Felix's ominous words returned, until the housekeeper added, "But her maid found a bag missing along with clothes and toiletries."

"So, she meant to leave?"

"It seems so." She took out a handkerchief and wiped the tears from her cheeks. "There was no news even though your grandfather tried to find her. Rumours began to circulate she must have had…a lover and left the earl to live with him."

"But did she seem to be the kind of woman to do that?"

The housekeeper squeezed her hand. "I wouldn't have thought so, but we never know what folk are really like, do we?" She gave a sigh. "This was such a happy home, full of music and laughter and in the space of a few weeks it became a mausoleum."

"What did my grandfather do?"

"He waited two years and then humiliated, he petitioned Parliament for a divorce through desertion."

Antheia had come across this many times when helping her father in his parish. Unhappily wed couples who could do nothing to end their marriage. She knew only the wealthy could obtain a divorce by the passage of a private act through Parliament. It didn't seem fair to her, but her father had reminded her that marriage was 'till death do us part'. But fathers still deserted their families.

"Ah, I see. My mother was against my grandfather obtaining a divorce. But she would have missed..."

Mrs Hadwin gripped her hand tightly. "No, my dear. It was the fact your grandfather wanted to remarry that upset your mother."

Antheia felt aghast. "But surely not! How could she deny him happiness after what he had been through?"

The housekeeper shrugged. "It was the way it was. We heard them arguing and it wasn't pleasant."

"And the woman he wanted to marry?"

"She isn't nobility by a long chalk. He had met her...well, she was a seamstress from Liverpool and some twenty-five years younger than the earl."

"He still deserved to be happy."

Mrs Hadwin nodded slowly. "They married the same year as your uncle, and your mother decided to stay long enough to see her brother and Lady Frances wed, but refused to stay for her father's nuptials. She left, but fortunately we knew she was going. She didn't just disappear like her mother did. Of course, we didn't know where she went and knew nothing of her until his lordship informed us her daughter, you my dear, was to reside at the Abbey with us."

Antheia's thoughts returned to her grandmother. "How old was my grandmother when she disappeared?"

Mrs Hadwin thought for a moment. "Well she was ten years younger than the earl so in her early forties."

"Does a woman of that age take a lover?"

The housekeeper's eyebrows raised in disapproval. "Ah, you believe love, romance, even passion belongs to the young. Well, let me tell you this, Miss Antheia, a woman can take a lover at any age." She looked aghast and stuttered, "Oh my, listen to me talking about lovers to a young, innocent girl like you."

"Helping my father in his parish opened my eyes to the facts of life." She leaned closer. "You wouldn't believe what some of them got up to."

Mrs Hadwin's eyes opened wide. "Really? You must enlighten me one day."

Antheia looked at the parquet floor trying not to smile. "Even so, my grandparents must have been married quite a while."

"Over twenty years."

Antheia shook her head slowly. "It just seems so strange my grandmother would up and leave without an explanation." She took in a breath. "Was he married to his second wife for long?"

Mrs Hadwin paused causing the young girl to look at her in surprise. Her expression seemed to be of someone who had detected an unpleasant smell. "They were married about five years until the earl died and your uncle took the title."

"Well, I'm sorry, Mrs Hadwin, but I have to disagree with my mother's actions. My grandfather was simply seeking comfort in his later years. My mother was wrong to behave so…so selfishly."

Mrs Hadwin shrugged. "It's all so long ago now. But you wished to know and now you do."

"Yes, I do and thank you." She had an inspired thought. "Perhaps you could show me the secret door to the inner courtyard. I'd love to explore it."

The housekeeper threw back her head, laughing. "It's hardly a secret door and it will take you just a short while to explore."

"Lead on MacDuff," said Antheia, gesturing to the exit of the ballroom.

The courtyard was more of a delight than she expected. Sitting in the pergola, she enjoyed the tinkling of the fountain and the aroma of the herbs and plants surrounding her. She knew she would spend a lot of time in the large garden at the rear of the house, but she had an inkling this place would become special to her.

She mulled over what the housekeeper had told her and still stayed firm to her opinion her mother had behaved selfishly by denying her own father happiness in his later years. His torment at the betrayal of his wife must have cut him sharper than a knife. What was strange was her mother hadn't been a selfish person. In fact, she could be exceptionally understanding and tolerant. Only now and again did Antheia see a frustration in her as though she had something important to do but was unable to do it.

Antheia caught her breath as she remembered the notion she had had the night before. Could her mother have had suspicions the earl had had a hand in his wife's disappearance? Felix was convinced about it.

Something else came to her. Mrs Hadwin had said, 'She isn't nobility by a long chalk,' when speaking of her grandfather's second wife. Isn't? Present tense! Antheia shook her head in exasperation. That could simply mean the dowager countess was still alive and living elsewhere. After all, she might only be the same age as her uncle.

A gentle cough made her raise her head and Joel was standing a few feet away.

"Sorry, I didn't want to disturb you. It's nearly lunch and I reckoned I'd escort you to the dining room."

She looked at her fob watch. "We still have fifteen minutes." Patting the seat next to her, she invited him to sit.

"Thank you, ma'am. You're very kind. My, this is a lovely place. I've always thought so."

"It is and will you call me Antheia. Ma'am makes me sound like the queen."

"That's how they address the monarch?"

"I believe so."

He cleared his throat. "I wanted to search you out since I wondered if I was being too forward asking you to write to me while I'm away."

"Oh, no, I would be delighted to. I've read serving soldiers value letters from home."

"They sure do." He paused before adding, "I'm also here to inform you of our plans. We talked it over in the library this morning. The three of us will depart at the end of next month and travel as far as Birmingham where young Felix will travel onward to Cambridge. Will and I will continue on to Southampton. He bound for Naples and I for New York."

Every word he said made tears come to her eyes and she blinked rapidly. "Of course, you all have things to do. Wonderful things to do." She became whimsical to hide her pain. "I wonder if I could follow Will to Naples and become part of the dig or perhaps I could follow you to America and become…a nurse for the wounded…"

He sensed her anguish and took her hand. "Will and I agreed it's hard to leave you alone, but we'll return."

"Not for a while."

"Felix will be home at Christmas." Nothing he could say removed the loneliness from her eyes. "I promise to come back as soon as I can."

She looked into blue eyes that were sincere. "I would like that, Joel. It was only when you and Will arrived I believed the Abbey could really become a home to me. But as you say, you're not leaving until the end of September. That gives us a month to enjoy each other's company and we must make the most of the time we have left." She pulled herself together. "Now, shall we go into luncheon."

He helped her to her feet. "Yes, ma…Miss Antheia."

"You're impossible!"

Taking his arm, they walked slowly through the courtyard and into the main part of the Abbey.

One month, thought Antheia, four weeks before she would be on her own and she decided she would enjoy the time they had together. This included a visit to St James's Church in Brawton for the Sunday service when Antheia wore her best felt hat with ostrich plumes and a scarf tied round the brim and flowing down her back. When she had packed it in the trunk, she had thought she would look stylish, but the housekeeper had told her a milliner would call at the Abbey in a few days to design her half a dozen new hats. She couldn't help feeling the entire wardrobe she had brought with her would be consigned to the parish poor before long.

The Reverend Horace Longmire was a portly man in his early thirties with a moon-like face and although Antheia enjoyed the hymns and said a silent prayer for the souls of her mother and father, she squirmed at the Reverend Longmire's sermon. It was full of death and damnation as he extolled his parishioners to look to their sins for the way of the flesh would ultimately lead to the fires of hell. She glanced at Will who pulled a face trying to make her laugh. He might be in his twenties, but he could be a clown at times.

As they came out of the porch of St James's she was introduced to the Reverend who took her hand and welcomed her to Brawton. She thought his hand rather moist and tried to ease herself away from him whilst remaining polite.

"I hate shaking that man's hand. It's wetter than a fish hauled out of the estuary," Will grimaced, on their way back to the Abbey in the carriage.

Lord Sedgwick grunted. "I can't disagree with you there. Perhaps we should start having services in the chapel again."

"What chapel, Uncle?" asked Antheia, intrigued.

He turned to her, smiling. "There's a private chapel, my dear, in the Abbey next to the ballroom. Have you not come across it yet?" When she shook her head he continued, "It was used extensively in the last century and the first couple of decades of this. But it fell out of use when the family decided to worship at St James's."

"I must go and see it." Her eyes lit up. "Did you and...Lady Frances marry there?"

"No, we married in the Church of St Nicholas in Newcastle, since my first wife was the only daughter of the Earl of Stannington so it was appropriate."

"What about my grandparents?"

"Yes, now I come to think of it, my mother and father did marry in the family chapel. And my sister and I were baptised there." A frown crossed his face. "You've made me think of my mother's siblings, my dear. Aunts and uncles, not alive now I should imagine, but I have cousins I've not seen since my marriage to Frances. It's such a shame how families lose touch."

The countess spoke for the first time since leaving the church. "And why would you want to meet them again. They refused to come to our wedding and that's a slight I will never forgive."

"Now, now, Cora don't be like that. They gave their reasons for not attending," said his lordship, but turned his head to view the passing scenery as if he didn't want to talk further on the subject.

Why didn't the family want to attend her uncle's wedding to his second wife? It was such a mystery but rifts in a family can stretch in every direction and rifts often turned into wide cracks impossible to traverse as time passed. A feeling of melancholy pervaded Antheia's senses and she tried to shrug it away. After lunch she would find the family chapel. Perhaps it would be interesting and a place she could escape to for private prayer.

But after luncheon, her cousins and Joel suggested a walk and thoughts of finding the chapel went out of her mind. Time with her cousins and Joel was precious and she didn't want to waste one second.

CHAPTER EIGHT

It was the start of many trips they took together over the next four weeks and Antheia couldn't have been happier. Her uncle smiled as he watched them setting off on their jaunts, often with his niece taking Joel's arm and he would rub his beard in speculation. The young man was intelligent and came from a good family of New England sailors and soldiers. He would have wanted a title for Antheia, but never having a daughter, he felt he should leave her to follow her heart's desire.

The day before they were leaving, Antheia couldn't believe how fast the month had gone. The following day she was to see them away on the train at Carnforth Station and she knew she would find it difficult to hold back her tears. But they had this one day left and Joel had already furnished her with his mother's address and she promised she would write as soon as possible.

That day at the end of September was beautiful, the air becoming still with hardly any breeze allowing the earth to soak up the last sunshine of summer. After breakfast, they set off for their final walk together, the men taking turns at carrying a small picnic basket and spurning Antheia's insistence she should take her turn. But none of them, even Felix, would contemplate the idea.

With Will leading the way, they started their walk towards Brawton. From the village, they crossed open fields that gave them a wonderful view across the estuary, but as they reached the end of the field they could see a secluded cove with a cave halfway up the limestone cliffs. Antheia was enchanted and wondered if they could go into the cave, although it seemed a steep climb.

They made their way down to the cove onto the shingle and stared up at the cave.

"I'm game if you are." Will winked at Antheia.

Joel came to her defence. "That's unfair. You've been in that cave many times and besides, Antheia isn't dressed for climbing."

Rising to the challenge, she bent forward and dragged the back of her skirt through her legs and tucked it in her belt. How pleased she was she had worn a simple navy blue straight skirt and plain white blouse that day, a shawl thrown over her shoulders shielded her from the slight breeze coming up the estuary.

"Well, look at that," smiled Will.

"Looks like the pants the men wear in the Middle East," said Joel thoughtfully.

"And why women can't wear trousers I'll never understand," added Antheia hotly.

Felix wasn't impressed. "Women wearing trousers…how ridiculous."

Giving them a haughty look, she scrambled up the rocks and hauled herself into the cave. She was surprised how small it was although easy to stand up in. The men had left the picnic basket at the base of the cliffs perched on a rock and followed her up, but stopped at the mouth of the cave when she pointed to a pile of clothes at the side. Walking tentatively across the pebbled floor she moved the pile with her foot, realising they weren't clothes, but dirty blankets. By the side was a box of matches and a half burned out candle stuck in a saucer; the saucer drawing her eyes. In its day it would have been an exquisite piece of crockery with a delicate garland of small forget-me-nots painted round the edge.

"Someone lives here," she murmured. "Who would make a home in a cave?"

Will sucked in a breath. "Could be just a harmless vagrant." He winked at Antheia. "Hopefully not an escaped convict running from the law."

"Perhaps we ought to leave," she replied, fearful whoever lived in the cave might return.

The others agreed and they helped her down the rocks to the cove, where she straightened her skirt. Collecting the picnic basket, they didn't speak as they made their way back up to the field and followed the lane, before Will led them through a gate and across another field giving them spectacular views. How many times had the boys come here over the years? Their sure steps and confidence made her think it must be hundreds of times and she knew this excursion had two reasons; to show her the area and also to say goodbye to the places they loved.

Will pointed. "Morecambe Bay. Perhaps Father will take you to visit Morecambe before the winter comes." She sensed his melancholy and squeezed his hand. They followed the track along the field and Will pointed yet again. "Warton Sands."

Antheia smiled. "Where your father found Fred?"

It was Felix who spoke up. "Yes, and I've never seen a dog in such dire straights. Half starved and bedraggled. We think someone tried to throw him in the estuary, but he managed to scramble out."

"Antheia doesn't need to know that," snapped his brother.

She nodded. "George told me Uncle had saved him."

Felix persisted. "Good thing he wasn't thrown into the quicksand. He'd have been sucked down to hell."

Antheia gasped and Will turned on his brother, but Joel held his arm and pulled him away. "He's trying to antagonise you. Just ignore him."

"But sinking sand," said Antheia, "Imagine being trapped and there's no one to help you escape."

Joel glanced at her and then gestured to the basket. "Shall we have our picnic now?"

They made themselves comfortable on the grass and opened the basket. Soon they were tucking into pork pies, chicken sandwiches, followed by fruit turnovers and cheesecake, all washed down with flasks of cranberry juice.

After they had finished and repacked the basket, Will led them along the field and down a shallow incline to the shingle. Looking around Antheia felt she knew this area. Wasn't it the one she had explored the day after she had arrived at Sedgwick Abbey? They examined the rockpools and Felix scooped out a worm and a snail, watching them wriggle and crawl, until he was pulled away by the others. They continued their walk along the shingle and Antheia thought of the tide sweeping in and covering the very ground they were standing on. Walking for a time they reached the trail that would take them back up the cliff and suddenly Antheia knew where she was. A short way away she could see the derelict chapel and the old graveyard.

"Oh, we've come full circle," she said, entranced. "This is where we first met."

Will couldn't help grinning. "Yes, this is Far Field and you were lying on the sarcophagus over there like Snow White."

"She was what?" asked Felix, looking askance at Antheia.

Will coughed apologetically. "I exaggerate. She was enjoying the sun…with her eyes closed. Nothing more."

Antheia looked about her, taking in the vista. The woodland in the distance seemed to stretch for miles protecting the Abbey from the wind and rain coming up the estuary. And there were quite a few fields between the woods and the cliff edge each divided by hedges of yew.

"Why is this called Far Field?"

"I have no idea and I don't think Felix knows." His younger brother shrugged in reply. "But the woods are criss-crossed with trails and secret paths. Felix and I must know everyone of them."

Felix grinned. "We certainly do."

Antheia glanced at Joel and he smiled at her. It was an attractive smile, warm and friendly, his blue eyes sparkling under the brim of his military hat.

They crossed Far Field and since the ancient burial ground was on their way back to the woods and the gardens of the Abbey, they stopped to take in the lonely abandonment of the place. Antheia couldn't prevent herself from walking towards the sarcophagus and placing her hand on its cool, flat top. Where the tears came from she couldn't understand. They seemed to spring from her eyes as the desperate feelings engulfed her once more. Such a feeling of loss and despair swept through her. She gave out a sob.

Joel heard and hurried over to her. "Antheia? What's the matter?"

She turned a tearstained face to him. "I don't…know. I just feel…" She fell against the front of his jacket and he put his arm round her to steady her.

Will and Felix raced across the graveyard towards them.

"Is she ill?" asked Will. "Perhaps we should carry her home."

Antheia swallowed and was relieved to feel the emotions subsiding. "No, please. I'm all right. I can walk. But I think I'd like to get back to the Abbey as soon as possible."

Will took charge. "Felix run ahead and inform Mrs Hadwin Miss Antheia isn't well."

Felix didn't wait but sprinted across the field towards the woodland. In minutes he had disappeared from view.

"I am feeling better," whispered Antheia, ashamed at causing so much fuss.

"Could be the heat," nodded Joel.

In a repetition of when they first met, the three walked arm in arm across the field, through the woodland and into the gardens, where Mrs Hadwin came hurrying towards them, her face blanched, her expression pained, until Antheia waved to her with a reassuring smile.

"What happened? Did you feel faint?" Mrs Hadwin fussed over her as Antheia pulled off her boots whilst sitting on the edge of the bed. "Is it your monthlies, my dear?" she added almost in a whisper.

Matty hurried to take the boots away to be cleaned, tutting at the state of them.

"Oh no, it wasn't that. Besides it wasn't a physical pain it was…well, I have no idea what happened and I certainly didn't feel faint. It was more a feeling of desperation."

"Desperation?"

Antheia found it difficult to explain. "I was overwhelmed by a grief that was hard to bear, as though I was never going to see those I loved again. A dreadful loneliness and a wretched urge to be…"

"What, my dear?" Mrs Hadwin had helped her to remove her skirt and blouse and pulling a face decided they had better go to the laundry too. The young girl's sudden halt in her explanation made her turn her head. "Urge to be what?"

"Heard," whispered Antheia. "Someone was calling out to be heard."

The housekeeper gave a sigh and made her lie down, covering her with a blanket. "You need to rest before dinner. You're worn out and it's putting fanciful thoughts in your head. You'll feel better after a sleep." She drew the curtains. "And besides, I think the departure of the young men in the morning is affecting your emotions. I know you'll miss them dreadfully."

After she had left, Antheia rolled over onto her side and curled up in a ball. The kindly housekeeper had been speaking the truth when she said she would miss the boys, but it was more than that. The month or so they had been in the Abbey had been her life blood, had been her reason for living. The thought of them leaving filled her with dread. What would she do once they were gone? Her father had always said, 'The devil finds work for idle hands', and she must find something to do. She refused to float about this enormous house like a lost ghost looking for redemption. It might take time, but come what may, she would be gainfully employed by Christmas.

Her good intentions faded away in the early hours of the morning as she stood at the window watching the sky slowly turn from purple to blue. There were two windows in her large corner room; one facing south and one west. This meant she had the benefit of the sun all day plus a view of the gardens on the west side, and on the south side a partial sight of woodland through which a glimpse of the estuary could be seen. Although she always enjoyed the view from her window, this morning she felt dispirited. Today Will, Joel and Felix were leaving.

She met them downstairs for breakfast and then it was out into the chill air as they piled into the landau with a waggon following with their trunks. The earl and Mrs Hadwin stood at the door and waved them off, but it was Antheia who would accompany them to the station in Carnforth.

They kept up an excited banter all through the four miles to the station, although she was sure Joel studied her thoughtfully at times. But when she turned her head to look at him, he would become absorbed in Will or Felix's conversation. When they arrived at the station the porter organised the luggage onto the platform and Antheia forced herself to keep smiling despite her torn feelings. The train squealed into the station far too soon to say farewell and she watched while their trunks were loaded into the luggage waggon at the rear of the train where the guard sat. As they climbed into a first class carriage, she kept up her happy demeanour, waving until the train was gone and she stood alone on the platform. Turning on her heel, she made her way out of the exit, acknowledging the stationmaster as she past him and smiled through misty tears.

"Take me home, Wilson, please," she whispered, as Charlie helped her into the landau.

Wilson touched the brim of his hat with the handle of the whip and urged the horses forward. Tears trickled down her cheeks and she wiped them away with her gloved hand. Drawing in a breath, she knew the future beckoned. She would write to Will and Joel often and there was no reason why Felix shouldn't receive a letter now and again. She would fill her time. She wouldn't be idle she promised herself. Her life must count for something or she might as well leave the Abbey and take her chances elsewhere.

CHAPTER NINE

Letters were written in the morning room, with a huge writing desk, the pigeon holes filled with notepaper, envelopes, the red wax and seal, plus all the equipment needed for writing.

Making herself comfortable in the leather chair, Antheia pulled a sheet of buff, headed paper towards her and dipped the pen in the inkwell. She had decided to write to the Reverend Brown again, since her first letter had been a brief one and only mentioned she had arrived safely at the Abbey. The pen dangled in her hand and she turned her face to the window, her thoughts distant. Had her mother sat in this very chair writing letters to her friends? It seemed possible. Had she written to anyone about her qualms at her father's impending marriage? She had left home and made her own way in the world and for a young girl to take such a drastic action must have meant circumstances were dire. Was she worried or fearful? Did she fear what had happened in the Abbey? That's if anything had happened. Antheia couldn't believe her mother could be so vindictive as to oppose the happiness of her own father.

Sighing, she returned to the task in hand and after twenty minutes of constant writing, the letter was completed and she folded the paper and placed it in the envelope, sealing it with the wax seal of the Earl of Sedgwick. Carefully, she wrote on the front of the envelope; The Reverend and Mrs T Brown, The Vicarage, Bromyard, Herefordshire.

In the letter she had poured out her heart, telling the Reverend and his wife about the departure of her cousins and a good friend who had become special to her. How she would miss them, she had told them. She had tried to keep her news happy, but it had been difficult. Her spirits were so low. She would write to Will and Joel in a few days when she had more to say. After all, they wouldn't have left England yet.

She took the letter into the hallway and placed it on the occasional table ready for the footman to take to the Post Office in Brawton after luncheon. For a moment she stood in the hallway and listened. There was no sound at all although she knew below stairs it would be a hive of activity with Cook and her maids busy preparing luncheon and more maids doing the laundry, the footmen cleaning the silver and going about their duties. All cleaning of the main rooms was done early in the morning and the bedrooms were tidied as soon as the occupant had gone down to breakfast, but it seemed she saw little of the servants who appeared to be invisible.

Antheia felt horrified there were now only three members of the family and over twenty household staff to look after them. She felt the urge to join the servants in their domain below stairs just for the company, but knew she would be severely reprimanded if she did, as well as not being welcomed by the servants. Remembering the courtyard garden, she decided to sit in it for a while and allow herself a moment of contemplation. She passed her uncle's study, the breakfast and morning room and turned down the wide, beautiful corridor with the doors to the ballroom and courtyard. But then she saw the wooden door on the north side of the Abbey, the one she knew led into the chapel. She had never explored the chapel and changing her mind, she pushed the door open.

The sudden chill caught her unawares and she pulled her shawl more closely round her. It was an austere place with a vaulted ceiling. In front of the altar there were three rows of hard wooden pews and the space behind was free of chairs. She noticed the door to the outside and realised the outdoor staff would use that door, whilst the family could use the inner door, making themselves as comfortable as they could in the pews. The unfortunate servants would have stood at the back throughout the service and how uncomfortable that would have been for them.

Everything was clean, not a bit of dust anywhere. No doubt the maids dusted in here too, but it felt neglected, unused. There was a narrow stained-glass window above the altar letting in a little sunlight, but everything seemed to be cast in gloom. Although the chapel was constructed mostly of stone, the walls had been lined with wood from floor to halfway to the ceiling. She took a seat in the front pew and stared at the altar with a simple wooden cross in the centre. It looked as if the chapel had been stripped of anything of value and a sadness pervaded the place along with the chill. Not a friendly place to worship, but when she thought of it in its day, with vases of flowers and candles and an altar cloth. Perhaps then it would have been a beautiful chapel.

On the wall above every wood panel there was Latin writing; *dona nobis pacem deo maii tempore interitu*. This was easy to translate; may god grant us peace in time of turmoil. To Antheia it made a poignant maxim, since the family was torn by war in the fifteenth century during the Wars of the Roses. No doubt this chapel had given the family a place of peace during the turmoil of those times. But she couldn't think it was the family motto.

She noticed a vase of dahlias in the corner and walked across to smell them. And then she saw the vase in which they stood wasn't a vase. It was metal and quite ornate, but looking at it closely she realised what it was. It was a brass censer with the chain snipped off and used in the Catholic Church to burn incense during certain services; when swung by the chain the incense was released. Now it had been turned into a flower vase. Antheia looked about her and was drawn to the simple wooden cross on the altar. Peering at the four arms she could see the holes where the figure of the crucified Christ would have hung. The holes had been filled and the entire cross varnished, but the indents were still visible. She looked about her knowing this was once a place where the family worshiped during the time of Queen Elizabeth's reign when Catholics were persecuted and executed, especially their priests.

Antheia knew she couldn't use this chapel for private prayer. It was too bleak and far too cold. She walked across to the outside door and turned the handle, but it was locked. She was fairly convinced the door would lead out into the gardens, since the chapel was situated in the north west corner of the Abbey. It was time to leave as the chill was starting to seep into her bones. She made her way to the door she had used to enter the chapel and wondered from where the draught was coming. It was strong enough to blow a ship off course and running her hands over the wooden panels she felt cold air coming from behind one of them. The walls to the Abbey were thick, but obviously the wind could whip round the corner and find any nook and cranny available. She shivered and looking at her fob watch realised it was time for luncheon.

How glad she was to leave the dismal atmosphere of the chapel and follow the corridors to the dining room where Winder nodded at her as he opened the door. Her uncle was standing at the sideboard helping himself to a selection of meats and potatoes.

"It seems it's a buffet luncheon for you and me today, my dear. My wife is eating in her room as usual."

Antheia picked up a bowl and ladled a good amount of chicken soup from a large silver tureen into it. And followed this by taking a warm roll from under a cloth placed over the platter. She joined her uncle at the table and tucked into the soup, relishing not only its delicious taste but also the warmth it spread through her chilled body.

The conversation between her uncle and herself was amicable as he requested details of the departure of the boys, but she could only inform him they had caught their train on time and that was that. He wouldn't want to know the pain she felt at their absence and how empty the Abbey appeared. Perhaps he did. Antheia sensed in him loneliness too and knew he missed his elder son. He seemed filled with sadness and she feared he would revert to his former demeanour towards her. Would he be indifferent to her wellbeing from now on? Perhaps she would have to wait for Will's return before his previous happy self appeared once more.

Replenished with a warm meal inside her she thought she would take a walk in the gardens and probably have a chat to George. Fred would be out there with him too. Fetching her cloak from her room, she hurried downstairs and almost ran to the far side of the house to the rear exit.

She walked slowly down the paths and through the rose trellis. The last of the blooms were glorious and spread out in front of her were the herbaceous borders still full of colour.

"Miss Antheia! Miss Antheia!" She turned to see Matty running towards her and stopped walking to allow the maid to catch up with her. "Miss Antheia, her ladyship wishes to see you in her sitting room immediately."

"What does she want with me? She's barely spoken a dozen words to me since I arrived."

The maid shrugged. "I got the message from Patience, miss. Only you're to go straightaway."

Antheia giggled. "It's like a summons from the queen, isn't it."

Matty grinned. "More like a summons in front of a judge. I do hope you get a fair trial."

Antheia grimaced and turned on her heel to make her way back into the house. Once in the hallway, she threw her cloak over a chair determined to continue her walk after her audience with the mistress of the house. Lifting her skirts she took the stairs quickly and hurried down the corridor to her ladyship's apartments. Knocking on the double doors made her quake a little, but drawing in a breath she steeled herself.

Patience opened the door and smiled. "Miss Antheia, you got the message?"

"Yes, and I pray this won't take long."

Her ladyship's voice came from within. "Do bring her in girl, and then fetch a tray of tea."

The maid pulled a face. "Keep your eyes on your cup. Don't let the old witch drop any poison into it."

Shaking her head in amusement, Antheia slipped into the room and dipped a curtsey. "Good afternoon, Aunt. Are you well?"

Lady Sedgwick grunted. "I would be well enough if that idle so-and-so didn't dally with her duties." She looked at the young girl standing in the middle of the room. "Don't just stand there, sit by me." This had never happened and with trepidation, Antheia took the seat indicated, smoothing out her skirts to give her hands something to do. Lady Sedgwick noticed. "I see you're better presented now you have a new wardrobe. You could pass for the niece of an earl. And I must say Miss Sill has done you proud. You look quite becoming in the lavender."

"Thank you, Aunt."

"I don't think a young girl should wear complete black. It's too melancholy and as your uncle said, we rarely entertain and never venture to London now. We are quite isolated here." Patience came in carrying the teatray and placed it carefully on the occasional table and when the countess waved her away, she hurried from the room as though a bear was chasing her. "The reason why I've asked you here is because I want to know more about your life in Boxwood."

"Bromyard, my l…Aunt."

"Ah, yes. I'm sure it's a pretty village. Tell me about the vicarage and how your mother fared being the wife of a clergyman."

What could she say? It didn't take long to give the details of her upbringing, her happy childhood and how at the age of twelve she had helped her father in the parish. The countess listened intently and Antheia was incredulous she should be interested. More questions followed, but she was quick to notice the countess always turned the conversation round to her mother. Why would her aunt be bothered about a woman she had never met, albeit her sister-in-law? As she sipped her tea and answered the questions fired at her, she began to feel uncomfortable. Suddenly she wished to be out in the open; to walk the paths between the flower borders and look at the fountain. And if George were about, she would love to have a chat with him; even take Fred for a walk if it was acceptable.

Her thoughts became distant as she sipped her tea and she hardly absorbed her aunt's next words.

"I've volunteered your help at St James's. The Reverend Longmire is in desperate need of assistance."

Antheia nearly dropped her cup in her lap. She paused before stuttering, "But...surely his curate..."

"Did your father have a curate?"

"Yes, he had three over the time he officiated at St Peter's."

"But you still helped him?"

"I was his daughter and felt it was my duty to assist him."

"The Reverend Longmire has no curate since he died last year. You have the experience and you can start tomorrow. Take the gig or whatever vehicle suits you and be at the vicarage by ten o'clock."

Indignation made her speechless and she had a mind to tell her aunt, quite calmly, she appreciated the gesture but must decline. She had hoped to find something to do, but to help the Reverend Longmire with his moist hands and rather musty odour was the last thing on her mind. Her memories returned to the time she had spent with her father in the parish. She had been happy and contented. Perhaps helping a clergyman again would be beneficial since if she occupied herself with visiting the parishioners and helping in the community, she might only see him now and again.

Her resentment faded as she worked through her thoughts. Yes, she would do it and if anything it would make her acquainted with the folk in Brawton and give her something to write about to Will and

Joel. And the Reverend Brown. How surprised he would be when he received her next letter.

She nodded and smiled. "Thank you, Aunt. I was wondering what I would do with my time and helping in the parish will suit me perfectly."

Lady Sedgwick inclined her head in acknowledgement. "Excellent. You may leave. I need to rest."

CHAPTER TEN

The bell tinkled on the door to the apothecary as Antheia swept in. She loved the shops in Brawton, but some she loved more than others and the apothecary was one of them. She enjoyed breathing in the aroma of fresh herbs, tinctures and ointments, mostly prepared in the dispensary at the rear of the premises.

Wide shelves against the wall contained gleaming blue glass jars of whale oil, camphor and lavender and above these were smaller jars of potions and many types of seeds. Antheia knew the green glass jars on the top shelf indicated a poison and were treated with great respect. There were a few customers in the shop and she waited patiently as each was served at a polished mahogany counter. It seemed every available surface was filled with all the apothecary could sell from barley sugar sweets to smelling salts, from soap to shaving implements.

Antheia dipped into the basket she carried on her arm and studied the paper on which was written a list. The customer in front of her moved away and smiling she stepped up to take her turn.

"And what can I do for you, Miss Vale," said Mr Armer, leaning his huge bulk on the counter. He always enjoyed the company of such a pretty young woman.

"I have three prescriptions to collect," she looked at the paper in her hand, "peppermint lozenges for Mrs Bellis, ointment for Miss Hicks and a bottle of laxative for Mr Lowis."

Not taking his eyes from her, he shouted to his assistant and in moments the three items appeared on the counter. He checked them to make sure they were correct before placing them in her basket.

"There you are and all paid for in advance." He paused before adding, "How are you enjoying your work for the Reverend Longmire?"

"Am I working for him? I certainly don't get paid."

He raised bushy eyebrows in surprise. "But you're here in Brawton nearly every day."

"Even so, I don't get a penny."

She left him grumbling it didn't seem fair to be used so and made her way out of the door onto the main street.

In the two months since she had started working in the parish she had discovered two wonderful facts. The first was her meetings with the vicar only extended to a morning cup of tea with him when she arrived at the vicarage. And his housekeeper, Mrs Sisson, was always about to chaperone her. The tall, slender widow with a constant serious expression had become a barrier between the vicar and herself and she was grateful for it. Only once had Longmire ventured too close to her. It was the morning when the housekeeper was otherwise engaged and the vicar had walked behind Antheia's chair and placed a sweaty palm on her neck. She had pulled away from him, eyes narrowed in anger. He had apologised profusely, his excuse being he was simply straightening the collar of her jacket.

The second wonderful fact was her growing knowledge of the residents of Brawton. Of course she knew the landlord and landlady of the Red Lion public house, but slowly over the two months she had come to know many others. And their problems. It always surprised her how the folk of the village would pour out their woes to her when discovering she was working on behalf of the Reverend Longmire and had been a clergyman's daughter. Many of their complaints were minor although she had to admit some suffered ill health. And none more so than in the poor quarters of the village at the bottom of the main road in Slee Court.

Here were the poorer cottages with families of eight crowded into two rooms. When she arrived back at the Abbey she felt ashamed such an enormous amount of room was available to so few people. In order to compensate her guilt, she would often visit these cottages and take whatever she could scrounge from the kitchens of the Abbey. Cook was happy to fill her basket with bread and potatoes, pies and sausage since it was for a good cause.

The one thing that amused Antheia was although she had taken to wearing the clothes she had brought with her to Lancashire, since they were simple and comfortable, she was now dispensing those with good wear in them to the poor of Brawton. The families saddened her, especially the ones with many children. But it was Mrs Thornborrow who worried her.

Antheia had seen the wizened old woman many times as she carried out her duties, but coming out of the apothecary that chilly morning, they almost collided outside the shop. Stooped and using a stick, it seemed the residents of Brawton avoided her, even moving away from her as she approached. Antheia stood her ground and smiled, nodding a greeting. The elderly woman didn't return her smile, but stared at her for a few seconds before continuing on her way.

She watched her shuffling along, before spying the vicar rounding the corner. She gave an audible groan. Her morning was nearly over and she wanted to get back to the Abbey as soon as possible.

"Ah, Miss Vale. I'm just on my way to have luncheon. Would you care to join me at the vicarage?"

She rarely stayed in the village in the afternoons unless she had something important to do. Her eyes flicked to the elderly woman slowly making her way down the lane.

"Mrs Thornborrow is always alone. Does she not have any family or friends?"

He followed her line of vision and pulled a face. "I don't think she has any of either."

"So, you don't know much about her?"

"Well, she arrived in the village about thirty years ago, but she keeps herself to herself."

"I feel so sorry for her."

His laugh was almost a snarl. "She's an old witch and best avoided."

Anthea felt appalled. "Oh, no, she's an elderly woman who needs our help not our censure."

He reached to take her hand and his touch felt uncomfortable. It took all her effort not to pull away, although the sweaty smell from his body made her tilt her head away.

"You have such a kind heart, but she doesn't deserve your pity. She has a colourful past that would be best left unsaid."

Anthea's heart went out to her. "But she makes potions and medicines for those who can't afford apothecary prices. And I know she also treats those who can't afford the physician."

"As I said she's a witch."

Anthea felt only contempt for him. "Oh dear, and there's me thinking it's 1863 and not 1663."

He stared down at her and she shrank from his gaze. For all his rotund shape and moon-like face gave him a jovial appearance, she suddenly believed he could be violent when he felt the need.

His expression changed and he was once more the pleasant vicar of St James's.

"You didn't answer my question about luncheon."

"I must be getting back to the Abbey after I've delivered this medication." She patted the basket in emphasis.

She was glad to be away from him and quickly walked toward the home of Mr Lowis to deliver his laxative. It wouldn't take long to dispense with the other two and then she would jump in the gig, waiting for her at the stable, and travel back to the Abbey. Antheia was awaiting the arrival of a special letter.

Joel's first letter had arrived a few days after he had left. Sent from The Star Hotel in Southampton his words had conveyed a warmth that made her glow, even though his news only informed her their journey south had been fairly pleasant. Since they had to wait over an hour for their train at Birmingham they were able to see young Felix away on the train bound for Cambridge.

Now ensconced in the hotel, he would say farewell to Will the following morning with his own ship leaving the day after. Antheia had replied immediately sending the letter to Joel's mother in Cape Elizabeth, Maine. Never in her life had she written to foreign parts although she couldn't decide if America was a foreign country. To her utter surprise, another letter had arrived only one week after he had set off and this had been written aboard ship. She had wondered how they posted letters aboard ship, but guessed they must pass the bag of mail to a ship going from New York to Southampton. It seemed a lovely idea.

Joel had spoken about the Cunard Line ship RMS Scotia, about his bunk in a cabin with three other men and how the ship was both steam and sail. The crossing was going well and the sea mostly calm. He hoped to dock in New York in eight or nine days after a two-week crossing. He would then travel to Maine by train to spend time with his mother before reporting for duty.

This had made Antheia gasp since she had tried to put it out of her mind he was enlisting into the Union Army. She wrote her reply that afternoon and again, sent it to his mother. She spoke of her work with the Reverend Longmire and of the people of Brawton. She wondered if he knew any of them and couldn't help mentioning Mrs Thornborrow and the fact had she lived two hundred years ago she might have been persecuted as a witch.

His next letter came four weeks later. It had been the beginning of November and the summer was long behind her, the leaves fluttering to the ground in a cascade of brown, gold and yellow. The fact she had had to wait a month for his third letter drew on all her patience. She knew he had the journey to his mother's home, plus all he needed to do to prepare for active service, but it was the longest four weeks of her life.

In this letter he said he had arrived in Cape Elizabeth safely, but had had to wait a few days before her letters had caught up with him. He was enjoying home cooking while he waited for his orders and his uniform to arrive from the tailor's and yes, he remembered Mrs Thornborrow and had always felt sorry for her. But he expressed surprise she had decided to help the Reverend Longmire. Antheia thought she detected concern along with surprise and puzzled over this. Perhaps Joel didn't trust the Reverend.

Having escaped lunch with the Reverend Longmire, she arrived back at the Abbey and searched eagerly for a letter. But the silver salver on the hallway table was depressingly empty. She had hoped another letter would have arrived since it was three weeks since the one he had sent after reaching Maine. Antheia had soon come to realise letters from America would be spasmodic and had decided, although she longed for his letters, she wouldn't wait for his replies, but would write every two or three days. In this way there would be a flurry of letters from her crossing the Atlantic.

Even so, she was sure one would arrive from him soon and decided to spend the afternoon walking round the garden and chatting to George who was deadheading the last of the roses. It was getting cold and she thought how strange she had no desire to walk through the woodland, across the field and down the cliff to stand on the shingle of the estuary. Since the boys had left, she had stayed away. And as for the derelict chapel and cemetery? She felt it better to avoid that place at all costs.

When the butler brought a letter to the breakfast table the following morning, she almost grabbed it from him.

Her uncle chuckled. "Don't mind her, Winder. My niece is hungry for news from a certain young man."

The butler's face was impassive. "Indeed, my lord."

Antheia turned it over in amazement. "It's thicker than normal. How many pages has he written."

Lord Sedgwick didn't answer, but continued buttering his toast. She broke the seal and took out two neatly folded pieces of paper. She opened one and saw it was from Joel, but she was intrigued by the second. Opening it carefully, she was surprised when a small photograph fell out onto the lap of her chocolate brown skirt. She picked it up and gasped at the portrait of a serious but handsome young man now sporting a becoming moustache. His jacket was double-breasted with two rows of shiny buttons and underneath the high collar was the hint of a shirt. She could just see the hilt of a sword strapped round his waist. But it was his hat that brought tears to her eyes. It was the same hat he had always worn but now with a cord round the base of the crown and an insignia sewn on the front.

Antheia passed the photograph to her uncle as she unfolded the letter accompanying the photograph. She was surprised to see it from Joel's mother since Mrs Newton had never written to her before. She read with great interest.

Dear Miss Vale,

I trust you are well. My son has been very busy preparing for joining his regiment, but I persuaded him to go to the photographer's studio and have his picture taken. I needed a memento of him since I don't know when I will see him again. He caught the train from Portland yesterday and he so reminded me of his father, I found it difficult to keep the tears at bay. My love and heart go with my boy.

I enclose his last letter to you before his departure and I thought you might like a photograph too and took the liberty of getting a copy made. I find the moustache my son has grown quite the military officer and Joel has it on good authority that an infantry captain must sport a moustache if he's to be taken seriously by his men.

Take care my dear girl. I will forward my son's letters to you the moment they arrive.

Yours sincerely
Martha Newton

Antheia smiled as she read. Martha Newton sounded a lovely woman and the kind of mother who would have a son like Joel.

Joel's letter was brief.

My dear Antheia,

Please forgive me for my tardiness at answering your letters. As you can imagine I've been preparing to start my duties and tomorrow I will journey to Alexandria in North Virginia to report for duty.

It was wonderful reading all your news and my mother sends her regards. Whatever you do, Antheia, my dear friend, please keep your letters coming. And do not worry. I'm sure this war will soon be over and when that happens I promise to return to England and to you.

Kindest regards
Joel Newton

It was a lovely letter although it was short and to the point. Antheia smiled and placed it back in the envelope. He promised to return and it was all she needed to know. Her uncle took a sip of tea as he handed the photograph back to her. She studied it and thought how handsome Joel looked.

"He's a fine young man," nodded her uncle. He squeezed her hand. "It's hard not to worry when you have a soldier for a suitor."

She felt alarmed. "He's not my suitor. He's a good friend."

He let it pass. "My mother said she was extremely anxious when my father went off to Waterloo."

"My grandfather fought at Waterloo! I didn't know he was a soldier."

He cleared his throat and smiled. "He wasn't a career soldier as such, but when Napoleon escaped from Elba he thought he ought to serve his country."

"My grandmother must have been heartbroken." She knew exactly how she had felt since didn't she feel the same now as she waited for news from Joel? And it was an unpleasant feeling.

"She was expecting me when he marched away. And believe it or not I was born three days after the battle. When he came home, he had a family."

"I'm so pleased he survived...or my mother wouldn't have existed...and therefore me." It was a salutary thought.

"Yes, and they enjoyed over twenty years of marriage before she..." He glanced away and a stillness filled the room.

Antheia didn't want to dwell on the fate of her grandmother and turned her thoughts to Joel.

"I am worried about Joel, Uncle. He's not a soldier. He's a Doctor of Archaeology and how is he going to manage in a world he doesn't understand."

"Now what makes you think he doesn't understand soldiering?"

"Because he was at Cambridge from the age of seventeen. Oh, I know his father was a soldier, but that's a different matter."

"Did he tell you where and how he was educated?" The earl narrowed his eyes at her.

"No, nothing at all."

He sighed and shook his head in amazement. "He went to West Point as a cadet when he was only ten years old. He graduated from the academy at sixteen." Rising to his feet he chuckled. "Don't worry, my dear, he knows what it's like to be in uniform and I'm sure drilling and marching and everything military will return to him." He threw his napkin on the table. "Now, I must leave since I have much to do." He caressed her cheek briefly and left the room in a hurry.

She smiled watching him go. Her fears he would be indifferent to her had disappeared since his melancholy state had only lasted a week after the boys had left. Now he seemed content, even happy in her company. Had she taken Will's place in his affections? She didn't think so, but it had entered her head perhaps she had become the daughter he would have liked.

Even so, he had eased her worries. Yes, it was ten years ago when Joel had worn the grey uniform of a West Point cadet, but surely with further training he would have all the skills to get him through the war. But deep down she wanted the war to end. Before Christmas would be wonderful. Reading the accounts of the battles in the newspaper, she doubted it would be over in 1863. There was always 1864. Yes, perhaps hostilities would cease the following year.

CHAPTER ELEVEN

Felix arrived home at the beginning of December and queries on how his first term had been were greeted with a shrug.

"I keep failing in my Latin," he admitted.

Antheia didn't want to offend him but felt the need to help. He had wandered into the library as she was in the process of research and she quickly noticed his dejected demeanour.

"Why don't we spend an hour every day after luncheon here in the library and I can tutor you."

He looked askance at her. "But it's the holidays!"

"My father taught me a wonderful way to learn Latin. I can teach you."

"But an hour every day!"

"What about two hours every other day?" She tried not to smile.

He nodded reluctantly. "Very well. But as the family motto tells us, *quia viribus tuis*."

As he walked away, Antheia shook her head in dismay. If she could fool him so easily, how would he manage as a solicitor? But the family motto intrigued her. *Quia viribus tuis*; know thy strengths. Was Felix saying the law wasn't for him? She couldn't worry over her younger cousin and turned her attention to the large atlas spread out on the table. It had been her Bible ever since Joel had arrived back in America. She had traced his route from New York to Cape Elizabeth and discovered it was over three hundred miles and later she had done the same with his route from Portland to Alexandria in North Virginia. Another five hundred and fifty miles. The distances seemed immense but she had come to understand the states of America covered an unbelievable landmass.

From then on she had scanned the newspaper and much to her uncle's distress, had followed the battles from state to state. The gains and losses, the casualties and death toll. Even though her uncle said it served no purpose she couldn't help herself and the atlas remained open permanently on the large table in the library.

Christmas at the Abbey was going to be a subdued affair although that didn't stop the servants from placing candles round the rooms and filling bowls with dried rosemary and sage. The hallway and main rooms were decorated with holly and ivy and in the drawing room stood an enormous fir tree; its branches filled with the family's treasured glass ornaments collected over twenty years, plus small silk bags of sweets, candy canes and gingerbread men.

Antheia sent gifts to the Reverend Brown and his wife and also to Will and Joel, although she couldn't think when they would receive them. Letters had come from Will in an ad hoc fashion and he seemed to be enjoying his time in Italy and learning a great deal at the dig in Pompeii.

On Christmas Day they travelled to St James's in the closed coach with the coat of arms emblazoned on the doors. A gentle snow had started to fall, but nothing too serious to impede the church-bound traffic. Once inside the church, singing *Once in Royal David's City* and *Angels from the Realms of Glory* compensated the congregation when the Reverend Longmire spent a good fifty minutes slamming his hand down on the pulpit and spouting about the overindulgence at Christmas. Antheia was amused since they hadn't even had their Christmas dinner or opened their gifts and they were already being made to feel guilty about it.

She thought of the folk living in Slee Court. What kind of Christmas would they have? The weeks before the festive season had been busy for her. She had continued begging spare food from Cook and old blankets and shawls from Mrs Hadwin. All her gowns from her time in Herefordshire were now dispersed amongst those in need. In her room was an exceptionally thick woollen shawl in purple with yellow tassels round the edges. She hoped to give this to Mrs Thornborrow, but the old lady had not answered the door when Antheia had visited her. She was determined to try again after Christmas.

While the Reverend expounded his disgust at parishioners who thought only of themselves, Antheia glanced at her aunt. The countess looked splendid as she sat regally in the front pew with the rest of the family. Decked out in jewels and a beaver fur hat with matching fur on the gold-coloured coat's cuffs and collar, her attire seemed to make her glow. Antheia had decided to wear her burgundy cloak with a wide hood since the sleeves of her gown were too wide for her coat.

Her attention went back to the Reverend who had thankfully finished his sermon. Suddenly, Felix rose from the pew and stood in front of the congregation. The organ began to play and Felix gave a wonderful and touching rendition of *O Holy Night,* a carol her parents had loved. Tears came to her eyes as she was filled with memories, on this the first Christmas without them. Her cousin's beautiful voice echoed and soared to every part of the church and made many of the congregation reach for their handkerchiefs.

The final prayer and blessing followed and then her strong boots crunched through the snow as she came out of the church, lifting her face to catch the falling snow on her tongue.

"How are you enjoying your time with the Reverend Longmire?" The words came out of nowhere and it was a few seconds before she realised she was being addressed by the countess.

"It's interesting, Aunt. I'm getting to know the folk in Brawton."

"But what about the man himself? Do you work well together?"

She didn't like to say she tried not to work with him and kept her distance as much as possible. In fact she had been successful in avoiding him from the start. "Amicable enough," she lied.

"He tells me you've refused to take luncheon with him although he's asked you for a good few weeks now."

"I...like to get back to the Abbey for luncheon." She didn't see the point of telling her she hurried home in order to see if there were any letters waiting for her.

"I'd like you to start having lunch with him. It's impolite to turn him down and unbecoming for the niece of an earl. After all, he's only looking out for your comfort."

Antheia couldn't see how having a meal with the obnoxious Reverend Longmire was adding to her comfort, but inclined her head in acknowledgement. It would be easy to avoid him or make an excuse. She could always forget the time; forget him. There was no possibility she would sit for a meal with him.

"Mrs Thornborrow! Do open the door. I need to speak with you." Antheia stamped her feet trying to bring some sensation back into her frozen toes. It was New

Year's Eve and the snow had lain since Christmas Day.

"Go away!"

She paused before knocking again. "It's so cold out here. You're forcing me to freeze to death."

"Are you deaf? Go away!"

"If I do, then you're forcing me to take luncheon with the Reverend Longmire."

There was silence for a few seconds before the door creaked open. "Hiding are you? Then you'd better come in." She opened the door wider allowing Antheia to pass into the interior of the small cottage.

The first thing she noticed was how clean and tidy it was. The fact Mrs Thornborrow lived in one room didn't prevent her from organising her living quarters to the best of her ability. A cast iron range stood against the wall, a roaring fire in the grate. The kettle on the hot plate steamed ready for a pot of tea, the door of the adjacent oven was closed with the aroma of baking bread making Antheia breathe deeply. There was a small truckle bed in the corner and the walls were of plain plaster with two windows, one at the front and one at the back. The floor was stone slabs and scrubbed to whiteness, as was the table in front of the range. Along with an old armchair and an even older straight-backed dining chair, there was very little furniture. But the elderly woman had made it homely with cheap landscape prints on the walls and a vase of flowering winter heather in pink and mauve on a far shelf. At the far side of the room was a long bench and above it a shelf filled with jars like those in the apothecary although smaller, containing dried seeds and other substances. Bunches of herbs dangled from the ceiling with pieces of twine.

Antheia held out her hand. "We've never been introduced. I'm Antheia…"

Mrs Thornborrow pointed to the armchair. "I know who you are. No need to be formal here. Sit yourself down. The kettle is boiling and I'm sure a slice of bread and butter won't go amiss."

Antheia nodded and shrugged off her coat, opting to sit on the dining chair rather than in the armchair. She watched as the elderly woman opened the oven door and lifted out two rounded loaves of bread and tipped them out onto a wire-cooling tray. She then busied herself with making a pot of tea.

It wasn't long before Antheia was tucking into a slice of warm bread smothered with melting butter and a cup of tea. The crockery was mismatched, the cutlery plain and unadorned, unlike the tableware at the Abbey, but she had never enjoyed a meal so much in all her life.

"So, you're escaping Longmire?"

Mrs Thornborrow had taken a seat in the armchair and there had been no discussion between them while she prepared the meal.

Antheia nodded and wiped a dribble of butter from her chin with her hand. "My aunt has requested…demanded I take lunch with him and I'd prefer not to."

Mrs Thornborrow chuckled. "Yes, best to keep away from that man if you can."

"Why?" What a silly question! She knew his wandering hands were a menace, but she wanted to know what the old lady thought.

"He has a history does that individual."

How strange the Reverend had said the same about her. "What kind of history?"

Mrs Thornborrow tapped her nose. "That would be telling."

Antheia remembered the shawl and reaching for her basket took it out. "I wondered if this would help you in the cold especially when you're out and about in Brawton."

She hoped her gift wouldn't be thought an insult to the old lady's independence and was relieved when she took it, turned it about to examine it and nodded.

"I give you thanks. Tis nearly New Year and there's still a while to go before spring."

"If you're in need of anything, then please let me know. The servants at the Abbey are getting used to me begging and foraging for items."

"The countess is agreeable?"

Antheia copied Mrs Thornborrow's former gesture and patted her nose. "What she doesn't know can't hurt her."

The old lady's eyes glazed over. "Her ladyship knows far more than the disappearance of victuals and chattels from the Abbey."

"What does she know?" The young girl smiled in amusement, but the woman shook her head and turned away. "Do you have family? I always wondered."

"I married Thornborrow when a young woman. He was a sailor from Liverpool and didn't come back with his ship."

"He died at sea?"

"Aye and buried at sea."

"Were you married long?"

"He sailed away two weeks after we wed."

Antheia's hand went to her mouth in dismay. "I'm so sorry."

"A woman marries a sailor she must expect it to be so."

The same with a soldier thought Antheia and pulled herself together. She wasn't married to Joel, but her emotions couldn't be keener.

She changed the subject and pointed to the bench at the side of the room. "You make potions and ointments for those in need and can't afford the apothecary. That's commendable."

"I do what I can to help. As well as birth the babies of mothers who haven't the wherewithal to pay the midwife or physician."

"Did you deliver Mrs Garnett's seven kiddies?" She nodded in the direction of the cottage across the lane.

"I did although she had the last one in a bucket before I arrived."

"A bucket!"

Mrs Thornborrow smiled showing broken and missing teeth. "She went for a pee and delivered the bairn instead. Easy as pie he slipped from her."

"Oh, my goodness!" Antheia didn't know whether to laugh or cry. "Were mother and baby all right? No harm came to them?"

"She managed to catch him and as you've seen, young Leonard is right as rain."

"He is although all of them could do with more food in their stomachs."

The woman filled Antheia's cup with more tea. "Unlike her ladyship, who I couldn't save."

Antheia had lifted the cup to her lips and almost dropped it. "You attended my Aunt Frances?"

She nodded. "I was the practising midwife in Brawton then and physician should have gone but he was in the next village."

The young girl placed her cup down on the cracked saucer. "You saved my cousin Felix and I'm sure my aunt would have forgiven you the loss of her life for her son's."

"She was a lovely lady, so sweet and gentle. But things were wrong…"

"What do you mean wrong?"

Mrs Thornborrow thought for a moment. "The bleeding wasn't right. At first I suspected a ruptured womb, but then I wondered…"

"Wondered what?"

She shook her head as though to disperse bad memories. "It was such a long time ago."

Antheia had an inspired thought. "Did you know my mother? The Reverend says you came to Brawton thirty years ago."

"Thirty-five years ago I came to Brawton, after Thornborrow was lost at sea. Yes, I did know your mother."

"And my grandmother?" Another nod followed. "The people in Brawton must have been well aware of my grandmother's disappearance and my mother's sudden departure from the Abbey. The belief is my grandmother left to be with her…lover. But I can't believe that."

Mrs Thornborrow carried the cups over to a bowl and placed them inside to be washed at the pump in the courtyard. She came back and her expression was dark. "Your grandmother didn't have a lover."

Antheia caught her breath. "I knew it! I don't know why, but it just didn't seem right." She sighed. "I don't suppose she's alive now. I wonder where she died and where she's buried and most of all what happened to her."

The elderly woman dropped heavily into the armchair. "I only have my suspicions. And it wouldn't be right to point the finger with suspicion only. Many an innocent person has faced the gallows simply through suspicion and very little evidence." She grinned. "I must ask you to leave. I'm sure the Reverend would have eaten his lunch by now."

Antheia rose to her feet and pulled on her coat. "Will you tell me your suspicions one day?"

Mrs Thornborrow smiled. "One day."

CHAPTER TWELVE

Friday the first of January 1864 was a stormy day of rain that seemed intent on washing away the Christmas snow. Matty had opened the curtains and the daylight coming in hardly lit the room.

"I think we'd better keep the lamps on, miss, while you dress."

Antheia opened her eyes and rolled out of bed. The family had barely stayed up the night before to see in the New Year, but even so Antheia had remained at the window of her bedroom until she heard the clocks chiming midnight. She wanted to send Joel a message via the moon for the New Year, even though she had already posted a letter and knew the time difference in America would mean 1864 wouldn't arrive for him for a few hours yet. Even so, she stood at the window and sent her love up to the moon, watching its soft silver light dancing on the landscape.

Yes, it was her love she was sending him; there was no doubt about it. Although she hadn't dared write the word in her letters, she longed to. But how appalled he would be if she did and perhaps the last thing he wanted to hear in all the turmoil of war.

Antheia yawned. "Has Patience mentioned my aunt's reaction to my avoiding luncheon with the Reverend Longmire?" She felt quite comfortable confiding in her maid.

Matty filled up the ceramic bowl with hot water from the jug. "No, miss, her ladyship wouldn't say nothing to Patience."

Antheia stepped across to the bowl and began to wash. "Now then, Matty, you know and I know Patience has a habit of listening at keyholes."

Matty's eyes opened wide. "Does she? Well, perhaps she does."

"So, what has she heard? I know the vicar called to see her ladyship yesterday afternoon."

"Yes, and we knew you had come back as Mr Winder saw you trotting up the drive. We searched for you a good twenty minutes."

Antheia giggled as the maid helped her on with her stays and petticoats. "I'm getting so good at hiding." She had stayed in the stables after returning from Brawton and being informed by the stable hands the Reverend had arrived unexpectedly. They had tucked her away in one of the stalls with her horse.

Matty sighed. "He's visiting again today."

Antheia turned her head to stare at her. "But why? Twice in two days!"

The maid lowered her voice. "You're right, miss. Patience was listening at the keyhole and it seems when we couldn't find you, her ladyship invited the Reverend for lunch today. You're going to be cornered in the dining room, as it were."

"Well, thank you for telling me. And bless Patience and her eavesdropping."

"You asked what they were discussing yesterday." Matty's face turned pale. "They were discussing marriage."

"Whose marriage?"

The maid couldn't hide her discomfort. "Your marriage to the Reverend Longmire."

Antheia looked at her in horror. "There is no way on God's earth I'll marry that man! And I'm only seventeen. I don't wish to be married yet."

Matty grinned. "We all know it, miss. That's why you can rely on any of us to help you out. We know your heart's set on Mr Joel. When he comes back from the war, that is."

"I don't think...I haven't contemplated marriage with...Mr Joel. We're friends, that's all." Antheia was relieved throwing the mauve woollen gown over her head and straightening it across the crinoline cage hid her burning cheeks.

The maid's face remained impassive as she placed the black shawl round her mistress's shoulders. "If you say so, Miss Antheia."

Her uncle looked sternly at her and Felix couldn't suppress his delight.

"Antheia, my dear girl. This is an unhealthy obsession and will only cause you distress."

Her cousin piled a spoonful of porridge into his mouth and spluttered with laughter, "Oh, Father, give her the newspaper. She'll only find ways to read it later. You know what she's like." He thought for a moment. "How incredible they're able to send reports back to England from across the Atlantic Ocean."

Lord Sedgwick held onto the newspaper. "They have war correspondents who telegraph the news to the newspapers here."

"Does a person need Latin to be a war correspondent?"

"No, but you need very good English to be a journalist," quipped Antheia. She turned her attention back to her uncle. "I'll compromise. Read me the account. I'll settle for that."

The earl shook his head, flicked open the pages and found the article. "All right. The Battle of Mossy Creek in the state of Tennessee, described as a minor battle on the twenty-ninth of December. The Confederates were forced back."

"A victory then," whispered Antheia. She added, "Casualties?"

Her uncle blew out an impatient breath. "The Confederate losses where approximately four hundred, the Union forces about one hundred."

"Doesn't seem like a victory," she said, taking a bite of her now cold toast. "Men still died." How she prayed Joel wasn't amongst them.

"It's war, Antheia. Men die in war," said Felix, nonchalantly. He jumped to his feet and began to sing *John Brown's Body* in his rich, tenor voice, his arms spread dramatically.

"Oh, do sit down, boy. Don't you realise you're upsetting your cousin!"

"He's not upsetting me, but I do wish Joel would write. His letters are spasmodic at the best of times."

Felix took his seat and murmured an apology. "He'll be on the move all the time and it must be difficult to write when you're living in a tent."

Antheia couldn't agree. "As a captain, he'll have to write daily reports. I'm sure he's used to it." She stood to take her leave and then suddenly remembered. "I won't...be taking luncheon today." She turned to Winder and made her directions precise. "I think I'll...have a sandwich in my room. I need to visit...some folk in Brawton." The butler nodded, his smile barely perceptible.

"You're going to the village on New Year's Day?" asked Felix, pulling a face. "And in this weather!"

She nodded sharply and left as her uncle and cousin started a discussion on the merits of a civil war and the impact on the ordinary people. Making her way to the morning room, she sat heavily in the leather chair at the writing desk. She might not be receiving letters from Joel on a regular basis, but she was still keeping to her routine of writing every Monday, Wednesday and Friday. Today might be the New Year, but it was still Friday.

Her pen flew over the paper as she told him all her news. She normally told him everything in detail, describing whom she had met and what had been said, but this time she decided she wouldn't mention her aunt's plans for her to marry the Reverend Longmire. That was too disturbing for her to contemplate and to put it in writing would make it too real.

She wished a letter would arrive from him. There had only been one letter since he had left for Alexandria and that had arrived the last week of November. Five weeks of no news whatsoever, although she had sent up to fifteen letters to him. She had even included a few for Martha Newton and thankfully she had replied. She too spoke of not hearing from Joel and reminded the young girl correspondence in the time of war was apt to be irregular at the best of times and non existent at the worst. But it seemed Mrs Newton also followed the progress of the war and often mentioned the victories of the Union Army.

Antheia finished her letter, addressed and sealed it and stood. Picking up the envelope, she decided to take it to the hallway and perhaps have a stroll round the garden. She glanced at her fob watch. It was still three hours until luncheon and the dreaded appearance of the Reverend Longmire. How could she escape him this time? Perhaps take a walk through the gardens and woodland. Go down to the estuary? Of course, she could conceal herself in the gardens; George would help her.

Matty came running in, bringing a draught of chilly air with her. "Miss! Miss Antheia. He's here already! Three hours before luncheon would you believe! Mr Winder has shown him up to her ladyship's rooms!"

Antheia spun on her heel, fear making her mouth dry. "Oh, Matty. I must hide, but I haven't time to get to the stables." An idea came to her. "I know I'll...!"

The maid put her hand on her arm to stop her. "No, miss, don't tell me. Then I can't tell a lie."

Pushing the letter into Matty's hand she watched as she dropped the envelope into her apron pocket. And then both young women ran for the door and out into the corridor. Matty ran one way and Antheia took the opposite direction towards the family chapel.

She opened the door quietly and closed it behind her. It was then she saw the flaw in her plan. Although her gown was made of soft wool with long sleeves and she had a thick shawl round her shoulders, they were no match for the chill of the chapel. Antheia drew her shawl closer and wondered if she could stay a while before sneaking into the courtyard. Surely, the Abbey was big enough to find a place to hide!

Scuffling somewhere in the chapel made her hair stand on end. Were there mice or rats in the chapel with her? It was a possibility since they could make their way up from the estuary looking for bits of food from the kitchen. Normally she wasn't afraid of them, but hearing them scratching behind the wainscot made her wince. She walked about trying to discover from where the sound came and to her surprise it seemed to be coming from behind one of the panels. And if she remembered rightly, the very panel where she had detected a draught when she had first explored the chapel.

She bent and placed an ear against the panel. Yes, that's where the noise was coming from and by the sound of it, there must have been a dozen or so vermin in the wall. There was a loud squeak and horrified she stepped back. The panel was slowly opening and one thing she knew about mice and rats, they didn't have the ability to open apertures. Antheia hurried to the altar and hid behind it, her head turned to see what was coming out of the wooden panel in the family's cold, medieval private chapel.

CHAPTER THIRTEEN

It was a small and very dirty hand that appeared first, clutching a saucer on which was a stub of a candle flickering in the draught. An equally dirty head wearing a flat cap on short, lank hair followed this. The rest of the person came into view, wearing nothing more than rags for a serge coat, a pair of trousers and ankle boots with holes in the toes.

Antheia jumped from behind the altar. "Hey! What do you think you're doing!"

The small person shrank back in horror and stared at her with wide eyes that shone from the filthy face. In a moment he had dropped the candle extinguishing it immediately it hit the floor and disappeared back behind the panel, pulling it shut with a click. She rushed across and tried to pull it open, but it wouldn't budge. Antheia stared at the panel, rubbing her hands on the sleeves of her dress to warm them.

The door to the chapel opened slowly and Antheia received another shock when she realised she was to be discovered.

"What are you doing in here?" Felix stepped into the chapel, closed the door quietly behind him and looked about. "Let me guess you're hiding from Longmire."

"You've discovered my secret," she smiled.

"Thought so. But why in here, it's piercingly cold." He shivered to emphasise his statement. "I heard you shout out, so thought I'd better come and check on you."

"I appreciate that. However, we have an intruder in the Abbey." She examined the wooden panel. "And he's behind here."

Felix stared at the panel. "Behind the wall? Is there enough space?"

"There must be. For a child anyway. But one thing I'm sure of he's not going anywhere."

"He?"

She nodded. "I think it was a young boy but what I saw was so dirty it could have been either gender, except he wore breeches." She noticed the candle on the floor and stooped to pick it up, running her fingers round the edge of the saucer. "And do you recognise this?" When he shook his head she explained, "The last day before you, Will and Joel left. We explored the cave in the cliff. Remember we thought someone must have been living there? I remember this saucer with the garland of forget-me-nots painted round the edge." Horror overwhelmed her. "Oh, Felix, is he trapped behind the wall in the dark? Surely not!"

To her surprise, her cousin remained calm. "If he can open the panel then he isn't trapped, although he could be in the dark if he's lost his candle."

She placed the saucer back on the floor and put her fingernails behind the edge of the panel. "The hinge was on the left so if we pull together we should be able to get it open."

After a few seconds of strenuous effort, it was plain to see the panel wasn't going to budge. "No good. There must be another way to open it," said Felix.

Antheia swept her eyes round the chapel, thinking aloud. "In the sixteenth century this was a Catholic chapel and Catholicism was forbidden so Queen Elizabeth's militia and investigators could subject families to impromptu searches. The family would hide the priest in a priest hole. This must be one behind the panel."

"He would have had to escape quickly, if soldiers were banging at the door. There would be little time to hide him."

Antheia studied the panel. "Above every panel it says, *Dona nobis pacem deo maii tempore interitu.*"

Felix grinned. "May God grant us peace in time of turmoil."

Antheia feigned surprise. "Oh, my lessons have had some effect then?"

He shrugged. "That's simple Latin. It's legal Latin I'm finding difficult."

She let it pass. "But look. The words are not painted on, they're individual letters made out of metal and fixed with screws I think."

"Is that significant?"

"Perhaps the trick of opening this panel is in the words." She began to press each metal character, but nothing happened. "Oh dear, I was hoping one of these letters would trigger the panel to open."

"Wouldn't that have been too easy for the investigators?"

She glanced round the chapel. "Yes, it would. They were clever at working out where the priest holes were."

The next five minutes were spent in pressing more of the metal letters and discussing how they could open the panel. Finally the cousins took a seat in a pew.

"We shouldn't stay in here long. It's too cold," said Felix, rubbing his legs.

Antheia agreed and pulled her shawl closer. "But we can't leave on two counts. I don't want to be anywhere in the vicinity of the Reverend Longmire and we must find the little boy."

"What do you suggest?"

She shook her head slowly and found she had no answer for him. A few minutes passed as silence descended on them.

"May God grant us peace in time of turmoil," she whispered, concentrating on the cross.

"Amen," replied Felix.

"Pardon?"

"Sorry I thought you were praying."

Her eyes opened wide. "Praying? Yes, it's like a prayer isn't it. Praying, prayer. Pray?"

"I'm lost."

She turned to him, her face animated. "Pray for peace in time of turmoil. And Latin for pray is…"

"*Tandem*," he nodded confidently.

She jumped from her seat and crossed the floor to the panel. Skimming her fingers across the letters she said, "We can spell it out with these letters."

He had followed her and also studied the metal characters. "But how do we know which ones will work? There's two for every letter in *tandem*."

"I'll go from left to right." She pressed the first 't' along the line and then the first 'a' until she had spelled out *tandem*. To her disappointment the panel didn't click open. "How annoying. I'll try the second set that make up the word." Again, nothing happened even though they pulled on the panel to try and release it.

"This is impossible, Cousin. It's a lost cause. There must be thousands of combinations to try before we get it right." He turned away despondently.

But Antheia couldn't give up. It wasn't in her nature. She bent and studied the characters, before deciding to look at them side on, but facing the stained-glass window. "Although the maid has polished these, I can still see a slight wearing on the first set of letters." She straightened her back. "I think we're on the right track."

"You've already tried spelling out *tandem* with the first lot and it didn't work."

Her eyes lit up. "I'll try again, but this time...press them together." Placing a finger over every letter in the six-lettered word, she turned to Felix and breathed deeply. "Here goes."

All six characters were pressed simultaneously and there was a muffled click from behind the panel before it swung forward a few inches. Antheia pulled it open further and peered inside.

"Goodness, there's more room than you'd think."

Felix peered in too and both saw a space about twice the width of a man although only about four feet high. "The walls are much thicker on this side with it being the outside wall." He thought for a moment, before adding, "I remember Father saying the chapel is the oldest part of the house so the walls would be thicker." He peered into the hole again. "Wait a minute, where's the boy?"

In her excitement of opening the panel, she had forgotten about him. "He can't have disappeared. That's impossible."

"I'm going to take a look," said her cousin, realising he was the man in the situation and must show courage.

"Be careful."

Holding the panel open, she watched him dip his head into the hole before stepping inside. He looked about him and shrugged. "It's just a hole in the wall, but adequate for a priest to hide while the Abbey was being searched."

"And he would have taken any Catholic artefacts with him. The family could probably turn the chapel into a Protestant church in seconds," added Antheia.

She tapped her chin. "But where has the child gone? Run your hands over the walls. Can you feel a loose rock or something that might indicate another way out?" He did as instructed and then she looked down at his shoes. "What about the floor?"

He hunkered down and swept away a few loose stones. His cry was startling. "I thought the ground didn't feel like stone. There's a wooden hatch here."

Excited, she pushed her head further into the aperture. "Can you lift it?"

It took a few minutes before he found a way of levering up the hatch, but once found he had no difficulty lifting it. A blast of cold air hit him in the face and he turned his head.

"What can you see?"

"A ladder going down into darkness. Has to be a tunnel down there considering the draught coming up from it."

"It must have been an escape route for the priest if things became dire. Perhaps he received a signal from the family if the investigators were getting too close. We must see where it goes. We can't leave it there."

He dropped the hatch and came out of the priest hole. "We need light and warmer clothing." He pulled out his watch from his waistcoat pocket. "It will be luncheon soon and my father and stepmother will expect me to be there." He pointed at her. "As you are."

She shook her head. "I'm in Brawton, remember."

"I know Father won't mind, but my stepmother will be hopping mad."

"Not to mention the Reverend Longmire," she grinned.

"I'll get Matty to bring you warmer clothing and something to eat and after luncheon I'll return with some lanterns."

"Very well," she shivered. "Perhaps you should include a thick blanket along with warmer clothing."

He acquiesced and made for the door. She was surprised he glanced back at her over his shoulder and smiled as he turned the handle and disappeared into the corridor. Perhaps they had a better understanding now and he didn't think her a simple country cousin. She walked back to the panel and looked inside. She desperately wanted to lift the hatch and look into the tunnel. Believing there was nothing stopping her, she wedged the panel open with the saucer and candle and crawled back into the space. Lifting the hatch proved easy since she discovered finger holes at the side. She leaned the hatch on its hinges and stared downward.

The metal ladder stretched to the bottom but it was too dark to see where it went from there. Felix believed there was a tunnel and since she couldn't hear a sound, she had to assume the little boy had made his escape down the tunnel. But where did it lead? The child lived in the cave, she was sure of it and was using the tunnel to gain access to the Abbey. For what? He looked like a hungry waif and probably stole food from the kitchen and tried to warm himself by the fires. Poor lamb, she thought. How could a child end up in such a desperate way? The cold was more intense in the priest hole and Antheia wondered how the priest himself survived hiding in such a small space especially in winter.

Out of the corner of her eye, she saw the panel move slightly and heard the grating noise of the saucer moving. She lurched forward to grab the panel but was too late. The weight of the wood was too much for the fragile piece of china and she was plunged into darkness as the panel clicked shut. She cried out and rising to her feet, banged on the opening. Panic engulfed her, the darkness so profound she couldn't see anything, not even her hands.

There had to be a catch on the door since the little boy had used it to get into the chapel. She searched the entire panel, her fingers groping and tapping round the edges. Suddenly she realised she could see. Just a glimmer but as her eyes were getting used to the dark, she saw there was a small amount of daylight coming from the chapel and filtering through the edges of the panel. It was only a sliver of light, but enough to allow her to examine the panel more thoroughly. Where was the catch to open the panel? If a child could find it, surely she could? She searched the wall round the panel and her finger caught on protruding metal. She pushed it and then pulled it. There was a muffled click and the panel swung open flooding the priest hole with light. She crawled out and pulled herself painfully to her feet. She had never felt so cold in her life and knew she must get warm immediately. Remembering there were servants' stairs at the end of the corridor, she closed the panel door, picked up the saucer and candle and slipped out of the chapel.

It was wonderful to be running along the corridor and past the ballroom to the door at the end. Once through it the warmth coming from below stairs made her arms and legs ache as feeling started to return. Following the stairs down she found herself in a part of the house she was familiar with when raiding food from the kitchen. The whitewashed passageway with a red runner along the cobbled floor led to the many doors below stairs; the butler's pantry, the wine cellar, the boot room, laundry room and of course, the enormous kitchen. On the right through half-windows she could see the servants busy in the kitchen preparing lunch, but on the left a door was open. Peering inside she knew this was the housekeeper's small, cosy parlour with comfortable furniture, vases of ferns, many ornaments on a dresser and most of all a large grate in which burnt the most wonderful fire she had ever seen. Skipping across the rug, she left the saucer and candle on the dresser and bent over the fire warming her hands. The pain made her gasp as she rubbed and pummelled her fingers and arms.

"Miss Antheia! What are you doing here?"

She turned to see the ample shape of Mrs Hadwin standing in the doorway.

CHAPTER FOURTEEN

"I thought I'd visit for a cup of tea." She gestured round the room. "I always thought this a lovely parlour." She knew she had walked into a domain where only the privileged were invited and hoped the housekeeper wouldn't be offended.

"You're welcome. Let me call for a tray of tea." She made her sit in the large armchair. "Dear Lord! You're frozen! Where on earth have you been?" She had taken Antheia's hands as she guided her to the chair and was appalled at their lack of warmth. "I think you need more than a cup of tea, my dear." She pulled a blanket from the cupboard and wrapped it round the young girl's shoulders.

"I'm sorry to intrude on your privacy, Mrs Hadwin, it's just that…"

The housekeeper held up her hand. "I understand, Miss Antheia. We all do. Avoiding the Reverend Longmire is taking a lot of doing." She stepped out of the door and spoke briefly with a passing member of staff.

Antheia had almost forgotten the vicar's intentions in her effort to find warmth and the fear of being trapped in the priest hole.

"I've been hiding in the chapel."

Mrs Hadwin gasped. "No wonder you're chilled to the bone. The maids don't stay long in that place. Just enough to dust and sweep."

Antheia shivered and blew on her fingers. "Little wonder. You could store sides of beef in there."

The woman clicked her tongue. "No doubt, but folk tend to stay away. And when they clean, the maids must go in pairs. I agree to it since I know they believe it's too eerie and perhaps even haunted. It's a load of nonsense, but they're sure they've heard noises behind the walls. I tell them it's mice come up from the estuary, but even that scares them. Silly girls."

Matty entered with a tray, her face beaming. "Here's the tea and we're also preparing some lunch for you, miss. Your family is dining now. I think the Reverend will leave after he's eaten." She placed the tray on an occasional table and Mrs Hadwin nodded.

"Yes, Matty, Miss Antheia certainly needs some hot food in her."

Matty hurried out of the parlour and returned almost immediately with another tray containing cutlery, a napkin and a plate of food.

"Was anything said about my absence at lunch?" Her mouth watered at the sight of steak and kidney pie with rich gravy, potatoes and vegetables. It looked so delicious.

Matty pulled a smaller occasional table closer to her mistress. "Well, Mr Winder said your step-aunt was furious and the Reverend extremely annoyed. I'm afraid Mr Winder and Charlie found it difficult to keep their faces straight."

"You've all been so good. I don't know what I would have done without your help."

Matty and the housekeeper exchanged glances, but it was her maid who explained, "We want to see you wed to Mr Joel, miss. We all want to see you both happy."

Antheia shook her head and sighed. How easily the servants fell into matchmaking.

"We're friends I've told you."

Matty winked at Mrs Hadwin. "Of course you are, miss. That's why you keep his photograph by your bed."

Yes, she had placed it in a small silver frame and stood it on the nightstand, but that was only because she wanted to say goodnight to him. There was no harm in it, surely? Thinking of Joel made her feel melancholy. It seemed such a long time since she had received his last letter with the photograph.

She put a slice of pie in her mouth and enjoyed the delicious flavour. Suddenly she remembered Felix would return to the chapel after luncheon and they were going to explore the tunnel. She would need to return as soon as she had eaten.

"Master Felix asked me to bring food and drink and your warmest clothing to…the chapel," said Matty, frowning. "Is that where you were hiding or are intending to go out? Be careful you don't bump into the Reverend."

It was the last thing she wanted, but Antheia was filled with concern about the child. Here she was settled by the fire and enjoying a delicious hot meal. Warmth and the meal were reviving her, but as she felt more alive a terrible fear had taken her over. She had been chilled for such a short time, but that child had been living in the cave since September at least. Food and a roof over one's head were the basic essentials of life. Yes, he had a cave to live in, but how could he possibly survive through the rest of the winter?

Pushing the last of her meal into her mouth, she drank back her tea and made a decision. "Could you bring my outdoor clothing here please? Yes, I've decided to go out. Oh, and I'll need a blanket too."

"You can take that one," said the housekeeper, pointing to the one round her shoulders.

The maid nodded. "If you're going out I'll bring down your stout boots as well." Matty disappeared through the door and ran down the corridor.

"I need you to do something for me, Mrs Hadwin. Inform Master Felix that…that I've changed my mind and I'll speak to him this evening after dinner."

The housekeeper frowned. "Of course, my dear. But where are you going?"

Antheia rose painfully to her feet. "I have a mission and I just hope I can get to the stables and away before I'm seen by the family."

"I can show you out of the back way. You'll not be noticed," smiled Mrs Hadwin.

Matty returned in minutes and Antheia shook off her house shoes and laced up her boots, before tying the shawl round her shoulders, donning a warm cloak with a hood and pulling on her gloves. The blanket had been folded and carrying it, she followed Mrs Hadwin through the kitchen, with Matty carrying the tray of dirty plates and cups.

Antheia stopped when she saw the food on the table. "Do you think I could take a basket of bread and perhaps cheese? Apples too?" Collecting a basket from the side of the sink with a large pump, the housekeeper filled it with what was available. "What about a drink? Have you anything to keep out the cold?" asked Antheia tentatively.

The housekeeper frowned and called to Cook who was on the far side of the room supervising the dessert for upstairs. "Mrs Nelson, I'm taking the half bottle of brandy left over from making the Christmas cakes." She was answered with a raised arm and crossing to the cupboard, she took down the bottle from the shelf and placed it in the basket.

"Thank you and now I must get to the stables," said Antheia.

Mrs Hadwin folded her arms. "May I ask where you're going, my dear? I'm fair worried about you."

"Only to Brawton." She giggled. "I said I was going and so I am. I've given truth to my lie and my conscience is clear."

The housekeeper bit her lip but simply nodded and led her to the back door and out to the kitchen gardens. Antheia hoisted the blanket in one arm and holding the basket with the other ran towards the stables.

Mrs Hadwin watched her go. She had never met a young girl like Miss Antheia Vale in her life, but goodness; she had certainly livened up the Abbey. Such a shame she had lost her heart to a man thousands of miles away. But Mr Joel would return. She was sure of it. Walking back to her parlour she decided she had better continue with the weekly accounts. The ledger lay open in her office next door and she had been disturbed from her work when she had heard someone in her parlour. Sighing, she turned to the door and then her eyes were drawn to the dresser. Her eyes widened as she walked towards it. Was she seeing what she thought she was seeing? A saucer with forget-me-nots painted round the edge? Surely she must be mistaken! She hadn't seen this crockery since her lady had disappeared all those years ago. Tears trickled down her face as she picked up and caressed the small piece of Dresden china.

Antheia drove straight to Brawton and although it was bitterly cold, she was pleased the stormy weather had blown over with a few grey clouds chasing each other across a blue sky. She was determined to get to the cove and into the cave; she had to find the little boy and make sure he was all right. Too many people were found frozen to death in winter and she wouldn't be responsible for the death of a small child.

She drove to the outskirts of the village and tied the horse to a post outside the Red Lion public house. Holding onto the blanket and basket, she followed the track across the open field and came to the trail that would take her down to the cove. Joy swept through her when she saw the tide was out, but negotiating the incline was difficult, hampered by the basket and blanket and the fact it was slippery with the rain and snow since Christmas. She inched herself down, taking her time, but often her feet skidded under her and she had to stop to regain her balance. It was hard going and when her feet finally landed on the shingle, she blew out a breath of relief she hadn't slipped and broken her ankle, or worse. She made her way past the rockpools to the base of the cliff.

Antheia looked up at the cave and cupped her hands round her mouth. "Are you there? Will you come out and talk to me?" Only silence answered her shouts. Had the child not arrived back yet? "My name is Antheia. Antheia Vale and I've come to help you. I mean you no harm."

She glanced across the estuary and suddenly thought the water seemed to be closer. Placing the basket and blanket on the shingle she decided she would climb up. She had done it before and had managed it easily. She had put a foot on the first rock to haul herself up when a dirty face appeared from the mouth of the cave.

"What do you want?"

Stepping back she smiled and scooped up the basket. "See here. I've brought bread and cheese and apples. Aren't you hungry? Wouldn't you like some?"

The small face showed large hungry eyes and she held up an apple to entice him further.

"Are you bringing it up, then?"

Antheia dropped her chin and looked at him demurely. "You can't expect me to climb all the way up there. Not in these skirts. You'll have to come down."

She wasn't sure if it would work, but she knew from working in the parish with her father, food was always a wonderful enticement to get what was needed. She waited, still holding out the apple and tried to stem her excitement when the small figure lowered himself over the edge and came down the rocks at a speed that amazed her. Now she was staring at the tiny child she had glimpsed behind the panel in the chapel.

He held out a dirty hand and she placed the apple in his palm, watching him crunch into it hungrily. She looked out towards the estuary.

"I think the tide is coming in. Shall we climb back up to the field and then you can eat the rest of the food in my gig?"

He looked into the basket and nodded. Placing the blanket round his shoulders, they made their way along the shingle, up the incline and across the field. Before long he was sitting next to her in the gig, the blanket tight round him as he munched the bread and cheese. She took out the half bottle of brandy.

"A sip for you and a sip for me, eh!" She drank back a small amount and held the bottle while he took a sip. "What's your name?"

"Jeremiah," he said, grimacing at the taste of the brandy.

"Have you lived in the cave long?"

"Since the summer after running away from the workhouse."

"And where is this workhouse?"

"Lancaster." He helped himself to more cheese. "But I weren't happy so I ain't going back."

Antheia had heard of the workhouse in Quernmore Road and had had dealings with these institutions in Leominster when she had visited with her father. It wasn't a place she would like to live.

"I'll make sure you don't have to go back." She glanced at him, heartbroken at his pitiful appearance. "How long did you live there?"

"From being born. I were left on doorstep."

"How old are you?"

He licked his lips and thought for a moment. "They said I were found at Christmas, year of the big battle."

"Which battle?"

He blew out a breath. "When a terrible crime was done against someone called Sebastian. I remember the name cos a lad I knew was called Sebastian. He died."

Antheia grimaced at the kind of life Jeremiah had known. But one fact she was sure about, he was talking about the Crimean War and the battle must be the siege of Sevastopol. She remembered the siege had lasted a year and as good as she was with events historical, she would have to research the exact date. However, that put the lad at about nine years old. Now she had to work out what to do with him. She could take him back to the Abbey, but even if her uncle agreed to give him a roof over his head, her step-aunt certainly wouldn't and what's more would insist he be sent back to the workhouse. An idea occurred to her.

"I think I know where you can stay, but I'll have to speak to the lady of the house first."

"Nah, I can go back to the cave."

"No, you can't. It's too cold for you. Let me try my idea first."

He shrugged and she took advantage of his compliance by taking the reins and setting the horse on the main lane to the village. How quiet it seemed, everyone behind their front doors and by the fire. She pulled up inside the court and helped him down.

"Can I take the food with me?" He had become very attached to the basket.

She nodded and holding his hand led him across the cobbles to the door of the tiny cottage.

"Who is it now?" The angry voice in response to her knock was expected.

Glancing down at the small boy at her side she grimaced. "Don't take any notice she's always like that." She knocked again and called, "Mrs Thornborrow, it's me, Antheia Vale."

The old woman pulled open the door a crack and peered round. "You again? What's this, two days running you come and visit!"

"I need your help."

The woman looked at the small child. "What have you got there? Is that a black child?"

"I don't know what colour he is under all the grime. But I need your help."

Mrs Thornborrow didn't argue and pulled the door open. "In you come, then. Be quick and don't let the heat out."

It was so cosy and warm in the small room, Antheia threw back her hood and pulled off her gloves. The child went straight to the fire to get warm. It took only five minutes to explain the situation and when she had finished, she waited for the elderly woman's opinion.

"You want me to lodge him here?"

"I don't know what else to do. Would you keep him safe until I work something out?"

The boy had made himself comfortable in the armchair and wrapping the blanket tighter round his thin shoulders was dropping off to sleep. His dirty hand held onto the handle of the basket, which was wedged firmly between his legs.

"I see he's purloined my armchair already," she sniffed.

"He's cold and hungry and he's only a little boy."

Mrs Thornborrow's expression softened. "Aye, he's only a kid. About seven or eight?"

"I think about nine."

She nodded. "He can stay. Sit down and I'll make us some tea. Sounds like you've had an adventure."

"There's only the straight-backed chair. You must take that."

Mrs Thornborrow chuckled and threw some cushions on the floor. "You can use them."

Antheia lowered herself to the floor and onto the cushions. In five minutes the tea was made and she sipped the hot brew. "He wants to hold onto the basket, but there's half a bottle of brandy in it. I would find it and put it away for yourself if I were you."

She smiled as the elderly woman crept across to the sleeping boy, lifted out the bottle and grinned in delight before placing it on the shelf. She returned to the chair and stared down at the young girl.

"You look tired, girl."

"The first day of this New Year has been quite eventful." She gestured to the boy. "Thank you and I'll get some money for you. You can't expect to keep him for nothing."

Mrs Thornborrow took a gulp of her tea. "Before I married Thornborrow, I worked in a brothel." She waited to gauge the young girl's reaction and seeing her unaffected she continued, "Not exactly the workhouse since it was a good establishment and the madam looked after us girls. But I know how it feels to be trapped in a place you don't care for."

The Reverend Longmire had said the old lady had had a colourful past and it seemed he was right. But there had been 'ladies of the night' in Bromyard and Antheia had no revulsion for them.

"It must have been a terrible life. Thank goodness you married."

She chuckled. "He was one of the guests, as Madam liked to call them. A regular one, actually, but he took to me. I think he fancied having a woman to come home to, so I moved into his rooms, but…you know the rest."

"That's when you decided to come to Brawton?"

"Only because he left me a small amount of money but as time passed I couldn't afford the rent no longer. And I refused to go back to whoring. I'd helped deliver a few babies and heard the midwife in Brawton wanted to retire, so I thought I'd take my chance here. She was good was the old midwife. Gave me the benefit of her knowledge before she left."

"How long were you…in the brothel?"

She sucked in a breath. "I ran away from home at twelve. I was found walking the streets and taken in by the madam who put a roof over my head."

Antheia looked at her aghast. "Oh, goodness, she didn't make you…"

Mrs Thornborrow grinned. "She could have, but she didn't. No, I worked as a maid until I decided to join them at fifteen. As I said, she was a good madam and cared for her girls. But after seven years or so I was glad to marry Thornborrow."

"Why did you run away from home?" Antheia wondered if she should ask.

The elderly woman reached down to squeeze her hand. "Just be grateful for your happy childhood, my girl. It's a blessing that mustn't be taken for granted."

Antheia passed her cup to her hostess knowing it was time to leave. Jeremiah was still snuggled in the blanket fast asleep.

"Take care of him and I'll bring money as soon as possible for his food and clothing."

Mrs Thornborrow looked at the small boy in her favourite armchair. "I think I'll put the kettle and a few pans on to boil. He's going to need a good scrub before I put him in clean clothes." She tapped her chin. "I wonder if Mrs Garnett across the way has something I can have. Her Leonard is growing fast."

As Antheia travelled home the daylight was fading. She would take a bath herself when she arrived at the Abbey. Jeremiah's pungent smell was on her clothes. What would Matty think? That would set the servants' tongues wagging.

CHAPTER FIFTEEN

"The panel closed on you?" Felix couldn't hide his amusement. "You shouldn't have gone inside. It's too dangerous on your own."

"I only went to take a look and I wasn't in more than two minutes."

He puffed out a breath. "Well, at least you knew I was coming back and could let you out. What would you have done if I weren't and you couldn't find the release to open the panel?"

She thought about it, before saying, "I would have continued down the ladder and followed the tunnel."

He looked at her quizzically. "In the dark?"

"I'd have no choice."

The evening before, Antheia had wanted to escape her step-aunt's anger as soon as possible and after dinner the young couple had fled to the library when polite to do so. There she had related the events of that afternoon; of going to the cave and finding Jeremiah. She spoke of the conversation they had had and how she had found him a home.

But she had forgotten about her mishap in the chapel until they were standing by the panel.

His expression became stern. "Promise me you'll not go into the tunnel alone. You could have harmed yourself."

Antheia tilted her head, studying him. "I didn't know you cared."

He ignored her. "So, shall we proceed?" he said, nodding towards the priest hole.

They were standing by the wall in the chapel and he was holding onto the panel keeping it open. It had been easy to enter the code and Antheia realised she and her cousin were now accomplices in a mystery. But Felix had always believed the rumours that circulated the household; that their grandfather had murdered their grandmother and hidden her body. Mrs Thornborrow had her suspicions. Antheia was determined to pay another visit to Mrs Thornborrow, to check on Jeremiah and glean more information about her grandmother.

She gestured in compliance and watched him dip into the hole and lift the hatch. Passing him the lantern, he waved the light for a few seconds, before easing himself over the edge and onto the ladder. She followed him in and looked over the side, holding her lantern high. He was making his way carefully down to a depth of about seven feet.

He looked up and grinned. "There is a tunnel down here. And a well constructed one too."

She eased herself over the edge and hanging onto the ladder and lantern, took each rung carefully until she reached the bottom. The tunnel stretched out in front of them, sometimes rising slightly and then dipping again. But what was amazing was it was lined with brick, albeit only about four feet high. They would have to stoop to follow it.

"You're right, it is well made. But there was mining in these parts during the Elizabethan times and the miners could have easily built this tunnel," she informed him.

"How do you know that?"

He was leading the way and she was forced to speak to his stooped back. "Because my father educated me and had me writing copious essays on history, geography and many other subjects."

"Sounds worse than Eton."

"I found it interesting and…is there no end to this tunnel!"

"I think we're under the gardens."

"So, we're heading towards the woodland and the open field next to Far Field where the derelict chapel and abandoned cemetery is?"

"Yes, that field is called Sarah's Meadow."

"How...lovely."

"Sarah was our grandmother."

Despite her aching back, she smiled. Her middle name was Sarah and she now knew why her mother had chosen it for her.

It seemed they had passed under the gardens as suddenly the tunnel ended and before them was a shaft with a similar metal ladder. Felix climbed it while Antheia held both lanterns. Reaching the top, he banged on a square of wood.

"It's another hatch. Damn, I should have brought a crowbar with me."

"I don't think Jeremiah had a crowbar and he must have come out this way. Put some muscle into it! Push it don't bang on it!"

He looked down at her, narrowing his eyes. But he did as he was bid and pushed. The hatch came away easily and the fresh air gushed towards them. The piece of wood landed with a slap on the ground above and Felix stepped down a few rungs, collected his lantern and continued climbing. Antheia followed him and took his hand to haul herself over the edge, both laughing as they fell onto the mossy woodland floor.

It was such a relief to be out of the tunnel with the smell of the estuary wafting towards them. The woodland looked sparse, the trees devoid of leaves except for the conifers.

He looked at the hatch. "Goodness, I was born and brought up here, but I never knew about the priest hole or the tunnel and certainly not this hatch."

"Over the years it would have become covered by leaves and foliage. But I wonder how Jeremiah found it. Next time I see him I must ask."

He helped her to her feet and they blew out the lanterns.

Felix stared down at the hatch. "I think we should hide it."

"That would be a good idea."

Placing the lanterns on the ground, they scattered leaves and twigs over the hatch until Antheia spied a large boulder of gritstone. "We could put that on top to mark the place."

Dutifully he carried it across and placed it over the hatch. Pulling his penknife from his pocket, he opened the blade and scratched a large X on it. "X marks the spot, eh!" He picked up both lanterns and they started their walk through the woodland and into the gardens. "What now?" said Felix.

"You've found an excellent escape route should the constables come for you," she winked.

Shaking his head at her, he said, "I mean about the tunnel. Should we tell Father? Of course he might already know about it."

Antheia thought about this before saying, "Perhaps we'd better stay mum for a while. I don't know why, but I feel hesitant about proclaiming our find just yet. There will come a right time and place I'm sure."

His gaze became distant. "I'll be going back to Cambridge in two weeks. And I must say I've never had a holiday like this one. You certainly know how to shake up the old family seat, Cousin."

"Not intentionally, I assure you."

They passed George who was busy digging a patch of earth in the flowerbeds. He stopped as they said 'good morning'.

"Ah, Miss Antheia, they've been looking for you."
Dread filled her. Was she to be summoned to her
aunt's sitting room for a severe reprimand? George's
next words made her heart thump wildly. "Seems
something has arrived for you."

"A letter! He's written to me!"

She set off without ceremony holding up her skirts
to give her more speed. Felix and George watched her
go.

"I think Miss Antheia has no understanding news
from a country at war don't always bring good
tidings," said George.

Felix studied him. "Joel will come through this."
He handed the lanterns back to the head gardener.
"Thank you for the loan of the lights."

George rubbed his chin as he watched Master Felix
walking towards the Abbey. He had been surprised
when the young master had asked for the lanterns.
And he had seen the couple emerge from the
woodland. Had they found the tunnel? He didn't hold
with going along the tunnel. As far as he was
concerned it should be filled in. Especially if the
rumours were true.

Antheia flung herself through the door and hurried
towards the hallway. On the silver salver was quite a
bulky envelope and she recognised Mrs Newton's
spidery writing immediately. Grabbing the package
she hurried upstairs to her room, placed the brown
envelope on her bed and pulled off her gloves. Her
hands shook as she untied her cloak and lay it over
the chaise longue.

Scooping up the package she made herself
comfortable on the bed and slowly opened the
envelope to reveal the contents. To her utter
amazement there were ten letters inside and all from

Joel. She placed them in date order and saw the first one was dated the fifteenth of November. She remembered his last letter had informed her he had set off on the long train journey to North Virginia, so he must have written as soon as he had settled in Alexandria.

She read his first letter carefully.

My dear Antheia,

I've arrived safely and since Alexandria is a seaport, it feels very much like home. I'm undergoing a few weeks training before I receive my next orders. The training is very much like I experienced at West Point as a cadet, although not so much theory and bookwork.

I think of you often and our time together at Sedgwick Abbey. Believe me, my lovely girl, they are such wonderful memories I shall always treasure. Ma has now informed me she sent you a copy of my photograph. I do hope it pleased you. My moustache needs trimming regularly, but I share a tent with two other officers who have let their facial hair grow to enormous lengths. You would laugh if you saw them.

I will write again when I can and please do write back. You cannot imagine how soldiers enjoy letters from home.

Kindest regards
Joel Newton

His next letter was dated three days later and spoke mostly of the camp, the men and officers he met. She read the ten letters in date order and laughed when he spoke of the evening he and his fellow officers had gone into Alexandria to enjoy a meal since the camp food left a lot to be desired. His seventh letter had a change of tone and was dated the twenty-sixth of November.

Her heart speeded up when she saw his salutation had changed from My dear Antheia, to My dearest Antheia. Not only that but he had signed off with Fondest regards and given his first name rather than his full name.

My dearest Antheia,

I am the envy of every man in the camp. Whereas they receive intermittent mail and one letter at a time, a package of letters arrive for me in the mail call. Ma is obviously sending your letters in batches of seven and eight although I can see from the dates you are writing at least three times a week. You can't imagine how that makes me feel.

But now to the serious business of soldiering. I'll be shipping out in the morning at the head of R Company, but with my lieutenant and sergeant I feel confident. There are about a hundred men in my Company and they are fine fellows from all occupations and all ages.

I don't know how often I'll be able to write, but I'll do my best. Please don't forget me and if you can, perhaps you could send me a photograph of yourself. Not that I'll ever forget what you look like as your image is engraved on my memory. It's just that an actual photograph would be much appreciated.

Fondest regards
Joel

Should she reply in the same way? To call him My dearest Joel would be so wonderful and to end with

Fondest regards would say exactly how she felt. She was fond of him there was no doubt about that.

The next three letters she opened with trepidation. They were all dated December and short. She wondered if he was allowed to say much in his correspondence since he was now on active service. He talked about the weather and how they had bought a chicken from a local farmer and cooked it for all to share. The sergeant made up his tent every night and the soldiers would sing round the campfire.

Where was he going? It sounded as though his Company were on their way to meet a bigger army, but whatever it was, he certainly wasn't saying. A photograph? She had never been to a photographer's studio, but it sounded fun. Perhaps she could have it done for her eighteenth birthday. But that wasn't until March and she didn't want to wait too long.

Her attention was drawn to the window where rain pelted against the glass. What happened when a person had to live in a tent in terrible weather? And what was the weather like where he was heading?

She would go to the morning room immediately and answer his letters. Yes, it was Saturday and not her usual day, but she must reply as soon as possible. As he said, soldiers look forward to news from home. And she would start her letter My dearest Joel and end it with Fondest regards, Antheia.

CHAPTER SIXTEEN

Antheia stood outside her uncle's study, her hand raised ready to knock. She had decided not to approach him at lunch since what she needed to ask him was too private for the dining table. Now the time had arrived and taking in a steadying breath, she tapped gently. A quiet 'enter' summoned her into the earl's presence.

He lifted his head and smiled. "Ah, Antheia, my dear, did you wish to speak with me?" She nodded and he stood up and gestured to a seat on the long sofa by the wall. "Well, I can see by your face this is a serious matter."

He took a seat next to her and she tucked in her crinoline skirts to give him room, wondering at the difference between this interview with him and her first one on the day she had arrived at Sedgwick Abbey. Then he barely had time for her, now he was the affable uncle.

Plucking up courage, she said, "I wondered if..." She changed her mind and decided to broach the request in Joel's letter. "I wondered if I could have my photograph taken? Joel pointed out I have his likeness and he would like mine."

The earl's face lit up. "Why, what a splendid idea! I should have thought about that myself. Of course, we all had our photographs taken before my son and his friend left to go to Italy over two years ago. But we have none of you to add to our collection."

She had noticed the family photographs standing like a regiment of soldiers on the piano in the drawing room. There was one of the entire family, one of Will and Felix together and finally individual portraits of each member. But none of Joel. Perhaps because he wasn't a member of the family? Antheia felt sad he hadn't been included, but she knew her uncle liked matters to be correct. She had even studied the photographs in the servants' passageway next to the kitchen, comprising three; the first showing the entire indoor staff, the second, the outdoor staff and the third a huge photograph of all the servants working for the Earl of Sedgwick.

Antheia smiled appreciatively. "I know there's a photographer's studio in Lancaster. I don't mind travelling there. Matty can accompany me."

Lord Sedgwick stared at her for a few seconds before bursting into laughter. "My dear child, how refreshingly innocent and unassuming you are." Noticing her bemused expression, he explained, "I'm a peer of the realm. The photographer comes to me, not the other way round."

"Oh, I'll have it taken here?"

He nodded. "Yes, indeed. And he'll bring backdrops for you to choose, or he'll use attractive rooms of the Abbey. Probably the ballroom. Of course, if it were the summer you could have had taken in the rose garden. But never mind."

She looked down at her hands furled in her lap. Now she had to ask him the most delicate part of her interview. "Uncle, may I have some money?" She felt it better to spit it out.

He stared at her in horror for a few seconds. "What have I been thinking of! How remiss of me. It didn't enter my mind you would need funds, but of course you do. A young girl always needs cash for fripperies."

Her lips parted to remind him all her needs were catered for and if she did happen to purchase anything in Brawton, she could add it to her uncle's account.

Besides, she never had the urge to buy 'fripperies'. Her father had taught her at a young age the difference between wanting and needing something. Strangely, the money she required was both wanted and needed.

"I thought just a small sum," she asked. "To get me by."

Rising sharply, his tall, thin frame covered the distance from the sofa to the desk in seconds where he opened a drawer and brought out a metal cash box. Antheia stood and walked towards him as he unclipped the key from his watch chain and opened the box. She couldn't see the coins, but she did notice the wad of white five-pound notes and gasped at the fortune the residents in Slee Court would take years to earn. There came the sound of coin clinking on coin before he counted out gold sovereigns and held them out to her.

"Forgive me, my dear. I should have dealt with this when you first arrived. Here are three sovereigns and you'll get the same every month. I go to the bank in Lancaster at the end of the month to pick up cash for wages and deposit rents from the farms, so come to me at the beginning of February for your allowance. And every month thereafter."

Antheia stared at the three coins in the palm of her hand. She had never had so much money before and had it been for herself she would have given two coins back. But this money was sorely needed.

"Thank you, Uncle. I'll spend it wisely."

He shrugged. "It's yours to spend how you wish."

The fact she was visiting Mrs Thornborrow for the third day in a row didn't bother her one bit. The rain clouds had passed and now the sky was a brilliant blue with a crisp chill in the air. She made the horse canter all the way to Brawton and through the village to the far end where Slee Court seemed a pleasant place when the sun shone.

At the end of the court she jumped down and tied the horse near the trough, before walking past the dozen cottages to the one rented by Mrs Thornborrow. Standing on a stool and wrapped in a thick coat far too big for him, was Jeremiah. He had a woollen hat pulled down over his ears and was busy wiping the windows carefully with a cloth. Next to the stool was a bucket of soapy water with steam rising from it. She noticed the coat nearly reached his feet now clad in well worn but sturdy boots.

He turned his head. "Miss Vale! Granny Thornborrow wondered if you'd visit again. She said how you can't keep away."

Antheia chuckled and asked, "Granny Thornborrow?"

He jumped down from the stool. "That's what I'm to call her. It's nice having a granny."

Her heart broke that this child had not known a mother and father never mind grandparents. How could anyone leave a baby on the doorstep of an institution was beyond her. His mother must have been desperate.

"Well, is Granny Thornborrow at home?"

"Aye, she is and you obviously smelled bread baking!" The elderly woman appeared at the door and grinned. "Both of you come in. I've made cinnamon cake too. Leave the bucket there and I'll scrub the doorstep afterwards."

The warmth of the cottage and the smell of baking washed over Antheia in a wave of pleasure and glancing round the room she saw a small cot next to the woman's truckle bed.

She shrugged off her coat. "I've brought money for Jeremiah's upkeep. I said I would." Boy and elderly woman looked at her and then exchanged glances. "Have I said something wrong?"

Jeremiah watched her, still dressed in his overlarge coat and woollen hat, his dark brown eyes filled with mischief. Mrs Thornborrow moved behind him and placed tender hands on his shoulders.

"We have something to tell you," sighed the woman.

She lifted off the woollen hat and a pile of dark hair fell over the child's face. She removed the coat and to Antheia's surprise she saw a young boy dressed in a short red dress partially covered with a white pinafore.

"I don't understand," she stammered. For one ghastly minute she thought Mrs Garnett must have had only girls' clothes to spare.

"Let me introduce you to Miss Jemima Moffet," said Mrs Thornborrow, turning away to hang the coat and hat on the back of the door. "And yes, it was a surprise to me too."

The girl gave a sweet curtsey as Antheia stepped towards her. "But why didn't you tell me you were a girl when I brought you out of the cave?"

She shrugged. "I didn't think. I just wanted what was in your basket."

The elderly lady chuckled as she laid out the crockery for afternoon tea. "She had to say something before I put her in the tin bath. Otherwise I would have noticed a doe splashing amongst the suds rather than a buck." She called to the child. "Jemima, bring up the chairs and we'll eat."

Antheia came round the table and noticed there were two more straight-backed chairs. The tiny cottage was becoming quite cramped.

"Well, Jeremiah or Jemima, he...she seems happy."

The woman nodded. "It's a treat having her about the place and she's already made herself useful. My legs ain't what they used to be."

"And it's still all right if she lives with you?"

She looked at her visitor accusingly. "I would have told you straight off if I couldn't accommodate her. But then, how could I turn down the plight of a small child."

As Antheia took her seat and watched Jemima scramble up onto a chair, her eyes wide at the ham sandwiches, cinnamon cake and jam tarts laid out on the cloth.

Suddenly she remembered the money and went into her reticule. "Here's three sovereigns for you. I'll give you the same at the beginning of every month."

Mrs Thornborrow paused in her preparations and held the gold coins in her gnarled hands. "Is this your allowance?" Antheia nodded. "Me thinks this is it all?"

Antheia turned back to Jemima who sat patiently ready to tuck in. "I received it from my uncle this afternoon although I didn't tell him what I wanted it for. I'm not sure he would have approved."

The elderly woman stared again at the coins and after a moment of deliberation, handed two back to her. "One sovereign will do. She has a good appetite but nothing excessive. If you're determined to provide for her, then I won't accept more."

Jemima giggled. "The Garnett boys were so surprised when I turned into a girl. They said it didn't matter. They have three sisters so are used to girls. They laughed at my hair though."

Mrs Thornborrow poured out the tea and handed round the cups. "It'll grow and then we'll find some pretty ribbons to tie it up with."

Antheia took a sip of her tea. "Why did you pick Jeremiah as your name?" She held up her hand. "And please don't tell me he's a boy who died in the workhouse!"

The girl looked coy. "He's not dead. But they were sending him away to...a big city to be something called a prentice. I begged to go with him, but instead he cut my hair, stole the clothes and helped me get out of the workhouse."

"And this Jeremiah thought it better for you to be dressed as a boy?"

"He said the workhouse would be looking for a girl not a boy."

"How did you escape?" whispered Antheia, hoping the authorities wouldn't be knocking on Mrs Thornborrow's door.

Jemima thought for a moment. "Simple really. I hid in the cart that took him away, under the bones."

"Bones?" Antheia didn't know whether she should smile.

The little girl grimaced. "Yes, they used to be bones. But not when they're put in a sack."

Antheia glanced at the elderly woman, frowning in puzzlement. Mrs Thornborrow refilled her cup and grimaced. "She means the inmates would crush bones to make fertiliser. I know it's backbreaking work."

Antheia shook her hand sadly and then smiled at the little girl chomping on her ham sandwich. "I'm puzzled how you got your name if you were a small baby when you were found."

The child's eyes filled with tears and it was Mrs Thornborrow who explained, "When she was found there was a note pinned to her blanket. It said her name was Jemima and with it was a small crocheted heart." She cleared her throat. "Sometimes mothers leave a small keepsake with their babies should they be able to return and claim them."

Jemima nodded. "I thought my ma might come back for me, but then I knew she wouldn't. That's why I thought to get away from the workhouse and find a proper family of my own."

Silence fell round the table, until Antheia asked, "But what about the name Moffet?"

Again Mrs Thornborrow answered. "It was the name of the matron who found her."

It all sounded so sad and yet here in a small cottage in Brawton, life seemed more secure despite it being in the poorer part of the village.

Antheia decided to change the subject. "But we must think of the future and what to do with you. Can you read and write?" The little girl shook her head and Antheia turned to the elderly woman. "She needs a basic education."

Mrs Thornborrow nodded. "She does. I didn't learn to read and write until I was twelve and in the b...better place than my home." She thought for a moment. "There's a church school attached to St James's, but it's not free."

"Run by the Reverend Longmire, unfortunately," Antheia sighed.

She nodded. "Aye. And a few wives of the parish councillors."

"Could we teach her between us? You start her off with her letters and I'll help out when I can."

Jemima listened to the discussion intently. It was always the way, grown ups talking as though kiddies were not in the room. "I want to go to school."

The women turned to her.

Antheia pulled her reticule onto her knee and opening it took out another sovereign. "Take this and enrol her in the school. But make it after Easter and then we can teach her the alphabet at least."

Mrs Thornborrow took the coin and nodded. "She's a clever girl is our Jemima. I think by Easter we could get her reading."

"I'll borrow some books from my uncle's library. I'm sure he won't mind. My cousins have quite a few that will do well for her. *The History of the Fairchild Family* by Mary Sherwood and *The Children of the New Forest* by Frederick Marryat. And oh, she must read *Gulliver's Travels*." She turned to the little girl. "It's about a man who is shipwrecked and ends up in a land where the people are very tiny."

Jemima stared in wonder. "Do you mean they were kids?"

Antheia shook her head. "No, they were adults but small." She grinned at the child's incredulous expression and suddenly thoughts of the library reminded her. "Oh, I nearly forgot. I went into the library yesterday. The battle you mentioned was the siege of Sevastopol and it lasted for a twelve month. So, since you were found at Christmas, I reckon it must have been Christmas 1854 when you were born so that makes you nine last Christmas."

The little girl's eyes lit up. "I never knew how old I was."

"You should have a birthday, it's only right and proper," said Mrs Thornborrow. She rubbed her chin. "Christmas, you say?" Antheia nodded and the elderly woman turned to the little girl once more. "Would you like your birthday to be Christmas Day?"

Jemima nodded slowly. Taking a nibble on her jam tart, she lifted her head and stared at the two women, frowning. "What's Christmas?"

CHAPTER SEVENTEEN

The following two weeks sped by for Antheia. Her work in the parish and helping to teach Jemima seemed to fill all her time. She had brought the books and made it plain to the little girl books must be treated with respect and she must always wash her hands before using them. Jemima's progress was exceeding all expectations and within a week she had learned the alphabet and by the end of two weeks was able to read whole sentences. Antheia had started teaching her simple mathematics and enjoyed her role as teacher.

All through the two weeks, Antheia had worried the Reverend Longmire would impose himself on her again, or the countess would call her to her sitting room for a reprimand. But it didn't happen and even attending the services at St James's was uneventful. As the time came for Felix to return to Cambridge, she began to believe the vicar and her aunt had given up on the idea of pushing her into marriage.

Antheia accompanied her cousin to the station in Carnforth and it was while waiting on the platform he confessed his reluctance.

"I don't think it's for me. I really don't want to go back."

Her heart went out to him. "Perhaps you could use this term to decide. Would it be so bad to leave university?"

He shrugged. "Will completed his studies and went off to Italy straight after."

"Will knows he'll be the Earl of Sedgwick one day and is making the most of his time before having to take on the responsibility. You have more freedom to do what you like."

"My father believes I should make my own way in the world, but I've no idea what that should be."

His despondency made her take his hand and to her surprise he raised it to his lips and kissed her fingers. The train was approaching the platform and came to a halt. "Take care and think carefully what you wish to do with your life. The world is yours for the taking Felix Martindale."

He picked up his portmanteau, opened the door of the first class carriage and jumped inside, pulling down the window so they could carry on talking. "Thank you for a wonderful and eventful Christmas. I couldn't be more delighted to share an adventure with my country cousin."

She smiled and blew him a kiss as the locomotive pulled away and the carriages clanked together. Waving him off, she knew the term 'country cousin' was meant as an expression of affection and not used disparagingly. Suddenly she felt as though she belonged to the family and knew the months leading to spring and Easter would be full. She must continue Jemima's education and in a few weeks, the photographer was calling at the Abbey to take her portrait. And there were always the letters from Joel to look forward to. No more had arrived since the package of ten, but she felt confident one would be on the silver salver in the hallway any day soon.

Mr Powley, the photographer, was efficient to the extreme. His physique was like her uncle's and although he had no moustache; his beard was all encompassing. A chin-muffler, Matty told her as she helped her to dress.

Antheia didn't know what to wear for her portrait although her maid reminded her colour wouldn't matter. And so it was settled; she would wear her grey and purple check gingham dress since it was what she had worn at the first lunch she had taken with the family and the subsequent trip to Brawton when they had used the Red Lion's private garden. Added to this, Matty had coiled up her hair and placed the comb of purple silk flowers amongst the auburn tresses.

Matty accompanied her down to the ballroom where Mr Powley was fussing with his equipment, the large camera standing ready on a tripod and other paraphernalia scattered about. He had an assistant who seemed to be called Cas, the times the photographer called to the young boy to 'fetch this' or 'sort that', endlessly backwards and forwards as his employer directed him on setting up the backdrops.

"Ah, Miss Vale," said Mr Powley. "We're all ready for you. As you can see we have three backdrops for you to choose from." Antheia studied the large canvas and props. Two canvases showed landscapes with the Abbey in the distance, another a garden. "Of course you could stand by this column with a vase on top. We could position it next to the wall. Such beautiful walnut walls would set off your hair."

Antheia wasn't sure since all she could think was one of these photographs would go to Joel and he would probably carry it about his person.

Matty gestured over to where there was an arched trellis of silk roses with a small seat. "That's lovely, miss. What about sitting there?"

Mr Powley looked to where she was gesturing. "Indeed! We could place it by the window and it would suit you very well."

In moments the boy called Cas had arranged the seat and Antheia took her place, spreading her skirts elegantly. "May I smile?"

The photographer came out from behind the lens and frowned. "It's not usual. Can you retain your smile for twenty seconds?"

She nodded. She wouldn't, couldn't send Joel an unsmiling photograph of herself. And as the man and his assistant set up the shot, Antheia thought of the man she was growing fond of and kept her smile as the cap was lifted from the lens, the time counted and the cap replaced.

More poses followed for the sake of the family collection and before Antheia and Matty were released from the ballroom, Antheia reminded the photographer she needed a pocket-sized copy of her photograph to send to America.

Stroking his chin he said, "Then I'll print one that will fit in an oval leather frame to keep it safe. Now, the prints will be ready in two weeks and I'll get my assistant to bring them to the Abbey for you to peruse."

It seemed everything was in hand and they left the ballroom; the maid hurrying along the corridor to complete her duties upstairs and Antheia towards the library. She had told the parishioners in Brawton she wouldn't be visiting them, since she would be taken up with the photographer, but the weather from her bedroom windows that morning showed dark, threatening clouds heralding rain. It was mid February and it seemed to have rained for the last four days.

She wandered into the hallway. Winder hadn't removed the newspaper from the chair where her uncle had unceremoniously thrown it after breakfast and Antheia picked it up and immediately went to the news entitled 'Reports from America' and specifically to the accounts of the conflict. She knew her uncle was right and following the theatre of war did her no good, but she couldn't help herself. Flicking to the relevant page she saw there had been a Battle of Athens in Alabama at the end of January. She read it had been a victory for the Union, but she folded the paper and placed it back on the chair before she read the casualty numbers. Better not to know how many men had died.

Quiet sobbing from the landing on the floor above drew her attention and she could see the shadow of two figures. She climbed the staircase and immediately came across Patience with her arms round Matty who was crying uncontrollably into the maid's shoulder.

"What on earth has happened?" asked Antheia, walking towards them.

"Oh, Miss Antheia, it's dreadful," said Patience, her eyes pooling too. "Terrible to hear such news."

"What news?" Her heart speeded up. "Tell me!"

"Why it's about Mr Joel. He's been…killed, miss."

Antheia stared at her, hardly understanding, hardly breathing. "No! How do you know? Who told you?" She looked at Matty who had recovered and was wiping her eyes with a crumpled handkerchief.

Matty nodded. "Patience heard the countess telling his lordship."

Patience shook her head. "No, it was his lordship telling the countess."

Contradicting each other gave Antheia doubts although she had just read about the Battle of Athens. Was the 7th Maine Regiment embroiled in that battle?

"You've been listening at the keyhole again," she said, sighing.

The maids stared at her like two naughty girls.

"Sorry, miss, but it was such a shock whoever said it," admitted Patience.

Antheia decided to find out the truth for herself. "Come into my room and tell me everything." She shooed them in front of her as though she were herding geese and all three hurried down the corridor and into her room. One inside she closed the door and turned to them. "All right, I want to hear exactly what you heard."

Patience squirmed. "I wasn't exactly listening at the keyhole, Miss Antheia, they were almost shouting and it was easy to hear from outside the door."

"Continue," she urged.

Patience gulped before explaining, "I was taking in my lady's morning coffee and I stopped because his lordship was in there and I didn't know if I should interrupt them. They were going hammer and tongs, I can tell you. Your uncle was saying how you, Miss Antheia, didn't have any affection for the Reverend Longmire and her ladyship should get the idea out of head of any marriage between the two of you." Antheia breathed with relief; she had an ally in her uncle. "He then mentioned Mr Joel and how your heart was with him." She paused and swallowed.

Patience gulped before explaining, "I was taking in my lady's morning coffee and I stopped because his lordship was in there and I didn't know if I should interrupt them. They were going hammer and tongs, I can tell you. Your uncle was saying how you, Miss Antheia, didn't have any affection for the Reverend Longmire and her ladyship should get the idea out of head of any marriage between the two of you." Antheia breathed with relief; she had an ally in her uncle. "He then mentioned Mr Joel and how your heart was with him."

She paused and swallowed. "That's when her ladyship said how Mr Joel must have been...blown to bits by one of them..." She picked her words slowly. "Them...twelve...pound...Howitzers." She sniffed. "I don't know what they are, but if they're twelve pounds they can't be good for anyone."

Antheia nodded. "I don't know what they are either, Patience. But, you're right, they do sound lethal." She stared at them, biting her lip. "You two get on with your duties and leave it with me."

Patience's face became pained. "You won't say anything, miss, will you! That I was listening and told you?"

Reassuring her, she watched them go and walked across to the west-facing window of the Pink Room, staring out at the gardens. The conversation Patience had overheard was pure speculation and didn't mean Joel was a casualty in the war, but it brought home to her how far away he was and how much danger he was in. If only they had met months before instead of barely six weeks. Had it been six months she might have been able to persuade him not to go. Would that have been possible? If a man is set on serving his country, can he be convinced to do otherwise?

A twelve-pound Howitzer must be a type of cannon? It sounded frightening. She remembered reading about the Springfield rifle and the Colt although she couldn't remember where. Even so, the weapons of war in angry, determined hands could take a man's life in seconds. Panic filled her and she sped from the room and hurried to Lady Sedgwick's sitting room.

Patience was in the outer room and stared at the young girl who burst through the door.

"I need to speak with my aunt, now!"

Patience didn't answer but simply tapped on the door and stepped into the room. She appeared moments later. "She says she has no time this morning. She'll call for you when…"

Antheia pushed past the startled maid and burst into the room. Her aunt was sitting on the chaise longue and turned in annoyance at the intrusion.

"What is this? What do you mean by coming into my rooms uninvited!" Her ladyship rose to her feet. "Get out immediately?"

Antheia took in a breath and remained calm. "I will leave, Aunt, but only after I've had my say." She stepped closer to a woman whose face had reddened. "Firstly, there is no possibility of my marrying the Reverend Longmire. So, I would appreciate it if you'd forget that idea completely. Secondly, how dare you spread rumours about Mr Joel. He is a brave man who went to serve his country and should be praised not used as a tool to get what you want. He will survive and return to England." She felt compelled to say he had promised to come back, but she thought it sounded too personal. Instead, she turned on her heel and left the room, her grey and purple checked gingham skirt swirling round her small figure.

It was only when she came face to face with Patient's blanched face she realised what she had done. In effect, she had shown the maid to be an eavesdropper and caused her a great deal of trouble with the countess.

"Oh, Miss Antheia. What shall I do? I'll be dismissed for sure."

The countess ringing her bell summoning her maid caused the two young women to tense.

"I'll wait here. Go and see what she wants," said Antheia. She wouldn't let Patience be dismissed.

The maid disappeared into the room and came out moments later with the tray, smiling with relief. "She just told me to get rid of this," she said, nodding at the tray.

"Nothing else?" Patience shook her head. "If she says anything to you then tell me. I'm sure my uncle will not contemplate your dismissal." She had an inspired thought. "Perhaps she'll surmise Uncle Henry told me. Oh, my poor uncle. I hope I haven't got him into hot water too."

Patience giggled. "I don't think so. She's grateful to be married into such a prestigious family and having a title."

Antheia sighed. "Well, you did tell me at the outset she thought all her birthdays had come at once when she bagged my uncle."

A strange look crossed the maid's face as they walked out onto the landing. Antheia was about to make her way down the stairs and Patience to the service door that led to the servants' stairs at the end of the corridor, when she turned to Antheia.

"Miss, I didn't mean your uncle."

Antheia stopped in her tracks. "You didn't mean my uncle? I don't understand."

Patience adjusted the tray into a more comfortable position. "When I said she was grateful to bag the earl, I meant your grandfather, the late earl."

Antheia took a few steps towards her. "My grandfather?" Her voice fell to a whisper. "My aunt...the present countess...was married to my grandfather?"

The maid nodded and looked about her as though afraid they would be overheard. "Yes, miss. It's what I heard, although only a few are still here to know it all. She married your grandfather after his divorce

167

and then your uncle after your Aunt Frances died in childbirth."

CHAPTER EIGHTEEN

Antheia felt stunned as she walked slowly down the staircase. What Patience had divulged had rocked her foundation. Cora, the present Countess of Sedgwick had been part of the family for more years than when her uncle had married her. She remembered the conversation in the ballroom, when Mrs Hadwin had told her how her mother had packed her bags and left the Abbey because she disagreed with her father's second marriage. And the woman he was marrying was Cora! A woman twenty-five years his junior and once a seamstress in Liverpool. And years later, when her uncle had lost Aunt Frances he had married his stepmother! Antheia remembered discussing such marriages with her father. They were permitted, although considered 'voidable' if challenged by an interested party. Obviously no party was interested enough to challenge their union.

Felix and Will must know about their marriage and had never mentioned it. In fact, the entire household must know this history and had not divulged it at all. A seamstress in Liverpool? Mrs Thornborrow had been born and raised in Liverpool. She had had a chequered past, but her expression when speaking of the countess had been puzzling to Antheia.

As she reached the bottom of the stairs, she gripped the newel post in surprise. Yes, Mrs Thornborrow knew the countess when she became the second wife of her grandfather and later her uncle, but was it possible she knew her in Liverpool too? What did the elderly woman know? At her next visit to give Jemima her lesson, she would ask her outright.

Her uncle stepped out of the library. "Ah, my dear, there you are. I was about to summon Winder to fetch you."

She shook herself back to reality. "Did you want me?"

He beckoned to her. "Come into the library. I've something to ask you."

She followed him into the cavernous room and into the corner where there was a lectern on which stood a large, leather bound Bible. She had noticed it many times, but had never felt the need to study it.

He stopped at the lectern, turning the front cover and smiled as he gestured to the page in front of him. "This page is for the births in the family and when Mr Dodwell wrote to me on behalf of your father, I took the liberty of adding your name." She glanced at the page and saw she was the last entry. "And I must say I was pleased your parents included my mother's name in your name."

"I knew my mother was Anne Sarah, but I had no idea where the Sarah came from."

"Well, Antheia Sarah Vale you've been in the Bible for nigh on eighteen years." He thought for a moment. "Of course in March when you reach eighteen you could go down to London for the Season. You could be presented to the queen."

"Who would sponsor me? It must be a former débutante."

"Not my wife, of course, but I know ladies who I could call on."

She shook her head. "Thank you, Uncle, but I'm the daughter of a clergyman and the Season in London would scare me to death."

He chuckled and turned over two pages. "Now, on this page I entered the death of your mother which was a desperately sad occasion and filled me with regrets." He turned to the page before. "However, on this page is the marriages. And I need to know your father's full name and where and when your parents married." He walked across to the small table containing paper, pens and ink. Filling the pen from the inkwell, he returned carrying a larger blotter.

When he was back at her side, she gave him the information he required. "My father was called Walter Cecil Vale and they married on the fifteenth of May 1840 at the Priory Church in Leominster."

She watched as the earl wrote in copper plate the date of her mother and father's wedding day. As he wrote she noticed the entries above it. Her parents' marriage would not be in date order as she could see her uncle's marriage to Cora fell in 1845 with her parents' wedding day the entry below. She supposed it wouldn't matter, but watching him, questions tormented her. Why had he married Cora, his own stepmother? Had he been so distressed, so grief stricken he needed the comfort of a wife as soon as possible? As her grandfather had done after his divorce from her grandmother?

He blotted what he had written, closed the Bible and returned the pen and blotter to the small table containing stationery. "Thank you, my dear. You've been a great help."

"Are all the family in this Bible?"

He shook his head. "Only for the last two hundred years." He gestured to the shelf on his right. "At the top is a record of the family of the Earls of Sedgwick for the preceding two hundred years."

Her mind returned to the conversation with Matty and Patience. "Uncle, if anything…happened to Joel when would I hear?"

He stared at his shoes for a few seconds before answering, "It would be a few weeks I'm afraid. They would inform his mother first and she would write to you."

"Who are 'they'?"

"I do believe the senior officer writes to the family personally." She didn't answer and seeing her pensive expression, he caressed her cheek with his forefinger and tried to allay her fears. "This war has been going on for three years. It has to end soon."

As he left the library, she murmured. "But at the turn of this century we were at war with France for twenty years!"

She decided to stay in the library, hopeful the peaceful ambience would soothe her troubled heart. Patience had only heard the vindictive uttering of a woman who seemed to possess few feelings for her fellow human beings. Even so, the fears it evoked in her were more than she could bear. And the images of war and destruction; of men being blown to pieces plagued her thoughts. She opened the Bible and turned to the 'Marriages' page.

Her grandfather, Stephen, had married Cora two years after Sarah's desertion. That seemed reasonable, as he would have had to wait for his divorce from Parliament. And when Aunt Frances had died, Uncle Henry married Cora barely three months after her death! Shock swept through Antheia. He had not even mourned his late wife for the customary twelve months. She knew the family didn't seem to adhere to the social norms, but her uncle spoke of his late wife so lovingly.

As she closed the Bible, she was disturbed from her conjectures by Winder entering the room.

"Ah, Miss Antheia, there you are. Luncheon will be served in ten minutes. However, the afternoon post has arrived and you've received another package from America."

How she managed to swallow her meal she couldn't imagine. Her aunt had decided to eat in her rooms again and since it was only herself and her uncle, the earl was happy for her to curtail lunch and hurry from the dining room to the hallway where she scooped up the letter and rushed upstairs to her room.

Flinging herself on her bed, she carefully opened the package. There was a letter from Martha Newton asking after her welfare and giving her brief news from Cape Elizabeth. But there were six letters from Joel; the first dated the eighth of December. He seemed to be still on the move and spoke of incidental incidents en route; a waggon had broken a wheel and one of his Company, being a wheelwright, had it fixed it in no time. His horse had thrown a shoe and that had held them up for a time.

It was his second letter that seemed to tell her R Company had finally arrived at their destination. Antheia picked up small clues and specifically the fact names of other officers crept into his letter, especially a certain Captain Masters. Since she had assumed each Company had only one captain and he had only mentioned his lieutenant and sergeant up to now, she knew Captain Masters must have been leading another Company. And he and Joel had become firm friends.

She imagined a huge camp, brimming with soldiers and preparing for battle. The thought terrified her.

His third letter confirmed everything she feared.

My dearest Antheia,

Again I received your letters in a box sent by my ma. Along with your news, Ma had sent a ginger cake

173

and many other goodies I shared with the men. You might think me generous, but that is what happens in camp. We share any treats sent from home.

We also share news, but some of us find our letters too personal to share as I do with yours. Even though you speak of the Abbey, of Felix and your uncle and all the things you are doing, I'm reluctant to divulge anything in your letters. This has made me somewhat of a 'dark horse' amongst my men who nod and wink when I answer mail call. They are all very curious to know who is this young English lady who has stolen my heart. You say you are making arrangements to have your photograph taken and when it is done and I receive it, I might consider showing R Company your likeness. But that is all.

Keep writing my dearest Antheia. I look forward to your letters more than you can imagine.

Fondest regards
Joel

The young English lady who has stolen his heart! She read the sentence over and over again, before opening his last three letters. The next was dated the twentieth of December wishing her a Merry Christmas and the next was the first week of January and wished her a Happy New Year. His last letter in mid January, mentioned news from R Company and how Captain Masters had received news his wife had presented him with a baby daughter and another man had celebrated his twenty-first birthday and they had had something of a 'rumpus'.

Antheia placed the sheets of paper together and sighed. She remembered the Battle of Athens in Alabama had been at the end of January, so his last letter predated that. Was Joel in Alabama and had he taken part in that particular battle? She would know he was well once she had received his next letter. The waiting was putting her nerves on edge.

She had to be strong and not give way to these fearful thoughts. She would answer his letters and tell him she had had her photograph taken and would send him a copy as soon as the completed prints arrived at the Abbey. In one month she would be eighteen and Mrs Thornborrow and Jemima were planning a birthday tea for her. Felix would be home before her birthday for the Easter holidays and her uncle had suggested a birthday dinner and a theatre trip to Lancaster. There was much to look forward to.

Casting her thoughts back to Mrs Thornborrow, she knew her friend was reluctant to speak about the disappearance of her grandmother, Sarah. But perhaps in a week or so she could broach the subject, especially if she told her she now knew that her aunt had been the second wife of both her grandfather and uncle. What's more, she was now convinced Mrs Thornborrow knew Cora in Liverpool. How had their paths crossed and had they been friends? Antheia knew it was important to discover what the elderly woman knew and the knowledge would bring her closer to discovering what happened to her grandmother.

CHAPTER NINETEEN

Antheia woke up to gales howling round the Abbey on the first morning in March. She lay in bed curled up under the covers and listened. It sounded like lost souls screaming for mercy and it made her shiver. The door slowly opened and a figure floated past her causing her to pull the blanket over her head and hide, before feeling silly.

"Good morning, Agnes." She sat up in bed.

The young maid jumped to her feet. "Oh, sorry, Miss Antheia. I was trying to be quiet and not disturb you."

"You were very quiet. I thought you were a ghost."

"Shall I carry on?"

"Please do."

Agnes knelt at the fireplace, cleared the grate of ashes and shovelled them into a bucket before laying the fire with the paper and wood she had brought in a second bucket. She put a match to the paper and the flames took hold immediately. Antheia watched from the bed remembering how many times she had lit the fires in the vicarage and could have done this work herself. But Agnes being a lowly housemaid made up all the fires on cold winter mornings. When the wood caught, the maid placed coal from the scuttle carefully onto the flames; one piece at a time so she didn't smother the fire.

"There, miss, the room will be warm in no time. I'll just take your chamber pot."

Antheia pulled the covers up round her chest. "Thank you. How long have you worked at the Abbey?"

Agnes seemed to puzzle over this. "I came summer before last."

"Are you happy here?"

Again she frowned. No one ever bothered to ask her about her welfare. "Yes, miss, but I'd like to make parlour maid one day."

"I'm sure you will."

She grunted. "Not if Mrs Hadwin has her way. She was fair angry with me yesterday."

Antheia snuggled down and smiled. "What did you do to upset her?"

The maid walked towards her and bending down, took the chamber pot from under the bed, placed it carefully in the bucket containing the ashes and covered it with a beige cloth.

"I was dusting and polishing her parlour and saw a dirty saucer and a stub of a candle sitting there on the dresser, so I took it away to throw out. She was so cross with me."

"Why would that upset her?"

"I don't know, miss, but I thought I'd be dismissed on the spot, except I knew where I'd put it and went through the bin and found it." She shook her head. "Why she's so fond of such a filthy object I can't imagine." Antheia didn't know how to answer and jumped out of bed to open the door for her. "Why, thank you, Miss Antheia." The maid picked up the buckets and left the room while Antheia jumped back into bed, pulling the covers over her.

She stared at the flames now licking round the coal and casting shadows on the pink orchids and cyclamens on the wallpaper. Her thoughts turned to Mrs Hadwin's obsession with Jemima's candle and saucer. She had completely forgotten she had left it in the housekeeper's parlour the day she had driven to the cave to find the child she believed lived there. In

177

her letters to Joel she had told him about the tunnel and asked if he knew about it and also she told him about Jemima and the fact she had found a home for her, even helping her with her education before she joined the church school after Easter.

The last two weeks hadn't been fruitful when speaking with Mrs Thornborrow. Tentatively she had asked about the elderly woman's suspicions concerning the disappearance of her grandmother, but she had simply raised her hand and told the young girl it wasn't the time and place to divulge what she thought she knew. The fact she had told Antheia she didn't believe her grandmother had a lover, created more of a mystery. Why had her grandmother disappeared leaving behind all those she had loved? Had she been murdered? But by whom? Surely not by their grandfather. Antheia could only surmise Mrs Thornborrow didn't want to tell her yet, since those who were responsible were still alive and could be brought to account. She couldn't help thinking they should. No one should escape justice after committing such a despicable crime.

Antheia scrambled out of bed and threw back the dusky pink velvet curtains on the west window. Part of the garden she could see looked forlorn and empty, but she knew the spring flowers would be pushing their way through the soil soon. The day before she had walked in the woodland and noticed the beginnings of the primroses. She longed for the warmer weather to come and most of all she looked forward to Felix arriving home from Cambridge. He was due three days before her birthday and Mrs Hadwin had brought a menu to her and they had discussed her birthday dinner.

Her uncle had spoken further about attending the theatre in Lancaster and she had readily agreed that

Shakespeare's *A Midsummer Night's Dream* would be perfect. She had never visited a real theatre and her only experience was the amateur plays put on in the church hall in Bromyard. The Grand Theatre in Lancaster was said to be the best theatre in the county of Lancashire.

It was at breakfast Antheia glanced through the long windows and saw the boy called Cas riding up the drive with a satchel across his shoulder.

"My photographs have arrived!" Her heart beat furiously. How she hoped they would be suitable, especially the one to be sent to Joel. If they weren't she would have them done again.

Five minutes later Winder entered the breakfast room and handed a pouch to the earl.

"Ah, now let's see what we have here." He ordered the footman to clear a space as he lay out the six portraits in a line so he and his niece could view them. "Well, these are tremendous."

Antheia felt colour rush to her cheeks as she viewed her image captured by the camera. "Do you like them, Uncle?"

He picked up a larger portrait and nodded. "This will be framed and placed on the piano in the drawing room next to the others. And, oh my, look at this one." He put down the large portrait and held up a small oval one encased in a leather frame. "Now, is this for a certain Captain Joel Newton?"

The blush became more pronounced. "I asked for a smaller one to send to him."

"He will love this one. And he'll be the envy of every man in the regiment."

Winder gave a polite cough. "The boy is waiting below stairs, my lord. He says any you don't like can be taken away with him."

"I think we'd like to keep this one," he pushed the large one to one side, "and of course the small one in the frame. What do you think, my dear? Do you wish to keep any others?"

"I'm happy with your choice." She scooped up the one for Joel. "Excuse me, Uncle, but I need to write to Joel and send this, before I set off for Brawton." She hurried from the room in a swish of silk skirts.

Lord Sedgwick watched her go. "You know, Winder, I really hope this doesn't end badly. Despite the victories of the Union, I feel this war might last a while yet."

The butler didn't feel the need to answer.

In the morning room Antheia studied the photograph. The leather frame made her likeness seem elegant, showing a young girl sitting next to a trellis of roses in a checked dress with a comb in her hair. She had maintained a half-smile so she seemed...what? The only description she could think of was wistful. How she hoped Joel would like it and keep it near him.

With the letter written and the photograph enclosed in a package, she left it on the hall table before going round to the stables to collect the horse and gig. Although the wind whipped at her hat and coat, she cantered the distance to Brawton and felt relieved when she arrived outside the vicarage. To her relief the Reverend Longmire wasn't at home since he had been called to the home of a dying parishioner to give the Last Rites. She collected the sheet of instructions from the housekeeper and left immediately to continue on to Slee Court.

Leaving the horse at the usual trough, she walked towards Mrs Thornborrow's cottage, only to notice young Leonard Garnett waiting outside the door of his mother's cottage. The young boy jumped with

180

excitement and disappeared inside. In moments he was outside again accompanied by two of his brothers and one sister. They stood in front of Antheia expectantly.

She smiled and pulled out a paper bag from her basket. "I have some toffee for you."

Seven-year-old Leonard took it and then his older sister nudged him. "Thank you, miss," he added hurriedly.

It seemed that wasn't the end of it as the children didn't move away to enjoy their toffee. "Was there something else?"

The eldest amongst them, eleven-year-old Edith lifted her chin and said, "Please, miss, can we join Jemima with her lessons. We want to learn to read and write too."

Antheia felt stunned. Of course, their parents wouldn't be able to afford the cost of the church school, not for seven children. And there wasn't a 'ragged' school in Brawton catering for the poor. In her conversations with Mrs Garnett she had discovered of the three older children, one had married, one had gone to work in a factory in Manchester and another had gone into service in Lancaster. The busy mother was now left with the four youngest ones who were now staring at Antheia with eager eyes.

Owen who was a year younger than Edith pointed across the lane to Mrs Thornborrow's cottage. "Jemima said you might teach us and we can all squeeze round the table."

Antheia's heart was breaking. Yes, the children might all fit round the table if the elderly woman agreed to subject her home to noisy children. But it was what was needed to teach them that worried her. Books she could borrow from her uncle and the slate, chalk and an abacus she had bought from the Post Office. Could she afford more after paying Mrs Thornborrow for Jemima's upkeep?

"Let me speak with Mrs Thornborrow first. And then I'll come across and have a word with your mother. Agreed?" The children nodded and ran inside to enjoy their toffee.

She knocked on the door and Jemima opened it. Her hair had grown and now bounced on her shoulders in soft brown curls. Mrs Thornborrow had pinned a blue and white checked bow to one side that matched her dress and pinafore.

"Miss Antheia! I read a whole page of *Gulliver's Travels* and I've even started on the Bible."

"You're reading the Bible?" smiled Antheia.

"Granny said I should. We were supposed to in the workhouse, but they made us work instead. I've been reading about Christmas and how Jesus was born in a stable with the animals! And that's when it's my birthday too."

"I know." She stepped into the room and saw the table was set for a lesson. "I just need to talk with Granny first and then we'll start."

Mrs Thornborrow called across to her from the bench with her jars of seeds and herbs. "Can you make the tea? I must finish this preparation of bee balm for Mr Saul's bad head cold."

Antheia crossed to the kettle bubbling on the range and made the tea, before setting out the cups and saucers. How could she ask her about the Garnett children? Would they all fit in this small room?

The elderly woman finished her work and came to sit at the table. "Well, that's a penny earned." She chucked Jemima under the chin who answered with a giggle. "She's been working hard. She seems to read faster and faster each day. By the time she goes to the church school she'll be the cleverest in the class." She sniffed disapprovingly. "It's a shame girls can't go to university and enter male professions."

Antheia grimaced. "Elizabeth Blackwell obtained a medical degree in New York some fifteen years ago."

"America ain't England. I can't believe a young girl is banned by the men of this country to better herself. You take Mrs Garnett's older girls. Ivy was married at sixteen and Freda, only fourteen, sent to Lancaster to be a scullery maid."

"The boy was sent away too," said Antheia pouring out the tea.

"Aye, young Percy. Gone off to Manchester to work in a cotton mill."

Jemima raised her head from her book. "That's where Jeremiah went. I wonder if they met each other. I do hope so and they became good friends."

Antheia blew on her tea and said softly, "They probably became very good friends."

The lesson started with reading and writing practice, followed by thirty minutes on the abacus. But Antheia couldn't resist giving the little girl a short history lesson about the wives of Henry the eighth; a lesson Jemima seemed to enjoy especially when it came to the fate of his second wife, Anne Boleyn.

"Well, I must go," said Antheia picking up her reticule. "I have some errands to run in the parish. One of them is to read to Miss Hicks. Her eyesight is failing and we're halfway through *Moll Flanders*."

Mrs Thornborrow raised her eyebrows. "The unmarried ones are the worst." She opened the door to see her visitor out. "Goodness, why are the Garnett kiddies waiting in the court? They're stood there as if they're expecting the queen to pass."

"They're waiting for me," admitted Antheia. She closed the door and faced the elderly woman. "They want to know if I'll teach them too."

"They want lessons in here?" She glanced round her small room.

Antheia nodded. "They mentioned it, although I do believe they simply want lessons with Jemima."

Mrs Thornborrow blew out a breath. "It's a pity you couldn't rent the cottage at far end of the court. It's been empty a good month now."

"And make it into a schoolroom? What a wonderful idea."

"But you can't set up a school without funding either by the parents or a patron."

Antheia opened the door and stared at the delegation of four children still waiting. "What can I tell them?"

The old lady shrugged. "I'm sorry, but my cottage is too small to allow for a class of kiddies. As much as I'd like to I can't have them around my herbs and potions. Some of them are poisonous and I would be too worried. Jemima is all right as she lives with me and she knows what she mustn't touch. But as for the Garnett kids...no, I can't risk it."

Antheia respected her opinion and nodded. "You took in Jemima and I'm grateful for that. I wish I could use one of the rooms in the Abbey, there's plenty to choose from. But my aunt would be horrified." She was struck by the elderly woman's expression, that unfathomable look in her grey eyes.

Antheia opened the door and stepped outside. Squeezing her hand, she reassured her. "I'll work something out. Please don't worry about it." She looked across at the children. One thing was sure she couldn't let them down. "Who's the landlord of the empty cottage?"

"The Reverend Longmire." Mrs Thornborrow couldn't help smiling.

Her visitor sighed. "How unfortunate." Antheia looked away momentarily and gathered her courage. "I know Aunt Cora married my grandfather before marrying my uncle."

She made to turn away, but was held by her arm. "I think we should have that talk soon. Perhaps after your birthday?"

Antheia nodded and went to speak with the children waiting eagerly for her.

CHAPTER TWENTY

Matty helped her into a dark blue gown trimmed with lavender lace and pinned up her hair with silk pansies.

"It seems so strange to get dressed for dinner when there's only three of us," mused Antheia, turning about and viewing herself in the chevel mirror.

"His lordship always expects it and you do look very pretty, Miss Antheia."

"Thank you, Matty, but I think most of it is down to your skill."

The maid stood back and studied her mistress. "When do you finish your year of mourning?"

"In June. The last day of June to be precise."

"That means you can go into lighter clothes on the first day of July. The seamstress will call and make you summer clothes."

"There doesn't seem much point."

Matty was aghast. "Oh no, miss. His lordship will insist on it. You must uphold the dignity and respect of your family and wear clothes that suit your station in life."

Antheia turned to her puzzled, "But I travel into Brawton almost every day and work amongst the parishioners. I feel more like a clergyman's daughter then. I only slip into the persona of niece to an earl when I'm in the Abbey."

Matty would have none of it. "Even so, your work in Brawton is classed as charity work and quite seemly for your status. Anyway, miss, you'll look lovely in lighter clothes. Pinks and soft blues would suit you."

Antheia couldn't help laughing at the maid's enthusiasm. "I suppose so, but I do seem to have plenty of clothes." She bit her lip before saying. "I've been teaching a little girl who's living with Mrs Thornborrow."

Matty nodded. "The one you found in the cave? You thought it was a boy but it was a girl?"

She turned her head to stare at her maid. "How did you know that?"

"Postmaster's wife told Agnes and she told Patience and she told me."

"Does everyone know?"

The maid thought about this before answering, "All below stairs do and the stable lads. I'm not sure about the earl and countess."

"The trouble is more children want to join in and there's not enough room in Mrs Thornborrow's cottage. And besides she's worried about her medicines. Some are quite potent and she doesn't want any of the children to come to harm."

Matty adjusted the lace on Antheia's sleeves and agreed. "No, you wouldn't want them to become curious and try tasting anything." She shuddered. "Mrs Hadwin said it's only a matter of the dose what make a substance beneficial or fatal."

The subject was getting rather grim and Antheia decided to go back to their former topic. "I do have a dilemma, though. I can't say no to the kiddies who want to learn. But what can I do."

Matty handed her the fan she and the housekeeper had found for Antheia's first dinner with the family. "I suppose you could use the schoolroom."

"What schoolroom?"

"In the tower, miss. You get to it down a small passageway between the morning room and the old chapel."

"I went down that passageway when I was exploring the building. I tried the door, but it was locked."

"It's always kept locked now. I was told the tower was added a hundred years ago so the earl could climb to the top and view all his lands.

Antheia realised the earl Matty spoke of must have been her great-grandfather.

"My cousins were taught in the tower?"

"Until they went to Eton."

"They never mentioned it."

Matty giggled. "Who wants to talk about their schooldays, miss. I went to the parish school in Carnforth and I can't say they were the happiest days of my life."

Antheia thought about this. The tutoring she had received from her father had certainly been the best days of her childhood, but she could understand not everyone felt the same.

"Shall we explore tomorrow after breakfast?"

Matty's face beamed. "Yes, miss. Mrs Hadwin will have the key. The housekeeper tends to hold all the keys to the Abbey."

The following morning Antheia was the first to arrive. She had left after breakfast and gone straight to the short passageway off the corridor leading to the morning room and chapel. The passageway was about twenty feet long with a window at the end. The rush matting seemed rather worn and the door to the tower was small and might be mistaken for the entrance to a storeroom since the wood was painted and not varnished, as were the main rooms of the Abbey.

Footsteps and the swishing of skirts made her turn her head. To her surprise the housekeeper was leading the way with the maid a few steps behind.

"Ah, Miss Antheia, I hope we didn't keep you waiting. Matty says you wish to explore the tower."

Antheia nodded. "If it's no problem. I've been here nearly seven months and it must be the last place to visit."

The housekeeper smiled and lifted the large ring of keys attached by a chain to her belt. "Now then, where is the key. Agnes has the job of cleaning the tower and I know she gave me the key back. Ah, here it is." The two young women watched as she pushed the key into the keyhole and turned it with a crunch. Pushing the door open they were confronted by a winding staircase. "Lord Keasden and Master Felix loved to run up and down these steps."

With Mrs Hadwin leading the way, they picked up their skirts and climbed the thirty steps round the tower, the brick walls interspersed by oval windows. At the top there was another door and she turned the handle and pushed it open. Stepping into a round room came as a bit of a surprise, but it was plain to see Agnes, the lowly housemaid, had done a remarkable job of wiping away any dust and keeping the windows clean.

Antheia could sense the authority in the room immediately. There was a blackboard to the side and a large high desk to the left of it, the chair tall. This desk dominated the room and seemed to glare down at the much smaller desk facing it. There was intimidation in this room that made her shudder. An enormous print showing a map of the world was pinned to the whitewashed wall and near it standing on a cabinet, a large globe. On the far side was a substantial cupboard. Antheia stepped across to it and pulled it open. Inside were slates and boxes of chalks, rulers, and quite old pens although the ink had dried in the inkwells. There was even mathematical equipment and a large abacus meant for a class of children instead of the smaller one she used with Jemima. This was pleasing, but not so the dunce's cap on the top shelf and the cane lying threateningly next to it.

She heard Mrs Hadwin sigh behind her. "Doesn't seem five minutes ago they were small boys and being tutored here. And suddenly they're off to Eton and then Cambridge."

"I do hope the tutor was kind."

The housekeeper grimaced. "He was like all tutors. He enforced discipline in the schoolroom. Of course, with there being five years between the boys, Lord Keasden left for Eton just as Master Felix was old enough to be tutored. Such a shame they couldn't be tutored together."

Anthea blew out a breath and giving the cane a last glance, shut the cupboard door. "I'm supposing there's more to the tower. I heard there's a viewing point?"

Mrs Hadwin nodded and stepping across to another door opened it and they followed her up more winding stairs to the top. Here it was breezy since the top of the tower consisted of a viewing platform with unglazed apertures in the brickwork and a beamed roof covering all. The women spent the next ten minutes going to each opening and gazing out over the landscape. From one, Anthea could see the estuary and she even thought she spied the Irish Sea.

Their exploring over, they made their way down the spiral staircase and entered the schoolroom once more. Anthea looked about her knowing it was perfect, but would her uncle allow her to use it? She aimed to teach the poorest children in the parish and it wouldn't bring in a penny.

She couldn't remember when she thought of deceiving her uncle. Her dreams were disturbing, with Jemima and the Garnett children running across a battlefield with missiles flying about them and the little girl crying out they must hide in the tunnel. Whatever it was, her dreams or her common sense, she realised her uncle would never agree to her plan. And over the next two days she knew she had to teach the children in secret.

Slowly a plan formed, until she knew precisely what to do. The last thing she wanted was to get the servants into trouble, so she started by finding her way to the attic storeroom. Amongst the trunks and discarded paintings she discovered an old table and six worn chairs. The chairs she carried down one by one and hid in the chapel, thankful her aunt and uncle left her to her own devices.

The table was a different matter and she had to ask for help from the footman, Charlie, and also Matty who became joint conspirators in her scheme as they helped her carry it from the attic to the chapel to be placed with the chairs. This was followed by ten minutes of frantic cleaning as the dust of many decades was wiped from the chipped and battered furniture.

Borrowing the key from Mrs Hadwin was easy for Antheia; if the young lady wanted to visit the viewing platform again who was she, a mere housekeeper, to stop her. And with the means to gain access to the tower, she, Matty and Charlie carried the table and chairs up to the schoolroom. The small desk was moved over to the wall, before placing the table in the middle of the room with the chairs round it. She took the slates and chalks out of the cupboard and put them round the table.

"What about ink, miss?" Matty looked about the room.

"I'll have to do with the slates for now. Perhaps I can find paper and ink later." She looked at Matty and Charlie who had been a wonderful help. "If anything happens you'll not be blamed. After all you're obliged to follow my instructions." She looked at the key. "I'll not lock the door when I return the key to Mrs Hadwin. Let's hope no one notices."

"What about Agnes?"

"How often does she clean in here?"

Matty bit her lip. "The first of the month. She and Clara does here and the chapel."

"Good. It's a while till the first of April. By then I should have thought of something else."

Charlie nodded. "We wouldn't want you to get into trouble, Miss Antheia, but what puzzles me is how you're going to teach the kiddies. They live in the village and they'll not be welcome walking through the Abbey grounds."

Antheia smiled at him.

It was only a week until her birthday and she had decided to give Jemima a ride in the gig to see the Abbey gardens. But she had an ulterior motive making her feel guilty. The blustery weather had disappeared and the spring sunshine was glorious as she cantered the horse, the little girl sitting next to her in the oversized coat and bonnet. Mrs Thornborrow had tried to give it back to the Garnetts but Jemima held on to it. For some reason she felt safe and secure in the folds of the woollen material.

After pulling into the stable and leaving the horse and gig, they set off to explore the gardens. The crocuses looked wonderful against the daffodils and the beginnings of hyacinths emerging from the flowerbeds. Jemima was entranced with the fountain of Puck pouring wine for King Oberon and Antheia briefly told her the story; of fairies and spells; of romance and mischief, until the little girl continued her skipping along the paths. The sun came out to warm them as they reached the woodland where the primroses bloomed.

"I like seeing the garden properly," smiled the little girl.

"Do you mean it's better than sneaking into the Abbey?"

Jemima nodded slowly. "I didn't like doing that. But I was so cold and hungry." She glanced around. "The opening is here."

"Shall we find it?"

They walked further into the wood until they found the place. Jemima smiled at the large stone placed on top with a cross etched into it from Felix's penknife.

"I could find this place if it was dark," said Jemima, brushing the leaves from the surface.

"I know it only because it's just left of the trail through the woods and of course, we marked the spot." They sat down amongst the primroses and Antheia watched as the little girl picked a bunch. "Jemima, I'm thinking of using the tunnel for you and the Garnett children. Then you can all come secretly to the Abbey and have lessons in the tower."

Her eyes opened wide. "We're going to sneak in? Like I did before?"

She sighed to hide her guilt. This was against her better judgement, but she couldn't think what else to do. She couldn't risk her uncle refusing her permission.

"What would you say to bringing the Garnett children to this hatch and showing them the way through the tunnel and into the chapel. I'll wait for you and take you up to the tower for your lessons."

Her excitement was palpable. "What time should we come?"

"I think you should wait until the church clock chimes eight and set off from Brawton then. It's only a mile from the village to the Abbey. I'll keep to the same times and days I teach you since you know the routine."

"We could take the track across the fields. That's the way I came when I sneaked into the chapel before." Her smile was bright with the thought of such an adventure.

"Yes, that would be all right. It will be dark in the tunnel. We must organise a light."

"Where's my saucer and candle?" She looked accusingly at the woman sitting next to her. "I should have it back then I could use it."

"It's in the Abbey quite safe. But I could place a lantern at the bottom of the ladder here ready for you."

Jemima nodded. "Yes, Miss Antheia." She grinned. "Can we start tomorrow? It's so exciting."

"Yes, tomorrow." She had an afterthought. "How did you find the tunnel in the first place?"

"I was here looking to see how I could get in the big house for some food and I thought someone was coming from the garden. I ran and tripped over it."

"And where did you find the saucer?"

"It was in the tunnel. I thought it was so pretty. Please could I have it back Miss Antheia? I really liked it."

"I'll check with the housekeeper. I'm sure she's kept it."

They sat together listening to the birds nesting in the trees, as Antheia mulled over the fact the saucer

Jemima had found, certainly didn't come from the Elizabethan times, when the priest would have escaped through the tunnel. So from where did it come? And who had used the tunnel prior to the little girl?

CHAPTER TWENTY-ONE

She was up early the following morning and went to the schoolroom before going down to breakfast in order to light the fire with the paper, wood and coal she had placed there the evening before. She crossed to the blackboard and moved it a little closer to the table. Finally she checked the alphabet prints she had pinned on the walls. The room looked much friendlier than it had done when first she saw it and she was convinced the thick walls would hide any noise the children made. The only thing that worried her was the fire. She wondered if the smoke would be noticed from the chimney, but she reasoned the chimneys were in groups of four and perhaps it would be overlooked.

"You haven't asked after the news for a while, my dear. Have you lost interest?"

Antheia took a bite of her toast. She had written to Joel only the day before telling him about her plan to teach the children in the tower and in her letter she had told him to keep safe. No, she hadn't lost interest; her mind was simply engaged elsewhere.

"Is there…any news, Uncle?"

He frowned in puzzlement and turned to the newspaper. "There was a battle in Virginia in February at a place called Morton's Ford, the outcome undecided."

Suddenly, she wished she hadn't asked. "Thank you. Perhaps you're right and I shouldn't become involved. It's quite worrying. I think from now on I'll just wait for Joel's letters."

"Very sensible. You can't do a thing about the war, so you might as well get on with your life." He smiled. "I forgot to say I've booked three tickets for the theatre. I'm assuming Felix will want to accompany us."

She sighed. "I wish Will was home."

"In his last letter he thought he'd be home in the summer again when it starts getting too hot in Italy."

She sipped her tea and watched her kindly uncle as he turned the pages of the newspaper. Should she ask him about teaching the children? He might agree and she could meet the children and lead them through the garden in a crocodile line. That would amuse the gardeners. What would George think? But she couldn't risk her uncle's anger or that of her aunt at the thought of the children of the poor 'infesting' the family seat. Better to carry on with her plan, deceitful as it was.

The evening before, she had taken a stroll through the woodland, pushed the stone to one side and lifted the hatch. Staring down the metal ladder she had almost lost her courage. How could she let small children travel through the tunnel? But before taking Jemima back to the cottage they had confirmed the details. Jemima must lead the way with the lantern and Edith being the eldest at eleven years old must bring up the rear. And they must be as quiet as mice.

She had climbed down the ladder and left the lantern at the bottom, but had placed the box of matches inside the lantern for safety. The lantern was similar to the one she and Felix had used and she had taken it from the workshop when the gardeners were busy. Its design comprised a small door that opened to light the candle inside and it would be much better than an oil lamp. It also possessed a ring on the top enabling it to be held or hung on a hook. Only Edith, as the eldest, was permitted to strike a match against the brick wall, as she was proficient at lighting the oil lamps in her home. Glancing down the tunnel had made Antheia shudder and she was glad to climb out and close the hatch.

The clock on the mantelpiece struck eight and she knew the children would be setting off from Brawton. Looking across to the window she was pleased it was a beautiful morning, the sky blue with only a few white clouds; no rain threatening. She stood and folded her napkin on the table.

"Must be on my way, Uncle. I have a lot to do today."

"You spend a lot of time in the village. Is the Reverend Longmire keeping you busy?"

"Well, as you know, my work is on an ad hoc basis. I go in when there's things to do."

She left him quickly before she needed to tell a lie and went straight to the chapel, closing the door quietly behind her. It still seemed cold inside, but not as glacial as it was in the winter months. Perhaps in summer it became warmer as the stone walls heated with the sun. She pressed the letters spelling out *tandem* and swung open the panel to its widest, crawled inside and opened the hatch. A chill breeze hit her in the face as she caught her breath and eased herself over the edge and down the ladder. Standing at the bottom she searched the tunnel for light and movement. Although the children had been told to be quiet she surmised she would hear them, children could never be entirely silent.

And when stifled giggles echoed along the tunnel ten minutes later and she saw the swaying of the light, she breathed a sigh of satisfaction. Jemima was the first to appear the lantern clutched in her little hand, the Garnett children following closely. Antheia held out her arms as they approached feeling pleased and proud of them. She took the lantern from the little girl and helped her climb the ladder, followed by the four Garnett children. And then she climbed a few rungs and handed the lantern to Jemima who was looking over the edge of the hatch. The children pulled her out and she slammed the hatch closed, before crawling out through the aperture and into the chapel. Straightening her back, she closed the panel and caught her breath. The children stood quietly, but she could see they were amused about something.

"Well done, children." She blew out the lantern and placed it on one of the pews. "Did you remember to bring the matches with you?" Edith slipped her hand into the pocket of her coat and handed her the box. Antheia placed them next to the lantern. "I'll leave these here for your return journey."

Jemima grinned and pointed. "Oh, Miss Antheia, just look at your clothes."

Glancing down she realised her white blouse had a smudge of mud on it and pushing her hand into her skirt pocket, she pulled out her handkerchief and tried to wipe it away.

"It won't hurt, anyway it'll come out in the wash," she smiled.

Suddenly she realised all five children were dressed in their best, the boys in well-washed but pressed coat and breeches; the girls wearing their newest dresses and pinafores under their coats. And remarkably there wasn't a mark on them.

"Well, it seems the teacher is the one to be reprimanded for coming to school in an unacceptable condition," she said, fixing a loose curl behind one of the pins holding up her hair. "But you five get full marks."

The children broke into smiles, but it was Jemima who spoke for them. "It was exciting, miss. Perhaps you should wait for us at the top of the ladder so you don't spoil your pretty blouse."

Antheia couldn't agree more. "Yes, perhaps, but I worried about you."

"But Granny came with us although we told her we'd be all right on our own," said Jemima, sounding older than her nine years.

Antheia had crept to the door to see if the coast was clear, but turned on her heel. "Mrs Thornborrow came with you?"

Jemima nodded. "She said she wanted to see the tunnel too. She even climbed down the ladder to take a look."

"Poor Mrs Thornborrow. How did she manage with using a stick?"

It was Edith who answered. "We helped her down and then pushed her back up. She was puffing and panting a lot, but she said she had to see the tunnel."

Antheia had never thought of Mrs Thornborrow as a curious person, but perhaps the thought of a tunnel from a priest hole intrigued her. She turned her attention back to the door. Opening it slightly she saw everything was quiet.

"All right, children, out you go. Aim for the passageway on the left and wait outside the door."

The five children raced out of the chapel and disappeared down the passageway. When the last one had gone, she closed the door behind her and joined them. Soon she was shooing them up the spiral staircase in the footsteps of her cousins and into the schoolroom where they gasped as they looked round the spacious area. The fire was now blazing and welcoming them into a room and the gift of education.

It wasn't long before the Garnett children were settling down to learn the alphabet and Jemima was reading *The Water Babies* by Charles Kingsley; a book new out the previous year and Antheia had bought her as a belated birthday gift. She had also chosen a dozen more books from the Abbey's library. How grateful she was her cousins had nearly every book available to children and she knew they wouldn't be missed since they had been relegated to a place on the corner shelf.

They had been working for about an hour when the door opened and Antheia gasped and then breathed with relief when Matty breezed through the door carrying a tray.

"Oh, Matty. I think we ought to have a special knock when you come in. I nearly had a heart attack."

The maid grinned. "When Mrs Hadwin went for her morning tea I decided to sneak some tumblers of milk and biscuits for the kiddies and a cup of tea for you." She placed the tray on the table. "I'm sure you've all been working very hard."

The children nodded in agreement and as the women handed out the drinks they tucked into the shortbread biscuits. Antheia drank her tea back with relish and helped herself to a biscuit.

"Has anyone noticed anything?" she asked.

Matty shook her head. "You're out of the way here. I couldn't hear any noise from the spiral staircase and I wondered if you had decided not to go through with it."

She took the maid to one side. "I've loved every minute so far, but I'm on edge we'll be discovered."

Matty thought about this. "Only me and Charlie know at the moment, although I think we'll have to bring Agnes into it. I guess we'll have to hope for the best."

Yes, it was going to be a strange situation, but she had decided the few days she taught the children would be enough especially if she set them work to do while at home.

The family was expecting Felix home in three days' time on the Saturday and the following Tuesday it would be her eighteenth birthday and her special dinner and trip to the theatre in Lancaster. There was a lot to look forward to and plenty to tell Joel. She couldn't wait to write to him about the first day of her subterfuge and how guilty and scared she had been. Would he be disgusted with her for deceiving her uncle? She hoped not. Knowing Joel, he would be enjoying her little adventures. In a strange way, perhaps it was helping him in that terrible conflict so far away across the ocean.

CHAPTER TWENTY-TWO

The next few days fell into a routine and the children soon adapted to their journey through the tunnel and seemed to look forward to their lessons in the schoolroom in the tower. But Antheia couldn't reconcile herself to the secret she had to keep and often wondered if she should summon the courage to tell her uncle what she was doing. But to see his disappointment in her, was more than she could bear.

It was Saturday and the day Felix was returning home. She had completed her morning's work in Brawton and was keen to get back to the Abbey to greet him. The weather was still breezy, but the apple blossom was starting to bud on the trees and the gardens were filling with daffodils as the stable boy helped her up in the gig. She made herself comfortable in the seat when she saw the Reverend Longmire coming towards her.

"Miss Vale, are you leaving already? I thought I would ask you to lunch yet again."

She had to admire his persistence although she felt alarmed. Since she had confronted her aunt the month before, the vicar had become aloof, simply giving his instructions in the morning and leaving her to get on with her work. He seemed displeased with her, but this didn't bother her one bit. She much preferred his ire to his fawning attention.

"My cousin is arriving home from Cambridge today. I'm keen to get back to the Abbey to see him."

"Indeed you must be I'm sure. But couldn't you spare another hour? I have something to discuss with you."

She sat for a few seconds, the reins lying idly in her hands. It was irksome to have to make excuses. Perhaps she should say to him what she had said to her aunt? Set him straight.

"Just this once Reverend."

He helped her climb down, his moon-like face beaming. "I told Mrs Sisson to expect a guest."

It was rather presumptuous of him but she let it pass. No doubt the poor housekeeper had been preparing for a guest at luncheon every day for months.

"But after I've eaten I must be on my way."

"Certainly. Although a little bird has told me you're eighteen this Tuesday and I took the liberty of buying you a small gift."

She felt shocked and heartless. He had bought her a gift for her birthday! Perhaps she was too quick to judge people. He offered his arm and she took it, walking with him towards the church of St James and the vicarage next door.

It was quite a lovely house reached through a gate and a garden filled with spring flowers and a cherry tree in the middle of the lawn. The front door was varnished and sported a huge brass knocker in the shape of a bell. The windows either side and on the next storey gleamed in the sun, the whole topped with a red tiled roof. She had visited the vicarage many times and annoyingly, Antheia couldn't help thinking this would be a wonderful home for any woman who could suffer being the wife of the Reverend Longmire.

He opened the door for her and they passed through the hallway where he helped her off with her coat. Antheia patted her hair into shape under her mauve felt hat with a bow at the back and straightened her skirt. She should look presentable.

"Let's go into the sitting room and have a glass of sherry," he said, smiling. "Mrs Sisson has everything prepared and will act as a chaperone for you."

She wanted to get the meal over with, but felt she had no choice but to agree. And once in the sitting room she graciously accepted the crystal glass of amber liquid and took a sip. She often had a sherry before dinner at the Abbey, but declined alcohol at other times. The biting warmth on her empty stomach took immediate effect.

"Now then, do you have anything planned for your birthday?"

She nodded. "A special dinner on Tuesday evening and seats at the theatre in Lancaster on Saturday."

"Sounds a real treat." He stared down at her sherry glass. "I'll give you my gift now. I do hope you like it."

Opening a drawer in the sideboard he pulled out a small package beautifully wrapped. Her heart skipped a beat at the thought this might be a betrothal ring. But no it couldn't be; he would have had to ask her first after which, he should approach her uncle for his permission. Only then would she see a ring. Assuring herself this wasn't what she thought, she unwrapped the box and lifted the lid. Inside was a stunning gold brooch studded with tiny diamonds and emeralds and in the shape of a butterfly.

Colour flooded her cheeks. Didn't he know a gentleman must never give such expensive gifts to a young lady he was neither related to nor betrothed to since it smacked of buying her affection? This gift must have cost a small fortune and she gave a half smile.

"I'm pleased you like it. As you know butterflies are abundant in these parts in the summer." He took the box from her. "Here. Let me pin it to your bodice."

She didn't like this idea, but steeled herself to feel his fingers on her as he pinned the jewellery to her cotton and lace bodice. She shuddered as he touched her. How grateful she was when the housekeeper called them for luncheon.

He was as good as his word and Mrs Sisson stayed in the small dining room as they ate the chicken soup, pork cutlets with vegetables and finishing with apple tart.

Their conversation had been mundane throughout the meal until he asked, "I hear you're teaching young Jemima Moffet, who I'm delighted to say will be joining us at the church school after Easter."

"She's a clever girl and I'm sure will be a credit to you."

"And a credit to your teaching I think. How wonderful that Mrs Garnett has taken her in, especially with her having four young ones of her own."

Mrs Garnett? Had Mrs Thornborrow asked Mrs Garnett to pay the fee for Jemima's schooling and say she lived with them? Antheia closed her eyes briefly in awareness. Of course she might do that knowing the Reverend oversaw the church school. She would be afraid Jemima might be refused attendance simply because she lived with a woman the Reverend despised.

"Yes, she's very kind," she said in a low tone, taking a sip of her wine.

"Have you ever thought of training as a teacher? I think you would do well."

"It has crossed my mind at times."

"If you need a reference to enter any teaching college then I would be more than happy to oblige. You've certainly done sterling work in the parish."

She felt stunned. "Thank you. You're very kind." It seemed he wasn't going to mention marriage and if he didn't she would have no need to refuse him and set him right.

"Whitelands College is excellent and one of the oldest higher education institutions in England. Do you know it was founded in 1841 by the Church of England's National Society as a teacher training college for women? A veritable flagship for women's education."

"Where is it?"

"It's situated in a beautiful Georgian building in the King's Road, Chelsea."

"Chelsea! But that's in London."

He feigned surprise. "My dear Miss Vale, last summer you travelled all the way from Herefordshire to live with your uncle. Surely travelling down to London would be nothing for an intrepid young girl like yourself."

She didn't know how to answer. Not only had he offered her a reference but had suggested she move hundreds of miles away and study in the capital. Suspicion coursed through her. Why would he want her away from Lancashire? And why did she think her aunt was behind this? She had told her categorically she would never marry the Reverend and perhaps the countess was trying a different strategy to get rid of her.

Mrs Sisson's gave a cough attracting their attention and Antheia glanced at the housekeeper, her jet-black hair scraped back from her face and moulded into a severe bun at the back of her lace cap.

She had never seen the woman smile and wondered if she ever did.

"You said I needed to remind you, sir. You have an appointment."

Longmire's eyes opened wide. "Oh, goodness, yes. I'm afraid I do. I'm so sorry Miss Vale I must curtail our lunch."

He was throwing her out! And yet she felt grateful. "Not at all, Reverend. We had finished and I'm eager to get back to the Abbey."

In the hallway he helped her on with her coat. "Please give young Felix my regards."

How glad she was to be in the gig and urging the horse through the village and onto the lane that would take her to the Abbey. She guessed her cousin must be home now and when she reached the stables she was informed Master Felix had arrived only twenty minutes before. But her thoughts prickled when she was told he had brought two trunks of possessions with him. He had brought his trunks home? At Christmas he had left them in his lodgings and come home with a portmanteau containing only what he needed. This didn't bode well.

She made her way to the hallway in order to find her cousin, when her attention was arrested by the brown package on the silver salver. Joel's letters had arrived. Picking up the envelope she looked towards her uncle's study where there came a murmur of male voices. Obviously Felix was discussing his studies with his father and Antheia felt she had plenty of time to take the letters to her room to enjoy.

She opened the package sitting on the chaise longue next to the coat she had discarded and placed over the back of the seat. There were only four letters this time and she stared at the envelopes in surprise. Firstly none of them had stamps, but across the tops of each in bold writing was 'SOLDIER'S LETTER' and each envelope was decorated with a print drawing of a battle. She picked up one depicting the Battle of Gettysburg and the date, 1st–4th July 1863. The other three envelopes had similar drawings and she frowned. It was good of the army to allow soldiers to send their letters free of charge, but reminding them of the battles in which many men had died seemed insensitive.

Even so, it was the contents she longed to read and as usual she put each sheet of paper in date order. The first thing she saw was Joel's fourth letter was dated the fifth of February and she remembered the Battle of Athens had been at the end of January. She breathed out in relief since had he been embroiled in that conflict, he had come out unscathed. However, his first letter was dated the eighteenth of January.

My dearest Antheia,

Again there were eleven letters from you in the last mail call and I was delighted to receive them. I still await your photograph which I'm sure is on its way to me by now.

You write so vividly of Sedgwick Abbey and the folk in Brawton I feel I'm there with you once more. In my dreams I walk with you in the meadows and along the trails that follow the estuary. Sometimes I'm sure I can smell the sea. And in my dreams I walk with your hand in mine. And then I wake to the sound of the camp stirring to life. I feel my existence comprises the conversation of soldiers, of orders been called and answered, of the jingling of harness and the whinnying of horses.

I dream of the day I will return to England. I feel the Union is making good ground in this conflict, but all of us want to go home.

I look forward to your letters so very much. Keep writing my darling girl. And take care of yourself, for my sake as well as yours.

Fondest wishes
Joel

Yes, she would do that. When he came back to England she would walk with him and if they were in the gardens she would take his hand. It wasn't what she should do, but surely in a private garden with the gardeners about it would be acceptable even though a young woman did not hold the hand of a gentleman she wasn't engaged to. But they could always slip arm in arm if they met anyone. How she longed for his return. She missed him so much.

His second letter included news of the camp; his world. One soldier of R Company had lost his mother and been sent home for her funeral. She didn't realise the army did that and it seemed remarkably civilised when on a war footing.

His third letter was incredulous that she had found a priest hole and secret tunnel from the chapel to the woodland.

In all my visits to the Abbey over ten years I had no idea it existed. And obviously the boys didn't since you say you explored it with Felix. What an adventure for you. I can't wait to see it for myself.

You also say you went back to the cave and found a child living there. I was horrified we didn't investigate further. But you found Jeremiah who turned out to be Jemima. She sounds a lovely little girl and although I didn't know Mrs Thornborrow except by sight, at least she now has a home and an education if you're teaching her as you say. Living in a tent is not the most comfortable of abodes, but I couldn't imagine making my home in a cave.

Antheia had always believed it was thoughtless of her not to discover the inhabitant of the cave sooner, but she could never blame the boys. They were travelling on their individual journeys the following day and had no time. But she should have investigated the situation. She shuddered at what would have happened if she hadn't been hiding from the Reverend Longmire that day and seen Jemima emerging from the priest hole. Would she have lasted the winter? Antheia thought not and the death of a small child would have been on her conscience when a tiny frozen body was found in the cave.

Joel's fourth letter worried her as after some brief news he finished with:

I dare not make any promises, my darling girl, since war heightens a man's senses and ordinary events that he took for granted in civilian life, now seems sweeter and fills him with yearning. Home is all we talk about. We all have someone to go home to. Most of all Captain Masters who has not seen his baby daughter yet. All we can do is our duty and pray it ends soon. Please don't forget me.

How could she forget him? However, this didn't sound good as he had promised in his earlier letters he would come back to her. He seemed melancholy and perhaps he had good reason. Was R Company heading for another attack with the Confederates? He sounded like a man who was preparing for something.

The last time she had asked her uncle about the war in America, he had mentioned a battle in February called...she thought desperately. Something Ford...Morton's Ford. Horror swept through her. If R Company was taking part...had taken part in that battle, what had been the outcome for them? It was then she decided not to read the news any more. It was too painful and because of the time constraints in their letters she found herself on tenterhook with anxiety. Did she love Joel? She felt she did. He had certainly become more of a friend to her. Only when they saw each other again would they discover their true feelings for each other.

Hurried footsteps down the corridor and a door slamming brought her back to reality. It must have been Felix since she knew only a member of the family felt they had the right to slam doors; the servants never would.

Tucking the letters in her dressing table drawer to be answered later, she stepped out of her bedroom and in seconds was knocking on her cousin's door.

CHAPTER TWENTY-THREE

Their greeting wasn't as she had expected. Felix opened the door with a face like thunder although he attempted a half-smile when he saw her.

"Welcome back. I've missed you," she said, trying to read his expression.

He opened the door wider. "You'd better come in."

The two trunks he had brought home still stood in the middle of the floor. She gestured to them. "It looks like you've come home permanently."

He walked about the room agitated. "He won't listen! I explained how I hated Cambridge but he wouldn't have it. He wants me in a respectable profession."

She took a seat on the sofa. "But I thought Uncle Henry wanted you to make your own way in the world."

"Yes, as long as it's my brother's way." Seeing her confusion, he explained, "I don't want to be a solicitor, or become a barrister and judge in time. I want to…"

"What do you want to do?"

"You'll laugh."

"I won't. Just tell me."

He sat next to her his face alight with enthusiasm. "This term one of my old tutors from Eton visited Cambridge and our paths crossed. We went to the nearest public house and had an illuminating conversation." She nodded in acknowledgement and he continued. "He was puzzled why I was taking a law degree. I think he remembered how appalling my Latin was."

"He taught you Latin?"

"No, he taught music. I was in the choir at Eton and he remembered I had a good voice."

"He was right."

"Thank you. To cut a long story short, at Trinity I joined the choir so I've been singing with them since I arrived at Cambridge. My old tutor thought I would have gone to the Royal Academy of Music in London and not to university."

Antheia sat up and smiled. "The Royal Academy of Music! Yes, you should train there and then you could join an opera company."

"Such as Covent Garden?"

"Why not?"

His face became dark. "Because, dear cousin, my father said he'd rather see me burn in hell than disgrace our family with a career on the stage."

Antheia fell silent. Yes, her uncle would think that. She remembered as a child hearing about Jenny Lind and her beautiful voice. How she would have loved to go to Covent Garden and hear her sing. But a life entertaining an audience would be thought demeaning for the son of an earl.

"Uncle must know opera is respectable."

He snorted. "To watch but not if you're a performer."

"What do you plan to do?"

He shrugged. "I have no idea. Perhaps I can change his mind and ask him to transfer funds from Cambridge to the Royal Academy, but I doubt it."

"Could I give it a try? Perhaps I could offer another point of view."

His cry of relief echoed round the room. "Would you? Even if you don't succeed nothing is lost."

They stood and he glanced at the brooch pinned to her blouse. "That's pretty."

"Birthday present."

"Oh, yes, it's on Tuesday isn't it?" He bent closer. "I must say Stepmother is being very generous. That brooch is real emeralds and diamonds, not paste."

"Your stepmother?"

"Yes, her jewellery used to be my mother's and before that our grandmother's. But of course Stepmother inherited it when she married Father. She must be warming to you if she's given you such an expensive gift. I've seen her wear that piece many times, so she's quite fond of it."

Antheia walked along the corridor and down the staircase, unpinning the brooch as she went. How pleased she was when she met the housekeeper in the hallway carrying a vase of fresh flowers from the garden.

"Ah, Miss Antheia, Master Felix is home. Did you know?" She placed the fresh flowers on the table against the wall.

"I do, Mrs Hadwin, I've just finished speaking with him." She held out the brooch. "Would you return this to her ladyship please."

The housekeeper's expression showed utter surprise. "You've found it!"

"Was it missing?" Antheia tried to keep the disdain from her voice.

"Well, it's only this morning Patience said it was gone from her ladyship's jewellery box."

"And what did my aunt say about that?"

"Patience was very worried she would be accused of negligence. But the countess has not mentioned it. We hoped to find it before she realised it was missing."

Antheia couldn't answer since anger made her grit her teeth, otherwise she might say something she would regret. It was obvious something was going on between the Reverend Longmire and her aunt. Had her aunt given her the brooch as a gift she would have accepted it graciously. After all, it was a piece of jewellery that once belonged to her grandmother and it would have been a wonderful gesture on her eighteenth birthday.

She looked towards the study. "Is my uncle still working?"

"He is and he's not in a good mood if you wish to speak with him."

For some reason, seeing the brooch in the housekeeper's hand made her remember something else. "Mrs Hadwin, do you still have the saucer I left on your dresser the day I took lunch in your parlour?" The housekeeper didn't answer at first and turned away as if she couldn't look her in the eye. Antheia explained, "If you've thrown it away then that's all right."

"I would never throw it away, miss," she whispered.

"And why's that?"

Mrs Hadwin stared at the young girl assessing her. "Could we speak in the library, Miss Antheia?"

Antheia nodded in agreement and led the way into the room on the opposite side of the hallway. There the housekeeper became agitated and took out her handkerchief to wipe her mouth.

"I was fair shocked when I saw that saucer I can tell you."

"You recognised it, didn't you?"

Tears welled up and Antheia could see she was struggling with her emotions. "I told you that day in the ballroom about your grandmother taking certain possessions with her when she... left the Abbey." Antheia nodded, remembering. "When she and your grandfather were married they were given a thirty-six piece teaset in Dresden china. Your grandmother was very fond of it and when she left, one cup, saucer and tea plate were missing."

"She took it as a memento you think?"

The housekeeper's face filled with pain. "When I saw that saucer in my parlour my heart nearly stopped beating and I had to go straight to the cupboard and compare it with the other thirty-five pieces in the set." She sighed. "Even so, I was in no doubt where it had come from."

Antheia knew the implications of this, but needed to speak the words. "So, that saucer was in my grandmother's possessions when she left?"

"Yes, and that's the shock of it. Where did you get it, miss? I always meant to ask."

Walking into the middle of the room, Antheia debated her answer. Finally she came to a decision. "I can't tell you just yet, but one day the truth will come out. Please keep it safe."

"Of course, miss. Although it's a mystery."

They left the library together and Mrs Hadwin walked towards the stairs leading to the kitchen area. Antheia stared at her uncle's study door. If he wasn't in a good mood then it was better to leave her intended conversation with him for another day, especially as her thoughts were concentrated on the saucer found in the tunnel. She bit her lip. Despite Mrs Thornborrow suspicions, wasn't it possible her grandmother had escaped the Abbey through the tunnel? Whether to live with a lover or not, it would be a good way of leaving the Abbey without being seen. And in the attempt had dropped the saucer from the Dresden set. Perhaps her bag had come open. Should she mention the origins of the saucer to Felix? No, she wouldn't tell him yet; he had enough problems of his own. She would enjoy her birthday and wait for that all-important discussion with Mrs

Thornborrow. Perhaps then they could put the clues together and work out what had happened to her grandmother.

The following day she attended St James's with the family as normal and kept her distance from both the Reverend and her aunt. Her thoughts didn't make for sociability and she felt silence would heal the hurt and confusion. But she knew she must be on her guard against them. They might easily convince her uncle that marriage to a clergyman was beneficial and without his support she would be lost. In which case she would have to follow in her mother's footsteps and leave the Abbey.

After Sunday lunch, she realised her uncle was donning his coat and top hat.

"Uncle, are you intending to take a walk?"

He turned at the door. "Yes, my dear, I thought I'd walk through the gardens and woodland. I need a breath of fresh air."

"May I join you? Unless you want time alone and then I'll understand."

He nodded. "Certainly, I would enjoy your company."

In her room, she pulled on her boots, collected her cloak and grabbed her straw hat. In minutes she was downstairs and they made their way to the rear of the house and through the exit to the gardens. They strolled slowly enjoying the spring weather and the flowers emerging from their winter sleep and the trees budding. They stopped while her uncle had a word with George, before they continued on towards the woodland. Following the trail Antheia smiled and nodded as her uncle told her of the last time he had sat in the House of Lords, in March the year before, when questions had been asked about disturbances in

Ireland. She tried to keep her eyes on him and not glance in the direction of the hatch now hidden by leaves and broken ferns.

Finally they emerged onto Sarah's Meadow that led them to the cliff face and the track leading to the shingle. It wasn't to be this time as the tide was in and Antheia found herself looking across a flooded expanse, where the geese and curlews swam, peacefully waiting for the tide to go out so they could reap the bountiful harvest below them.

Uncle and niece stood in companionable silence; her hand through his arm. He smiled at her. "I have enjoyed your time here in the Abbey, my dear. I was dubious when I received the letter from Mr Dodwell, but now I can see how beneficial it was to us all."

He didn't know half of what she got up to and the thought made her wince. In the morning she would wait for the children to come through the tunnel and then it would be three hours of teaching in the schoolroom. What would he think if he discovered the truth? But she had other matters to worry about and decided to be frank.

"May I speak to you about Felix? He's not happy at all."

"I noticed. He's not spoken to me since our conversation yesterday."

"Was it awful?"

"I lost my temper," he admitted, watching her.

She looked out across the estuary and felt the wind on her face. "You don't like the thought of him studying at the Royal Academy of Music?"

He blew out a breath. "Singing is acceptable as a pastime and entertaining dinner guests, but how can he earn a living on the stage?"

"Many do. At Covent Garden."

He thought about this. "Frances and I went to Covent Garden about a year before Felix was born. We saw Weber's opera *Der Freischutz*."

"Did you enjoy it?"

"We did."

She smiled. "I think when it comes to the arts, whether it's painting and sculpture or music and writing, it's the inspiration that is important rather than the remuneration." She had his attention and pushed on with her argument. "My father used to say many folk have an ability. A good blacksmith can fashion the most incredible artefacts in metal and a carpenter can style stunning objects in wood. But these skills are learned and Father used to say there were also people who were gifted and that gift came from God. And if you're blessed with such a gift, as Felix is with his voice, then it must be used and not squandered."

He turned to her. "But to sing on the stage?"

"I'm sure he's willing to work hard at the academy. Singing is something he enjoys and I believe he must discover whether he can make a success of it. If he doesn't at least he made an attempt. If it's not what he expected perhaps he can go back to university and take his law degree."

"It seems a terrible waste of money."

Silence fell between them as they started their stroll along Sarah's Meadow, their gaze still on the water and the wildfowl skimming its surface. Antheia could see he was thinking over her words and felt reluctant to disturb him.

An idea came to her. "Why don't you give it twelve months? Let him start in September and by this time next year you'll know if his tutors think he has possibilities."

"Did he tell you what he intends to do before September?" He grinned at her and when she shook her head, he explained, "He thinks he can work at the Princess's Theatre in London's Oxford Street. The tutor he met said he could find him work as a stagehand, fetching and carrying."

"Excellent! That will give him a taste of theatre life. If he can work at menial tasks until the autumn and still want to train at the academy, then you'll know he's serious."

"After Easter they're starting rehearsals for *The Beggar's Opera* and he believes he might get a small part in it."

"Even better."

They turned to make their way back to the woodland and he became quieter. As they emerged from the woodland he looked out over the garden and finally up at the Abbey.

"I will think about it and make my decision tomorrow. If you speak to my son about this as I'm certain he must have asked you to fight his corner, then tell him to be patient. I have much to consider."

It was all she could hope for. She wanted Felix to be happy and when Will returned from Italy and Joel from America, she would never ask for another thing in her life. She would speak with Felix and reassure him she had done her best to persuade his father. She also wondered if she should tell him about the saucer found in the tunnel, but decided against it. It was her birthday in two days and they had a theatre outing on Saturday. She would enjoy reaching eighteen years and take up the mystery of her grandmother's disappearance after the celebrations were over.

CHAPTER TWENTY-FOUR

To say Felix was happy was an understatement, although Antheia didn't know about his delight until mid-morning of the following day. She had prepared the schoolroom as usual, met the children out of the tunnel and escorted them into the schoolroom. The lessons had gone well and Antheia was pleased with the progress of the Garnett children. They were enthusiastic and wanted to learn which made her efforts easier.

For the last thirty minutes she had been writing addition and subtraction sums on the blackboard, the children copying them onto their slates. The previous afternoon she had cut out paper pork pies and the children had been taking part in a practical lesson of passing them between each other, adding and subtracting the number of pies each had in front of them. It was coming up to the time when Matty brought the milk and biscuits, when Jemima mentioned the viewing platform at the top of the tower.

"Could we go up and see, Miss Antheia? The view must be tremendous."

The teacher smiled. Jemima had started using a different vocabulary of late, learning from the copious books she loved to read.

"I think we could. Leave your work, children, and you must put on your coats. It will be cold up there."

Excitedly, they got ready and Antheia led them through the door and up the spiral staircase to the viewing platform. The children had never seen the countryside from that height and their eyes became wide with wonder. Although she had to hold up the younger ones so they could see through the apertures, everyone was able to look across to the estuary and the rooftops of the Abbey. They could even see the buildings on the outskirts of Brawton.

She had left the door open to the viewing platform stairway and when she heard the door to the schoolroom open and close she collected the class together. "Come on, children. I believe Matty is here with your milk and biscuits."

Antheia let them go down first and followed, closing the door firmly behind her. She turned expecting to see Matty placing the milk and biscuits on the table, but instead her cousin stood in the middle of the room staring about him with a look of incredulity.

"Felix! Oh, my goodness!"

"Well, this place has changed."

She knew she must concentrate on the children first. "Take off your coats and settle down with…carry on with copying the sums I've written on the blackboard and then work them out. And yes, Cyril, you can use your fingers if you wish."

She gestured to Felix and he followed her to the side of the room. "What made you come up here?"

"Before I answer, what are you doing here? I can see you're teaching but…who are these young ones?"

"Oh, Felix, please understand. They're the children from the village who want to learn to read and write."

"And Father gave you permission to use the schoolroom?"

She shook her head. "Not exactly." She went on to tell him how they were using the tunnel to sneak into the Abbey.

He threw back his head, laughing, "Cousin Antheia, you'll never fail to surprise me."

"Sometimes I doubt the wisdom of my actions."

"I won't tell." He looked about him. "It seems warmer and friendlier somehow."

She paused before asking, "I take it your tutor was strict?"

Felix pulled a face. "I guess he wanted results, otherwise he would have been dismissed. He wasn't cruel and often he was kind."

"I saw the cane and wondered…"

"No, he never used it on me. But I think Will received its sting once or twice."

"He did?" For some reason she had thought her younger cousin would have suffered punishment more at the hands of the tutor.

Felix grinned again. "I heard he stole a pair of father's long johns, tied them to the cane and was caught waving them from the viewing platform."

"Oh dear. But it was just a mischievous prank. He shouldn't have been beaten for that."

"If I remember rightly, Father's valet complained to Mrs Hadwin's predecessor that his lordship's underwear was missing and she tore a strip off the poor scullery maid who did the laundry. Will was punished for getting the servants into trouble not for the misdemeanour itself."

It made sense. She glanced round the room. "I enjoy teaching the children, but I've been on tenterhooks at the thought I'll be found out."

"No one can hear a thing from downstairs. The walls of the tower are very thick."

"So, what made you come up here?"

His face changed from thoughtful to ecstatic. "Father spoke to me this morning. He's agreed to my going to the academy and not only that he's amenable about the job at the Princess's Theatre. And I know it's all down to you." He took her hands. "Dear country cousin, how would my life have been if you had never come to the Abbey!"

"Oh, Felix, I'm so happy for you."

His hands dropped to his side and he frowned. "I came up here...do you know, I don't know why, except I was searching for you to tell you my good news. No one knew where you'd gone. I suppose my feet led me here, although I was surprised to find the door unlocked. I thought it was always kept secured."

"It is. But thankfully no one checks."

He looked at the blackboard. "Arithmetic? Ugh!" To her horror he crossed the room to the children, pulling up her chair to sit with them. "Now then, do you know the song *Lavender Blue*?" When they shook their heads, he smiled. "Listen."

In his beautiful tenor he sang:

Lavender's blue, dilly dilly, lavender's green,
When I am king, dilly dilly, you shall be queen:
Who told you so, dilly dilly, who told you so?
'Twas mine own heart, dilly dilly, that told me so.

In only a few minutes they were singing along with him and knew the song by heart. By the time Matty arrived with the milk and biscuits, Felix had explained how a Round worked and pointed to each child to start them off.

Matty placed the tray on the table, her eyebrows raised.

"Music lesson," Antheia told her nonchalantly.

Her birthday the following day, was full of surprises. The gifts given to her at the breakfast table filled her with delight; a gold hair comb decorated with jet and diamonds from her uncle and a beautiful fan from Felix. Even the servants gave her little gifts, a box of

225

handkerchiefs from Mrs Hadwin and the maids and footmen had clubbed together to buy her a beautiful shawl. In the schoolroom the children gave her their small gifts. Edith and Jemima had knitted two woollen cosies to keep her boiled eggs warm and informed her Mrs Garnett and Mrs Thornborrow had helped. Leonard had found an unusual stone by the cliffs and given it to her as a paperweight, while Cyril and Owen had fashioned a piece of wood to make a pencil box, telling her their father, a skilled carpenter, had helped them with the tools.

It was after lunch she was called to her aunt's rooms and she went with trepidation. The day before, she had written to Joel and told him how Felix had found them in the schoolroom and the wonderful news he was to attend the Royal Academy of Music in London. Would he be surprised? She was sure he was aware her cousin wasn't cut out for a career in the law and she was also certain he would be pleased about the academy. Before she sealed the envelope, she had pressed a kiss on the letter and then held it to her heart. She didn't expect another batch from him until April since his mother seemed to collect up his letters and send them once a month.

She made her way to her aunt's room and waited to be announced by Patience, who whispered that her ladyship seemed to be in a happy mood.

"I don't know what's come over her, Miss Antheia. It's scary."

Antheia smiled. "Mrs Hadwin gave you the emerald brooch?"

"Yes, and thank goodness you found it. I don't know what she would have done if she had found it missing. I don't think I would have lasted long in my position."

Antheia squeezed her hand, knowing she hadn't been apprised of the full story. "Do you know why she's summoned me? She rarely leaves her rooms except for dinner and church."

"I think she's got a gift for you."

Surprised, Antheia passed through into the green and yellow parlour where Cora, Countess of Sedgwick sat on the sofa as usual, dressed in a vivid tangerine gown with white bows down the bodice. She didn't raise her lorgnette, but patted the seat next to her.

"Come and sit here, my dear. And may I wish you a very happy birthday. We haven't seen eye to eye, have we? But it's your birthday and I thought we could make a new start." Antheia sat but felt her skin crawl at being so close to a woman she didn't trust. "But first your gift." She called for the maid and told her to bring in the parcel. Patience brought in a package and gave it to her mistress, but as she turned away, rolled her eyes at the young girl sitting next to her. This didn't bode well. The countess offered her the parcel and Antheia smiled as she opened it. It was a bolt of heavy satin material in white, along with a roll of luxurious lace. "I thought Miss Sill could make you a summer gown for when you come out of mourning." She glanced at the dark blue gown Antheia was wearing. "You'll look pretty in a lighter colour."

Antheia fingered the material and had to admit to herself it was beautiful and the kind of cloth her mother could never have afforded. Only a year ago she would have been overjoyed to receive this gift and she decided she would accept it in the same frame of mind.

She smiled brightly. "Thank you, Aunt. This will make a stunning gown."

She ran her hand over the shimmering satin and then glanced up to see the countess smiling smugly. It sent shivers down her spine. Had her aunt expected her to reject the gift? Not that she would since she had been brought up to be grateful for any acts of kindness. Also, Antheia refused to give the countess any ammunition to fire at her uncle.

The countess patted her hand. "Are you looking forward to your birthday dinner tonight? Normally we would hold a ball in your honour and invite all the young folk from the neighbourhood, but alas, we live a quiet life at Sedgwick Abbey."

Antheia noticed her mouth dip downwards and knew her aunt regretted their isolation. Coming from humble origins, she had accepted her new life, but now it occurred to her perhaps it was unusual for a prestigious aristocratic family to bury themselves away in their stately home. What had Mrs Hadwin said? When her mother, Lady Anne, had lived in the Abbey there had been plenty of entertainment. The housekeeper had said there had been balls and parties every week. What a different place it would have been filled with laughter and music. Why had it stopped? She couldn't help thinking it was after her grandmother's disappearance. And something like that, plus the divorce would shame a family.

"I don't need a ball or party, Aunt. All my other birthdays were spent quietly with my parents."

"And have you heard from Captain Newton? It seems such a long time since he left for the war."

Antheia swallowed and cleared her throat. "He's been gone nearly six months, as has Will. It'll be lovely when they both come back."

"So, Joel is planning to return to England at the conclusion of the conflict?"

She nodded. "In his letters he says he will."

The countess seemed to be thinking this over. "Of course, America is a goodly distance and anything could happen. Oh, I'm not saying Captain Newton will come to any harm, I'm sure he knows how to keep his head down. But if he should meet a suitable girl over there and decide to stay, would you be disappointed?"

It was a stupid question and Antheia tried to stem her irritation. "Of course I would, Aunt. I've grown fond of him."

She patted the young girl's knee. "I'm sure you have. I'm just preparing you, my dear, for what you might have to face."

By the time Antheia left her rooms she felt like one of Cook's blancmanges. Yes, she had considered all the countess had said to her, but decided always to hope for the best. What else could she do? It was out of her hands. She went straight to her bedroom where Matty was placing clean linen in the chest of drawers.

The maid glanced at the parcel in her hands. "She gave it to you, then?"

Antheia dropped the bolt of material on the chaise longue. "Yes, and I'm sure Miss Sill will enjoy making me a summer gown."

Matty crossed the floor and examined the material. "A summer gown, eh?"

Antheia noticed the maid's mouth was twisted in a strange smile. "What's wrong, Matty?"

The maid sighed. "I shouldn't say, miss."

"Out with it."

Matty closed her eyes briefly before explaining, "It was Mrs Hadwin who went to the Post Office to collect it and she knew straightaway." She paused, but her mistress remained silent. "She saw the material was from London. Spitalfields to be exact. And the lace is Honiton lace from Devon."

"And what's the significance of that?"

"Mrs Hadwin remarked it's exactly the same material and lace what was used for Queen Victoria's bridal gown." Seeing the colour drain from the young woman's face, she decided to change the subject. Lifting a maroon gown out of the armoire, she held it up. It was adorned with black lace across the skirt and an off the shoulder neckline. "Are you wearing this tonight, miss? I could do your hair and set it with the comb his lordship gave you. You'll look such a picture."

Antheia nodded, her mind numb. What devious schemes was the countess plotting now? What web was she spinning to ensnare her? As she prepared for the evening, she tried to feel happy. It was her birthday and she had the theatre to look forward to. And there was always Joel's letters to brighten her day. She would read them again when she retired for the night. It made her feel close to him, but her aunt's gift had unsettled her and filled her with foreboding.

CHAPTER TWENTY-FIVE

It was four days after her birthday, a gift from Joel arrived. It was an oval box of marshmallow sweets and she smiled as she took off the lid, but his letter that accompanied it made her laugh and cry.

My dearest Antheia,

I've asked Ma to place this letter with your gift and I hope you enjoy the marshmallows. I would have liked to send you something more personal, but I understand there's a protocol in England in how gifts are sent between couples and I wouldn't want to offend you.

I know your name Antheia is for the goddess of flowers, blossoms and the marshes. I felt marshmallows would make you smile. To be named after a goddess suits you, my darling girl.

I do miss you with all my heart and I wish you a very happy birthday. Although I'm not with you in person, I'm there in spirit and I pray we'll be together soon.

Fondest wishes
Joel

She had written to him immediately, thanking him and giving him further news of the Abbey and village, before sharing the sweets with the family and Matty. She realised in the turmoil of war, her letters were a distraction and reminded him normal life was continuing. Not that she could call her life normal. Sneaking five children into the Abbey under her uncle's nose wasn't exactly usual, but at least it would entertain him. She imagined him laughing aloud at her exploits.

Two weeks after her birthday, she took tea with Mrs Thornborrow and Jemima. Antheia was acutely aware from the elderly woman's thoughtful demeanour, the time had come for their talk. Both women were relieved when Jemima finished her tea.

"May I go out and play with my friends? Edith has chalked a game on the court and she's going to teach me something called hopscotch."

"Off you go, then," smiled Mrs Thornborrow, opening the door for her. After she had gone, she added, "Now, it's not often I get a bit of peace, but it's lovely when it happens."

"You're managing with her?"

"She's a treasure. And not having kiddies of my own, I appreciate her." She turned to pour hot water into the teapot. "So, you've had a busy time since your birthday? Everything seemed to happen at once."

"Well, I'll always remember the theatre trip. It was a wonderful performance and we laughed throughout. It's so strange since I've read *A Midsummer Night's Dream* many times, but seeing it on the stage was a different experience. And my cousin was entranced by what the backstage people were doing. He studied every scene change with interest."

"He's gone now?"

Antheia nodded sadly. "Yes, he planned to go straight after Easter and he left yesterday, bound for London and the Princess's Theatre. I've never seen him so excited. And in September he'll start at the Royal Academy of Music. He's going to board with a friend he knew at Eton. But I do miss him."

"He does have a remarkable voice. I always enjoyed it when he performed a solo in St James's." She pushed the teacup towards her.

The younger woman sipped her tea. "I'm looking forward to Will coming home. And…Joel, of course."

Mrs Thornborrow reached across to squeeze her hand. "Your young man will come home safely, I'm sure."

Antheia carried on sipping her tea. Only when Joel's letters arrived did she know he was all right. Even so, they were so out of date she wondered what he was doing at that moment. She was having a cup of tea; what was he doing? The elderly woman's next words called her back to the present.

"I think it's time to tell you more about your grandmother and what I suspect."

Antheia put down her cup, her heart beating rapidly. "If you think it the right time."

"I do. But please remember these are just my suspicions. I have no firm evidence." Antheia stayed silent allowing her to sit comfortably in the armchair and continue her story. "You know something of my history, but what I didn't tell you is that your step-aunt is the daughter of the madam who ran the bordello."

"She wasn't a seamstress! She was a…"

Mrs Thornborrow held up her hand. "Now don't go jumping to conclusions. We must look at this from an objective point of view. No, she wasn't a whore. Being the daughter of the madam gave her some sort of status over us. The madam had the money to send her to the best schools. Unfortunately, despite her privileged education she learned very little. She must have been Jemima's age when I first went to work in the house and about fifteen when I left to marry Thornborrow."

233

Antheia studied the elderly woman, remembering she was only twelve when she ran away from home and went to work as a maid in the brothel. In fact, Cora was only a little younger than Mrs Thornborrow, but the years hadn't been kind to her friend and sadness made tears come to her eyes.

Thankfully, Mrs Thornborrow didn't notice and concentrated on the fire burning in the grate. "Cora always wanted more for herself. Expected more. I don't mind that as I believe it's a good thing to improve yourself. But I always felt Cora didn't care who she hurt or climbed over to get what she wanted."

Antheia finished her tea and nodded. "She does seem to have a strange way with people. She wouldn't make a good diplomat."

"Would you like another cup of tea?"

Antheia nodded and said, "You stay there and I'll get it." She busied herself filling up their cups and returned to her seat at the table to listen further.

"So, I married Thornborrow and after he was lost at sea I came here to Brawton as midwife. I didn't live here at the time. I rented a lovely cottage down Patterdale Lane."

"Round the corner from St James's," Antheia mused, more to herself than her friend. The homes in Patterdale Lane were spacious with good-sized gardens.

The elder woman sighed. "I had a parlour and separate scullery. And I could grow what I needed in my garden. I didn't have to forage for herbs in the woodland and meadows." She paused, reflecting, before going back to her story. "I didn't see Cora again until...well, until she came as lady's maid to your grandmother some years later."

Antheia blew out an incredulous breath. "She was Grandmother's lady's maid!"

The elderly woman chuckled. "I suppose she must have learned a thing or two in the years we hadn't seen each other. It seems she was a seamstress for a while, but decided to aim higher and become a lady's maid. "

"Did you recognise each other?"

"We did and she was as pleasant as could be. Kissed me like she had met an old friend. Seemed a completely different person and I thought she must have changed. But a leopard can never change its spots can it?"

"So, she became my grandmother's lady's maid. Oh, dear, why does that make my blood grow cold!"

Her smile was askew as she explained, "Well it might, my dear. That was my first suspicion, as I knew from my discussions with her, she aimed for the top of the tree and a good marriage. The higher the better."

"Uncle Henry?"

"Your uncle was about twenty years old when she arrived at the Abbey and away at Cambridge, but yes, she had her sights set on him. She was some two years older, but it was plain to see her plan. Every time she opened her mouth it was, Lord Henry this and Lord Henry that."

"I take it he spurned her?"

"His future was already set out and besides his heart was with Lady Frances."

"Cora and my grandfather married the same year as Uncle Henry and Aunt Frances."

"They did. Your grandmother's desertion broke your grandfather, as well as the divorce that followed. I believe Cora found herself available to comfort him during this time."

"But you don't believe my grandmother did desert my grandfather?"

"That was my second suspicion. I knew your grandmother. She adored her family and wouldn't have brought such shame on them." She pointed across to the workbench were she made up her ointments and potions, the mortar and pestle to one side. "Cora was interested in my herbalist skills. She would visit me in Patterdale Lane and sit in the scullery having a cup of tea, much as we're doing now. And she would ask me about the plants I grew in my garden and what they meant. I didn't mind, I thought it good to understand about flora and its benefits."

"Perhaps she was gaining more knowledge," said Antheia.

"I thought so too, but then I realised she was asking about cat mint and foxglove. The first is used for insomnia and the second for slowing the heart. She also asked about the poppy I make opium from and you know the effects of that."

Antheia nodded. "For pain."

"Yes, it helps those in need of relief from pain, but I'm sure you know it can be addictive."

"I do, we had a man in Bromyard who died from an overdose of opium."

Mrs Thornborrow sighed. "After your grandmother disappeared and your grandfather married Cora, I thought back to all I had taught her. Perhaps I gave her the knowledge to use…" Tears trickled down her wrinkled cheeks.

"Whatever happened it wasn't your fault."

She turned a weary face towards her. "Wasn't it? I knew Cora and I should have had an inkling she was up to no good. She wouldn't use her knowledge of herbs for the benefit of the household, only to benefit herself."

Antheia stared at her. "The nub of your argument is that you believe Cora poisoned my grandmother?" She didn't answer, but the look in the woman's eyes told her everything. "As you say, it's all suspicion."

"Yes, all suspicion, but then there was your Aunt Frances."

Antheia's stomach did a flip. "You think she…Oh, no!"

The elderly woman shook her head. "Again, all suspicion. Your Aunt Frances had a difficult time when she birthed your cousin, but she came through it and I was confident of her survival. The bleeding surprised me and I couldn't stop it." Her voice raised in the horror of the memory. "I tried, I did try. She slipped away from me with the excessive bleeding."

Her tears came thick and fast and Antheia jumped up and knelt by the chair, taking her hand. Moments of silence passed. "What could have caused excessive bleeding."

"It could have been sweet clover. It's used for thinning the blood. Oh, God, what have I done! I've given the devil the instruments to do terrible harm."

Antheia stayed on the floor holding her hand. She needed to think logically. "You said they're only suspicions."

"But Cora married your uncle only months after your aunt died. I would call it all too much of a coincidence."

The younger woman couldn't disagree with that. "What can we do? It seems only we two have these misgivings."

Mrs Thornborrow pointed to the workbench. "There's a letter in the drawer. Bring it to me will you." Antheia did as she was bid and fetched the battered and dirty envelope, bringing it over to the elderly woman. "Read it."

Antheia opened it and gasped. It was from her mother and dated the twelfth of December 1845. She took it back to her seat to read.

Dear Ursula,

I haven't written to you in all the time I've been away and now I feel I must. I am married and expecting a child in the spring. After losing two babies, I pray this child will live and thrive.

It's wrong of me to lay this burden at your doorstep, but even though I feel this child will survive, I myself might not. And I must rid myself of the thoughts that plague me.

When I said farewell to you, I said it was because I disagreed with my father marrying my mother's lady's maid. I have been suspicious of her from the start and I cannot believe my mother would have deserted us.

I had to leave otherwise my mistrust would have torn the family apart. But I've kept my eye on the newspapers and I've discovered lovely, sweet Frances has been taken from us after providing my brother with two sons. How I wish I could have met my nephews and I pray for their safety and wellbeing every day.

Now I discover my stepmother has married my brother, Henry, and I don't know what to make of it. Nothing seems as it should be and I must ask you, my good friend, to watch out for the family I left behind. Perhaps I shouldn't have left the Abbey and followed my suspicions to their conclusion. I feel as though I've abandoned them.

I leave it in your hands.

Your good friend
Anne

"My mother believed it too! And that's why she left," said Antheia.

"She did, but even after receiving her letter, I…did…nothing…about…it." Her fist thumped the arm of the chair accompanying the last five words. "I locked myself away in my cottage and continued birthing the babies and dealing out physic to those who couldn't afford the physician and apothecary."

"What could you have done?"

"I could have watched out for your cousins as she asked. But I chose to ignore her appeals."

Antheia thought about this. "I don't think my cousins are in any danger."

"No, unless she decided to do away with your uncle and marry your cousin, Lord Keasden."

"I think not," said her visitor, smiling slightly, before becoming serious again. "But we must face the truth there could be a murderess living in the Abbey."

Mrs Thornborrow nodded. "There could be. It's all suspicion. Unless…"

"Unless?" repeated Antheia.

"You can find out more."

"But Grandmother has been gone over twenty years!"

"Since 1836, so that's almost twenty-eight years. And your aunt Frances has been gone nearly nineteen."

"I have discovered a few things. I found the priest hole and the tunnel."

"Ah, the tunnel. I found it interesting."

"The children said you took a look at it."

239

"I needed to surmise if it had another purpose other than the escape of Jesuits. It's a convenient way out of the Abbey when someone can't use the front door."

"Yes, not to mention to sneak children in." This reminded Antheia of the saucer Jemima had found and what Mrs Hadwin had told her. In minutes Mrs Thornborrow knew it too. "You see, my grandmother might have used the tunnel to escape and dropped the saucer in her hurry."

It was time for Antheia to leave and they stood, the elderly woman crossing to the door peg to fetch her visitor's coat. "That's if we hold to the story she deserted her family for another life." She watched as her young guest adjusted her hat and collected her beaded reticule. "I do believe you were sent here for a purpose, my dear. Somehow the good Lord knew you would be needed at the Abbey. You must solve this mystery."

As Antheia left the cottage the words spun in her mind. She must solve the mystery? But how and could she do it alone? The answer arrived the following day.

CHAPTER TWENTY-SIX

After a restless night, Antheia needed to go for a walk and set off immediately after breakfast, to take her usual route through the gardens and woodland to Sarah's meadow.

The tide was out, but she had no desire to climb down the trail to the shingle. Sitting cross-legged on the grass, her skirts tucked round her, the short jacket snug against her to keep in the warmth, she looked out over the estuary, breathing in the air laden with the tang of salt and mud. It would be the first day of April on Friday and she hoped to have a word with Agnes about cleaning the chapel and schoolroom. Only a few knew what she was doing, but it seemed more would be implicated before she was done. Despite the risk, she knew she couldn't give up teaching the children. She loved the work and seeing them develop each day, made her feel her life had meaning. Of course, she would lose Jemima the following week when she started at the church school, but she would have the four Garnett children.

Her conversation the day before with Mrs Thornborrow took over her thoughts. It seemed it was down to her to discover the truth. But how to do it? Find the poisons her aunt would have used? No, they would have been disposed of. Place a notice in *The Times* requesting any knowledge about her grandmother? If she had left the Abbey, she must have lived somewhere. She would have had neighbours and friends, perhaps not alive now, but they might have had children who remembered Sarah. Antheia was certain of some facts. Her grandmother, mother and aunt were now dead and Cora and her uncle weren't going anywhere. In a strange way she had plenty of time to discover the truth.

"I hope you saved some marshmallows for me."

She turned her head slightly and smiled. "Now, how did you know I had marshmallows?"

Will closed the distance between them and dropped onto the grass next to her. "Matty told me when I asked where you might be."

"I might have a few spare." She studied his features. His black hair and grey eyes seemed in contrast with his tanned skin. "It's so good to see you, Will. When did you arrive back?"

"Late last night. You'd already retired and I didn't want to disturb you. But Father and I became involved in a long discussion and it was the early hours before we went to bed. I overslept and had some breakfast brought to my room."

Antheia realised why she had breakfasted alone, but couldn't understand why Winder hadn't told her of Viscount Keasden's arrival. No doubt he wanted it to be a surprise for her and didn't wish his young master troubled after his late night.

"Are you home for long?" Her voice caught in her throat. How tired she was of all the farewells.

He grinned. "I'm home for good."

She couldn't hide her delight. "Oh, Will, I'm so pleased. I've missed you all so much."

"It must have been lonely for you."

"I've kept myself busy," she smiled with amusement. If only he knew.

"I've brought you a birthday gift from Italy."

"What is it?"

He wagged his finger at her. "You'll have to wait and see. I know it's past your birthday, but I want it to be a surprise. Matty has put it in your room."

"Then I thank you in advance." She linked her arm through his. "It's so good to have you home."

He looked out over the estuary as he spoke. "I made a deal with Father I would go on the digs after Cambridge and then return to the Abbey to help with the estate. We had a steward but he left a few weeks before you arrived and George has been taking the reins. It's too much for a man of his age and although as head gardener he's excellent, the roll of steward is one he'll surrender willingly."

"Uncle Henry seems to be good at making deals. He's made a deal with Felix to try out his new venture for twelve months."

Will turned to her, his eyes shining. "Yes, he told me. So, my little brother has gone to London to seek his fortune. Or more specifically, tread the boards. I'm surprised my father agreed to that." He squeezed her hand. "Why do I have the feeling you had something to do with it."

She refused to answer and said simply, "Felix must march to the beat of his own drum."

A minute of silence passed until her cousin asked tentatively, "Talking about marching to the beat of your own drum, I've had only two perhaps three letters from Joel and he says very little. I'm assuming he keeps more in touch with you. How is the old man?"

Antheia sighed. "He seems all right, but his letters are weeks old. I want to know what's happening to him now not months ago."

"The war won't last forever. And I know he'll come to England when he can." He bit his lip, before asking, "And you two? Are you courting by correspondence?"

"Courting?"

"Some of the most passionate romances were conducted by letter. Josephine and Napoleon one of them."

She hesitated a moment. "I care for him a great deal, Will. Sometimes I wonder if I do love him. But can a girl fall in love with a man so quickly?"

He nodded. "Mmm. Would you take his place on the battlefield?"

"Oh, yes. In a heartbeat."

"Then you love him."

"How so?"

"You're willing to sacrifice your life for him. You only do that when you love someone. When his life is more important than yours." Antheia felt her cheeks flush and stayed silent. Will smiled at her. "So, tell me more about your teaching."

Startled she stared at him. Did he know? "My teaching?"

"In your letter you spoke of finding a child in the cave and he turned out to be a she and you're teaching her before she attends the church school."

Relieved, she nodded. "Oh, yes, Jemima. She's a good pupil and starts at the church school this Monday. I'm sure she'll do well."

"And she's living with Mrs Thornborrow, the witch of Brawton?"

She released her arm from his and turned on him, anger making her cheeks red. "Don't you dare call her that! She's a kind, honest and caring woman who's become a good friend to me."

He pulled back in surprise and then raised his knee, resting his arm on it. "I apologise. As children that's what we called her. It was wrong of us and especially now, since I should know better."

She accepted his apology gracefully. "I forgive you, dear cousin." She took his hand. "If you need any help running the estate, I'm happy to offer my services."

"Thank you. I might accept your offer. But will you have time? Father said you're kept busy with your charity work in the village."

"I could fit it in somehow."

He studied her. "What made you go to the cave to find the little girl?"

She thought for a moment. Felix knew about the tunnel, as did Matty, Charlie, Mrs Thornborrow and the children. What did it matter if he knew. The next ten minutes were spent in telling him about seeing the child pop out of the hatch and then her adventure with Felix exploring the tunnel.

"I'd really like to see it too?" said Will, his eyes shining.

She pointed over her shoulder at the woodland in the distance. "The entrance is in the woods. We could have a look if you wish."

He jumped to his feet and helped her up. "Absolutely! My goodness, a person thinks they know everything about the place in which he was born and brought up and suddenly this happens. And if my little brother is in the know I must be too."

They walked across the meadow and reached the woodland. In moments they had found the boulder marking the spot. Will removed it and lifted the cover. He peered down at the shaft and ladder.

"Well, would you believe it! I wish we'd found this as children. Felix and I would have had great fun." He winked at her. "I'm going to take a look." He swung his legs over the edge and lowered himself down, reaching the bottom of the ladder in seconds. "Goodness, it's dark. Oh, hold on, there's a lantern down here." Her breath caught in her throat as she heard the match strike on the brick wall and flare into life. He opened the door in the lantern and lit the candle. She could see his face looking upwards, his features illuminated by the yellow glow. "Why is this lantern here? How strange. Did you and Felix leave it when you explored the tunnel?"

How was she to explain it? She wasn't teaching the children that week since it had been Easter Sunday only a few days ago. But they would arrive the following Monday.

"I think we might have. How careless of us," she said, biting her lip.

"Are you coming down? Or do you want to close the hatch and I'll meet you in the chapel?"

She hadn't expected him to want to explore. "The tunnel leads to the priest hole and then there's a catch on the wall on the left hand side of the panel. You need to pull it to open it," she told him. Suddenly she wished she hadn't told him. "I'll meet you in the chapel."

Closing the hatch, she placed the boulder on top and scattered leaves and ferns over the surface. From there, she hurried with as much dignity as she could muster, through the woodland and garden and into the rear entrance of the Abbey. In minutes she was in the cold of the chapel and could hear scratching behind the panel. Pressing the characters for the code, the panel swung open and there stood her cousin, a look of amusement on his face.

"That was interesting." He looked about him. "So, the priest hid in this tiny place, but if he was about to be discovered he would escape through the tunnel?"

"We think so."

"I couldn't find the lever in the dark." He studied the wall. "Ah, I see it. But how did you open the panel?"

She helped him out at the same time as explaining the code and how she and Felix had worked it out.

His eyes shone. "I'm impressed although I think Felix would have been no help with Latin." She decided not to answer and busied herself slamming the hatch and closing the panel. He opened the lantern's door and blew out the candle. "I'd better return this to the garden workshop."

Antheia stared at him and then at the lantern. "It's needed."

"Why? Do you often take trips through the tunnel?"

A saying came into her mind; might as well be hanged for a sheep as a lamb and she took in a steadying breath. "Leave the lantern there and I'll show you." She turned on her heel. "Did you bring the box of matches with you?" He nodded and took them from his pocket. "They can be left too."

She faced ahead as she led him through the door and along the passageways to the door of the tower. Climbing the staircase, she opened the door to the schoolroom and held it wide so he might pass inside.

"Our old schoolroom! Well, what's going on here!"

She stood quietly by the table, tidy with slates and chalks at each place and watched as he walked about, studying the wall map of the world and the alphabet prints.

He closed his eyes briefly as it dawned on him. "You're teaching here? But not just one little girl I surmise."

"Four other children."

He nodded. "This is a secret isn't it? I mean, Father doesn't know about this?"

"I daren't tell him."

He thought this over. "I'm not sure what he would say." He burst into laughter. "The children come through the tunnel?"

She nodded in agreement. "I want to carry on with what I'm doing, Will. It's important to me to continue teaching them. The Garnett kiddies can't afford to go to the church school. I believe all children should have an education and at least be able to read and write."

She had become fierce in her argument and he grinned, standing back with his hands up. "I understand and I agree with you."

"You do?"

He came forward and took her hand, kissing her fingers. "Dear cousin, I wouldn't have expected any less of you. And I admire the way you set your feet on a course and refuse to be deviated."

She hung her head in despondency. "But one day your father is bound to discover the truth and then what will I do!"

He shrugged. "Father has a tendency to ignore what he doesn't want to know. And if he finds out we'll face that problem when it arrives."

"We?"

"Yes, it seems I'm part of your little conspiracy now." He tilted his head at her. "And there's me thinking being home would be boring. I should have known better."

As they made their way down the stairs and back into the main part of the Abbey, Antheia wondered if she should confide in him about her mother's letter and the revelations from Mrs Thornborrow. He never believed Felix's theories and in fact, had reacted vehemently against his brother. She would wait and enjoy him being home. Perhaps in time she would have the confidence to tell him all, since there was one thing she was certain of, she would be glad of his help. But how could she tell him not only might his grandmother have perished at the hands of his stepmother but also his own mother? It would be a bitter pill to swallow.

CHAPTER TWENTY-SEVEN

Antheia gasped as she opened the parcel placed on her bed. It was the most magnificent parasol she had ever seen. Made in black silk with a gold frill round the edge, it had a carved ivory handle that felt snug in her hand. The black silk was decorated with exotic flowers in threads of gold; the whole exquisite and Italian in design.

"It's so beautiful," said Matty, touching the frills gently.

"I've never seen anything like it either. It's perfect. I do hope we have a wonderful summer with sunshine every day."

"Shall I put it with your summer hats?"

Antheia passed it to her and watched as she placed it back in the box and walked across to the wardrobe. "I need to talk to Agnes. It's April soon and I must apprise her of the schoolroom. I do hope she's amenable to joining our little conspiracy."

Matty closed the cupboard door and turned to her. "I thought you might want to speak to her, miss, so I took the liberty of telling her so this morning."

"I did think of speaking to her when she came to light the fire, but I lost courage."

"Why was that, miss? I think you the bravest woman I've ever met."

"Foolhardy more like."

Matty grinned. "I've always thought that when you need to do something unpleasant, it's better to do it straightaway. The longer you linger the worse it gets."

"Wise words, Matty. So, fetch her and we'll get it over with."

Five minutes later, Agnes stood in the Pink Room, wondering why Miss Antheia needed her. She was nothing but the lowliest housemaid and was more used to being ordered about by the housekeeper and butler. Antheia explained the situation carefully as Matty watched on.

"So, you see, Agnes. The tower schoolroom is being used now."

"And it's a secret, miss?"

"I would like it to remain so. Only Matty and Charlie know."

"None of the family?"

She felt caught out as she admitted, "Well, my cousins know." She tried to clarify. "But they would wouldn't they. It was their old schoolroom."

Agnes thought about this. "You want me to clean but not take any notice?"

"I would be most grateful."

"What about Clara? I clean chapel and schoolroom with her."

"Could you make an excuse and say you want to do it on your own?"

Agnes visibly shuddered. "Go into the chapel and schoolroom by myself! Oh, miss, I couldn't. It's too scary. There's evil spirits there."

Antheia tried not to smile, but knew she had to compromise. "I'll clean with you."

"You, miss? But you mustn't. Isn't right, you being niece of his lordship."

She wouldn't hear of it and said firmly, "On Friday I'll meet you in the chapel and help you dust and clean and then we'll go to the schoolroom and do the same."

"But we do it after I've laid the fires and taken the chamber pots away. It'll be early."

"Excellent. I'll be up and dressed and ready to help you. Afterwards I'll go down to breakfast and no one will have an inkling what I've been doing."

Agnes looked at Matty who had remained silent throughout. "Is it allowed?"

The maid smiled. "You, me and Charlie are part of a big secret. Isn't that exciting."

Antheia could see the housemaid was dubious and tried to put her mind at rest. "I promise none of the servants will get into trouble over this. Only I will take the blame."

This seemed to put Agnes's mind at rest and she nodded. "Very good, Miss Antheia. If you instruct me, I must do as you say."

Everything turned out far better than Antheia expected, since good fortune was with them. The fact Clara had developed a bad head cold and was confined to bed, helped the situation enormously; at least for the month of April. And on Monday morning, that first week of the month, she waited patiently in the chapel for the children to arrive. She felt sad Jemima wouldn't be one of them and was eager to know how she had fared at the church school. However, the rustling sound and occasional giggle along the tunnel made her smile.

And when they arrived, she realised although losing one pupil, she had gained two more. A small boy and girl followed Edith, Owen, Cyril and Leonard Garnett up the ladder. All six children seemed scrubbed clean and in their best clothes.

It was Edith who explained. "Miss Antheia, this is Thomas and Beatrice Hugill. He's eight and she's seven and they so wanted to come with us. I hope you don't mind."

Antheia stared at the two tiny figures, the boy holding his cap to his chest, the girl studying her with large brown eyes. The teacher nodded. "Excellent, we have slates and chalks for everyone."

That was the start of many contented weeks for Antheia and again, she was amazed how the new pupils to the class absorbed their lessons like a sponge. The weather was getting warmer and she longed to take the lessons outside. The woodland was filling with bluebells and the garden's herbaceous borders with spring flowers of hollyhocks, snapdragons, marigolds, pansies, hyacinths and lilies. In the inner courtyard garden, irises and sweet peas had been planted. And as spring took hold of the Abbey, she found herself in the courtyard garden many times, thinking of Joel. This was a special place for her, where she could remember him more keenly and feel close to him. She knew his letters would be on the way to her soon and she watched for the post every morning, much to the amusement of her cousin.

Will had settled down to his life as steward and one morning, she accompanied him to a small outbuilding on the far side of the stables. He had turned it into a workable office, clearing away the clutter that had accumulated and filling the small bookshelves with files and documents. A large walnut desk stood near the window. His eyes bright with enthusiasm, he was delighted to explain to his cousin how much he was enjoying the responsibility. He had taken charge of the upkeep and daily running of the estate and had already organised the rebuilding of the stone walls, damaged during the winter storms, and spoken to the four tenant farmers. He thought they should take on more outdoor staff and casting his eye over the accounts, he knew there was enough money to employ at least three more men.

It seemed the entire family was contented, since Felix also wrote of his enthusiasm for his backstage life in the Princess's Theatre. He had already made many friends and being young and strong, was called on to do a great deal of lifting and carrying. But during the rehearsal of *The Beggar's Opera*, he had been put in charge of the curtain ropes. There was even talk of him playing the part of Crook-Finger'd Jack, a small part, but his first on the public stage.

It was ten days into April when Joel's next batch of letters arrived. As usual, Antheia ran to her room to read them in solitude, lying on her bed.

My dearest Antheia,

I regret to say we've had a bout of dysentery in the camp. I was suspicious of the river after realising it flowed near the place of a former battle. Some of my men had already jumped in to swim and others filled their canteens, when a dead horse floated by. I told them to empty their canteens immediately and ordered the men out of the river. Thankfully, no harm came to R Company. They are a rough and, might I say, tough breed and yet the privations of camp have tested their endurance. I'm grateful there has been very little illness in R Company, but not so T Company, as Captain Masters has lost five of his number through disease.

My sweet girl, here I am talking of infections in the camp and it must make you so worried about my welfare. Trust me, I am well although Ma has had to send me new combinations as my underwear is in rags. Being in the saddle takes its toll on my pants, although my jacket is holding up well.

It has been rather cold and wet here for the last week, but generally the weather is fine and we are able to wash and dry our clothes easily.

I am still waiting for your photograph and I'm sure it will arrive soon. I long for it to arrive. I will write again in a few days.

Fondest wishes
Joel

Dysentery? She had forgotten it could be the scourge of an army on the move. Many men had died from it in the Crimean War some ten years ago. Only the ministrations of Florence Nightingale and her ladies had kept much of the infection at bay, with their cleaning and scrubbing.

His next letters were more news of the camp, but it was his last letter that made her cry with delight.

My dearest Antheia,

Seven letters arrived from you in the mail today and with it, what I've been waiting for. What a beautiful photograph and so well worth waiting for. And displayed in a leather frame that will stand the rigors of camp life. Of course, the men wanted to see and I indulged them, although I feared their grubby hands would destroy it and had to save it from their handling almost immediately. My friend and fellow officer Captain Masters, studied it with delight and advised me I had a treasure in my possession.

I shall keep it close to my heart and look at it every day. Aaron (Captain Masters) is quite correct. I do have a treasure to come back to and when I do return to England, I hope to make plans for the future. But we can discuss these when we meet again.

Fondest wishes
Joel

He wanted to make plans? Her heartbeat quickened. Did his plans include herself? Folding the letters, she wondered what she would do if Joel proposed to her. Would she accept? She had always been sensible in her approach to life and she knew Joel was the same. When he returned to England, they would have to take their time and build up their relationship. They were friends and she mustn't start having romantic thoughts. It would be devastating if he came back, only to find they couldn't progress further than friendship. But her feelings had gone further than that. She knew it. Oh, the damned war! How many romances had been blighted because of a conflict? She had half a mind to jump on the next ship and follow him across the ocean.

She slipped off the bed and pushed her feet into her house shoes. She was being silly. There was no possibility of her travelling to America. Her uncle wouldn't allow it and until she was twenty-one he would have the last say as her guardian.

A knock on the door startled her and she called for them to enter. It was Matty who came into the room, her face white as a sheet.

"Miss Antheia, her ladyship would like to see you."

Antheia sighed. "Oh dear, another royal summons!" Matty didn't answer and looked round the room moistening dry lips. "What's the matter?"

"I'm not sure, miss, but Patience thinks it's to do with the school."

She stepped forward in horror. "She knows about the children?"

Matty nodded. "The Reverend Longmire is with her and they've been talking together this last hour. Patience tried to listen but they kept their voices quite low. But she did hear the countess say the word 'school'."

Antheia caught her breath and tried to think clearly. "Jemima started at the church school after Easter. It could be something to do with that."

"But why would the vicar want to talk to her ladyship about a young girl living in Slee Court. She wouldn't be interested," said Matty, pulling a face.

"Yes, you're right."

Thoughts whirled round her head. Had Jemima said something? Perhaps in her excitement at being in school, she had told the teacher or her friends about the tunnel and the schoolroom in the tower? There was only one thing to do - obey the summons. But after her conversation with Mrs Thornborrow, she did not trust her aunt and in many ways, feared her. She was conniving and cunning, but was she dangerous? Antheia knew she would always have to be on her guard when it came to her step-aunt and if she crossed her, how threatening would that make her?

CHAPTER TWENTY-EIGHT

It did feel like a royal summons and Antheia couldn't think she would be any more nervous if she had been called to an audience with Queen Victoria herself. It seemed every time her aunt ordered her to her rooms, she would enter with trepidation and leave in an agitated state she couldn't shake off for hours.

This anxious feeling became more acute as Patience showed her into the sitting room, where the Reverend Longmire rose to his feet at her entrance. He smiled smugly. Her aunt studied her through narrowed eyes.

"Sit down, Antheia," ordered her aunt, indicating the velvet chair near them.

She did as she was told and decided to stay silent. What she had done wrong she couldn't imagine, but she had certainly done something to displease her aunt and amuse the vicar.

"How are you, Miss Vale?" he took his seat, straightening his jacket.

She smiled at him. "I'm well, Reverend." She turned to her aunt, hoping she would get on with it.

The countess took in a breath. "It's about the child, Jemima. The Reverend has told me you were teaching her." Antheia nodded in agreement. "And she lives with that witch, Ursula Thornborrow!"

Antheia's heart started to beat rapidly. "I can't see it being a problem. I found her starving in a cave and Mrs Thornborrow was good enough to take her in."

The vicar's face remained impassive as he said slowly, "Why didn't you correct me at our luncheon, when I mentioned the child was living with Mrs Garnett and her brood? You led me astray."

The young girl frowned. "I didn't think it mattered where Jemima lived."

"And how is an old woman with very little income, affording the upkeep of a small child and paying for her education?" Her aunt raised her lorgnette, as though she needed to see her answer as well as hear it.

Antheia shrugged. "She must have something put aside."

Her aunt persisted. "I know your uncle gave you an allowance." She glared at the young girl sitting near her. "Are you spending your allowance on the upkeep of this urchin and, what's more, giving good money to a woman of dubious morals?"

Antheia tried to look surprised. "Oh, so you know her history, Aunt."

The countess's face flushed slightly. "She's obviously told you what her…occupation was in her youth!" Antheia decided not to answer although she was tempted to remind her aunt, she herself had benefited from the earnings of a bordello. "Does your uncle know on what you spend your allowance?"

"He said it's mine to spend as I wish."

"I'm sure he'll not be pleased to discover you're wasting it…"

Antheia couldn't help interrupting. "How is providing food, shelter and clothing for a child wasting money? How is paying for elementary education throwing money away?"

The Reverend Longmire raised his hand. "Your ladyship, Miss Vale. Do we need harsh words over this?" He studied the countess. "We made an agreement."

Another agreement thought Antheia. The Abbey was ridden with deals and agreements.

"I shall leave her to you, then," she said, turning her face away. After a moment she rose from her seat and the vicar stood too. "I shall visit the kitchen and have a word with Cook. That should give you plenty of time to sort out your business."

She swept from the room and Antheia watched her with dismay. She disliked her aunt, but equally she didn't like the thought of being left alone with the vicar. She didn't care to hear his deal. Now that her aunt and the Reverend knew Jemima lived with Mrs Thornborrow and she and the elderly woman had become good friends, how much power would they have over her? If a deal was imminent, then it was a deal with the devil.

The Reverend took his seat once more, placed his fingers together and steepled them under his chin. For a short while he waited in a similar way he waited for his congregation to settle down, before delivering his sermon.

He smiled in a reassuring manner. "Miss Vale, you must know my feelings towards you? I've made it quite plain I find you attractive and quite appealing. And of course, being a daughter of a clergyman you are well suited..." Antheia closed her eyes briefly, steeling herself. "...to be the wife of a clergyman."

"If that's a proposal of marriage, Reverend, my aunt already knows my opinion on marriage to you and I'm sure she's told you."

A gleam came into his eyes and Antheia was shocked when she understood the meaning. He was enjoying her reluctance and stubbornness. After all, the thrill of the hunt was in the pursuit before the kill. No hunter found satisfaction in easy prey. And if it came to it, she was sure the vicar would be more than pleased to subdue her feisty nature and bring her to heel.

"Her ladyship has apprised me of your feelings, but I thought you might reconsider."

"Why?" As firm as she tried to keep her query, she felt her voice break.

"Because, my dear, I know the landlord of the humble cottage in which Mrs Thornborrow resides. An upstanding member of the Church of England believe you me and if I told him Mrs Thornborrow's dubious history, he wouldn't hesitate to throw her out within the week." He leaned forward. "And then what would she and your little protégé do?"

Anthea's mind spun, her mouth drying. "You couldn't do anything so cruel!" But his raised eyebrows told her differently. "I'll ask my uncle if he has any cottages for rent on the estate," she spluttered.

This amused him. "The rent would far exceed the income of Mrs Thornborrow. And if you're thinking of asking your uncle for more allowance, your aunt will put paid to that immediately. Besides, I can't see him dolling out money to you, to pay rent on his cottages. It wouldn't make economic sense."

Anthea looked down at her fingers twisted in her lap. "My heart is with another," she whispered desperately.

He threw back his head, laughing. "It's highly unlikely Captain Newton will return from the war never mind America. He's a lost cause and I advise you take my offer." She glanced up and saw the Reverend's expression turn from amusement to pity. "I have a good income, my dear and before Christmas I'm hoping to take up another living."

"Where?" She caught her breath.

"In London. Chelsea to be exact. All Saints and an old church. By the river so we could go on a boat and view the sights of the capital." He hurried on, "And there's no doubt young Felix will be a constant visitor. Why, we could even attend his recitals at the Academy."

Realisation washed over her. So that was why he had suggested she attend the Pupil-teacher College in Chelsea. Another plot to trap her. But she could spawn her own plots and besides what alternative was there at the moment? She couldn't see Mrs Thornborrow thrown out of her home.

She steadied her breath. "Very well, Reverend, I accept your proposal."

His reaction was utter astonishment, before he jumped to his feet, took her hand and left a wet kiss on her fingers.

"Thank you, my dear. I feel lucky beyond words." He sucked in a breath. "I shall request an interview with his lordship immediately. Perhaps he could accommodate me now."

She inclined her head in acknowledgement. All she wanted to do was remove herself from his presence. And when she left her aunt's sitting room seconds later, she went straight to her room where she pulled the chamberpot from under the bed and emptied the contents of her breakfast into it.

Antheia had never felt so poorly and staggered across to the jug of water on the occasional table and poured herself a glass. She tried to put her thoughts into order. She had betrothed herself to a despicable man and as she thought of how she had been manipulated, anger filled her. She fetched her boots from the cupboard, slipped off her house shoes and fastened the boots tightly. Taking her cloak, she flung it over her shoulders and then noticed the chamberpot. It wouldn't be fair to leave it for Matty, so covering it with a handkerchief, she decided to take it down to the kitchen.

At the door she met Matty carrying a dark grey gown over her arm. "Miss Antheia, I've sewn the button back on…" She noticed the chamberpot and her mistress's pale face. "Oh, miss, have you been poorly?"

"I've been a bit sick, that's all. I'll take this down to the kitchen."

The maid lay the gown across the bed. "No, I'll take it, but you're going out! Shouldn't you be lying down? Is it your tummy?"

Antheia handed the chamberpot to the maid. "I'm all right. It's passed now and I must go out."

In moments she was hurrying through the Abbey, towards the stables and Will's office.

As she had hoped, she found him sitting at the desk, although had he been out she would have waited for him until doomsday. The door was ajar and she knocked gently.

He looked up and smiled. "Cousin! Just the person I need. I've added up this column of figures twice and can't get it right. Would you oblige?" He suddenly noticed her blanched face. "Goodness, what's the matter? Are you ill?"

He brought a spare chair for her, making her sit and fetched a glass of water. She drank thirstily. "Something dreadful has happened, Will. And I don't know what to do about it."

Will's expression matched hers, the blood draining from his face. "Oh, Lord. Not Joel!"

She held up her hand. "No, not Joel. The last news from him was he was quite well. It's something else." She continued to tell him about her interview with her aunt and the Reverend and how Mrs Thornborrow might lose her home.

Colour returned to his face as shock was replaced by anger. "That man! And that woman! They should have married. They certainly deserve each other!"

She gave a wan smile. "She's old enough to be his mother."

"I always knew Longmire disliked Mrs Thornborrow and to be honest, she was always regarded as...eccentric. But she mustn't lose her home. Did he say why she could lose the cottage? Although a landlord doesn't need much reason to throw out a tenant unfortunately."

"Her past is somewhat disreputable."

"Well, I'm sure when everyone gets to her age, they'll have skeletons in the cupboard."

"I don't suppose you have a cottage available on the estate?"

He paused before answering, a look of sadness sweeping across his face. "Antheia, the cottages on the estate have much higher rents than the ones in Slee Court. Besides, the estate workers have priority and there's none empty at the moment."

She turned her head and stared out of the window. Because the office was close to the stables, she could see the men taking the horses out for exercise. A dog barked and she recognised it as Fred, who must have left her uncle's side for a while to play with the other two dogs who lived in the stables.

"His lordship took in Fred when he was in dire straights. Perhaps he'll take pity on an elderly woman and a little girl," she said without hope.

He stood and came round the desk to kneel by her chair and take her hand. "No, he won't. Father does a great deal for the poor, but he knows he can't help everyone."

She looked down at him. "I've agreed to marry the Reverend Longmire."

If he hadn't been holding her hand, she was sure he would have fallen backwards. "You've agreed what!" He stood and went back to his chair, sitting heavily. "But I don't understand. What about Joel?"

She sat upright and for the first time that morning, spoke firmly. "I'll not betray Joel. He's too dear to me. But if I promise to marry the vicar then Mrs Thornborrow keeps her home."

Will held up his hands in surrender. "I've never understood the female mind. Please explain."

Lifting her chin she smiled. "Queen Elizabeth made many promises to the kings and emperors of Europe. She flirted with them, wrote them letters of affection, and used all her feminine wiles to keep them from declaring war on her country. She promised much and delivered nothing. I shall follow her example." He still looked confused so clarified, "I've only promised to marry him. Yes, we'll become betrothed. But a lot can happen between a betrothal and the wedding."

"So, you intend to hold him at arm's length. Until…?"

"Until I think of something else."

"That's risky."

Antheia leaned forward in her chair. "Will, can I rely on you as an ally?" She laughed. "Deals and conspiracies seem to be the mainstay of the Abbey."

He stared at her for a few seconds. "Of course, you can always rely on my support. But what about Joel?"

"That's my main problem. He might be thousands of miles away, but he could hear the news and it would devastate him."

"And you can't prevent it," he said angrily.

"True. And I'd like to write to him and tell him everything. Why I'm doing this and that it has no bearing on my feelings towards him. It's simply a means to an end."

"That would…well, he's involved in a conflict, Antheia. A man might not be able to cope with that kind of information or be able to absorb the details."

She shook her head. "You're right." Licking her lips nervously, she added, "And he could think me deceitful. Oh, Will, what shall I do!"

He thought it over while tapping his pencil on the desk. "You must continue writing to him as before. God knows he needs your letters. I only hope my stepmother doesn't write to the regiment's headquarters and pass on the news to Joel."

"Would she do that? It seems spiteful."

"She's certainly capable of it. Although she might have no interest now she's got what she wants. Mission accomplished as it were."

Antheia shook her head slowly. "*Dona nobis pacem deo maii tempore interitu,*" she whispered.

Her cousin frowned. "May God grant us peace in time of turmoil. What are you thinking?"

"I'm thinking I'll write something at the end of my letters. If repeated, hopefully it will penetrate Joel's mind and act as an anchor."

"Write what?"

"I know he reads Latin so I'll write," she paused thinking, "I'll write *cor meum semper sit vera.* Then surely it will always confirm my feelings for him."

Will smiled. "*Cor meum semper sit vera.* My heart will always be true. Well said, Cousin, well said."

CHAPTER TWENTY-NINE

They walked back to the Abbey for lunch, arm in arm. Will had qualms about his cousin's plans, but he would support her in any way he could. The one thing he was sure of was he wouldn't see her married to the Reverend Longmire. That odious man would never join their family and he wouldn't stand by and watch him make Antheia miserable for the rest of her life.

Luncheon was a pleasant meal, although she noticed her uncle kept glancing in her direction, his brow puckered in a worried frown. And after the meal when Will returned to the estate office, Antheia wasn't surprised when her uncle asked her to accompany him to his study. She followed him, steeling herself.

"Sit down, please." He indicated the chair and then sat in the chair behind his desk. She realised this was a formal interview and waited for him to open the conversation. "Before luncheon, I had a very interesting discussion with the Reverend Longmire. He asked for your hand in marriage. I was about to protest and throw him out, when he informed me, rather smugly, you'd accepted him. Is it the truth?"

How she wanted to scream the real truth at him; to tell him she was being blackmailed into a marriage she abhorred.

Instead she nodded. "Yes, Uncle, I accepted him."

He shook his head in dismay. "Why in God's name did you do that! I thought you were set on Captain Newton."

She licked dry lips. "Joel is a good friend, but he's fighting a war…"

He held up his hand to stop her. "You don't have to tell me what he's doing! What I want to know is what you are doing!"

"It seemed a good match." Her voice caught in her throat. She mustn't cry or her uncle would know there was something dreadfully wrong.

But the earl had noticed her demeanour and the fact she was holding back tears. "My dear, won't you tell me what's bothering you? If I can help I will."

She was tempted. If she told him everything; about Mrs Thornborrow and Jemima being at risk of losing their home, would he understand? Perhaps he could give them a home? But she had used her allowance to fund Jemima's upkeep and education. Not to mention the fact she was sneaking six children into the Abbey and teaching them in the tower schoolroom. That would have to be admitted too and he wouldn't take kindly to such deception. He would stop her lessons immediately. He held the purse strings, he had the control and power and she couldn't risk his displeasure.

"I'm content with my betrothal to the Reverend, Uncle."

He studied her for a few seconds. "Do you wish a betrothal ball? We could use the ballroom and invite the young people from prestigious families in Lancaster.

Her head snapped up. "No!" She calmed herself. "I'm not used to large parties. A family dinner in the same vein as my birthday dinner will suffice."

He nodded. "A quiet family dinner, then. A party would be unsuitable anyway and would have to wait until after our period of mourning."

His words filled her with hope. Of course, celebrating an engagement elaborately would be thought indelicate when in mourning and that didn't

268

end until the first day of July. And it was only April now. She had over two months of breathing space. To think what to do!

"I'll write to Felix, Uncle." Yes, she would tell him exactly what she was doing. Both her cousins must know her plan.

"Longmire told me he's to go to another living before Christmas. To London. I must admit I never thought of losing you so soon." He played with the papers on his desk, before asking, "When will you set a date?"

"Not until my mourning is over," she said firmly.

He stood and walked round the desk to stare out of the window at the lawn and driveway leading to the front gate. "You truly want to marry that man?" She nodded and then realised he hadn't turned to look at her.

"Yes, she murmured."

This time he did turn to face her. "I will give you away, of course. But I tell you this. I'll ask you regularly if you wish to go through with it. Even at the church door, I'll need your reassurance all is well with you."

It was something to hold on to and as she left his study, she smiled at the thought of reaching the church door and spinning on her heel to race through the graveyard. It would be regarded as terrible behaviour by society, but anything was better than marrying the Reverend Longmire.

If there was any custom Antheia was pleased about, it was the one dictating a couple must wait fourteen days before an engagement is announced. Normally, this was because either party could change their minds, but for Antheia the following two weeks gave her time to calm down and think. She knew she would often seem aloof to her family and pupils, her thoughts distant and preoccupied.

She had written to Felix and told him what she was doing and his reply had been filled with alarm, but with a postscript that if she needed someone to punch the Reverend on the nose, he would travel from London immediately. She answered the letter in the same vein, thanking him for being her 'hero' and asking him to mull over the problem for her and should he come up with any ideas, she would gladly consider them.

Her letters to Joel were more strained and she prayed it didn't show. She had always given him news of everything she was doing, but her betrothal was one fact she had to keep secret. After writing 'Fondest wishes' and her name, she wrote, C*or meum semper sit vera*. My heart will always be true and she would kiss the letter before sealing the envelope. And she repeated this with every letter she wrote from then on.

Two weeks passed and she delighted in the improvement of her pupils and the news from Jemima how she loved school and was aiming to be top of the class. But eventually the engagement had to be announced which meant a small section printed in *The Times*. This was fraught with danger and she had asked her uncle to make it no more than a few lines, hoping it would be overlooked. Very few people knew her and even less knew she had lost her heart to Joel. She prayed it wouldn't occur to anyone to think anything was untoward.

What surprised her was the utter shock of the servants.

"Miss Antheia, can it be true?" The housekeeper's concerned face made her bite her lip. "I know it's not the place of any servant to question a member of the family. But we thought....well, that another wedding would happen at some time."

"It's true. And I'd rather there was no speculation below stairs."

"It's difficult to stop speculation below stairs, miss. But I'll do my best." Mrs Hadwin passed the menu to her. "This is the suggestion for your betrothal dinner on Saturday. I've shown it to her ladyship and she advised me to consult you."

Antheia took the menu but barely glanced at it, before passing it back. "If her ladyship is agreeable with the choice, then I am too."

The housekeeper narrowed her eyes in thought. This wasn't how a young girl due to be betrothed should behave. Where was the excitement? Where was the joy of finding a man to spend the rest of your life with? This was certainly a peculiar situation.

With her maid Antheia was more honest.

"You do understand don't you?"

Matty stared at her. "But it ain't right, miss. You can't marry him because Mrs Thornborrow might lose her home."

"Who said I was going to marry him? I'm simply getting betrothed. Whether we marry or not is a different matter." She put her finger to her lips. "But this is a secret. You mustn't tell anyone. Not even Charlie and Patience."

"So you've promised to marry him while you think of something else to do? To save Mrs Thornborrow and the little girl from losing their home?"

Antheia nodded. "It's a terrible thing to do. But I couldn't think of what I could do at the time."

"I already knew, Miss Antheia. I already knew why you're marrying the vicar. So does Patience," said Matty guiltily.

271

Antheia let out a long breath. "Patience was eavesdropping?"

Matty nodded. "Only after you had been left alone with the Reverend Longmire. When she saw her ladyship leave the sitting room, she guessed what was happening. Guessed, but couldn't believe it. She felt she had to know."

Antheia walked to the window and looked out on a glorious morning. It was the last week in April and she hoped May would be beautiful. Life always seemed better, more hopeful, when the sun shone.

"So all the servants know?"

The maid twisted her hands together. "No, miss. Patience told me and we've kept it to ourselves. We were so shocked we couldn't believe you would be forced into such a situation. It doesn't even sound legal."

She turned and smiled. Matty and Patience had kept it secret. For Patience this must have been difficult and she admired her.

"Well, thank you for that. I know folk will be surprised now the announcement is made, but my true reason must be kept between us."

"Yes, miss, of course. But what are you going to do? After you're out of mourning, you'll be expected to set a date."

"I have two months until then and I can always make it as late in the year as possible. Or even next year. Some couples have quite long engagements."

"Somehow, I don't think the Reverend will be happy with that," said the maid. "He'll go by society's customs, but not give an inch more."

Antheia grimaced. "You're right, Matty. So I must come up with a plan as soon as possible."

It wasn't a happy prospect. Horace, since now he insisted on her using his given name, would be impatient once July arrived and she was out of mourning. But if she insisted on marrying in October, it still gave her time. She had allies; her cousins and the lady's maids knew her dilemma, so she wasn't alone.

Until then, she had to get through the betrothal dinner and she supposed Horace would present her with a ring. The idea made her smile. Would her aunt be rummaging through her jewellery box at this very moment, searching for a suitable ring? If it were anything but a simple gemstone, she would be suspicious.

And when the evening of the betrothal dinner arrived, she steeled herself to sit next to her intended and smile as toasts were made and congratulations given. The fact it was only five of them eased her conscience and the compliments from her fiancé were bearable. She wore the same gown she had worn for her birthday; the maroon with black lace across the bodice and the jet and diamond comb in her auburn hair. Before he left the Abbey, the Reverend Longmire placed a ring on her finger and she was relieved it was a simple love knot with a tiny diamond in the centre. But when she went to bed, she took it off and placed it on her dressing table.

CHAPTER THIRTY

Mrs Thornborrow was more astute than she gave her credit for.

"If you've affianced yourself to that despicable man you have a reason."

Anthea had called in only to leave some liquorice for Jemima when she came home from school. She had taught the children in the morning and given out liquorice for their splendid work and she didn't want Jemima to miss out.

"Is it obvious?" She tried to grin and fell short. "Yes, I have my reasons."

"I thought you were already spoken for. The young American friend of your cousin?"

Anthea nodded. "Joel Newton. I suppose the whole of Brawton is buzzing with the news of my engagement."

"Words have been said especially as folk didn't think you liked Longmire. I've kept my own council and not said a word to anyone about your previous feelings towards the vicar or the American." She pointed the wooden spoon at her, halting her task of making a cake. "I've not even spoken to Mrs Garnett about it."

"Thank you for that."

There was a pause in the conversation, until the elderly woman said, "So, are you going to tell me why you've hitched yourself to a man you barely had time for?"

Anthea watched her folding the flour into the mixture and her eyes wandered to the small dish of sultanas and raisins ready to be added. She looked round the neat and clean one room Mrs Thornborrow lived in; the small bed and Jemima's even smaller bed in the corner. It wasn't much to call home and yet her friend had made the cottage her home and place of work. If she was thrown out, where would she go?

"I'm…a vicar's daughter and being a vicar's wife… seemed…practical."

"Ah, you're being practical, are you?" She narrowed her eyes. "You have a hidden reason, my girl. You're marrying him to get something or to prevent something being taken from you. But what could it be? You're the niece of an earl and have some influence, not to mention someone you can go to and ask for help if needs be."

"I don't have as much influence as you think and my uncle can't solve all the ills of the world."

"I know your heart, my dear. You wouldn't be doing this unless someone you cared for was at risk."

Antheia rose to her feet. "Now how do you know that? We've only known each other since New Year's Eve."

Mrs Thornborrow glared at her. "You're your mother's daughter. I saw it right from the start and marrying with a hidden reason is exactly what Lady Anne would have done."

"But you seem to forget, Mother left when she faced a problem."

"Only because she could see no way of solving it. And it was an act she regretted for the rest of her life."

The younger woman felt the need to leave. If she stayed, Mrs Thornborrow would wheedle the information out of her and there would be hell to pay.

"Suffice it to say I have a lot to consider." She smiled as she picked up her reticule. "Save a slice of cake for me."

After her visitor had gone, Mrs Thornborrow poured the mixture into the cake tin and put it in the oven. She heard the church clock chiming the half-hour and knew it was two-thirty. She could leave the cake and the washing up for a good thirty minutes and pinned her black hat to her thin, grey hair pulled back in a bun. She collected her shawl and walking stick and left the cottage.

It didn't take her long to make her way along the main street, past the butchers, apothecary, Post Office and other small shops to the Red Lion at the outskirts of the village. As expected, she saw the woman wearing black, sitting on a metal bench and looking out over the meadow and estuary beyond.

"Margaret."

The woman turned and hurriedly dropped a silver flask into her basket. "Ursula!" Her face reddened. "Just a little tot to get me through the rest of the day."

Mrs Thornborrow held up her hand in a non-committal gesture and took a seat next to her. "I've not come to chastise you about your afternoon sip of brandy. I need some information on your employer."

Mrs Sisson frowned. "Now, you know I don't tittle-tattle. Although there's many that do."

"Not gossip I assure you. All I want to know is surely in the public domain. I want to know where the Reverend Longmire ministered before coming to Brawton."

The month of May seemed to be passing all too quickly and it threw Antheia into a panic. Nothing had occurred to her to get her out of her predicament and she had suffered many family dinners with Horace at her side and taken lunch with him at the vicarage on a few occasions. Thankfully, she had managed to avoid driving out with him, with the excuse she was too busy with her work in the parish and helping her cousin on the estate. Most was partly true since she had gone to the estate office regularly and helped Will. There were times she became so desperate, she felt she must bare her soul to her uncle and throw herself on his mercy.

It seemed she was full of guilt and on top of this she had promised Mrs Thornborrow she would try and uncover the truth of her grandmother's disappearance. When Joel's next letters arrived, she was more than ready to receive them.

Opening the packet, she saw they were dated the tenth of March to the fourteen of April. The first one gave more news of the camp and the fact Captain Masters had received a photograph of his new baby daughter, held in the arms of his wife and had been in tears over it. But his second letter was dated the fifteenth of March; her birthday.

My dearest Antheia,

I write this in the early hours. Some of the men have not risen yet and those that have, are washing and shaving and preparing for our next orders.

I'm aware it's your birthday today and my love is winging its way across the large divide that separates us. By now you should have received the box of marshmallows along with my note. I was able to telegraph my order to New York City after Christmas and have it sent to Cape Elizabeth so it could be delivered in time for your birthday. I explained in my note, why I chose marshmallows and I hope you enjoyed them. You are the sweetest thing and I think of you often.

I'm endeavouring to keep your photograph clean and I believe I'm doing an excellent job and if this war ends soon it should be in good shape. I keep it in the inside pocket of my jacket, next to my heart.

I pray I'm with you soon to see you in person.

Fondest wishes
Joel

He sends his love across the wide Atlantic! They were words she longed to hear, but this time she felt cheap and dirty. Here she was reading love letters from one man whilst betrothed to another. But it was Joel she loved, Joel she yearned for and wanted by her side.

The next letter was informative.

I believe the mail is arriving faster and that is good. The more gains the Union makes the more we push back the Confederates. Yesterday, we discovered a young Confederate soldier lost in the woods having been separated from his Company. He was frightened and confused and we had to take him as our prisoner. We fed him and dealt with his wounds and he'll be sent with others to a camp until this is all over and then be allowed to return home. He was no more than fifteen and my heart went out to him. Are soldiers getting younger or am I getting older!

Antheia sighed sadly. No matter what side a man was on there was always suffering. What had the Duke of Wellington said as he surveyed the carnage of Waterloo? '*Nothing except a battle lost can be half so melancholy as a battle won.*'

His last letter was bright and full of enthusiasm.

My dearest Antheia,

What news you tell me! You're teaching children in your cousins' old schoolroom in the tower? And under the nose of your uncle. I admire you, my darling girl. Only you could think up such a scheme, although I'm sure the children will benefit from your teaching. But I would advise you not to keep it a secret and tell your uncle. He's not a tyrant and will understand. I say this only as I'm worried for you and I could sense in your letter you felt guilty. Guilt can eat you up and destroy your life and I want you to have a contented life.

You also tell me your uncle has agreed to allow young Felix to leave Cambridge and attend the Royal Academy of Music in London. I always believed he wasn't cut out for a profession in the law and he does have an amazing voice. When you write to him next, please send him my very best wishes and good luck in his new venture. I'm sure he'll enjoy being a stagehand at the theatre in the meantime. We must attend his performances when I'm back in England.

I trust you are keeping well and as ever, my love goes with this letter.

Fondest wishes
Joel

Antheia placed the letter down beside her and stared round the room. 'Guilt can eat you up and destroy your life'. He was almost on the mark, except another guilty feeling had taken over from those of the tower schoolroom. Perhaps in his next batch of letters, he would mention the Latin she had written at the end of each letter since agreeing to marry the Reverend. He might wonder what she was doing, but she had to impress on him she would always be true to him and no one else.

She glanced at the watch pinned to her bodice and realised she was late for the estate office, since she had promised her cousin she would check through the accounts for him. Antheia always enjoyed going to the office and was coming to know the duties of a steward. But she also knew her cousin relished the position. Young as he was, he was well respected by the workers and was making some amazing changes to the estate. Even her uncle had nodded in agreement at many of his ideas.

Picking up Joel's last letter, she wondered at his advice of telling her uncle about the schoolroom, but for her the main problem was her promise to marry Horace Longmire. Somehow the secret of the schoolroom seemed insignificant against that. Her uncle still had qualms and would often cover her small hand with his and ask if she was still agreeable. Sometimes it became irritating, but if he ever stopped asking, she knew she would be thrown into a panic. For it would mean he had accepted the situation and she couldn't bear the idea.

The walk round to the estate office eased her mind and the beautiful May weather filled her with hope. She still had June and anything could turn up. She smiled. She sounded like Wilkins Micawber, the clerk in *David Copperfield* by Charles Dickens, who always stayed optimistic with the belief 'something will turn up'. But perhaps it was the best frame of mind to be in.

She arrived at the office and found it empty. But on the desk the ledger was open and Will had left a note asking if she would add up four pages of figures. She got down to it immediately. When her cousin arrived fifteen minutes later, it was all done.

"I don't know what I did wrong," he smiled, as he entered the office.

She tapped the pencil on the large black ledger. "The actual figure was £467 13s. 2d, but you had put it as £476. You transposed the last two figures."

"I must remember to take more care."

She rose to give him his office chair, but he gestured for her to remain seated. "I still haven't thought of what to do about Horace," she said thoughtfully.

He made himself comfortable on the spare chair and sighed. "Me neither. Except the only way out is to remove Mrs Thornborrow and the little girl out of his clutches."

"I'd have to find her another home she could afford. And she's not living in Slee Court for nothing. She hasn't the income for anything more. She used to live on Patterdale Lane."

"Now, they are nice cottages."

"I believe she was happy there."

Silence ensued while they mulled over the situation. Antheia finally broke the silence. "Would Uncle buy the cottage off Mrs Thornborrow's landlord? Whoever he is."

"That would be too obvious. Father would get suspicious and want to know why you wanted him to buy the cottage." He paused. "Unless you do tell him everything. I'll back you up, you know that."

"I might need to." But could she trust her uncle? Her thoughts turned to her aunt and she glanced across at her cousin who had pulled the ledger towards him, studying her recent calculations. "Will, do you remember your mother?"

His head jerked up at the change in topic and he sucked in a breath. "I remember a kind, gentle woman who would put me on her knee and sing to me." His gaze became distant. "She would come into my room on a night and stroke back my hair." His hand swept across his fringe as though imitating a long lost memory.

"And what about Aunt Cora? How did you take to her?"

"I was only five when my mother died and my father remarried. I was too young to have any opinion about it."

"You do know your father married Cora within months of your mother's death?"

"I didn't understand until later when I was older and I decided my father must have been terribly lonely and needed to marry straightaway."

She was reaching the nub of her argument. "But are you aware our grandfather married Cora first, after our grandmother Sarah disappeared? She was Grandmother's lady's maid." Horror slowly etched itself across his face. "Yes, Will. Your father married his stepmother." His face turned white, but she pushed on. "I know you never agreed with Felix about our grandfather murdering Sarah and I'm not sure either. However, from evidence I've received, I believe it was Cora who had a hand in the disappearance of our grandmother and the death of your mother."

CHAPTER THIRTY-ONE

Will slowly rose to his feet and stared at her. "I didn't know Father married his stepmother. Except..." He looked out of the window. "Shall we walk?"

It was what she needed and happily agreed. In moments they were walking towards the gardens.

"Let's sit in the gazebo. It's out of the way," she suggested and they continued on to the far side near the woodland.

The gazebo was an elaborate metal structure painted white with lattice walls and a solid roof to keep out the rain. Inside there was not only a bench, but also a small table and four chairs. They decided to sit at the table and Antheia looked about her. The clematis was already starting to wind its way through the latticework along with roses and sweet pea. She had sat here many times in the days when she was discovering the joys of the Abbey.

She glanced at her cousin across the table. The colour had returned to his cheeks, although she could see the shock was still with him. "I didn't mean to upset you, Will."

He didn't answer for about thirty seconds and when he spoke he seemed in pain. "I remember a funeral. People dressed in black with sad faces. I must have been about three years old and I escaped my nurse and went to sit on the stairs. The many people who talked in hushed voices fascinated me. And then my mother appeared from the drawing room. I remember her smile and the lovely perfume she wore. She picked me up and carried me back to the nursery and sat me on her knee. She told me Grandfather had gone to live with the angels. I remember thinking it meant I wouldn't see him again. The gruff old man who smelled funny. I realised later it must be tobacco I could smell. He liked his cigars."

"What about his widow?"

He puzzled. "A tall, thin woman who glittered with jewellery. I'm sure I called her Grandmama, but suddenly there was another funeral and people were wearing black and very sad. This time it was my mother, they said, who had gone to live with the angels. But she'd left me a wonderful gift. I remember gazing at my little brother in the cradle and wondering when he would be big enough for us to play together."

"You were only five years old," she said softly.

Will stared at her. "But the tall, thin woman?" His eyes opened wide. "Suddenly she became Stepmother and I must have forgotten she was once Grandmama. But why did I forget?"

"Because you were young and accepted what the adults told you."

"And no one mentioned it from then on. I don't think Felix knows either."

"I'm sure he doesn't or he would have told us by now."

"But why has he always said Grandfather murdered our grandmother? I do wish I'd questioned him more rather than blown up at him like I did."

Antheia smiled. "You thought it all nonsense and he was being ridiculous."

"What kind of elder brother am I to ignore him like that."

"He said he was going to find our grandmother's body. That does sound amusing on the face of it. And besides, Felix had no proof either. In fact, everything is based on suspicion, although I've learned a few things since coming to live here."

"Tell me what you've learned."

She went on to tell him about the saucer in the tunnel and her mother's letter. Finally, she told him about her conversation with Mrs Thornborrow, her skill with herbs and her aunt's sudden interest in knowing about them.

He frowned. "Stepmother might have simply wanted to know about herbs…" He stopped, thinking. "No, she's never been the one to nurse us during an illness. If truth be told, she kept away if any of us were unwell." He considered the rest. "Your mother might have been wrong, after all what proof had she? And Mrs Thornborrow's misgivings are all conjecture."

Antheia sighed. "I suppose the only thing to do is join Felix in his efforts to find our grandmother's body."

"How do we do that? It could be anywhere."

She nodded. "And it happened such a long time ago, there won't be much of her left."

"Ugh!"

She looked askance at him. "I would have thought you would have been used to digging up bodies in Pompeii."

"I helped with uncovering a villa and some rather lovely mosaics."

She gestured out to the garden. "Well, she's out there somewhere. All we have to do is find out where."

"I like your optimism, but may I remind you we own 12,000 acres and besides, she could have been put in a boat and dumped in the Irish Sea."

"How horrible!"

"It is horrible. But conversely, she could have died in another town or even a different country."

"My mother believed she would never desert her family so cruelly."

"I could stay alert for any hiding places on the estate. Secluded locations at the edge of the property and wooded areas, would be a possibility. As steward I ride over the property all day."

She smiled. "That would be excellent." She thought for a moment, playing with a piece of lace on her cuff. "Since you've mentioned wooded areas let's speculate for a moment. If Grandmother was removed from the Abbey, isn't it possible she was carried through the tunnel and brought out in the woodland?"

"It's certainly a possibility."

"So the starting point could be close to the hatch?"

He nodded. "It's a place to start. I'll search the woodland tomorrow. Perhaps there's something amiss that might stand out." He linked his fingers and rested his hands on the table. "You say Stepmother might have had something to do…with my mother's death?"

"It's what Mrs Thornborrow believes. She couldn't understand why Aunt Frances didn't survive the birth of your brother. She bled too much for her liking." She licked dry lips and wished they had asked for refreshment to be brought to them. "There's potions that stop the blood from clotting. I think its called sweet clover."

Quietness settled over them again, each with their own thoughts. Antheia knew her cousin had much to think about, the worst of which was the fact his own mother might have died at the hands of the woman who was now sitting comfortably in her rooms in the Abbey.

"And what about your other problem?" His voice broke into her melancholy thoughts.

"I've no idea what to do about that."

"Time is marching on, dear cousin. We're already halfway through May."

Yes, she thought, *tempus fugit*, time flies and there were only six weeks before she would be coming out of mourning. She shook her head and tried to hold back her tears. But they were tears of anger for her stepmother and more so for her fiancé, the Reverend Horace Longmire.

Over the following month, two letters arrived at the Post Office for Mrs Thornborrow; the first reply came a week after she had written and the second three weeks later. She had become concerned the way April had slipped into May so quickly, but she knew she could rely on Orla Walsh. She had been the loveliest of the whores in the bordello and had been popular with the clients. Her red hair and green eyes had attracted many; bringing money into the house and her bright Irish personality and kind ways were a solace to the other girls. Although the madam was a considerate proprietor, it was to Orla everyone turned when needing support and comfort.

But the most wonderful fact about a house of disrepute was a sisterhood developed, each looking after the other. And when farewells happened; an inevitable fact since whoring was a temporary occupation, the 'sisters' kept in touch. Through Orla, Ursula Thornborrow had discovered the fate of many of the others. One had married and two had ended up working the streets of Whitechapel in London. But not Orla Walsh. She had set up her own 'gentlemen's club' in Islington, London and was doing very well for herself.

It was to Orla she had written when Margaret Sisson had told her the Reverend Longmire had been curate at a church in Harlow. It was twenty miles from London, but close enough for Orla to make some enquiries on her behalf.

The first letter Mrs Thornborrow received, told her Orla would do her utmost to find out the history of the vicar. The second letter told her what she needed to know. And with that letter tucked in her velvet bag, she set off for the vicarage.

She walked slowly, her stick tapping on the cobbles as she made her way down the main street, delighting in the cherry blossom now adorning the trees, and when arriving at the large house next to St James's church, she stopped to gather her courage. This could go very wrong, but she needed to do this. Fight fire with fire she thought, as she went up the path and knocked on the door.

Margaret Sisson answered. "Now, what are you doing here?"

Mrs Thornborrow looked askance at her. "Surely I can visit the vicar of the church I attend?" She tried to see past her. "Is he at home?"

"He is." She opened the door wider. "You'd better come in."

Mrs Thornborrow stepped into the ample hallway and looked about her. She couldn't see lovely Antheia living here and certainly not with the present incumbent of the property. The housekeeper had disappeared into what she supposed was the study and she could hear muffled voices; one rather angry. She smiled.

Margaret Sisson appeared. "He says you can go in, but he hasn't long. Ten minutes that's all."

Mrs Thornborrow ambled past her and entered the vicar's study with its musty smell of old books and lavender beeswax polish. The Reverend rose reluctantly to his feet, his expression one of disgust at having a woman such as Ursula Thornborrow polluting his home.

288

He tried to smile but it was an effort. "Take a seat er...Mrs Thornborrow. I'm always available for my parishioners."

She sat and leaned on her walking stick. "This won't take long."

"I'm pleased to hear it. I have a very busy morning ahead of me."

Mrs Thornborrow paused and said as seriously as she could, "I wondered what your preferred reading material was these days."

"I beg your pardon!" He sat back in his chair. "What are you talking about?"

She gave an exaggerated smile. "Do you still enjoy reading *Swell's Night Guide*? I've heard it's an interesting read for some er...gentlemen."

Anger suffused his face. "What the blazes...! Why are you wasting my time with accusations?"

Her eyes opened wide. "Ah, accusations, is it! Now, I would have expected a person such as your good self to query what exactly was *Swell's Night Guide*, but you obviously know. How interesting."

"I...I've heard of it. In the course of my ministry," he blustered.

"And used it from what I've heard. Frequently, whilst a curate at your last living in Harlow. And Harlow is but twenty miles from the fleshpots of London. Why, Swell's could be as popular as *Bradshaw's Railway Guide*, but not half as much fun."

"What are you saying, you old witch!"

She spoke in a hushed voice, not wanting to be overheard. "You have a hold over Miss Antheia Vale, a young girl who's become very dear to me. I don't know what that is, but now I have you in my grip. I know how you visited the brothels in London and how your Bishop sent you to this remote part of

England until you behaved yourself. And if you're a good boy you'll be allowed to return to London." She watched him as the colour drained from his face. "Now how do you think Miss Vale's uncle will react, if information comes his way that his niece's fiancé is not the upstanding, moral man he should be?"

"You wouldn't dare! You're a whore yourself."

She nodded. "I was, but a long time ago. And them what knows don't really care. No one is interested now. You see I'm no better than I should be, whilst you…folk think more of you than they do of me." She drew in a breath and let it out noisily. "The perils of trying to maintain a good reputation, eh!" She hauled herself to her feet and leaned on her stick. "Ooh, and the perils of growing old!" She rubbed her back. "I've heard you could be returning to London before Christmas. That's wonderful news and I'd be the first to wish you well. But I'd prefer it if you travelled alone and not drag Miss Vale along with you. I'll leave it with you since I'm sure you'll do the right thing."

She turned and walked to the door and through to the hallway. Margaret Sisson opened the front door for her and Mrs Thornborrow could feel her eyes on her along the path until she turned at the gate and headed up the main street of the village.

CHAPTER THIRTY-TWO

Why had she brought her wedding day forward? Why was she approaching the church porch on her uncle's arm? Her dress was beautiful, white satin and lace veil, but she could only feel horror at what she was doing. Her uncle would ask her if she were sure. He promised. But he didn't and suddenly they were walking up the aisle and towards the bridegroom who had the silliest grin. She turned desperately to the congregation. Everyone was there, Mrs Thornborrow, Jemima, Will, Felix and others from the village and the Abbey. All smiling, all happy for her. She reached the altar and she wanted to run, but her feet were stuck as though in the quicksand out at Warton Sands.

"I now pronounce you man and wife. You may kiss the bride," droned the vicar.

No! That was wrong she wanted to scream at him. She knew how the wedding service was conducted. They hadn't taken their vows and he should have asked if any person present knows of any lawful impediment to this marriage, they should declare it now. But he hadn't! Why had he left that bit out? Horace leered and grabbed her by the shoulders. She pulled away, but he tore off her veil and then the bodice of her dress. The church door banged open and she turned to see Joel striding along the aisle. He was in uniform, his sword strapped to his side. He looked dirty, tired and very angry, but she was relieved to see him. He was going to save her from this awful marriage. But instead of tackling Longmire, Joel grabbed her by the arms and started shaking her.

"Why did you do it, Antheia. Why did you betray me so? Don't you know how much I love you!"

Antheia gave out a scream.

"Miss Antheia, do wake up."

She opened her eyes to see Agnes looking down at her, holding her arms and still shaking her awake.

"Yes, yes, Agnes I'm awake."

"Goodness, you were thrashing about and shouting. I've never heard the like."

She pulled herself up on the pillow. "It was a dream. Actually a nightmare."

Agnes giggled. "It sounded like it." She became serious. "My ma used to say dreams show you the path through life."

"I can well believe it. However, that dream didn't tell me anything I didn't already know." She glanced round the room. "Open the curtains please. Let's see what kind of day it is."

The maid did as she was told and pulled the long velvet curtains to the side, allowing the sunshine to flood the room.

Agnes sighed. "A beautiful day. Truly lovely for the first day of June."

"It's June already?" Antheia swallowed hard. How could it be June so soon?

Agnes came to her side. "Yes, miss and it's the day I clean the chapel and schoolroom. I thought I'd remind you, just in case you wished to help."

Antheia smiled. She had helped in April and May and enjoyed the duties. On a school day, she would spend a little time in the schoolroom preparing for the lesson and since it was Wednesday, the children would be arriving through the tunnel that morning.

She climbed out of bed to get dressed. "How has Clara been about you cleaning on your own?"

Agnes picked up the chamberpot. She wouldn't make the fire that morning, as it wasn't needed. "She thinks I'm so brave," grinned the maid. "But she hasn't asked anything about it. I think she's happy to get out of doing it."

After she had seen the children on their way home, Antheia made her way to her room to tidy herself for lunch. The dream had stayed with her all through the lessons and although Agnes's philosophy about dreams showing a person the path through life was no doubt correct, she knew her path was still very rocky. On many occasions she had wanted to tell her uncle everything and hope he would come up with some ideas. And watching him reading the paper at breakfast, she felt tempted. Was she in too deep now? How could she extricate herself from this mess without destroying those she loved? By the time she went down to the dining room, she had lost her appetite and knew she would only pick at her lunch.

Passing through the hallway she wondered if she should take a walk after lunch and try and clear her head, and then she noticed the letter on the silver salver. It must have arrived in the afternoon post and Winder hadn't had time to bring it to the recipient yet. Antheia's eyes opened wide as she saw her name on the envelope and recognised Mrs Newton's handwriting. But Joel's mother didn't write to her with single letters; she always included a short note with Joel's letters in a delightful bundle she could take to her room to enjoy.

She broke the seal and carefully unfolded the sheet of cream paper.

Dear Miss Vale,

It saddens me to tell you...

Her legs gave way under her as she sank to the ground, knocking the vase and sending the flowers scattering across the floor, the water dripping over the edge of the small table and pooling on the tiles. She only barely heard the butler and housekeeper running up from below stairs and her uncle and cousin hurrying from the dining room. Who carried her to her room she couldn't tell, only she knew she was lying on her bed and Matty was hovering over her, her lips moving, but her words incomprehensible.

******

It was raining, but only a gentle rain for the beginning of May that bounced off his hat in a sparkling cascade. He had stepped out of the tent after writing a dozen letters to the wives and mothers of the men lost in previous conflicts. He remembered the names of every man lost in R Company, even though he had been their captain for only a short time. Often fresh recruits for the Union Army took their places. There were farmers, blacksmiths, wheelwrights and many more from all the occupations he could think of. Some were very young and some had seen a few summers.

He had come to know every one of them and writing the final letter to their families was the most difficult job of all. Five men had gone in the last skirmish and seven before that and he was resorting to platitudes; so difficult was it to find something different to say to those they left behind. What could he say? They were brave men and had done their duty? It seemed crass and he often tried to include some detail in the letters. How they would miss one man's terrible jokes; how another man was so proud of his children and had spoken of them often; another man delighted the Company with his tunes on the mouth organ. But how do you tell them someone they loved is no more? He couldn't tell them the truth. He couldn't describe the mayhem and acrid smell and smoke of battle; the noise of artillery and shouting men or how the wounded cried for their mothers as they waited for help. How the dying would stare up at the sky, their lips moving in silent prayer.

Joel glanced round the camp. Many of the men were cleaning their weapons. The two rules he had tried to instil into his men were to look after their weapons and also their feet. A soldier's rifle was his friend; healthy feet an absolute necessity. A few of the men were washing their clothes and two were cleaning the artillery gun, whilst another two were tending the horses. All was busy with the sound of men calling to each other and the neighing of horses. He felt he had been with these men, on the march or fighting, for a hundred years instead of five months.

He dipped into his inside pocket and pulled out Antheia's photograph. He had written how well preserved he had kept it, but that wasn't entirely true. It was getting rather grubby and the leather frame had a lot of nicks and scrapes. But her beautiful face shone out with an enigmatic smile like the Mona Lisa. He had enjoyed receiving the packets from his mother and opening them to find seven or eight letters inside. He would read each one at least three times, revelling in his darling's exploits. She had found a secret tunnel from the chapel to the woodland? And she was sneaking children into the Abbey to teach them? Although they had been together at the Abbey barely six weeks, he felt he had grown to know her so much better through her letters. Her last letter had been intriguing. At the end she had written, '*Cor meum semper sit vera*. My heart will always be true'. He couldn't understand why she had written that, since he knew her heart would always be true. Even so, he accepted it as a wonderful sentiment from the girl he loved.

One thing he was sure of was when this was over he would return to England to be at her side. Of course he realised he mustn't rush anything. They would have to start at the beginning, only this time he would court her in the proper way. Perhaps this time next year they would be making plans to marry, when his soldiering days were over and he could be plain Doctor Joel Newton at Cambridge University. His position had been left open for him and he hoped he would be awarded a professorship after his work in Pompeii. It would be delightful to blend into the fabric of the university building and teach once more. Would Antheia be happy as the wife of a university tutor? He hoped so.

He noticed Lieutenant Firth and Sergeant O'Connor talking by the horses and then the lieutenant was striding over to him.

"Orders have arrived, sir." He handed the message to Joel.

Joel read and raised his eyebrows. "Back to Virginia it seems and to where we started." He studied the young man who seemed older than his twenty-two years. War aged a man. "Ulysses S Grant fancies waging a war of attrition against Lee's army."

"Only way to drive them back I reckon."

The lieutenant saluted and went to order the sergeant to stir the camp and get them moving. It was only a one-day march to the rendezvous point. Joel pursed his lips. The last thing he wanted was to head into a war of attrition. Wearing down your enemy inevitably meant wearing down your own army;

exhausting men and lowering morale. But what could he do? He was nothing more than a humble captain.

Three days later on the 5th of May, R Company of the 7th Main Infantry Regiment found themselves taking part in Grant's Virginia Overland Campaign. Joel's Company along with thousands more were ordered to engage the enemy on the Orange Plank Road but were forced into dense woodland. Joel realised immediately the situation was impossible. Despite having the advantage of more men than the Confederates, the impenetrable undergrowth was making it difficult for a large army to advance in an orderly fashion.

As dawn broke, over 90,000 men waited behind barricades of fallen trees for the inevitable onslaught. Joel walked stealthily behind his men, resting his hand gently on the shoulder of a young recruit whose face was pale with fear, his hands shaking on his Springfield rifle.

Drawing his sword, he called along the line, "Don't fire until you get the order, boys. Aim true and hit your mark."

There was no doubt this would be a bloody encounter and God knows how many would come out of it alive. He looked across at Captain Masters standing behind T Company and they exchanged glances. Aaron's face looked pinched, his lips in a thin line.

And then they were coming, the wave of grey uniforms, flags flying and the shouts of 'Fire' echoed along the line in a wave. The noise was deafening; the sight of the enemy dropping to the ground in a bloody mess brought no joy to Joel, as three of his own men crumpled in a heap at his feet and were dragged to the back of the line by their comrades.

A bullet whizzed out of nowhere and his sword flew out of his hand and into the branches of a tree. He gasped and spun on his heel, before another bullet struck him in the side. He hit the woodland floor and looked up at the blueness of the sky, wondering where his sword had gone. It was a few seconds before he raised his torn and bloodied arm and wondered where his hand had gone also.

******

Lord Sedgwick watched his son carry Antheia upstairs followed by Mrs Hadwin and Matty, and stooped to pick up the letter from the tiles. He read it carefully and then followed the household to his niece's room. He remembered the battle to which Joel's mother referred. He had read about it in the newspaper some two weeks ago. The newspaper had called it The Battle of the Wilderness, although he could never work out how they named these battles. It was fought in early May over two or three days and both sides had suffered heavy casualties. The earl sucked in a sudden breath when he remembered the death toll being around 5,000. What was worse was the battle was tactically inconclusive, so no outright victory for either side.

He had long since stopped informing Antheia of the campaigns across the water. She hadn't asked for quite a while and he felt it was better that way. But this terrible and bloody battle had touched the lives of the people at Sedgwick Abbey. He shook his head and made his way upstairs, where he discovered his son hovering outside his cousin's bedroom door. Mrs Hadwin had sent him away after he had settled Antheia on the bed. Men were not needed here.

"What are we going to do, Father? The shock will be terrible for her. She'll never get over it."

The earl held up the letter. "Have you read this?"

"No I didn't. I was too busy lifting Antheia from the floor."

"Well, I need to speak to her and then to you."

"Why me, sir? There's little I can do except comfort her."

His father narrowed his eyes at him. "This ridiculous engagement with Longmire is getting out of hand. I've let it persist since I reasoned she would come to her senses. But this news," he shook the letter for emphasis, "has brought everything to a head." Seeing his son and heir's blank expression, he whispered, "There's something going on and I believe you know all about it. Wait for me in my study and you'll not leave until I know exactly why my niece has taken such drastic action, as to pledge herself to a man she despises. And I want to know it all, Will, no matter how painful and how many promises you've made to keep it a secret."

CHAPTER THIRTY-THREE

She crushed the letter in her hand, as she lay curled up on the bed. Mrs Hadwin had left to continue her duties, but Matty still fussed round her. She had never fainted in her life, but the shock of reading Mrs Newton's words had been like a lightning strike. Her uncle had been so kind and had drawn up a chair at her bedside and spoken in gentle words, asking her how much of the letter she had read. She had to admit to reading the first sentence only and a wave of relief flooded through her followed by tears, when he read the letter in its entirety. The letter was dated the twentieth of May 1864.

Dear Miss Vale,

It saddens me to tell you the terrible news that my son has been injured in battle on the 5th of May. I received word from his friend Captain Aaron Masters, who has assured me Joel was treated at a field hospital. But you must brace yourself, my dear, for he has lost his right arm above the elbow. It seems the surgeons couldn't save it although they tried and amputation was the only recourse.

I travelled to Virginia immediately where he had been taken to the large hospital in Alexandria. I am nursing him myself and my skills are keeping infection at bay. I hope to take him home to Cape Elizabeth at the beginning of June to recuperate.

He wishes to write to you, but I've persuaded him to wait until we're home and I've reassured him I'll keep you apprised of his progress.

I must admit I was alarmed when first I saw him. He looked poorly and the laudanum made him sleep a great deal. But slowly he improved and in the last four days, he's demanded to be allowed out of bed for an hour or so, since he wanted to visit the men of R Company who were injured also. He is with the officers, of course, but I walk with him to the other wards that deal with the private soldiers. He sits with them and talks to them and I've now seen how well respected he is. It brings me to tears when he sits with a young private who was blinded and reads to him.

As for your photograph, he will not let it out of his sight. Captain Masters visits frequently and often jokes how Joel will do anything to get out of the war and return to England and to the young girl in the leather frame. Even at the cost of an arm. It is taken in good humour and Joel is already learning to write with his left hand.

Kindest regards
Martha Newton

The shock had slowly abated as her uncle read the letter to her and had been replaced with embarrassment. Why hadn't she read the letter properly to begin with? How silly could a girl be! She reached out to caress Joel's photograph in the silver frame, running her forefinger down the side of his cheek. But one thing Antheia was sure of was Martha Newton's news had come as the last straw. Her mind and body couldn't take any more and had simply folded under the strain.

Her darling Joel had lost his arm and his right arm at that. But he was strong and would recover, she was sure of it. His mother would take him home to Cape Elizabeth and the sea air, wonderful nursing and nourishing food would make him better in no time. But what amazed her was Joel's last letters must have been sent days before Mrs Newton received the message he had been injured. In fact, while she was reading them, he was in hospital. She pulled herself up onto the pillow, shame surging through her. What had she been doing when his arm had been blown off? Betrothed to the Reverend Longmire that's for sure. She wouldn't put up with it any longer and to Matty's surprise, she jumped off the bed and pushed her feet into her house shoes.

"Oh no, Miss Antheia, you must stay on your bed. We don't want you fainting again."

Antheia shrugged her away. "I have to see my uncle and it must be now."

She hurried along the corridor and down the stairs, holding up her skirts as she raced across the hallway to the door of the study. She heard voices from within and surmised her uncle and cousin were having a heated conversation. She knocked and after some hesitation a gentle, 'enter' ushered her into the presence of the Earl of Sedgwick and Viscount Keasden.

They rose to their feet as she came into the room; the anger on her uncle's face and redness of her cousin's told her immediately what they were talking about.

"Antheia! How are you feeling?" Her uncle came round from the desk and studied her. "Are you sure you should be up and about?"

"I'm well, Uncle and needed to speak with you."

He nodded. "Will, bring that chair over here and your cousin can join our conversation."

It was when they were all seated Antheia discovered Will had told his father why she had engaged herself to Horace Longmire. Alarm filled her he might have divulged their suspicions concerning their grandmother's disappearance or the secret lessons in the tower schoolroom.

Lord Sedgwick sat back in his chair. "I know Mrs Thornborrow very well. She is an excellent midwife and I thanked her heartily for her care towards my darling Frances. She tried so hard to save her and the fact she couldn't saddened me, but I didn't harbour any resentment towards her."

Anthea held back her tears. "I'm so sorry, Uncle. I didn't know what to do. I didn't want her to be thrown out of her cottage."

"And the vicar threatened he would inform her landlord of her past, if you didn't wed him?"

She was wary. Had Will told him her aunt was also involved? She would let her uncle take the lead. "I thought I would consent until I could think of something else to do."

"Well, I believe the owner of many of the cottages in Slee Court is Sir Erasmus Kitching and he would have no qualms in throwing out a tenant who didn't come up to the mark."

"So, Horace was correct?"

Will spoke for the first time. "But that doesn't give Longmire the right to blackmail you into marrying him." He ran his fingers through his hair. "I should have done something about it! I should have acted!"

Anthea reached across to squeeze his hand. "You supported me and besides, I told you not to tell anyone. You kept my secret for as long as you could and I thank you for that."

Her uncle nodded. "Sometimes secrets can destroy a person's life. And the guilt."

She stared at him. Joel had said similar things and he had been right. But suddenly she felt her uncle was talking about something else; matters personal to him. She could see it in his face.

He shrugged away the feelings and smiled. "So, I think you need to break your engagement with the Reverend immediately. I'll send a note and summon him to the Abbey. It would be better if we make it a formal interview. And we'll find alternative accommodation for Mrs Thornborrow, in case he decides to retaliate."

"But where can she go, Uncle? There's nothing available."

"I own a cottage in Patterdale Lane. It's been empty for the last two weeks, so she can move into there."

She shook her head. "Mrs Thornborrow hasn't the income for the rent for anything in Patterdale Lane."

His lordship thought for a moment. "She can pay the same rent she's paying now. There's many things more important than money."

Antheia nearly jumped to her feet with joy, but instead clapped her hands. "Oh, that's wonderful. Thank you so much."

"Now then, I need to get on with my work and Will, I want to have a word with you before you go back to the office. We need to sort out the spring lambs." Antheia realised she had been dismissed and stood to leave. She crossed the room and was surprised when her uncle strode after her to catch her up. He opened the door for her. "By the way, why don't you meet the children at the gate and bring them down the drive for their lessons. Take them round to the servants' entrance, don't use the main door." She looked aghast at him, her mouth drying. "I don't like them using the tunnel. And since it's now summer, I don't see any reason why they can't have a few lessons in the grounds. Oh, yes, speak with Cook and

304

organise a meal for them in the kitchen before they leave for the day."

Antheia glanced at her cousin and saw he was as surprised as she and she knew for certain the information hadn't come from him.

"You knew?"

He grinned. "My dear, I have a way of finding out what's happening under my nose. There's not much escapes my attention."

"I don't know what to say. It's so kind of you."

He patted her hand. "I'll get Will to collect the keys for the cottage in Patterdale Lane. They'll be in the estate office and he can deliver them to Mrs Thornborrow."

"May I do that, Uncle? I want to see the look on her face."

He nodded in agreement.

So, her uncle knew about the tunnel! That had come as a surprise to her, but should she have been surprised? She reasoned that like her cousins, her uncle had been born and reared in the Abbey and must know it like the back of his hand. It seemed logical he would know about the priest hole.

But Antheia had many things to think about over the following week. Firstly, Mrs Sisson came in person in answer to the earl's note delivered to the vicarage. The housekeeper arrived at the Abbey in the late afternoon, after walking the lanes from the village and had informed Winder she must see Lord Sedgwick immediately. After she had left, the earl informed Antheia there was no need to acquaint her fiancé she was breaking their engagement, as the Reverend Horace Longmire had packed his possessions and left Brawton. His lordship's queries as to his whereabouts were answered with a shrug;

Mrs Sisson didn't know where he had gone, only she had seen the vicar packing his belongings in a great hurry. She had learned later he had taken a ride to Carnforth, probably to catch a train. She added that the vicar from the neighbouring village of Storth would officiate at St James's, until a permanent minister could be found.

The relief she felt at the news caused Antheia to dance round and round her room, grabbing her maid's hands to make her dance too. But the following morning she went with Will to the estate office to collect the key for the cottage in Patterdale Lane.

"It's a lovely cottage," he said. "One of the biggest, but you'll need to turn off Patterdale Lane on the left as its secluded."

She took the brass key in her hand and smiled. "Oh, I'm sure Mrs Thornborrow will know where it is."

He folded his arms. "I've never seen you glow so much, Cousin."

"Despite the news about Joel, I do feel happy. Everything is going well and when I hear from him again, I'll be able to assess how he is. At least the war is over for him, Will. And when he's better, he'll return to England and Cambridge.

"Will you go with him? To Cambridge?"

"If he asks me," she answered coyly.

He couldn't help smiling. "And I'm sure he'll ask you."

"You think so?" Her heart fluttered at the thought.

He nodded. "I don't think losing his arm will impinge on his work at the university. After all, there was a tutor at Cambridge who lost a leg in the Crimea."

She caught her breath. "How dreadful. It brings it home what men sacrifice in the service of their country."

Will stared down at his boots. "I'll be twenty-four on the twelfth of June and I thought I should look for a bride soon."

"You've plenty of time."

He eyed her carefully. "I always thought I'd marry you, my dear cousin. I think I've loved you since Joel and I first saw you lying on the sarcophagus in the old churchyard."

She felt shocked at his admission and for a moment felt speechless. "I know first cousins marry, but I think you can find a better bride than me."

"Oh, so you're suitable for a soldier-cum-university tutor but not for a viscount-cum-earl?"

"Your wife will be a countess one day. I don't think the title would suit me."

"You think so? From what I've seen you would make a perfect countess." Her lips parted to answer but he stopped her by taking her hand and kissing her fingers. "Yes, since that first day I met you you've become very special to me. However, I could see from the start how it was between you and Joel."

"How did you know?"

"The way you looked at each other," he sighed. "I knew I didn't have a hope in hell in winning your heart."

She squeezed his hand. "We will always be the best of friends and the most loving of cousins."

Her feelings were troubled as she collected the gig and horse from the stable and drove towards the village. Will had been in love with her from the moment they had met? How well she remembered that day, although it was Joel she only had eyes for. His slow and easy accent she found so attractive; his broad shoulders, brown hair and sparkling blue eyes. How she longed to see him again. And she would as soon as it was possible. He would travel to England as soon as he felt well enough and they would have to start their courting from the beginning. What joy that would be.

She reached Brawton and went straight to Slee Court, jumped down from the gig and tied the horse securely. Her heart was pounding as she knocked on the cottage door.

"Mrs Thornborrow, are you in? I have some wonderful news."

The door creaked open. "Ah, you've heard about Longmire. He's cut and run the coward." She opened the door wider. "I wouldn't have put it past him, mind. He wasn't the kind to face up to his responsibilities."

Antheia walked to the centre of the room and turned to face her. "Yes, I'm free of him, but I have better news."

The elderly woman grinned. "Now what could be better than that!"

She held up the brass key. "I've found you a new home."

CHAPTER THIRTY-FOUR

It was plain to see why Bluebell Cottage was so named, as it stood at the edge of woodland filled with bluebells in April. They were gone now and foxgloves and poppies took their place, covering the mossy ground in a spectacular spread of colour. Mrs Thornborrow was helped down from the waggon loaned by the earl and opened the door with quivering hands, calling to the estate workers who had come to help, to bring in the furniture immediately.

As Will had told his cousin, the cottage was down a short track halfway along Patterdale Lane and when viewing it, Mrs Thornborrow was almost speechless as she nodded and smiled. The fact it was isolated from the other cottages filled her with joy. She had loved the large parlour and modest sized kitchen with a small scullery to the side for doing the laundry. Up winding stairs were two bedrooms and Jemima couldn't believe she would have her own room. At the rear of the building was a substantial garden, now covered with weeds, but George had promised to visit and clear them for the elderly woman.

"Oh, everyone has been so kind," breathed Mrs Thornborrow, as the men carried in her armchair and large kitchen table.

Antheia nodded. "You have a good heart and deserve all the kindness in the world."

Mrs Thornborrow opened the back door leading from the scullery to the rear of the cottage. A gravel path ran down the edge of the garden and seemed to peter out at the tree line. "I'll grow my herbs in the half nearest the trees and the woods will provide anything else I need. And vegetables. We'll have lots of vegetables and I'll plant them in the half nearest the door. The front garden will be for flowers only." They surveyed the landscape; it was so peaceful with the blackbirds and sparrows happily chirping in the branches. "It's even got its own privy." She gestured towards the extension built on the right hand side of the cottage. "No sharing with the neighbours like we did in Slee Court."

The new tenant and her visitor looked up at the cottage. It had a thatched roof with whitewashed walls in the Tudor style and small panes of window glass. The front door was reached from the lane by a fenced gate and small path; the front garden filled with wild roses, hollyhocks and jasmine.

"I think you and Jemima will be happy here."

Mrs Thornborrow grinned. "Oh, we'll be happy here, there's no doubt about that. But I'm surprised his lordship is not asking for more rent. Are you sure it's only two shillings a week? Goodness, I paid six shillings when I lived in Patterdale Lane and that was some time ago."

"He seemed adamant about it."

"Well, I shan't quibble."

"I'll still give you a sovereign a month for Jemima's upkeep and another sovereign for the next term at school."

The elderly woman squeezed her hand. "I wish I had the money to pay for her myself."

"No, she's my responsibility."

"Well, Midwife has asked if I'd give her a hand over the summer and take on the extra births expected in September. The merriment of Christmas..." She quickly changed the subject. "And George from the Abbey is coming to help with the garden?"

"He volunteered to do it in his own time," said Antheia, trying to hide her smile.

"How kind."

They walked round the cottage to the front, just in time to see the men jumping aboard the waggon and setting off back to the Abbey. The women waved farewell, before entering the cottage through the front door, which lead straight into the parlour. Mrs Thornborrow went to the kitchen to light the range for a cup of tea, while Antheia started unpacking. In reality, the elderly lady hadn't much in the way of possessions and once the men had carried the beds and chest of drawers up to the bedrooms, the parlour was quite bare.

Mrs Thornborrow came from the kitchen and rooted about in a box. "I need my crockery for our tea." She looked about her. "Oh, dear. Do you think I need more furniture? My table has gone into the kitchen and all that's in this room is my armchair and a few odd chairs."

Antheia thought about this. "In the attic of the Abbey there's a sideboard and a couple of occasional tables. I can ask for them to be brought here. I'm sure you'll find a second hand sofa cheaply."

"Aye, that's all what's needed. Oil lamps on small tables and vases of flowers and my pictures on the wall. A sofa will make it just right." She looked across at the fireplace with a large mantelpiece and small tiles decorating the chimney breast. "I think this will be a really cosy room when I'm finished. We'll have a cup of tea and then I'll get the curtains up and make the beds."

"I'll stay and help you."

Mrs Thornborrow squeezed her hand in gratitude. "You're a good girl. My, I've never seen so many cupboards in a kitchen and a large pantry and cupboard for buckets and mops and a Welsh dresser! What's more there's room by the window for my workbench with three shelves above where I can place my jars and whatnot."

Her excitement was palpable and Antheia smiled. "Did you tell Jemima to come straight here after school?"

"I did and no doubt she'll run all the way."

Antheia stopped her unpacking. "Uncle knows about the tower schoolroom."

"He's not brought it all to a halt?"

"On the contrary. He's given me permission to let the children into the Abbey by the main gate and take lessons in the gardens on sunny days. Also, they're to have a meal before they leave."

Mrs Thornborrow's eyes opened wide. "Well would you believe it! The Garnett children will enjoy that." She continued pulling out the cracked and worn teapot, teacups and saucers, before rummaging for the cutlery. "So, your young man is out of the war?" Antheia nodded. "That's good. And no doubt he'll be back in England as soon as he can. But you must expect him to be different." Antheia raised her eyes in query. "What I mean is the experience of war changes a man, not to mention he'll be struggling with losing a limb. It'll be no mean feat."

"I know," whispered the young woman. She had often thought of Joel and his disability and all she wanted to do was to be with him and help him.

"How are you coming along with solving the mystery of your grandmother's disappearance?"

"Not very well. My cousin is scouring the estate for any nooks and hidden places where a body could be hidden."

Mrs Thornborrow pursed her lips. "It might be a lost cause, my dear. It was such a long time ago. But please watch that aunt of yours. Never trust the countess whatever you do!"

The first weeks of June proved to be a joy for Antheia. Firstly, visiting Bluebell Cottage always filled her with delight and the elderly woman was starting to make a wonderful home for herself and Jemima. Once the unpacking was done and the curtains hung, the sideboard and occasional tables were delivered, polished to perfection by Antheia and Matty. Soon they were adorned with lamps and vases of flowers. Mr Armer, the apothecary, sold his old sofa to Mrs Thornborrow, who had beaten him down from eight shillings to five. And Margaret Sisson donated a serviceable rug for the parlour. Two days after moving in, George Dent arrived in a cart with his garden tools, to tackle the garden. He worked all day, only complaining when he couldn't work out where the garden ended, but after being refreshed with many cups of tea and ginger biscuits and an afternoon meal of steak and kidney pie, it was decided the tree line would denote the end of the garden.

Teaching the children now became more than a pleasure. She would wait for them at the gate and lead them round to the servants' entrance, their small faces uplifted and eyes wide at the immense structure that was Sedgwick Abbey. The first half of the morning was spent in formal lessons at their slates, but after Matty had brought their milk and biscuits, Antheia would take them outside to the gardens. Often George would give them a short lesson on the plants and planting, even inviting one of the boys to plant a small tree. They would go into the woodland to study the trees and leaves and many times they went to Sarah's Meadow and played bat and ball. If the tide were out, they would make their way down the trail to the shingle and study the rockpools and the molluscs living in the salty water.

Because of the wide variety of lessons, Antheia would invariably find herself in the library in the late afternoon, her head bent over the many books and scribbling away frantically. It seemed the teacher needed to learn before she could teach.

By the middle of June, she was sure Mrs Newton would write soon. If she were taking Joel to Cape Elizabeth at the beginning of the month, it was possible she would write immediately, knowing Antheia was waiting to hear of his wellbeing. Of course, all their letters had to cross the Atlantic, but she knew three weeks from sending to receiving was about the right time. Yes, she should receive a letter by the end of June at least.

The day was so hot, Antheia decided to take the children down to the estuary, since a cool breeze would blow up the river. They formed a single line down to the shingle; the pungent, muddy smell of the sandbanks assailing their nostrils, and the children immediately engrossed themselves in lifting out the residents of the rockpools and placing them on the sand to study.

Thomas Hugill stood up after squatting by a pool. "Miss Antheia, can we walk along the shingle? There's more pools over there."

The teacher nodded and shepherded the children along the shingle where they examined every part of the sand and asked endless questions. Antheia had to admit her aptitude, other than reading, writing and simple mathematics, was mostly history and the subject she most loved when her father instructed her. The science subjects were not her strongest skill, but she had learned enough the day before to answer their questions.

Edith, the oldest of the group pointed. "Shall we explore up there, miss?"

Antheia pursed her lips. She knew where that trail took them. To Far Field and the old cemetery. But she always felt nervous about being on the shingle too long; her fear of getting caught by the tide had given her many moments of anxiety. They made their way up the narrow track and onto the grass, where the children whooped with joy and set off immediately towards the old cemetery and derelict chapel. She hurried to keep up with them.

The children wandered around the chipped stones and broken monuments.

"It's not looked after very well, is it!" said Edith in disgust.

"It's not used any more so I suppose they don't see any reason to look after it," said their teacher, looking about her.

"The chapel looks good. Can we explore?"

Antheia pulled young Leonard back. "No! It's too dangerous. Something might fall on you or trip you up." She sighed. "It really should be pulled down."

The children continued walking round the cemetery and tried to read the names that had almost faded to nothing with the wind and rain coming up the estuary. Antheia wandered over to the sarcophagus. She knew she shouldn't, but she was intrigued whether she would react in the same way as before.

"This one says 754!" called Thomas. "That's a long time ago."

Antheia smiled. "I think it will be 1754." She stood in front of the large tomb and slowly placed her hand on top.

She almost shrank back at the weariness flooding through her and the overwhelming feeling of grief and loneliness. This was the third time it had happened, but she was ready for it. It wouldn't catch her unawares again; she was determined of it. Filling her lungs with air, she assessed what was exactly happening to her, even though the desire to break down and cry was overpowering. She controlled herself and knew the feelings were coming to her from somewhere else. The sarcophagus?

"Do you like that grave, miss? Why are you touching it?" Edith's voice filtered through her turbulent feelings.

She pulled her hand away and stared down at the six small faces and gave a wan smile. "Well it's the biggest and the best. It must be an important person." She saw them frown and continued in a voice that sounded strained to her ears, "Shall we find out who's lying here?" They nodded and she stood back trying to read the inscription. It was so faint she resorted to tracing her fingertips along the inscription. "Oh goodness, I do believe it's one of my uncle's ancestors. Bartholomew, sixth Earl of Sedgwick born 1570 and died 1617. I can't read the rest I'm afraid."

"Is he one of your relatives too?" asked Leonard.

"In a way. My uncle is the eighteenth earl."

For the children, the sixth Earl of Sedgwick was of little interest to them. Leonard looked across Far Field. "Is that the woods over there where the hatch is?"

"It is. Shall we go back now? It's nearly time for luncheon."

The idea of sitting in the kitchen and being served a hot meal appealed to them and all six began to run across the grass towards the woodland. Antheia threw back her head laughing and picking up her skirts, she hurried after her small charges.

It had been a good day and exhausted as she was, she needed to spend time in the library before getting ready for dinner. The children had asked about the weather. Why was the sky blue? What was the sun? What were the clouds made of? Although she was aware of some facts, she knew she would have to revise for the next lesson.

Bartholomew, the sixth Earl of Sedgwick, came into her mind. Why was he buried in a small cemetery on the cliff? She knew the family had a mausoleum at the edge of the estate, where her grandfather and Aunt Frances were now at rest, but it seemed an ignominious resting-place for someone as prestigious as an earl.

She stood and searched along the shelves for the large volume on the history of the earls, going back to the Wars of the Roses in the fifteenth century between the Houses of York and Lancaster. Once found she lifted it down, placed it on the table and flicked through the pages.

"Ah, there you are," said Will, putting his head round the door. "Are you still working?"

"Mmm, the children want to know about clouds."

He took a seat at the table and stared at the book she was poring over. "You won't find anything about clouds in there. Clowns perhaps." He chuckled at his quip and pulled his mouth down when she gave him her best schoolmistress glare. "So, what are you looking for?"

"Bartholomew, sixth Earl of Sedgwick. He's buried in the old cemetery and I wondered why."

Her cousin closed his eyes briefly. "Ah, the black sheep of the family."

"Is that why he isn't buried in the family mausoleum?" When he nodded, she asked, "What did he do?"

"He murdered his wife."

CHAPTER THIRTY-FIVE

"Actually, I exaggerate somewhat," explained Will. "His wife disappeared and he was accused of murdering her and disposing of her body."

"She disappeared! Do you mean the same as…" She looked towards the door and lowered her voice, "what we think happened to our grandmother?"

He nodded. "The same. But Bartholomew was despised and by all accounts was an evil man and a brute. He wasn't above using his fists on his wife, children or any servant he took a dislike to."

"He does sound a horrible man."

"Have you heard of the Pendle witches?"

"I think I have. Early seventeenth century witch trials."

Will added to the story. "Yes they lived at Pendle Hill which is about fifty miles south of here. In 1612, nine were hanged at the castle in Lancaster and one in York. Bartholomew went to witness the hangings and it wasn't through a need to see justice done, but to enjoy the spectacle. I think he wrote he had a wonderful time, watching their feet twitch."

Antheia stared at him. "And when he died, they decided to bury him in the old cemetery?"

"They did. His son and heir couldn't bear him to be buried with the rest of the family."

"But what happened to his wife?"

"When his wife disappeared, many fingers were pointed at him he was so hated. But he was an earl and had influence. What's more they couldn't find any evidence."

"So, he lived a happy life?"

"I'm not sure he lived a happy life. But his wife turned up after he died. She had simply run away not able to take any more and gone to live in France. She returned to be with her children and become the dowager countess. Her oldest son was in his twenties by then and was completely different from his father. However, he forbade the family and servants to attend any executions from then on. As a youth, it had sickened him how his father had insisted he join him at any executions."

"Now, why are you young people talking about executions!"

They turned their heads to see the earl striding through the door.

Will rose to his feet. "I just wondered if there was one imminent, Father, since I missed the last one in March."

Lord Sedgwick chuckled. "How strange, but I intend going down to the Lords after the summer, to attend the opening of Parliament and take part in the debate of ceasing public hangings. If a law is passed to take executions within the privacy of a prison, we'll have moved closer in our attempt to become more civilised."

"How will justice be seen to be done, sir, if the people can't witness it?"

Antheia smiled at her cousin's question. Perhaps he should have been the lawyer in the family.

The earl puffed out a breath. "There'll have to be official witnesses, of course. I guess the people will have to take their word for it. If a man or woman is sentenced to die, then that should be the end of it. We don't need a spectacle to confirm it." He frowned at the two young people. "But why was the subject so interesting to you two?"

Antheia tapped the book in front of her. "We were talking of Bartholomew, the sixth Earl of Sedgwick and his burial on the cliff top in the old cemetery, and how he was suspected of murdering his wife after she disappeared."

She could have cut out her tongue when her uncle's face seemed to close up. His skin becoming drawn and his lips pulled back in what seemed to be a snarl, or his way of stemming a cry of alarm. She couldn't be sure. But why had she said that? She hadn't thought for a moment it would be too close to home for him. Even after all these years, the disappearance of his mother still hurt him.

"Uncle, I'm so sorry. I didn't mean..." She glanced quickly at Will, who had also turned pale.

"No doubt rumours have circulated since you've been here and I should have expected it. I hope you don't perpetuate these rumours by repeating such absurdities."

She had never seen her uncle so angry and stuttered her reply. "I don't repeat gossip and I wouldn't hurt you for the world."

Her words seemed to placate him and colour returned. He gave a sad smile. "It's time to get changed for dinner. Come, the pair of you and let's forget this nonsense."

Antheia wanted to make up to her uncle after her *faux pas*, since he had been so kind to her and those she cared for. She hated the idea she might have hurt his feelings and chastised herself at being so careless. Hadn't she and Will only just spoken of the similarity between the two events? And she had to open her mouth and speak the unspeakable to the one person who didn't need it said.

But as the days passed, it was slowly drawing close to the time of the anniversary of the death of her parents and her thoughts were very much with them and her memories. Her father had died first on the twentieth, her mother following him ten days later on the last day of June. Antheia expected the end of the month to be sad and decided to complete her year of mourning by sitting in the family chapel in solitude to remember them. It seemed a fitting place, as it was where her mother was baptised. The following day, she would start wearing the lighter summer gowns Miss Sill had been busy creating for her and along with many others, was a stunning evening gown in pink satin material. When she had tried it on, she loved the way it swished round her and adored the small white silk roses that cascaded across the skirt and bodice. She would wear it for the first family dinner she and Joel attended and she wondered how surprised he would be at the young woman she had become while he had been away.

It was on the last day of June and the anniversary of losing her mother, when a letter from Mrs Newton arrived. Matty had put her head round the door of the chapel.

"Miss Antheia, I don't wish to disturb you, but a letter has arrived from America."

She turned her head and smiled. "I'll collect it immediately."

"I've put it on your dressing table. As I said, I knew it was a special day for you."

Matty disappeared and Antheia turned to stare at the wooden cross on the altar. "I must go now Mama and Papa, but you will always be with me. It's just that now my heart is full of love for a very special person."

She stood and hurried to her room. Picking up the letter, she made herself comfortable on the chaise longue and broke the seal. Mrs Newton's letter was dated the third day of June.

Dear Miss Vale,

I'm so pleased to tell you we are home in Cape Elizabeth. I think Joel found the train journey arduous although he bore it well. He came home in full uniform with his father's sword strapped to his side, since he hasn't relinquished his commission just yet. I was very proud of him, as many gentlemen came to him to shake his hand and young ladies offered their kisses. Don't be jealous though, my dear girl, they were pecks on the cheek. I guess the fact his right sleeve was pinned up, gave testament to what he had sacrificed in this blessed war. However, his exhaustion was evident and by the time we reached home, he was glad to go to bed and sleep.

The days that followed were spent in resting and taking short walks. But he is getting stronger by the day. He talks of going to England and has already checked the sailings from Boston. I've advised him to wait a little longer, but I don't think I'll be able to hold him off past July. I do believe he'll be with you in August. And if that happens, I must ask you to be patient with him. I'm sure you will and he's told me of Sedgwick Abbey and its remote location and beauty. If he should leave New England and travel to Old England, I know you'll be mindful of his health. I do believe the Abbey will be a perfect place to complete his recuperation. And being with you can only aid his journey to full health.

My best wishes go with you

It was a wonderful letter, although Antheia felt alarmed he wished to travel so soon. Yes, she longed for him to be with her, but not if it jeopardised his health. Sighing, she realised she must trust Joel and his mother to make the right decision. How lovely Martha Newton was, but she had raised a son to be proud of. How she hoped to meet her one day and she was sure she would. Mrs Newton must visit Lancashire and enjoy the benefits of the Abbey. Antheia was sure she and Mrs Hadwin would get along extremely well.

The following day she decided to visit Mrs Thornborrow. There had been no lessons that day, although she had helped Will in the estate office that morning and then travelled to Brawton to complete her parish duties in the afternoon. She didn't need to visit the vicarage; a fact she was grateful for. The vicar of Storth only came to the village on Sundays for the service at St James's and there was no incumbent at the vicarage until a new one was appointed. Mrs Sisson was sole occupant of the house and Antheia had seen her smile when talking to the apothecary. It was a revelation, since her face, in a bright smile, seemed transformed beyond recognition. There was no doubt the departure of Longmire had broken few hearts.

She left the horse and gig by the Red Lion and walked about the village, while she did her shopping and performed her parish work. Deciding to leave her transport where it was, she walked towards Patterdale Lane, but as she turned into the lane, she saw a horse and phaeton coming out of the small track leading on to the lane. Aboard was her uncle. Why she shrank back and took cover behind the trunk of an apple tree she had no idea, but the need to hide seemed important. Lord Sedgwick snapped the reins and urged the horse into a canter, as he turned into the main street of the village. Antheia could see his expression was serious, almost desperate. But there was one thing she was sure of. By driving out of the small side road into Patterdale Lane, he could have been visiting only one person.

"What a pretty gown," said Mrs Thornborrow, as she opened the door to her visitor.

Antheia couldn't help smiling. "I'm out of mourning. Do you like it."

The elderly woman nodded as Antheia did a twirl round the parlour. Her gown was in pale lemon with mauve ribbons decorating the skirt, the bodice tight with the same mauve ribbons around her neckline and sleeves. Over the top of the bodice, Miss Sill had made her a matching mantle trimmed with lace and braid, in case the weather turned a little chilly, as it was wont to do in Lancashire, even in summer. She had completed the ensemble with her favourite straw hat.

"Beautiful. Now take a seat." Antheia made herself comfortable on the sofa, running her fingers over the green fabric with the flower print. Mrs Thornborrow placed a tray of tea on the occasional table and Antheia couldn't believe how genteel she had become since moving into Bluebell Cottage. "So, he'll be here soon, your young man? Aye, he'll be able to recover his health at the Abbey."

Antheia stared at the teapot, steam issuing from the spout. "Yes, perhaps August if he can book a sailing." She wanted to ask about her uncle's visit, but since Mrs Thornborrow hadn't mentioned it, she couldn't see how she could.

"As I said before, you must be patient with him, my dear. He'll be weary beyond belief. Although he'll need your care and attention."

"That's what his mother said in her letter."

"A woman after my own heart. I've always thought a good woman makes a good man." She sighed. "Our gender has more power than folk realise. No matter we lose our property to our husbands when we marry and have no political say. I always thought I could have been happy with Thornborrow, if he hadn't been lost at sea."

Antheia took the offered teacup and sipped gently. "I don't think my step-aunt is good for my uncle."

"Ah, now she's something else. But your Aunt Frances was a treasure and had she lived, she would have been the making of his lordship."

The younger woman decided to gather her courage. "Why was my uncle visiting?"

Mrs Thornborrow looked startled. "You saw him?"

"I saw him turning out of the side road and...hid."

"Why did you hide?"

"I don't know. I felt it was an...intrusion into his affairs to make myself known. And his expression wasn't inviting. So, is it a secret why he visited? I can't think he called for any medication."

Mrs Thornborrow stayed silent for a moment, before saying, "He wanted to know about his wife and mother. He was very interested in the poisons inherent in some herbs. But mostly he was concerned about his wife and how she died."

"What did you tell him?"

"The truth. I felt it was the only way. What was the point in lying to him? He's well aware herbs like deadly nightshade and some of the ivy family, can be fatal. And there's many others that can be abused in the wrong hands."

Antheia swallowed with difficulty. "Do you think he's become suspicious of the fate of his mother and wife?"

She nodded. "It seems so and I took the liberty of showing him the letter from Lady Anne."

"My mother's letter! How did he take that?"

"He put his head in his hands and wept."

Antheia had no words to reply. Her uncle had been so overwhelmed by his feelings, he had actually cried. Her upstanding and stoic uncle? But if he now realised the women he had been devoted to, might have perished at the hands of his wife, then what would he do now?

She drank back the last of her tea and jumped to her feet. "Oh, I must get back! My uncle might do anything in that state of mind. Even try to choke my aunt to death."

"She'll deserve it," grunted the elderly woman, collecting up the teacups.

"But not to hang for it," came back the answer.

Antheia searched for her reticule as Jemima came bursting through the door.

"Granny Thornborrow! Granny Thornborrow! I've won a prize for the best pupil with my reading. Look what it is." She held up an orange.

Antheia had to leave and stroking Jemima's cheek in recognition of her award, she slipped out of the cottage. But not before turning to see the elderly woman hug the little girl, her face lit up with pride at her adopted granddaughter.

CHAPTER THIRTY-SIX

Everything was peaceful at the Abbey. Her uncle was working in his study and her cousin was still in the estate office. Antheia breathed a sigh of relief and wondered why she would think her uncle would harm his wife. But the news from Mrs Thornborrow had set her nerves on edge. Her uncle would only have suspicions about the countess, there was no actual evidence. Unless he confronted her and she confessed, only then would the truth come out and Antheia couldn't think he would do that.

After a restless night, she rose from her bed, tired and drained.

"Miss Antheia, you look as though you've not slept a wink. I do hope you're not worrying about Mr Joel, because I think he'll be as right as rain once you're together again."

Antheia nodded at her maid. "It seems once one problem is solved, another takes its place. Life can be so strange at times."

Matty lifted a pale blue gown out of the armoire. "Will this be suitable for today? Are you going anywhere special?"

"No, it's a simple ordinary day with the usual things to do."

But it wasn't to be a simple ordinary day, even though she was attentive to her uncle during breakfast. He showed no sign of his distress at Bluebell Cottage and discussed the issues concerning the estate with Will, as she buttered her toast and listened intently. And after breakfast, when she saw the envelope waiting for her in the hallway on the

328

silver salver, she hurried into the library, since it was the first secluded room closest to her.

Sitting at the table, she studied the address on the front of the envelope. It was Joel's writing and yet not his writing. Tears came into her eyes at the effort he was making to learn to write with his left hand.

The letter was dated the seventh of June and his writing was almost childlike, a spidery scrawl as he forced his left hand to form the words.

My darling Antheia,

Please forgive my writing. It's very strange using my left hand and it's as though my brain knows how to write, but can't form the words. But please don't worry about me, my darling, I'm improving with each day and each day brings me closer to you.

I've been in Cape Elizabeth just short of a week now and I'm enjoying taking walks and meeting the folk I've known all my life. They seem to hail me as a hero, but I don't feel like one. All I can think of is the men of R Company, those lost and those who now have a new captain to lead them forward in the war. I don't know him, although I trust he will do a good job with Lieutenant Firth and Sergeant O'Connor at his side.

Doctor Dwyer often calls to check on my arm and has said it's healing well. Despite being elderly, he's a veteran army doctor and knows a great deal about amputations, as you can imagine.

But I must tell you what happened while I was in hospital in Alexandria, since my mother tells me she didn't mention it in her letter.

Captain Masters came to visit me and believe it or not he had retrieved my sword. He had returned to the battlefield to bury the dead and collect the wounded, when he decided to find my sword. He saw it amongst the branches of a tree and Sergeant O'Connor climbed up to bring it down. Later, Aaron took it to a blacksmith to clean and reshape it. He brought it to me, knowing I treasured it since it belonged to my father. Because of my good friend, I was able to wear it when I travelled home.

My impatience to be with you amuses my mother and you'll be surprised to know I've checked the sailings and I intend to be with you in August. I will write when I've booked my passage.

Loving wishes
Joel

To be called 'darling' filled her with joy, even though the content of his letter was rather gruesome. But she understood his need to share it with her and she was relieved he didn't think her a dainty, fragile creature that fainted at the slightest mention of anything nasty or unmentionable. Perhaps American women were made of sterner stuff and he thought her one of their ilk. She must remember to ask him when they met again.

He was checking out the sailings and would be in England in August! She wondered if she should answer his letter, since he might be on the way before it arrived in New England. Yes, she would answer and Mrs Newton will return any letters arriving too late. Leaving the library, she went to the morning room to reply and then she would go and see Will and tell him the good news. She also needed to discuss her predicament over her betrothal. Should she tell Joel and would he understand?

But another thing she must do, was apprise her cousin of what she had learned the day before about

330

her uncle's visit to Mrs Thornborrow. The fact the earl was suspicious of his wife, had taken the mystery of her grandmother's disappearance to a more serious level. His distress over what he had learned, could only mean he believed the rumours were true.

And when she finally told her cousin, his face paled. "We must never mention this to Father, Antheia. He's not the kind of man to discuss these kinds of things."

"Family pride?"

He nodded. "He would be ashamed to think he'd married a murderess and we knew about it."

"He did put his head in his hands and cry. The poor man. So, what do we do?"

"We carry on as before. Try and find more evidence."

"It seems hopeless. I don't think we'll ever discover the whole truth."

He held out his hands and she took them in hers. For a few seconds they stayed as they were, silent and thoughtful.

Her cousin gently squeezed her fingers and smiled. "We'll be seeing Joel very soon. Perhaps his presence will be a distraction and he can give a different perspective on our mystery."

Her heart lifted. Mystery or not, she yearned for him to be back at the Abbey and his next letter couldn't come soon enough.

Antheia couldn't understand why the time she had been engaged to be married had passed so quickly; so fraught was she in ending it and saving Mrs Thornborrow's home. But now the days of July crept by. She longed to hear Joel's plans and eagerly watched out for a letter or any message telling her he was on his way. Would he write again or send a telegram? And when his next letter arrived on the seventeenth of July, she gave a cry of pleasure.

Tuesday 21st June

Darling Antheia,

I trust you'll receive this letter in three or four weeks, in time for my wonderful news. I've booked passage on the clipper ship Flying Cloud, bound from Boston to Liverpool. I set sail on the 24th of July, but I will keep writing to you until three weeks before my departure. After that any letters I send, will arrive in England after me. If all goes according to plan, I should disembark in Liverpool on the 3rd of August. The Flying Cloud is a fast ship and should cross the Atlantic in just over a week. My mother insists on coming with me on the stagecoach to Portland, but it's less than ten miles and it'll be a very different farewell from the last time she waved me off at that train station.

It seems strange, but when I sent the telegram to book my passage and also the hotel in Boston, where I shall stay the night before, I suddenly realised I shall be on my way to you. It will be almost a year since we first met and so much has happened to us since then. I look forward to gentle walks and long talks with you.

My darling girl, how I long to be with you.

Loving wishes
Joel

She had been given the letter by the butler at breakfast and opened it immediately, while her uncle and cousin sat quietly as she read. Will cast her an amused glance, but the earl seemed subdued, his thoughts often distracted. She wondered if his visit to Mrs Thornborrow was finally taking its toll on him.

Antheia lifted her head, her eyes sparkling. "He's arriving in Liverpool on the third of August aboard the clipper ship *Flying Cloud*. Goodness, he'll be setting off in just a week."

Her uncle nodded. "He'll have quite a journey in front of him. Train and ship."

"I do hope he's well enough. We could have waited another month," she said apprehensively. "He was injured in early May so that's only three months."

"He's made of tough stuff," grinned Will.

Lord Sedgwick took a mouthful of kipper and thought for a moment, studying the worried expression of his niece, as she read the letter to herself.

"There's no reason why you and Will can't travel to Liverpool and meet him off the clipper. We could check the times and if it's early morning, you could stay in a hotel overnight."

Will was enthusiastic. "We could stay in the Adelphi Hotel and be on the quayside to meet him." He turned to his cousin. "Although you must understand a ship is not like a train."

She feigned astonishment. "Really? I wouldn't have noticed."

He flicked his napkin at her. "What I mean is a train arrives on schedule. They pride themselves on it. But a ship can dock hours before or after they say." He hesitated before adding, "Sometimes they can be days late. Sea travel tends to be flexible."

Antheia didn't care if his ship was delayed a day or two as long as he docked safely. She felt it in her heart they would do as he said in his letter. Gentle walks and long talks. It sounded wonderful.

"I'll book rooms in the Adelphi for the second of August. Are you agreeable?" asked Will, breaking into her happy thoughts.

Antheia nodded and then a memory stirred; something she had read in the newspaper the year before. Yellow ribbons. Yes, she would need to visit the haberdashery shop in Brawton. Thirty, no forty yards should suffice. Matty would help, but how puzzled she would be. And how surprised Joel would be. Taking in a deep breath, she stemmed the excitement building up inside her. A little over two weeks and they would be on their way to Liverpool.

CHAPTER THIRTY-SEVEN

The morning was overcast and threatening summer rain, when they climbed aboard the landau with enough luggage for an overnight stay. Even so, Antheia couldn't hold back her joy that the journey had begun.

It had been a long two weeks, especially when the day dawned and she knew Joel was setting off on his journey. On that day, she had thought of him constantly, imagining his journey by stagecoach from Cape Elizabeth to Portland and his sad farewell from his mother at the railway station. And then arriving in Boston and booking into the hotel. Would he be all right with dressing? Surely the hotel would have valets to aid those guests who needed help with buttons and laces! But the following morning when she thought of him boarding the clipper, her heart went out to him. She knew the east coast of America was five hours behind English time, but that made no difference. She was with him in spirit if not in body. And now their physical presence was converging. Only twenty-four hours to go.

The cousins arrived at Carnforth and twenty minutes later boarded the train to Lancaster and from there the train to Liverpool Lime Street station. A short cab ride took them to the Adelphi Hotel. Antheia thought the railway station a bustling metropolis in itself, but staring out of the window of the hackney cab, she couldn't believe how busy the city of Liverpool was. It seemed impossible to make progress with the amount of traffic on the roads and tradesmen calling their wares to the many pedestrians that thronged the pavement. The shops were brimming with folk going in and out and the noise was deafening.

Will smiled at her, amused at her wide-eyed scrutiny. "Would you like to live in a city like this?"

She turned to him. "I certainly wouldn't. Bromyard was only small and Leominster was the busiest place I visited. I need space and a place to move and think."

"London is busier."

"I can imagine. Although Felix writes how much he enjoys the capital."

"He does and one day I aim to visit him. Perhaps you and Joel will accompany me before you…well, you decide what you're doing."

Antheia swallowed with difficulty. "I can't believe I'll be seeing him tomorrow. Oh, Will, what will happen if we find we don't like each other any more!"

"That's hardly likely to happen."

"It's been ten months since he set off for America and the war. We've both changed."

He shook his head slowly. "If there's one thing I know about my friend is that he's constant. But providing you take your time in getting to know each other again, I'm sure there'll not be a problem."

"I'm getting such advice constantly." She hated these doubts. They cast a shadow on her happiness.

"Wise words I reckon." Will smiled and gestured. "Ah, the Adelphi Hotel."

She looked out of the window in amazement, since their journey had been only a few minutes and they were already drawing up at the front of a substantial hotel of seven storeys and made of Portland stone. A commissionaire stood at the door, directing porters in their duties of unloading luggage for the guests arriving at the entrance.

Making their way inside a marble foyer enhanced by columns, Antheia followed Will to the reception desk and while he signed the register, she glanced into the interior rooms that seemed to be constructed of marble panelling and arches. It was like a palace and seemed more opulent than the Abbey.

"We have rooms next door to each other," said Will. "They're still serving luncheon and I've been informed the evening meal is at seven o'clock and breakfast from six."

"When do we have to go to the port?"

Will turned to the young man behind the reception desk and asked.

The man nodded. "We receive telegraph reports regularly, my lord, updating us on the arrivals of ships. It would be better for you to check with me later tonight when we receive the shipping details for tomorrow."

It was all in hand and after they had gone to their rooms and freshened up, they went down to the dining room for lunch. They were shown a table and as they studied the menu, Antheia smiled at the shining brass and glass room with glistening chandeliers and busy waiters. She had never eaten in such an opulent place and after they had ordered their food, Antheia noticed the other diners were smiling in their direction.

"Is there a smudge on my face?" She reaching for her handkerchief.

"No, why?"

"Everyone is looking at us."

Will turned quickly and grinned. "They think we're married and you are the new viscountess."

"How do they know you're a viscount?"

"I signed the register, remember. And it gets about very quickly."

"I hope you'll put them right."

He didn't answer and concentrated on the mushroom soup brought to their table.

"What do you want to do this afternoon?" he asked, dabbing his mouth with his napkin.

"I noticed a large building near the station. It had a great deal of columns."

"That would be St George's Hall. It's only a few minutes' walk from here. Would you like to take a look and perhaps there's a concert this afternoon or evening."

She nodded in agreement.

Stepping out of the main door of the hotel, her eyes and ears were filled with the mayhem of the city, but taking Will's arm she was mindful of her uncle's instructions to his son to take care of his cousin. And she knew he took his responsibilities seriously.

St George's Hall seemed far bigger when standing up close than when she had seen it from the hackney. The many columns gave it a classical look and if it was as beautiful inside as outside, any concert should be a delight to attend.

Will studied the poster outside the main door. "Ah, William Thomas Best is performing Handel at four o'clock. We could get tickets. He's the local organist." When Antheia nodded, they went into the booking office and came out moments later, with tickets for the recital that afternoon.

From St George's Hall, they strolled round the shopping area and Antheia enjoyed peeping into the many windows and perusing the displays. It was after visiting the Georgian Town Hall and they were passing a church, when Antheia saw a sight she would never forget. Sitting on the stone step that led to a wrought iron gate leading along the path to the church entrance, were three small girls. They were

338

barefoot, faces dirty, their clothes torn and filthy and their tiny hands stretched out, as they begged for money. She had seen much poverty, but never children like these. Not even in Slee Court. Their eyes held a dejected, desperate look and her heart broke.

She went into her reticule, but Will stopped her. "No, don't, Antheia."

"But they look as though they're starving to death. Surely a penny or two won't hurt!"

He looked about him. "If you give them money, then a horde of them will follow us along the street begging for more."

She looked about in fear. "What shall I do?"

Will pointed to a bakery on the corner. "Buy something for them to eat. It doesn't do to show you have money on you."

They hurried over to the shop and Antheia bought six currant buns with sugar sprinkled on the top. Taking the bag back to the little girls, she gave it into their grubby hands and watched as they pulled it open and peered at the treat inside. They were munching into the buns in seconds and she was relieved to see they shared the bread between them.

How old were these children? Four perhaps five? And where were their parents, their mother? It was a desperate sight and her thoughts turned to Ursula Thornborrow. From what she had been told, she believed the elderly woman's childhood had been wretched; so much so she had run away from home at twelve years old. Had she also been forced to sit on the kerbside begging for food, for help? And over fifty years later, these little girls were living a childhood no better than Mrs Thornborrow's. Would these girls be forced into prostitution too? It didn't bear thinking of and as Antheia watched them munch on the sugared buns, she felt desperate to help them.

"You can't help everyone, dear cousin," said Will, taking her hand. He knew that expression on her face very well.

She turned to him, tears in her eyes. "Oh, Will, I never realised. But something must be done for them. Perhaps when you're the earl you could go down to the House of Lords and pass a law to help them."

"It's the Commons that create the laws, but yes, I can use my influence to do something." He smiled he had managed to change her expression from one of despair to one of happiness. He wanted to make this trip a wonderful memory. But there was no getting away from the poor of Liverpool. "Do you fancy a sugared currant bun? I know I do. Let's find a teashop and have a pot of tea and then it'll nearly be time for the recital."

"Yes, I'm looking forward to it."

It was another early start, since the receptionist informed them a message had been received the *Flying Cloud* had been spotted in Liverpool Bay and was making its way along the Mersey by tug. It should be safely in Victoria Dock by six o'clock at the latest. They had ordered a pot of tea and slices of toast to their rooms, but it wasn't long before they were in a hansom and speeding the five miles to the docks. They were dropped off and all Antheia could see was the bustle of a port with its stevedores, dock workers and the forest of masts and funnels of the many ships already docked.

Will pointed. "There she is and just docked by the looks of it."

Antheia's heart speeded up, but Will was right. The gangway hadn't been put in place yet and the passengers were standing at the rail looking out over the port. She couldn't see him at first, as her eyes swept along the many people laughing and gesturing from high above her, the relief on their faces plain to see their voyage was behind them. And then she did see him. He was standing a little way from the main throng of passengers, wearing a brown suit with a cream waistcoat and cravat. She smiled he still wore the military hat he had worn the year before and right through his time as a soldier, only this time she saw the glint of the regimental badge and the gold cord round the base of the crown.

"He hasn't seen us," smiled Will. "What a surprise he's going to get."

They waved and to her dismay, Joel seemed to be occupied with looking out over the dock. Perhaps he was studying where he could get a cab to the railway station, but vehicles waited outside the large port building dealing with the needs of passengers coming and going from the docks.

He had shaved off his moustache and she was wondering why, when his gaze shifted to the quayside and a look of utter surprise crossed his face. He moved along the rail and waved and then he called something the cousins couldn't hear; his words lost in the noise of a busy port. But his smile was one of delight and when the gangway was pulled into place and the passengers streamed along it, they waited for him to come down.

Antheia had forgotten how tall he was and as they hurried towards him, she held back her tears at the sight of his right sleeve pinned neatly in two. Will put his hand under her elbow and guided her towards their visitor and when they met, offered his hand to his friend. Realising he couldn't shake with his right, he exchanged it for his left.

"You'll have to get used to this, old friend," said Joel, his voice husky. He turned to Antheia and noticed her eyes pooling. His expression softened. "Now I hope those are happy tears. I don't want you to feel sad for me," he said gently.

His face flushed slightly and she realised he had suddenly become embarrassed at the loss of his arm. She smiled and before she knew it, she flung herself forward and her arms encompassed him as she pressed her cheek on the front of his jacket. His arm came round her and held her close. Even though he only had one limb, she was aware his embrace was tight and his strength amazed her.

"We're being left behind," laughed Will, looking at the passengers disappearing into the port building. "But I guess we have time."

Joel caressed Antheia's face and as she looked up into his, she saw something different in his eyes. A man who had experienced war didn't come home unscathed. The experience would live with him for the rest of his life.

"Welcome back," she whispered.

His lips brushed hers ever so slightly and a warm feeling gushed through her. Joel lifted his face and grinned at his friend. "This is wonderful. I didn't realise I would be met. I was contemplating the journey to the train station."

Will came closer and nodded. "We've left our luggage at the Adelphi so we thought we would go back for breakfast, before starting our journey home."

"That's a good idea. Now where's my trunk?"

Antheia was more than happy to leave her cousin to sort out the luggage and with Joel's arm still round her, as if he was reluctant to let her go, they followed him towards the port building and the waiting cabs.

CHAPTER THIRTY-EIGHT

Antheia could hardly remember the walk through the port building or the cab ride back to the hotel. But once there, she heard Will ask the cabby to wait for them and then instruct the commissionaire to take their bags out to the cab, before going into the dining room for a substantial breakfast.

"Did you have a good voyage?" she asked, after they were settled with plates of toast, egg and bacon and a large pot of tea and another of coffee.

Joel nodded. "It was a fine crossing, except for one night and one day of rather blustery weather. I had a cabin to myself and believe it or not, a steward to look after my needs."

She saw him trying to cut his bacon. "May I help you?"

He looked up quizzically. "Ma warned me as she waved me off, I mustn't be too proud to ask for help."

Antheia reached across and cut his bacon into bite size pieces. "It serves as a lesson to walk in someone else's shoes and experience what they experience. Young Leonard decided to come to school and spend the entire lesson with his eyes closed, after he met a young boy who was blind. He wanted to know what it was like to be without sight. He had to do his arithmetic in his head and that was fun." Was she babbling? She hoped she wasn't making a fool of herself.

Joel chuckled. "Your tower schoolroom? How's that going?" He turned to his friend. "I heard you know all about it."

"Everyone knows about it now," grinned Will.

Yes, thought Anthea, a momentous day when receiving news about Joel's injury; her uncle's revelation he knew about the children and the day Longmire...Her heart speeded up. She had a great deal of explaining ahead of her.

Anthea quickly told Joel how her uncle's kindness had made everything so much easier for her and added, "I didn't mention it in my letters as I thought it would be clearer to explain it to you in person. And to tell you the truth, all I could think of was your coming to England."

"Ma brought your letters to me, while I was in hospital, and read them to me. And then when I arrived home, there were more waiting for me." He squeezed her hand. "Your many letters helped me during the war and afterwards, while I was recovering."

Their eyes met and they only looked away from each other when Will coughed. "I never realised how difficult it is being a chaperone."

"You'll get used to it," smiled Anthea.

"But not too quickly, eh? I want to take my time getting to know you all over again," added Joel.

The journey home to Sedgwick Abbey was spent pleasantly, although Joel fell asleep on the train to Lancaster. The cousins stayed silent and let him rest, realising three months was not a long time to recover from an amputation. But he was fully awake as they trotted down the lane towards the wrought iron gates leading into the grounds.

Joel sat forward. "Well, would you look at that!"

Anthea smiled. "Do you like them? I read that's what they do in America for returning soldiers."

He pulled her close and kissed the top of her head. "It's amazing. Thank you, my darlin'."

The gatekeeper had opened the gates and nodded as they passed the fluttering streams of yellow ribbons tied to the swirling metalwork of leaves and flowers.

Antheia chuckled. "Matty helped me although she wondered at the strange traditions across the Atlantic."

"A tradition only started during this conflict I believe," nodded Joel. "I guess it will die out once peace comes."

Antheia didn't answer. The war raging in America seemed such a long way away and didn't seem to matter now that Joel was at her side.

When they arrived home Antheia was delighted how Joel became the centre of attention, even though at times he seemed amused at the fuss made of him.

Mrs Hadwin had prepared his usual room and Lord Sedgwick had appointed Charlie as his valet, a role he enjoyed when valeting for Viscount Keasden when he was home. Two young gentlemen were no problem to a footman who relished the promotion and felt he had kudos over Albert, the earl's rather stuffy valet.

But after dinner, Joel needed to go to his room early and although Antheia missed his presence in the drawing room after the meal, she understood he would need to rest a great deal while he recuperated.

She slept badly that night, her thoughts turbulent at the decision she had made to tell Joel as soon as possible about her betrothal.

By five o'clock she couldn't stay in bed any longer and crossed the rug to draw back the curtains. It was a beautiful summer's day and she decided to get dressed and go out into the garden. Washing her hands and face, she slipped into her simple blue gown and tucked her hair into the gold-coloured hairnet.

She collected her cloak and boots as she left the room and crept past the other bedrooms and down the stairs, only stopping to sit on the bottom step to put on her boots, before leaving the Abbey at the rear entrance. The sun was on the far side of the Abbey and much of the garden was in shadow, but it was still warm and the rain shower in the night caused an overwhelming perfume to fill the air.

She strolled through the trelliswork of blooms and made her way towards the fountain of Puck and Oberon. She was almost at the gazebo when she heard someone chuckling.

"You're wearing the same clothes you wore when I first met you."

Antheia turned her head to see Joel rising from the bench. "Oh, you're up early." She walked towards him, took his hand and they sat comfortably together. Looking down at her dress, she nodded. "Yes, this was what I wore that day. I'm surprised you remembered."

"I remember everything about that day."

"And what a fool I was lying on Bartholomew's tomb."

"Bartholomew?"

"Will told me it was the tomb of the sixth Earl of Sedgwick."

"I thought the earls were buried in the family mausoleum?"

"I'll tell you the story one day." She squeezed his hand. "Did you sleep well?"

"Unbelievably well. It's so peaceful here. I was asleep as my head touched the pillow and didn't wake up till gone four. I've always been an early riser and the army made it more so." He smiled at her. "So, you're up early since you have school today? I would love to see your amazing tower schoolroom."

Antheia laughed. "It's August. Summer holidays."

"Indeed it is."

Silence fell between them as they studied the garden stretched out in front of them. George passed them pushing his wheelbarrow and doffed his cap, a huge grin spread across his features.

"The servants think we are a…well, Matty thinks we're like Elizabeth and Darcy in *Pride and Prejudice*."

"I thought Elizabeth didn't care for Darcy at the beginning," he frowned.

"I think she means we're a great love story."

He went quiet for a few seconds. "And is it a love story, Antheia?"

She raised his hand to her lips and kissed it. "I do hope so. I realise our courting has been mainly by correspondence, but I know I had feelings for you long before you left for America."

He removed his hand and placed it round her waist. "The disadvantages of having one arm, is I can't hold you in my arms, plural, as much as I'd like to."

"We'll get used to it." She changed the subject. "When do you return to Cambridge?"

"Not until after October."

She tried to remain nonchalant even though it seemed too soon. "Plenty of time then."

"Yes and I did hope perhaps this time next year, you would be in a position to accompany me."

Antheia turned her head to stare at him. "Is that some sort of marriage proposal Captain Newton?"

"I don't want to rush it, ma'am. We've a lot to consider. For example, will you be happy leaving Sedgwick Abbey and living in Cambridge?"

"I think I might," she said coyly.

They burst into laughter at the absurdity of their conversation and then the smile faded, as Antheia knew she had to clear the air before they could go any further.

"Do you remember my letters when I wrote *cor meum semper sit vera* at the end?"

He nodded. "I do. My heart will always be true. I thought it a wonderful sentiment. But I was confused why you wrote it." She rose from her seat and walked to the entrance of the gazebo. She must tell him and now. The longer she left it the worse it would be. "What is it my darlin'? You can tell me anything, you know that."

She turned and gritted her teeth. "I wrote it because I wanted you to be absolutely sure of my feelings towards you."

"Yes, I understand," he said, watching her.

She spoke hurriedly. "Especially since I...I became betrothed to...the Reverend Horace Longmire."

His expression changed from one of love to confusion. "You're engaged to be married to the vicar of St James's?"

She couldn't sit next to him and drew up a chair. "Only for six weeks and I had my reasons."

He narrowed his eyes at her. "Well, soldier, they'd better be good or you'll be digging latrines and standing extra hours on guard duty for the next month."

She bit her lip. "This is serious, Joel!"

He tipped his head and the brim of his hat fell across his eyes. "Serious! Then it could be a more severe punishment, such as standing on a log and wearing a placard."

"What would the placard say," she asked hesitantly.

"How about 'I love one man but decided to become betrothed to another'?"

He needed her explanation and so she started from the beginning and told him everything. About the terrible day she was called to her aunt's rooms and their threats against Mrs Thornborrow. How she couldn't bear for her to lose her home and had promised herself to the Reverend Longmire, only until she could decide what to do.

"And what did you decide to do?"

She shrugged. "Well, it kind of worked itself out. For some strange reason Longmire left the area. I don't know why, but suddenly he was gone. And then my uncle offered Mrs Thornborrow and Jemima a lovely cottage in Patterdale Lane."

"Would you have married him if he hadn't disappeared?"

She stared at him. "Certainly not!" Sighing, she stared down at her clenched hands. "I got myself into such a pickle. But I wouldn't have married that despicable man believe you me."

He reached across and enclosed his hand round hers. "I knew you didn't like him and guessed immediately you wouldn't have engaged yourself to him without a good reason."

"You know me very well." She glanced at the flowers surrounding her. To talk about Longmire in such a beautiful place seemed a travesty. "I'm sorry Joel, It was the last thing I would have done. Will knew what I was doing and why. He supported me and tried to help me find a solution."

"I think I ought to have a word with your aunt."

She jumped up from the chair and sat next to him. "No, please, don't do that! You see, Will and I have another problem to deal with. A mystery actually, concerning the countess."

"Tell me."

"Not before you say you forgive me. Please say you do."

His arm slipped round her. "What you're forgetting, my darlin', is you hadn't promised yourself to me at the time. We were friends. Loving friends, granted, but you were free to do what you wished."

"But I wrote and told you how much I cared for you."

He shook his head slowly. "You were still a free woman and had you written to say your attentions had turned to another man, then I would have had to accept it."

"I wouldn't have done that to a man fighting in a war!"

He thought for a moment. "I've known many a woman pledge herself to a man serving his country and come to regret it in time. I wouldn't have wished that on you."

She raised her face to kiss his cheek, but he turned and their lips met. His arm tightened round her and she relaxed against him. How different Joel's kisses were from Longmire's, even though the vicar had never kissed her lips. She shuddered at the thought.

Their kiss ended and he raised his face. "Does that show you I forgive you?" When she nodded he said, "So, what's this mystery you and Will are involved in?"

"Perhaps Will and I should tell you together. After breakfast. It's a mystery that happened before I was born and it can wait a little longer."

"Suits me fine."

They rose from the bench and arm in arm, made their way back to the Abbey.

CHAPTER THIRTY-NINE

Later in the estate office, Joel was told everything. "It seems circumstantial evidence," he said. "Not much to go on at all."

Antheia glanced at Will and sighed. "We know. The saucer in the tunnel and Mrs Thornborrow's suspicions as well as my mother's letter, doesn't amount to much. But it's all we've got."

"And your father married his stepmother?" said Joel, disbelieving.

Will nodded. "A fact I learned only recently."

"And quite permissible under the law," added Antheia. "The common denominator is everyone can't believe my grandmother would leave her family. So if something happened to her then she must…have been disposed of."

"And I've been searching the estate for any possible ways to dispose of her."

"You're talking about nearly thirty years ago," sighed Joel.

Antheia looked at him seriously. "Yes, and in normal circumstances we would forget it, since it's possible the perpetrators are long gone. But suspicion has fallen on my aunt and she's still very much alive. And if she did this awful thing, then she should be brought to justice." Antheia thought of her uncle's visit to Mrs Thornborrow. "Perhaps my uncle is already suspicious." She turned to her cousin. "Should Joel know?" Will agreed and Antheia told Joel what she had witnessed that day, when she had seen her uncle at Bluebell Cottage. "Mrs Thornborrow said he was interested in her potions and he asked questions about Aunt Frances and our grandmother."

"And by all accounts was very distressed about it," Will murmured.

"He would. It's not something a man wants to hear," said Joel. "But you still don't know if it's the truth or how significant this is."

Will blew out a breath. "And that's the problem."

Joel studied the young couple and sadness swept through him; their faces so full of concern. Perhaps it was the war, but he wanted to think of the present and the future not the past. He had never taken to the countess; finding her haughty and unfeeling, but a murderess? It was a far stretch and useless to speculate. He glanced at Antheia and thought of their future together. They had such a lot to look forward to.

She realised he was looking at her and smiled. "What do you want to do today?"

"I'd like to go for a walk along the cliffs. Perhaps go down on the shingle if the tide is out."

She took his hand. "Then that's what we'll do."

Will shooed them out of the office door. "Yes, go and leave me in peace. Some of us have work to do. Don't forget to collect Matty on your way out."

Antheia pulled a face at Joel. "I drive myself into the village regularly and run a school, but when it comes to you, I must have a chaperone."

He answered with raised eyebrows.

In effect, Matty proved to be an excellent chaperone and sat on the cliff top, while her mistress took her beloved down to the shingle. She could see them foreshortened, looking at the rockpools and picking up shells. As she enjoyed the sun on her face and a little time to herself, she smiled at the couple on the sand. They were well suited and she wouldn't be surprised if a betrothal wasn't announced quite soon. She turned her head as movement by the trees caught her attention. For a second or two, she thought a dark figure hovered, waiting and watching. But when shielding her eyes from the sun, there was nothing there.

It was at lunch when Antheia noticed Joel's pale and tired face, his demeanour sagging under the busyness of the morning.

"Would you do me a favour this afternoon?" she asked.

He turned to her. "Anything you ask."

"I promised your mother I would be mindful of your health and I would like you take some rest this afternoon."

He stirred his coffee. "You think I look tired?"

"Not tired, just weary. And if you take a short nap, you might be fine for staying with me after dinner this evening."

"A good trade off." He tried to stifle a yawn. "Yes, you're probably right. Perhaps a short nap wouldn't go amiss."

"Excellent. I'm going to drive into Brawton. I've realised I promised to buy some more yarn for one of the parishioners. She's knitting for her new grandchild and can't get out much because of her poorly legs."

He squeezed her hand. "Then you go to Brawton and I'll see you for afternoon tea."

They stood together and walked out into the hallway. She watched him climb the stairs and was grateful she had made the suggestion. The last thing she wanted was for him to do too much and jeopardise his health.

Charlie came from below stairs carrying a pair of boots.

"Oh, Charlie, Mr Joel has gone up to his room. Will you make sure he's all right?"

"I will, Miss Antheia. I'm going up now and I'll see him settled."

She paused before asking, "Have you seen his...wound?"

He nodded, "Yes, miss, last night and Mrs Hadwin was there too. She wanted to check how he was."

"What's it like? His arm."

"According to the housekeeper the surgeon did a fine job. It's almost healed, although there's a bit of scarring. But all in all a tidy piece of work." He added casually, "Of course his second wound is hardly noticeable."

She let out a gasp and rocked back on her heels. "His second wound!"

His eyes opened wide. "Yes, he was struck in the side, although it seemed the bullet went straight through. Lucky that. Half an inch and he wouldn't be here now."

Antheia didn't know how to answer and dismissed the valet with a half-smile.

"Ah, you've made him rest for a few hours?"

She turned to see her cousin at her shoulder. "Yes, I thought it for the best." She added tentatively, "Will, did you know he'd received two wounds."

Will nodded. "He told me."

"Oh, what has my poor love been through. How is he going to manage at Cambridge?"

"He wouldn't appreciate your pity, Antheia and he's an incredibly strong man, both physically and mentally. And an excellent tutor."

"What I mean, is how will he manage in a world where men aren't considered men, unless they're whole both in body and mind?"

"He'll have you."

She didn't feel appeased. "He lost his hand, but the surgeon had to remove almost his entire arm to save his life. It doesn't bear thinking about."

Will studied his shoes and smiled. "Did he tell you what happened in the hospital, when his friend returned his sword?" When she shook her head he continued, "I know you're not of a squeamish nature, so I'll tell you. When the sergeant climbed the tree to remove the sword, they were amused his hand was still curled round the hilt, as though he didn't want to let go, although in truth I suppose he had no say in the matter."

She tilted her head. "And what did they do with his hand?" Her tone was flippant, belying the feelings of horror that swept through her. How could soldiers be amused at something so terrible?

Will chuckled. "Well, they didn't give it back to him. I guess they buried it on the battlefield." Seeing tears in her eyes, he added gently, "He carried his father's sword with honour, dear cousin, remember that."

He raised her hand and kissed her fingers before leaving her. Antheia stood in the hallway for a short while, her eyes on the stairs Joel had climbed minutes before. Yes, he had her support and comfort and she would stay by his side until the day she died.

Glancing at her fob watch, she realised she must collect her outdoor clothing and be on her way. But as she travelled to the village, she couldn't understand why Joel hadn't told her about his second wound. How close he had been to death. Even without the injury to his side, he could have died from the amputation. He had been saved and now he was here with her. How grateful she felt.

Her chores completed, she decided to visit Bluebell Cottage before starting back to the Abbey. She longed to tell Mrs Thornborrow how the journey to Liverpool had gone and how Joel was faring.

The elderly woman listened with a smile, as Antheia enthused about the trip to the port and meeting Joel.

"And how was Liverpool?"

"Quite an experience I can tell you. But I was glad to be back at the Abbey."

"Well, Liverpool isn't a place I'll return to. I'm happy here."

They were standing in the back garden and Antheia couldn't believe what progress her friend had made; the garden dug over and ready for the herbs and vegetables that would grow the following year.

Squeals came from the trees where Jemima, the Garnett children and Thomas and Beatrice Hugill were taking turns on a rope swing tied to a large oak.

"They're enjoying themselves," said Antheia.

"They've been out there all morning. My, it's good to hear kiddies enjoying themselves." She took her visitor's hand. "Now, yesterday Jemima spent quite a few hours baking you some biscuits and she wants you to take them home with you."

"Oh, how sweet."

Mrs Thornborrow grinned. "Take them, but I doubt you'll eat them."

"Why ever not?"

The elderly woman gave an enigmatic smile and led her into the kitchen. The shortbread biscuits were laid out on a plate and looked delicious.

"You can try one if you wish. They won't kill you." Antheia reached for one and took a bite. They were nice to a point and then she pulled a short piece of thread from her mouth. Mrs Thornborrow nodded. "Yes, she decided to add pieces of chicken."

"Chicken!"

"I told her not to, but she insisted chicken shortbread biscuits were special."

Antheia stared down at the plate on the table. "I'd better take them. I wouldn't want to hurt her feelings."

"Brave girl," grinned her friend, pouring them into a bag and watching as Antheia put them in the pocket of her skirt.

"Perhaps I could give them to the dogs. I'm sure they'll love them."

Mrs Thornborrow patted her arm. "As long as you tell her you enjoyed them, I'm sure she'll be content."

Antheia spent the journey back to the Abbey laughing to herself. Trust Jemima to add chicken to shortbread biscuits, but she was sure Fred would enjoy them.

When she arrived at the Abbey she left the horse and gig at the stables and went straight to her room. She decided to freshen up and poured water from the jug into the bowl and washed her hands and face, before tipping the water into the bucket under the washstand. She looked in the mirror and tucked some stray auburn curls back under the gold-coloured hairnet. Leaving her room she made her way down to the hallway, wondering where Joel would be. If he were still sleeping she wouldn't want to disturb him.

She saw Winder coming through from the library. Often the household would leave books around the Abbey and the butler would collect them and place them back on the shelves.

"Where's Mr Joel?"

Winder thought for a moment. "He's up and about, Miss Antheia. I do believe I saw him walking in the gardens with Lord Keasden. I just happened to peer out of an upstairs window."

Antheia left the Abbey and made her way to the gardens. She looked across the expanse of flowerbeds and walked between the shrubs searching for them, but all was quiet and still. Suddenly, George came into view, carrying a shovel on his shoulder.

Antheia strode towards him. "Have you seen Lord Keasden and Mr Joel?"

The head gardener nodded. "They were walking towards the woodland, miss. Perhaps they've taken a stroll to the cliffs."

Antheia thanked him and hurried past the fountain and into the woods. But out in Sarah's Meadow there was nothing but the butterflies and bees floating between the buttercups and daisies, hollyhocks and poppies. She looked over the cliff, and not seeing them, took the trail down to the shingle and gazed across the salt marshes. Continuing her search, she followed the shingle, until she reached the incline leading to Far Field and the old cemetery. But they weren't there either and despondently, she decided to go back to the Abbey. This had been a silly venture as it was. She should have waited at the Abbey in the first place and not been so impetuous. She turned and started back across the field to the woodland.

The hand across her mouth and the hessian hood suddenly pulled over her head shocked her, as she was plunged into darkness. Her fingers clawed at her face, trying to remove it and she felt strong arms come round her and push her forward, forcing her to the ground. An arm came round her throat and began to choke her. She tried to fight back and in the hood, she screamed. Struggling, she found she couldn't reach the person who was now kneeling on her and pressing the air from her body. Gasping, her mouth open, she found it hard to breathe and as she fell into unconsciousness her last thoughts were, who would do this to her?

Will opened the panel with the catch and it swung open into the family chapel.

Joel followed him out. "Clever. Certainly an excellent way to escape the Abbey."

Will blew out the candle he had purloined from the kitchen. "And allow kids in as my dear cousin did at the start."

Joel grinned. "That's my Antheia for you. Full of ingenious ideas." He looked about the chapel. "We've not been in here much, so I guess the tunnel could have remained a mystery forever."

"If it hadn't been for a little girl called Jemima, who lived in a cave."

"I must meet this Jemima one day."

"I'm sure Antheia will take you to visit Mrs Thornborrow sometime soon. My cousin has made quite an impression on the folk in Brawton."

"Well, she's made quite an impression on me," smiled Joel.

Will looked at his watch. "It's time for tea."

"The quintessential English tradition."

They left the chapel and walked towards the drawing room, where afternoon tea was always set out on a large occasional table sporting a white tablecloth, Wedgwood china and silver cutlery. Tiers of sandwiches, small cakes and tarts sat amongst a large pot of tea.

"Where's my father? He's usually the first here." Will summoned the butler. "Have you called his lordship?"

"He's not at home, sir. His lordship took her ladyship out for a drive in the phaeton."

"But my stepmother never goes out unless to church."

Winder shrugged. "We were surprised, sir. But it's a beautiful day and perhaps his lordship thought it would do her good."

Will sat next to Joel and helped himself to a sandwich. "That's strange and where's Miss Antheia? Do you know?"

The butler nodded. "Ah, now she returned from Brawton and asked where Mr Joel would be. I mentioned I'd seen you both going out into the garden."

Will turned to his friend. "We must have been on our way to explore the hatch in the woodland. Not to worry, she'll be here any minute."

The maid served them tea and Joel looked towards the door, his unease growing by the minute. He wasn't worried about the earl and countess, but Antheia was a different matter. If she didn't appear in ten minutes he would set off to look for her.

It was dark and Antheia blinked hard, wondering if she had actually opened her eyes. Reaching up, she felt smooth marble only six inches above her nose and then her hands worked their way round, to feel the smooth coldness on either side of her. Where was she? She shuffled and realised what she was lying on, was sharp and dug into her hip. Tentatively, she slipped her hand under the small of her back and felt rough, dry cloth, causing her to pull her hand away in disgust.

After a few minutes of catching her breath and calming herself, she examined what was under her again and felt the dust encrusted cloth more carefully. She lifted her back slightly and was certain under the cloth there were jagged lumps, although she couldn't work out what.

And then a miracle happened. As her eyes adjusted to the darkness, she realised there was a small amount of light filtering into her prison. A small sliver of light in the marble, three inches above the side of her head. She lifted herself on her elbow and peered through a gap, some six inches long and an inch wide. What she saw made her cry out in fear. Broken and leaning gravestones and monuments stretched in front of her and as her heart thumped wildly making her gasp, she knew where she was. She was in the sarcophagus in the old cemetery and the lumps under her, were the bones of Bartholomew, the sixth Earl of Sedgwick.

Joel drank back his tea. "I'm going to find her. I can't sit here when I feel something is wrong."

Will agreed. "Better to go in search of her. This is very unlike my cousin."

They left the drawing room and headed out to the garden. Even though it was a splendid afternoon, the sun making the colours of the flowers vibrant, Joel scanned his eyes along the paths, his concentration only on one person.

They strode quickly between the borders and beds, searching the gazebo and any other areas where Antheia might be. Turning the corner they came across George squatting by a flowerbed, pulling out weeds and throwing them into a wheelbarrow. Fred was sitting in the sun on the path and came to his feet as the men approached.

"Have you seen Miss Antheia?" said Will, stroking the dog's head.

George gestured towards the woodland. "Well, sir, she asked where you might be and I thought you'd gone into the woodland. The last I saw of her, she was going in that direction."

"Then so will we," nodded Joel. "Perhaps she's gone down to the shingle and forgotten the time."

"She's always preparing for her lessons," said Will hopefully.

"But there's no lessons at the moment," replied Joel. "It's the summer vacation."

"So it is." They started towards the woodland, but Will stopped and whistled. "Come on, Fred, we have need of you." The dog dutifully bounded towards him and got a pat for his obedience. "Where is she, boy? Where's Miss Antheia?"

Joel's heart beat furiously. Every instinct was screaming at him and yet he couldn't let himself believe she had come to any harm. They'll find her walking on the sands of the estuary. It would be as simple as that. They would find her and then he would chastise her for worrying him, before holding her close and kissing her face, cheeks, eyes and lips. He tried to shake off the ominous thoughts, but anxiety made his mouth dry and his breathing arduous.

CHAPTER FORTY

Antheia tried not to panic. She had a small amount of light filtering in when, whoever had put her in the sarcophagus, hadn't replaced the lid fully. But what would she do once the sun went down and she was plunged into an unbearable inky blackness? She thought of Joel and her cousin. They would miss her and surely look for her, but would they think to come into the old cemetery? They must, since the thought of being buried alive horrified her. She would have air, but she had nothing to drink and thirst was already making her throat dry.

She coughed and the smell of the tomb rose up to choke her. It was the stink of death and decay, of dust and the debris of a tomb that had not been disturbed for many centuries.

Placing her lips as near to the gap as possible, she called as loudly as she could. "Help! Please help me!"

Looking through the opening, all she saw were the gravestones and she knew help wouldn't come from the inhabitants lying peacefully beneath the soil.

They made their way down the track to the shingle and hurried along, the Irish Setter ambling after them. They had resorted to calling for Antheia, but it was plain to see she wasn't near.

Will looked down at the dog. "Come on, Fred, find her! You're bred for hunting, for goodness sake!"

Joel's eyes swept across the sand. He didn't like the thought, but they needed to examine the rockpools. Some were shallow; others were quite deep and could swallow a person. He was relieved when no rockpools near the cliff contained anything untoward and suggested examining those a little further out. Again, nothing disturbing floated in them.

Finally, they reached the incline half a mile along the shingle and climbed it to Far Field. In the distance was the chapel and cemetery.

Will gestured towards the burial ground. "We'd better go across and search the graveyard and perhaps the chapel. If she's taken ill, she might be lying behind one of the monuments."

The horrifying idea made Joel pick up the pace across the field, leaving his friend to catch up.

Antheia tried to push her fingers through the gap and when that didn't work, she raised her knees to attempt to push the top to one side. But there wasn't room and her knees simply slid off the marble.

The voices from outside made her inhale painfully. She couldn't work out who they were although it was men's voices. And then she saw them making their way round the monuments and she knew they were searching for her.

"Joel! I'm here! I'm here!"

She could see him and Will too, but they were too far away to hear her. Their voices started to fade as they moved away and she gave out a desperate scream. She heard barking. They had Fred with them! Groping into the pocket of her skirt, she found Jemima's biscuits and spilt them across her chest. She pulled off her hairnet and wrapped a few biscuits inside, twisting them in a small bundle and finally pushing it through the gap, but holding tightly to the hairnet.

"Well, she doesn't seem to be here," said Will. "Look, old friend, let's go back to the Abbey. She's probably there now waiting for us."

"I guess she could be," said Joel reluctantly. The thought raised his hopes. And no doubt she would chastise them for wasting time searching for her, when she had been in the library all the time. Or the morning room writing a letter. But if she had been in the Abbey, she would have come to the drawing room for afternoon tea. No matter where the family where, they would always meet up at mealtimes.

Calling Fred, they started towards the woodland convinced they had been on a fool's errand, but the dog's barking stopped them.

"Come on, you stupid dog!" shouted Will. "We're going now." But Fred wasn't having it and kept sniffling round the sarcophagus. "Oh, blazes! He's probably going after a rodent. We'll leave him to it. He knows the way home."

Hearing Fred's bark heartened her. She had managed to squeeze the biscuits through the gap and her intention was to lure the dog, but hang onto the hairnet in order to alert Joel and her cousin. It wasn't long before a sniffling and snorting made her shout with delight, as a wet nose appeared at the gap and began to chew on the hairnet.

"Fred! I'm in here." Fred stopped, his front paws raised to lift himself to the small gap. But he wanted the delicious biscuits and went back to his chewing. He angled his head so the net was in the corner of his mouth and pulled with all his strength.

Antheia let out a scream as the hairnet was wrenched from her fingers and Fred's snuffling moved away and silence ensued. She lay back and tears trickled down the side of her face, to drip on the cloth under which lay the bones of Will's ancestor. Her hand dropped to her side and she knew all was

365

hopeless. How could anyone find her in this marble tomb?

Her hand fell to the side and slid off a ledge. Surprised, she felt about her and realised the sixth earl must have been placed in a casket and she was lying on it. But if the earl was in a casket then what were the sharp objects underneath the blanket on which she lay? Had the coffin lid caved in? To the side of her, she could feel marble and not the inside of a coffin. Leaning to one side, she stretched her arm over the edge until her hand touched an object lying at the bottom of the sarcophagus. Feeling about, she recognised it as a bag and by the texture a carpetbag, the metal clasp open. Her fingers explored inside and hooked a piece of crockery. Pulling it towards her so she could see it in the ray of sunlight, she gave out a gasp. It was a china teacup with a garland of forget-me-nots painted round the edge.

Once in the gardens, they decided to go their separate ways. Will to set up a search of the entire Abbey, Joel to sit in the gazebo while he waited for his friend to return. He and Antheia had sat together there that morning making tentative plans and the very thought made him clench his fist. He had arrived at the Abbey only the day before and surely nothing terrible could have happened to her. He studied his boots.

"Where are you, goddammit!" he whispered. "Antheia, please come back to me." He saw Fred ambling along the path, throwing his head from side to side and now and again, rubbing his jaw on the concrete path. "What's the matter, boy, come here." Joel sighed, as the Irish Setter loped towards him.

Fred lifted his head and Joel noticed he had something caught on a tooth; something that dangled down his face, dark with saliva. Grimacing, Joel unhooked it and spread the piece of netting through his fingers, ignoring the brown, slimy liquid oozing through it. He frowned and then giving out a cry, jumped to his feet to hurry across to the fountain where he plunged it into the water and swished it backwards and forwards. The material was in tatters, but he could still see the gold colour of Antheia's hairnet.

He stared at Puck and Oberon for thirty seconds, thinking, before turning on his heel and striding across to the head gardener still kneeling at the flowerbed.

Giving orders came easily to him. "George, go to the Abbey and find Lord Keasden. Tell him to meet me at the old cemetery in Far Field. And I want you to collect a crowbar and follow him. And hurry!"

George rose to his feet. "Yes, sir. I'll go now."

Joel barely watched him hurry down the path, before he was running towards the woodland.

Antheia lay quietly, holding the teacup to her, caressing its smooth surface. She thought about her abduction and being flung to the ground, the bag pulled over her head. But anger filled her when she remembered the hand over her mouth was cold and clammy and the distinctive body odour, before being rendered insensible. Yes, she had had to suffer the Reverend Horace Longmire too many times to mistake his obnoxious proximity. But why would he do this to her? Unless he knew of Joel's arrival and was filled with bitterness and rage.

"Am I going to die in here?" she whispered into the silence. "Please someone find me."

She felt someone's presence. A warm and comforting presence. She heard a voice, although she couldn't work out if she was hearing it or feeling it.

367

The sound floated around her in a soft echo, almost a sigh.

"Hold fast, dear child. Stay strong. I am here. You are not alone."

"Who are you? Mother?"

"Evil can win battles, but never the war," the voice said and faded to a whisper.

"Don't leave me. Stay with me." Antheia felt sure it was her mother's voice she heard.

She closed her eyes and calmed herself.

Noise from outside drifted into the sarcophagus and Antheia lifted herself on her elbow and looked through the opening. A bright light swept across her eyes and for a moment she saw the shimmer of a regimental badge.

She pushed the handle of the cup through the gap and rattled it against the marble, calling Joel's name as loudly as her dry throat would allow her.

"Antheia! Darlin', we're going to get you out. George is bringing a crowbar. Just wait a while longer."

She heard other voices and then the grind and crunch of the marble slab being lifted. The sunlight and fresh air rushing into her tomb, making her cry out with relief. She flung her arms round Joel's neck and he lifted her out in one swift movement, her long auburn hair sweeping over his shoulder, as she clung onto him for dear life. How he managed to hoist her out with one arm, she couldn't imagine, but suddenly her body was tight against him and she buried her face against his chest; his warmth and firmness the most secure thing in the world. She didn't want to let go. For a few seconds he held her close, before setting her on her feet, his arm still tightly round her. She turned to see Will and George staring at her in bewilderment.

In minutes, she had told them what had happened and who had done it.

"He's going to have to answer to the law," said Will, bitterly.

"Providing I don't get to him first," breathed Joel through his teeth.

Antheia looked up into Joel's face and saw a look of hate she had never seen before. The fact he only had one arm, wouldn't have deterred him from meting out his own form of justice.

"Leave it to Will. And Uncle Henry is a magistrate. They'll find him and he'll pay for what he's done," nodded Antheia.

"That's if we can find Father and Stepmother," murmured her cousin.

His statement didn't impact on her, as her eyes had turned to George and his expression of complete horror. He was staring into the sarcophagus and Antheia followed his gaze and grimaced. She was looking at a piece of white bone sticking out from the tattered and dirty tartan blanket.

"There's something there," she whispered.

Will stepped forward and leaned over to draw back the rotten fabric that came away in his hands. Underneath was a small skeleton, dressed in a dirty and stained nightgown, with long sleeves and the remnants of embroidery across the bodice and frills at the collar.

The four standing at the sarcophagus stared at each other.

Antheia lifted the cup she hadn't been able to let go of. "It's Grandmother." She turned to Will. "We've found her."

CHAPTER FORTY-ONE

The earl and countess were missing and Will rode to the village to make enquiries, while George and his men fetched a cart and carried the remains of Sarah, Countess of Sedgwick, back to the Abbey. Within two hours the lid of the sarcophagus was replaced, leaving the sixth earl to his rest.

Antheia went straight to her room and Matty prepared a bath for her. Even clean and dressed in fresh clothes, she wondered if she would ever forget the smell of the tomb or the horror of being incarcerated.

Although Matty suggested she rest, Antheia knew she wouldn't be able to close her eyes and insisted on joining Joel in the drawing room. Sitting on the sofa together, they waited patiently for Will to return. And when he finally jumped from his horse, all he could tell them was his father and stepmother had been seen in the village. In fact, the postmaster had told him the earl had gone into the Post Office to send a telegram and the landlord of the Red Lion said he had seen the earl and countess in the phaeton and heading for the estuary and more particularly Warton Sands.

"I've come back to tell you I've collected a band of men together and I'm leaving immediately to join the search."

Joel rose to his feet. "I'll join you."

Will took him to one side. "I know you would, my dear friend, but you are still recuperating from your injury." When Joel made to protest, Will added, "Besides I'd like you to stay here with my cousin. We can't leave her on her own after all she's been through. She'll need your company more than ever."

Joel glanced towards Antheia still sitting on the sofa and noticed her pinched, white face. Yes, she had been through too much and he should stay.

Nodding in agreement, he put his hand on his friend's shoulder. "Then God speed and I pray they haven't come to any harm."

As Will rushed out of the room, he went to sit next to Antheia and told her what Will had planned.

She gave a sigh. "It's not like my uncle to be away without saying where he's going. And my aunt rarely leaves."

He took her hand as Matty came through the door carrying her sewing basket. She grinned at the couple. "Mrs Hadwin has given me chaperone duties, Miss Antheia, but don't you worry. I'll sit over here and be as quiet as a mouse."

They smiled as she made herself comfortable in the armchair by the window and promptly opened her basket to start her embroidery.

Antheia turned to Joel. "I think I heard my mother's voice when I was trapped." She thought for a moment. "Or it could have been my grandmother's."

He raised her hand to his lips and kissed her fingers. "You were in shock and that can play havoc with your mind. I know of soldiers badly injured, who said they heard their mother's voice calling to them, while they waited for help."

She mulled this over. "But do you remember my reaction whenever I was close to the sarcophagus? I had the most overwhelming feelings of desperation, of loneliness and despair."

He nodded. "Indeed you did."

"I've never believed in the supernatural, but do you think it could have been my grandmother calling out to me to find her."

"My mother would agree. She firmly believes in the spirit world."

"And now she is found and when arrangements can be made, she'll be laid to rest with her husband."

Winder entered the room. "Dinner is being served, madam, sir."

Antheia giggled and Joel was pleased to hear her laugh. "Oh my goodness, we haven't changed for dinner. We completely forgot about it."

Joel helped her to her feet. "I'm sure Winder will forgive us this once."

Will arrived back at the Abbey at ten that evening. They had given up the search since the light was failing and while he was served a very late dinner in the dining room, Antheia and Joel decided to sit with him to keep him company and to hear what he had to say.

The fact he had little to tell them was ominous. The men on the estate and in the village had scoured the area almost to Morecambe, but there was no sign of the earl and countess.

Will pushed a small roast potato into his mouth. He found he had little appetite, but Antheia had encouraged him to eat to maintain his strength.

"What do you plan next?" she asked.

He swallowed his food. "If they haven't returned by the morning and we've had no word from them, then we're continuing the search at first light." He took a bite of carrot. "Where's Grandmother?"

Winder stepped forward. "We've placed her in the wine cellar, my lord. Mrs Hadwin is going to make her as presentable as possible for burial. That's if she can stop weeping. I've never seen her so distressed."

"I'll go down and see her. Poor woman," said Antheia.

Joel turned to Will. "Is there anything I can do?"

"Would you send a telegram to Felix tomorrow? He needs to come home. And perhaps see the undertakers since we'll have to make arrangements for the funeral? I've already informed the constabulary in Lancaster about Antheia's abduction and the discovery of our grandmother. They're sending someone as soon as possible, which means we'll have a few policemen about the place asking you questions, Antheia."

Antheia nodded, understanding. "I guess I'll have to make a statement. And then they'll try and find Longmire."

Joel nodded. "And when they do, he'll be going to prison for a long time."

"But how would it have been if I hadn't been found! Perhaps I would have been in the sarcophagus until the end of time." The thought of the marble tomb, now it was dark, filled her with horror.

Joel squeezed her hand. "I wouldn't have rested until I'd found you."

Tears pooled in her eyes. "God bless Jemima's chicken shortbread biscuits and Fred, of course." She looked at her cousin. "All we need to do is find Uncle Henry and Aunt Cora."

She left the men to talk in the drawing room, while she went below stairs to the kitchen. Mrs Hadwin was in her parlour and when Antheia stepped through the door, they were hugging, before the young girl had time to know what was happening.

"She's come home, Miss Antheia. Now we can give her a proper burial. But how are you? The servants can't believe what's happened since Mr Joel arrived."

"It's been a momentous day, I'll give you that."

"Is it true you were lying on your grandmother's bones?"

"I was. Not very comfortable, I assure you."

"But your grandmother was the kindest, gentlest soul. She wouldn't want you to be afraid of her."

"I don't think I was. In fact, I think she helped me to stay strong until I was found."

"And you found the missing pieces of the teaset. The one she loved so much and we thought she had taken with her."

"I found the cup."

"George found the plate. So, we have it intact again." Her face filled with pain. "You never told me where you found the saucer."

"In the tunnel that leads from the private chapel to the woodland."

Mrs Hadwin's eyes opened wide. "I know about the tunnel although few do. Oh, dear lord, my lady must have been taken through the tunnel and the saucer was dropped. And then she was placed in the sarcophagus. But who would do such a thing?"

"The police are arriving tomorrow and they'll discover that, as well as join the search for the Reverend Horace Longmire and my uncle and aunt."

The housekeeper shook her head. "It doesn't bear thinking about. Such evil."

"Evil can win battles but never the war," murmured Antheia.

Mrs Hadwin opened her eyes wide in surprise. "A saying your grandmother used."

Antheia couldn't believe how anyone slept that night and at breakfast it was only Joel and herself, since Will had left at dawn. How grateful she was to drive them to Brawton in the dogcart, with Matty sitting serenely on the box seat, again acting as chaperone.

They went straight to the Post Office and sent a telegram to summon Felix home and from there to the Funeral Directors to arrange an appointment for the undertaker to call at the Abbey.

While Matty did her shopping, promising to meet them outside the public house for the return journey, Antheia and Joel visited Bluebell Cottage

"I've seen you often young man and I knew I'd meet you one day," said Mrs Thornborrow.

"I'm pleased to meet you, ma'am. Antheia has told me a lot about you."

She made them sit, while she bustled into the kitchen to make a pot of tea, but Antheia insisted on helping her. "We've heard all the news here in Brawton. You being incarcerated in the old tomb and the finding of the countess's bones. And now his lordship and his wife gone. Whatever will happen next!"

Antheia set out the cups. "Once my uncle and aunt are found, we hope that's an end to it."

"Does your young man know the full story?" She glanced towards the parlour and whispered, "about her ladyship and my suspicions?"

"Yes, and it seems you might be right."

Antheia carried in the tray of tea and placed it on the occasional table.

Joel watched Mrs Thornborrow pour out the tea. "I'm afraid I overheard you and we can't be sure if her ladyship was responsible for the death of your grandmother," he mused.

Antheia smiled at him. "No, we can't, but someone ended her life." Her hair stood up on the back of her neck. "I hope to God she wasn't put in the sarcophagus alive, as I was."

Mrs Thornborrow shook her head. "I don't think that's a possibility. You were placed there out of revenge. Longmire had been spurned and the arrival of Mr Joel would have spurred him into action."

Joel sipped his tea. "But why was your grandmother put there?"

Mrs Thornborrow gave a twisted smile. "It has to be Cora. It can't be anyone else. She had set her sights on marrying the old earl and becoming a countess right from the start." She scrutinised the young man sitting on the sofa. "Are you thinking of getting a prosthesis? I've heard they've made some remarkable advances especially in America."

Antheia felt shocked at such forthrightness, but Joel seemed unaffected by her remarks and glanced at Antheia. "I wanted to speak to you about that."

"Oh, you must do what you want to do, my love," she whispered.

Mrs Thornborrow nodded. "One newspaper I read, praised the Douglass artificial limb. They said it looked almost real."

Joel sighed. "Yes, I discussed it with the surgeon and he said it's difficult to distinguish the artificial arm, from genuine flesh and blood. Quite inconspicuous." He turned to Antheia. "It's so I can blend into society without offending strangers with knowing I'm an amputee."

Antheia felt incensed. "Please don't do it on my account or society's. If we can manage when we live in Cambridge, then I'm happy for you to stay as you are." She grinned. "And may I remind you that our Lord Nelson lost his right arm and his eye, but continued with an illustrious naval career."

Joel put down his cup and ran his forefinger down the side of her face. She suddenly realised she had already got into the habit of sitting on his left side and took his hand, kissing it. Mrs Thornborrow watched with interest. There was a great deal of love between them and she nodded in satisfaction.

Jemima burst through the front door, but skidded to a stop when she saw Joel. "Oh, are you the American soldier who has one arm?"

"One and a half arms to be precise," he said, as seriously as he could.

Mrs Thornborrow put a hand on her shoulder. "Now you be polite and say hello properly."

Jemima dipped a curtsey. "I'm so pleased to meet you." She grinned. "Will you be marrying at St James's? I do hope so. Please don't get married in America. It's too far away."

Mrs Thornborrow grimaced. "She's an impossible child."

Antheia and Joel exchanged amused glances. It was Antheia who said, "When we've decided about our wedding, we'll let you know."

Joel nodded towards the little girl helping herself to a biscuit. "The child in the cave I take it?"

"Perhaps I should have left her there," laughed Antheia.

Jemima lifted her chin defiantly. "I came to tell you there's hundreds of policemen riding through the village and I think they're going to the Abbey."

Antheia sighed and placed her cup on the table. "Not hundreds I think, but time for us to go."

Antheia gave a cry of joy as she manoeuvred the dogcart into the stables and saw the phaeton.

"Oh, Joel, they're home! But I wonder where they've been?"

Joel was more hesitant. "Well, their vehicle is home. I guess we'll find out if your aunt and uncle returned with it."

He couldn't have been more astute, as they were told on entering the building, there had been no sign of the earl and countess and in fact, the horse had been found meandering home along the road from Carnforth to Brawton. Since it was only a distance of four miles, it was believed she must have been tied up somewhere and released herself.

In the Abbey there were two uniformed policemen and one inspector and immediately Antheia gave her statement wanting to get it out of the way. The inspector had already viewed the remains in the wine cellar and after speaking with Antheia, he and the constables left to join in the search for Longmire and the Earl and Countess of Sedgwick.

And as the second evening of his lord and ladyship's disappearance descended on the Abbey, the residents were filled with foreboding; the servants moving quietly about their duties as though afraid to speak aloud their terrible fears. For Antheia, Joel and Will waiting for news, any information would have been welcomed. And that would come the following morning.

CHAPTER FORTY-TWO

Mr Hayton, the family solicitor, arrived from Lancaster when the family were at breakfast and before Will was about to join the men in their continued search.

Rotund and balding with a red face caused by his exertions, he hurried into the Abbey, shedding his coat and hat as he went, but held onto a document wallet tucked under his arm.

"I must speak to Lord Keasden. Is he here?" he asked Winder, as the butler placed the coat and Bowler in the hallway cupboard.

"Yes sir, his lordship is in the breakfast room."

"Then fetch him, if you please."

The butler hurried towards the door and came back moments later with Viscount Keasden.

Will held out his hand. "Hayton! What are you doing here?"

The solicitor shook his hand and took out his handkerchief to wipe his perspiring head. "Forgive me, my lord, but I've been away in Leeds and only arrived back in Lancaster yesterday evening quite late. That is when my wife gave me your father's telegram. I had no choice but to get the early train this morning. I should have come two days ago when the telegram first arrived."

Will rocked back on his heels. "My father sent you a telegram?" He suddenly remembered the postmaster had said his father had gone into the Post Office.

Mr Hayton nodded. "And I must speak to you and your brother."

"Felix is still in London, but we're expecting him soon."

"Well, I don't think this can wait and I'd suggest, my lord, we speak in private."

Will gestured towards the earl's study. "We can go in there."

"Where's my cousin?" asked Antheia, as she and Joel left the breakfast room.

Joel listened carefully. "I think he's in your uncle's study. There's voices coming from inside."

"He must have company."

He listened again. "Well, I'll be damned. I'm sure Will is speaking to Mr Hayton."

"Who's Mr Hayton?"

"Family solicitor." He pulled his watch from his waistcoat pocket. "He's visiting early."

The door to the study opened and the solicitor came out with his arm round the young man's shoulders. Antheia crossed the floor swiftly at the sight of Will's pale face. He looked as though he would empty the contents of his breakfast any minute.

"Will! Are you all right? You look poorly," she said, resting her hand on his arm.

"I think we need to take his lordship into the drawing room," said the solicitor kindly.

The four walked into the drawing room and Will sat heavily in the armchair, leaning forward, elbows on his knees with his head in his hands.

Antheia took a seat next to Joel on the sofa giving him a quizzical glance. He replied with an imperceptible shake of his head.

"I think you'd better tell us what's happened." She couldn't prevent the slight hitch in her voice. The situation was dire, that was plain to see.

Will lifted his head. "Mr Hayton, you'd better tell them what you told me. I have too much to think about at the moment. Sit if you wish."

The solicitor studied the young people; his lordship in the armchair and a young couple his lordship had told him was his cousin and her intended.

"I'll not sit, sir, if you don't mind."

Will waved his hand in a noncommittal gesture. "As you wish."

Three pairs of eyes turned to the solicitor.

"Sirs, madam, my good friend and client the Earl of Sedgwick called at my premises in Lancaster approximately one month ago. I was surprised, as I usually attend him. However, he left me instructions. Should I receive a telegram from him then I must deliver a letter personally into the hands of his elder son and heir. Unfortunately, I only received the telegram when I arrived back from Leeds last night, otherwise I would have been here sooner."

"What was in the letter?" asked Antheia.

"I have it here," he said, patting the document wallet. He turned to Will. "Should I read it, my lord?" Will nodded. The solicitor's lips pressed into a thin line, as he untied the pouch and took out the letter. Filling his lungs with air, he said in a sombre tone, "It's very distressing and you need to brace yourselves."

Antheia slipped her hand into Joel's.

5th July 1864

My dear son and heir,

I leave this correspondence in the safe hands of my solicitor, in the sure knowledge he will follow my instructions to the letter.

I make this confession knowing I can leave the welfare of Sedgwick Abbey and all that reside there,

381

in your capable hands. You must look to the welfare of your brother and cousin for now you are the nineteen Earl of Sedgwick.

A cry echoed round the room and the solicitor looked at Antheia. "Are you all right, Miss Vale?"

Antheia nodded. "Yes. It came as such a shock." She paused. "Uncle is dead?"

Mr Hayton's expression didn't alter one bit. "I'll continue, shall I?"

My confession must start in 1836 when Cambridge was behind me and I was due to travel abroad for two years, before marrying my lovely Frances. I was barely twenty-one years old and full of pride and honour for the reputation of the family name and position in society.

When Cora, my mother's lady's maid, stirred me from sleep in the early hours of the morning and told me to follow her, I could do no other. But what I discovered, filled my heart with grief and dread.

My mother was lying in bed, her hands crossed on her breast. I saw liquid dribbling from the corner of her mouth and on her night table were many other bottles, all empty. She had consumed everything and now lay dead.

Why my mother would take her own life, I couldn't imagine and I immediately thought of the reputation of the Earls of Sedgwick and the shame to the family. At the time, there seemed to be only one course of action. I carried my poor mother's small, slight figure on my shoulder and into the private chapel. From there I took her out through the priest's tunnel and into the woodland. I thought to let the tide take her out into the Irish Sea, but instead I decided to carry her to Far Field and place her in the tomb of the sixth earl, as much as it was repugnant to me.

Cora was helpful and followed me with a carpetbag filled with my mother's possessions to make it look as though she had left the Abbey. And that's how it seemed for the family. The following morning, I had to suffer the anguish of my father and sister and pretend to search for my mother, knowing all along where she lay.

A month later and with great relief, I left for the Continent and was gone for two years. I came back to marry my Frances, although I was sad that, Anne, my sister, hadn't had a good time of it while I had been away. She had argued incessantly with Father, believing something terrible had happened to our mother. How my heart ached to tell her the truth.

My sister saw me married and then departed Sedgwick Abbey, never to return. As you know, I never set eyes on her again.

The fact my father married Cora the same year I married Frances, quite startled me. He had pushed a divorce through Parliament even though he should have waited the required seven years. His influence circumvented the law and he put his case that he needed to get on with his life.

They were married for five years before Father died and I took the title. Cora seemed content to become the dowager countess and so it was for another two years. But then Frances died shortly after giving me a second son. My grief was beyond imagining and when Cora persuaded me into marriage, for the sake of my boys, I agreed. I now know my mental faculties were impaired and I should never have ventured into such a disastrous marriage. But what was done, was done.

What I did as a young man haunted me and our lives became quiet and secluded. No more entertaining, no more balls and parties. I lived with my shame as best I could.

The arrival of my niece, Antheia, changed everything. She was a breath of fresh air and breezed through the Abbey, chasing away the cobwebs and casting light into all the murky corners of these ancient bricks.

Life was bound to change and with it the thought I had to put right what I'd done wrong. I counselled my wife we should confess my mother's suicide and allow her a decent Christian burial. I couldn't think after nearly thirty years it would matter if she were interred in the family mausoleum next to my father. Cora simply sneered at me and her mocking laugh shocked me. She then told me, when lady's maid to my mother, she had visited Mrs Thornborrow in Brawton and gained knowledge of certain herbs. She went on to tell me how she had given my mother a concoction of potions that would end her life. I was horrified and more so when she turned the knife by saying she had dispensed with my wife, Frances.

She sounded utterly insane and I decided to visit Mrs Thornborrow, since she had attended my wife at the birth of Felix and I respected her greatly. I demanded the truth and she told me plainly her suspicions.

And so, my dear son, I come to the end. For it is the end and my cruel secret must now be known to all. You will find my mother's remains in the tomb of the sixth earl and my wish is that she lies next to my father. It is where she belongs.

As for Cora, I have lulled her into thinking she is forgiven and all is forgotten. But not so. Her madness and my shame cannot be endured. I intend driving her out to Warton Sands and there we will die together in the quicksand. I believe it's the only unconsecrated ground we deserve.

Please forgive me, but all is settled in my last will and testament. Take care of the family and I hope one day you will think kindly of me.

Your loving father
Henry, Earl of Sedgwick

CHAPTER FORTY-THREE

Even after reading his father's letter, Will continued the search with extensive examination of Warton Sands and the stretches of quicksand. But nothing could be found. He began to believe his father had set up a decoy and in fact, the earl and countess had simply gone to live on the Continent. But a perusal of the family accounts showed all was as it should be and no monies withdrawn. They would have needed money to live on, although Joel was quick to point out Lord Sedgwick might have had other accounts, unknown to the family, secreted away in France or Italy. They would never know. Over the next ten days, a silence settled over the Abbey, the residents speaking in whispers, as though laughter and even smiling was painful to do.

Felix returned home and although his speculations didn't prove completely accurate, he felt vindicated in his suspicions about his grandmother's unwarranted burial. Antheia found it was her younger cousin she had to comfort more, since his distress at his father's disappearance and supposed demise was difficult for him to endure.

For Antheia, the arrest of the Reverend Horace Longmire came as a relief. Stopped at Dover before crossing the Channel to France, he now awaited trial at Lancaster. She knew with Joel's support, the coming trial would be easier to bear.

Two days before Sarah's funeral, they collected in the drawing room to hear the earl's last will and testament and Antheia discovered she had inherited the sum of £6,000 plus Bluebell Cottage, all put in trust for her until her twenty-first birthday or when she married. Will was to be the trustee and she knew her legacy couldn't be in safer hands.

Antheia and Joel came out into the gardens, walking slowly through the trellis of roses, their thoughts distant. That morning they had attended the funeral of her grandmother and seeing her interred next to her husband proved healing. More so for Antheia, as she thought of the woman who had died long before she had been born and whose tomb she had shared for three hours that fearful afternoon.

But that beautiful day in the middle of August, they had snatched some time alone together, as they made their way to the gazebo and took a seat on the bench.

"All this will pass, my darlin'," said Joel, holding her hand.

She nodded and brushed an imaginary piece of thread from her black gown. "I know, but why is it everything happened when I arrived here? Did I stir up the muddy waters? Perhaps I should have let things be. Folk were content enough before I arrived."

"You heard what your uncle said. You were a breath of fresh air to blow away the cobwebs and cast some light on the matter."

"But everything happened such a long time ago." She thought for a moment. "Although I must admit I'm more than relieved my grandmother has been laid to rest."

"I think it was meant to be. I believe that's why you came to the Abbey in the first place. To put right what was wrong."

"That's what Mrs Thornborrow said." She looked up into blue eyes and saw his love for her. "It feels strange we're returning to normal life. Well, as normal as it can be. Felix is leaving soon for the academy."

"Not until next month and I won't be going until October. Will is staying and you must continue with your teaching."

"I shall miss you so much when you do leave."

"I'm only going to Cambridge and I want you and Will to visit me, with Matty in tow of course. And I'll be here at the Abbey every holiday. Your cousin has given me an open invitation."

"Felix has said we must travel to London and attend his performances." She nodded. "Yes, life goes on." She gave a sigh. "At least you're not crossing the Atlantic to fight in the war."

"I thank God for that."

"And we have Miss Sill's wedding to enjoy," she said brightly.

In two weeks' time, Miss Eliza Sill would marry her fiancé and Antheia had gifted her the bolt of heavy, white satin material and luxurious lace, given to her by her aunt all those months ago. The delight on the seamstress's face was a joy to see and helped Antheia to start the healing process.

From under his military hat, his eyes sparkled. "I have other plans too. In the spring I want you to come with me to Cape Elizabeth and spend time in my home town and meet my mother." He grinned. "And Matty too, of course. I wouldn't want to offend."

Her breath hitched. "Cross the Atlantic? Oh, my!"

His expression softened as he enjoyed her excitement. But then he became serious. "I want the most important women in my life, to be there when I see the appropriate folk for an artificial limb."

Antheia frowned. "But I told you it wouldn't..."

He placed a finger on her lips to stop her and then followed this with stroking them gently with his thumb. "No, Antheia, I've given it plenty of thought." He glanced at his jacket sleeve pinned double. "It won't be any help to me, but it will make my uniform appear more acceptable." He smiled mischievously. "And I'll be able to put two arms round you."

"Make your uniform appear acceptable! But I thought you'd resigned your commission?" Was he re-enlisting? Surely not!

"I have. But I'm permitted to wear my uniform for special occasions," he chucked her under the chin, "including a wedding."

"Now whose wedding would that be?" she asked, trying to ignore her thudding heart.

"Ours, my darlin'." He turned and smiled at her. "As I've said, next summer would be perfect."

She narrowed her eyes. "Of course you've never actually proposed to me."

"Haven't I!"

She shook her head. "Not…officially. Oh, we've discussed many things about my living in Cambridge and other matters, but you've not actually said the words."

Joel looked about him, trying to keep his expression impassive. "How remiss of me." He reached up and plucked a deep red rose from the mass entwined amongst the metalwork and offered it to her.

Antheia smiled and bent to smell it, but pulled back in surprise. Nestled inside the rose was a gold ring with a diamond at its centre and an exquisite pearl each side of it.

Joel gasped. "Well, I do declare that George certainly has a way with flowers." He watched her hold the ring so that the diamond sparkled in the sunlight. "Well, ma'am, are you going to look at it or wear it?" He took the ring from her, holding it between his thumb and forefinger. "Miss Antheia Vale, would you do me the honour of becoming my wife?"

Shyly, she offered her hand. "I'm sure you know my answer."

"And I believe that makes it official," he grinned, as he slipped the ring on her finger.

"It fits perfectly!" she said in surprise. "How did you know?"

He raised his eyebrows. "I sent Matty on a dangerous mission." He enjoyed her chuckle before adding, "I asked permission of your uncle to marry you some time ago, but I decided to do the right thing and repeat my request to your cousin, since he's now your guardian."

She nodded and leaned towards him. Their lips met in a tender kiss, before she rested her head on his shoulder.

Closing her eyes to enjoy his closeness, she thought of their many letters crossing the Atlantic. They had become friends first, but slowly and imperceptibly they had fallen in love. Joel had suggested they marry next summer and she was happy about that. They would spend as much time together as possible and she could visit Cambridge and see the town as her future home. And Cape Elizabeth in Maine. At last she would meet Martha Newton.

"Will your mother have room for Matty and me? I wouldn't want to impose on her."

A frown flittered across his face. "What makes you think Ma won't have room for you to stay with her?"

"Well, I always assumed Cape Elizabeth was a small place and your mother's home would be similar to Bluebell Cottage."

He pulled back from her in surprise. "My darlin', Ma lives in a substantial seven-bedroom dwelling near the lighthouse. With three servants to help her."

"I'm sorry, I know your father was in the army so…"

Seeing her confusion he pulled her closer and kissed the top of her head. "Oh dear, I've been more remiss than I thought. I've never spoken to you much about my childhood home, have I."

She smiled. "Not really, I must admit."

Shaking his head in dismay at himself, he said, "It didn't seem relevant when I stayed at the Abbey before I joined the army, since we hadn't known each other long. And I never mentioned anything in my letters?"

"No, you spoke of R Company and Captain Masters and your lieutenant and sergeant, but only snippets from home."

"I knew Ma was writing to you, so I assumed she would tell you any news from Cape Elizabeth."

"She wrote very infrequently."

"Did she?" He took in a deep breath. "Well, Ma inherited a fishing company from her father, my grandfather and has been running it for as long as I can remember. She owns five sloops and employs fifty people in processing lobster and getting it sent out to customers and markets."

She was incredulous. "And you decided to leave all that to go to Cambridge?"

"After I left West Point, my mother agreed to allow me to come to England if I stayed twelve months working for her company and I did just that, both on the sloops and on land."

"But it wasn't for you?"

"I could never get rid of the smell of lobster from my clothes. Besides, my interest always lay in archaeology and my spare time was spent with my trowel and brushes, digging up the past."

"It seems digging up the past is something we have in common," she giggled. "Will you inherit the company eventually?"

"Under my grandfather's will, I receive an income from it, but whether I take up the reins remains to be seen. At the moment, Ma has adequate help and when the time comes, I may decide to sell."

"And stay in England?"

"Wherever you are I want to be too." His arm tightened round her. "I would have told you all this if we hadn't been taken up with other matters these last few weeks."

She blew out a breath. "A lot has happened since you disembarked at Liverpool."

"Ah, there they are," said Will, appearing round the corner.

"We said thirty minutes and that's all you're getting," Felix grinned.

Joel and Antheia rose to their feet and she showed her cousins her ring.

She felt the need to admonish them. "Now we're betrothed, we are permitted to spend a little more time alone together." Felix gave a whoop of joy and bent to kiss her cheek and shake Joel's hand. Will stayed silent but followed suit. "Where are you going," she asked.

Felix pointed towards the woodland. "All the guests have left and since it's so hot, we thought we'd walk along the cliff and go down to the sands. It should be cooler down there."

"Sounds like a good idea," agreed Joel. He turned to Antheia. "How do you feel about taking a walk? We've not been in that direction since…"

She gave a chuckle. "Sarah's Meadow, Far Field and the old cemetery, are all part of the fabric of the Abbey and I'm not afraid of my home. Yes, let's go and discover if the tide is out."

They walked along the path, passing the fountain and George wheeling his barrow. At the edge of the woodland, Antheia turned to look back at the Abbey, its many windows gleaming in the sunlight. No longer did she think it an ugly building, but a place to call home. The entire household was badly affected by the death of her uncle and she would never forget the tall, thin man who looked like President Abraham Lincoln and had been so kind to her.

The grief would live with them for some time to come. But the future beckoned and perhaps one day, the Abbey will come to life and laughter and joy will once again echo off the old walls; the ballroom will be filled with music and light and she and her new husband will dance under its amazing chandeliers at their wedding. Opening her black and gold Italian parasol, she slipped her hand through Joel's arm and followed her cousins towards Sarah's Meadow.

* * * * * *

ALSO BY JULIA BELL

A Pearl Comb for a Lady
Deceit of Angels
Songbird: (The Songbird Story – Book One)
A Tangle of Echoes: (The Songbird Story – Book
Two)
The Wild Poppy
Broken Blossoms
If Birds Fly Low
Nyssa's Promise
To Guide Her Home
When Lucy Ceased to Be
Harriet Grace

Previews of these novels can be seen below
These novels are available as eBooks and on
Kindleunlimited

A LETTER FROM THE AUTHOR

Dear Reader,

Thank you so much for choosing to read A Cruel Suspicion. I love writing but having my books read makes them come alive. Until they are read, the characters are only in my imagination and they need to live and be enjoyed. So, I hope you enjoy reading all my novels and you're able to spare a little time in telling me about it.

You can do this via my website or by leaving a review on Amazon.

Julia Bell
www.JuliaBellRomanticFiction.co.uk

PREVIEW OF OTHER NOVELS BY JULIA BELL

HARRIET GRACE
(in eBook and paperback)

When Harriet Grace discovers her grandfather is going blind and unable to operate the railway signal box, she decides to go against the rules and man the signals herself. This will set off a spiral of events when her deception is discovered and the authorities are informed. Harriet must attend a Board of Trade Inquiry and explain her actions. Forced to leave their small cottage, Harriet and her grandfather move to York to live in the same boarding house as the man she loves, Edward Hainsworth, a locomotive fireman.

But her move to York will be the catalyst for many changes in her life including the opportunity to work as a telegrapher and clerk with the York Constabulary. Meeting handsome Detective Constable Mackinnon Taylor brings her mixed emotions. And then on a visit to the signal box, Harriet intercepts a strange coded telegraph message leading to the discovery of a shameful secret, the implications of which will threaten the lives of Ned and herself as they pursue an abduction and possible murder.

A PEARL COMB FOR A LADY
(in eBook)

A pearl comb comes into the possession of three courageous and remarkable women over two centuries.

Living during the time of the Battle of Waterloo, Christabel is feisty with an overactive imagination. She's in love with a soldier who only wants to use her to advance his military career.

Victoria, living in the mid-nineteenth century, is sweet-natured but haunted by the loss of her child.

Finally there is Jenny, a 21st century career woman who is unable to sacrifice her pride and forgive the man she loves.

The pearl comb weaves its way through the centuries; a witness to the despair, loss, hope and dreams of these women. And the men they love.

THE WILD POPPY
(in eBook and paperback)

Melody Kinsman is determined to succeed as a newspaper reporter. But in 1864, a female reporter is unheard of and because of the prejudice of the male establishment Melody finds it difficult to persuade an editor to buy her articles.

When she accompanies her friend, The Hon Celia Sinclair to London, she uses it as an opportunity to report the news and events in the capital. She finally confronts the attractive but enigmatic owner of the Cork Street Journal, Guy Wyngate who reluctantly gives her the opportunity to prove herself. But first she must face the difficult challenges thrown at her, since Guy wants to test her commitment to the newspaper business.

This commitment will have consequences on her future happiness with the man she gave her heart to when a young girl and to another who is waiting to win her love.

SONGBIRD: (THE SONGBIRD STORY – BOOK ONE)
(in eBook)

In 2019 Songbird: (The Songbird Story – Book One) won a Chill Book Premier Reader's Award and in 2020 was a Finalist Winner in Historical Romance Readers' Favourite.

Isabelle Asquith has only one ambition in life and that is to become an opera singer. To do this she must attend The Royal Academy of Music in London and become classically trained. Isabelle is a widow and has a young son to support and the fees for the academy are beyond her means as a music teacher. Her only recourse is to apply for the annual scholarship.

In the summer of 1885 after losing the scholarship for a second time and eager to earn more money, she decides to answer a newspaper advertisement. This simple act and the meeting of a mysterious man will change her life forever.

In the coming years, Isabelle is destined to discover not only her true potential, but also the lengths she is willing to go to realise her ambition.

A TANGLE OF ECHOES: (THE SONGBIRD STORY – BOOK TWO) (in eBook)

As the granddaughter of both an earl and a viscount, Venice is not expected to take up a profession. But this has not prevented her from wanting to train as a doctor even though London in the 1920's doesn't completely accept women physicians and Venice has an uphill struggle to realise her ambition.

Blissfully unaware of her grandmother's secret and the actions she took forty years before, Venice concentrates on her dream to become a physician. Meeting the mysterious Tristan Cavell throws her into turmoil. She is not only physically attracted to him, but also intrigued by the secrets he seems to keep. Tristan comes from the poverty of the East End of London and is a veteran of the Great War. He has done well for himself and owns a lucrative hotel and nightclub. But he also owns a casino, an activity that is on the fringes of the law.

Her grandmother's secret waits in the wings to bring terrifying consequences for Venice. She and Tristan will have to face these consequences together and this will test their love for each other. The tangle of echoes from the past will change their lives even though the events occurred many years before they were born.

A Special Note from the Author

This story is the sequel to my third novel Songbird, but I firmly believe that you don't need to read Songbird to enjoy A Tangle of Echoes. In Songbird, I told the story of Isabelle Asquith, but in A Tangle of

Echoes, it is Venice's story (Isabelle's granddaughter) that takes centre stage.

If you've already read Songbird then I know you'll enjoy A Tangle of Echoes, but if you haven't then perhaps you'll feel intrigued enough to give Isabelle's story a try and discover how her secret came about all those years ago.

BROKEN BLOSSOMS
(in eBook and paperback)

At the age of fifteen, Katherine Widcombe, the niece of a baronet, is found missing from her bed whilst visiting her maternal aunt. She is returned to her aunt and uncle's home, Widcombe Hall, blindfolded and with the weight of a terrible secret on her young shoulders.

Six years later, she is invited to spend Christmas with her cousin, Philippa and her new husband Conrad, Earl of Croston. She is horrified when Conrad confesses his love for her. Dismayed by the awful truth of her past, Katherine returns to the Hall and decides to accept the marriage proposal of Sir Herbert Fox, a man thirty years her senior.

But marriage doesn't bring her the peace she craves and in fact, she discovers that her husband has secrets of his own and this will bring terrible consequences for Katherine.

These consequences will mean a perilous journey and privations that a woman of Katherine's wealth and rank would never be expected to endure and will draw on all her strength and courage to overcome.

IF BIRDS FLY LOW
(in eBook and paperback)

Since her mother's death, Charlotte has been reared by her Aunt Faith. But her childhood has been plagued by strange knockings on her bedroom door in the dead of night. A summons she never answers since she fears what might be waiting for her behind the door.

Meeting Noel Chandler, a tutor at the university in Cambridge causes tension, since Charlotte thinks him prejudiced against women. Noel is actually Squire Chandler and lives at Martlesham Manor a Tudor house in Suffolk.

It is while visiting Martlesham Manor with her cousin, Adele, that Charlotte learns the story of Prudence Chandler who, in the seventeenth century, was denounced as a witch by her husband and mother-in-law and consequently hanged.

Charlotte becomes absorbed with the story of Prudence and realises there are many mysteries at the Manor. Who is the woman who moves silently around the house at night? Why is there a terrible feeling of dread that permeates the old building? And why do the birds fly low since there is always a threat of rain hanging over the Manor?

As their love grows, Charlotte and Noel start to uncover the truth of his ancestral home. But the truth will involve Charlotte more intimately than she could possibly imagine.

NYSSA'S PROMISE
(in eBook)

Since childhood Nyssa has lived with her stepsister Gwen in a small house in Fulham, London. But Nyssa possesses the ability of a psychic empath and can read people's emotions through touch. This 'gift' has enabled her to pursue the work of a private investigator.

In the year 1904, she decides to take the position of companion to the Dowager Lady Kirby, living at Kirby House near Bodmin in Cornwall. Here she meets the dowager's two sons, Sir Howel, the sixth baronet and Captain Daveth Kirby, newly home from fighting the Boers in South Africa.

Although seeking a quieter life, Nyssa is drawn into the mystery of the disappearance of Lady Marie Kirby, Sir Howel's new wife. Her investigation involves her in the legend of the Beast of Bodmin Moor, a creature that supposedly prowls the moor. As the deaths mount up, Nyssa and Daveth must find the murderer before Nyssa, herself, becomes the next victim.

TO GUIDE HER HOME
(in eBook and paperback)

In the late nineteenth century Lydia has no ambition to settle down to marriage until she has travelled and seen the world. But her life and emotions are shaken up when she meets Doctor Russell Brooks. Unknown to Lydia, Russ is actually an electronics engineer and living in 1998. They are linked by Lydia's home, Prescott Grange on the outskirts of Worcester. In Russ's time, this has been converted into stylish apartments and he has discovered a winding staircase that leads him into the Victorian era.

Russ finds he's attracted to the beautiful fair-haired young woman; a woman very different from those he knows in the twentieth century. But is their love possible when it spans over one hundred years? Russ endeavours to turn himself into a nineteenth century gentleman hoping to win Lydia's heart by playing to her rules. A rival in the person of Doctor Aiden Kinkard spoils his endeavours since Kinkard is determined that Lydia will become his wife.

Russ hopes that one day he will persuade Lydia to live with him in his time, but this has terrible consequences for Lydia and will put her life in danger. As Russ learns more about Doctor Kinkard and begins to question the man's motives and identity, he comes to realise he has met pure evil.

WHEN LUCY CEASED TO BE
(in eBook)

Having lost her mother the previous year, twelve-year-old Lucy Paget tries to make a contented life with her father on their farm in Ilkley, Yorkshire. But her father, Sid, would rather spend his time and money in the public house.

One day in a fit of pique, Sid sets her up on a chair and tries to sell her to the men in the public house. There are no buyers until a certain gentleman shows an interest and decides to take up the offer. Edwin Beaumont has plans for poor Lucy and for the next eight years, she is trapped in a life of secrets and deceit as she adopts the guise of Edwin's daughter.

Meeting her 'cousin' Theo Keeton brings some consolation and over time, his friend Matthew Raynor wins her heart. But Edwin's deception will not only lead to heartbreak, but also Lucy has to face the truth that Matthew might not be the man she thought he was when he is suspected of murder and could end up on the gallows.

DECEIT OF ANGELS
(in eBook and paperback)

For nineteen years, Anna Stevens perseveres with a faithless husband in a marriage that destroys her plans to go to university and follow a career. When Anna escapes to Bristol to work for Jason Harrington, the attractive and wealthy owner of Harrington Rhodes Shipping Agents, she has finally made the decision to leave her husband and make a new life for herself.

But Anna has told Jason she is a widow and when she and Jason fall in love, Anna finds herself trapped in her lies. And then her estranged husband finds her. Anna must pay a devastating price for her deceit, a price that would have lasting consequences for herself and the man she loves.

Printed in Great Britain
by Amazon

18455683R00236